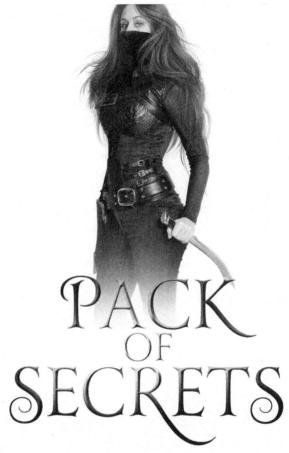

PACK
OF
SECRETS

CELESTIAL ARTIFACTS #1

AMARA MAE

COPYRIGHT

For Meltarrus.
My dragon.

PROLOGUE

Grace

A s the last rays of sunshine bled from the Seattle sky, I could practically hear the final minutes of my freedom ticking away. It was time to make a choice. Stay and commit or leave behind everything and everyone I'd ever known.

Forever.

Pausing in the center of a dilapidated street, I looked east. I'd grown up sheltered, but I wasn't ignorant. I knew the world was a massive place full of adventure and wonder. I'd seen maps and read travel books. There were so many places I wanted to see, but I'd never been outside of pack land.

And now, I probably never would.

A wolf needed a pack. More than travel or excitement, I needed my people.

Even if they rejected me.

My cell phone vibrated. I tugged it out of the pocket of my tactical pants to see a text message from my best friend. A smile tugged at my lips as I opened the messaging app. Okay, not all my packmates wanted to kick me to the curb. Mackiel had my back, and hopefully, he always would.

Mackiel: It's almost go time. Wish I could be there for you.

Me: Me too.

Mackiel: It'll be okay. I'll see you tomorrow. Then we'll get to endure two months of torture together.

I chuckled at his dry sense of humor.

Me: Can't wait.

He replied with a combination of laughing and death emojis, reminding me why I loved him so damn much. Mackiel made my pack bearable. We were inseparable throughout childhood, but it had been a year and ten months since he'd left for his mandatory two years of training.

My phone buzzed again.

Mackiel: Are you at the park yet? Don't be late.

I scanned the area, sniffing. Was he here? It would be just like him to jump out and surprise me. But I caught no hint of his scent. Regardless, he was right. I couldn't be late, yet there I stood in the middle of the street, debating whether or not to go like I had an actual choice in the matter. There was a reason shifters stayed close to the pack. In the twenty-three years since the war ended and the world was fractured to separate the magical and non-magical, Earth had changed. Monsters no longer hid in the shadows. On this lawless side of the fracture, might and savagery ruled.

I might have been little more than a prisoner with the pack, but at least I was safe.

Resolved, I shoved my phone into my pocket and picked up my pace. If I was late to my own ceremony, there would be consequences, and they would undoubtedly be painful. With one last glance down the road I couldn't take, I raced to the next block. The crumbling sidewalk felt uneven beneath my feet, but I knew all the right places to step to avoid rolling an ankle. Squeezing between two bushy evergreens, I burst into the clearing.

The city park was full. I appeared to be the last person to arrive, but at least my packmates hadn't taken their places yet. To my left, children under the age of ten played beside a mostly intact section of chain link fence. They didn't have full control over their animals yet, so several had already sprouted fur. One little wolf sprinted after a frog. He lost his balance and toppled sideways, plowing into a duo playing tug-of-war over a stick. Three fluffy bodies tumbled over one another until someone snarled and attacked. Nearby pups joined, forming a pile of nipping, snarling furballs.

The teenagers tasked with babysitting ignored the scrimmage and continued chatting amongst themselves. A pup stumbled out of the fray, set her sights on the adults, and bolted toward them. A teen boy plucked her up by her scruff and returned her to the puppy pile.

Although I'd grown up in this pack, I'd never experienced what it felt like to be part of the pile. I'd also never known the responsibility of watching pups. I was different, and wolves were wary of anything out of the norm.

Keeping my distance from the children and teens to avoid upsetting their parents, I took my place beside Daria. Tall, blonde, strong, and full of cocky attitude, she was my opposite. She was also the only other packmate who'd turned eighteen since the last full moon, so we'd be completing the ceremony together.

She glared at me and whispered, "Damn. I was hoping you wouldn't show."

Ignoring the bitch, I watched the pack line up. Pack structure fascinated me. I'd once read that wolf packs were family groups where only the alpha and his mate bred. Once pups came of age, they left to find a mate and start their own pack. Shifters were different. I knew nothing about how other packs worked, but our structure was like a ladder. A ladder you climbed by stepping on every pack member in your way. Nobody wanted to have one hundred and twenty-three asses in their face, so they bit and clawed their way up through the civilian and lieutenant ranks, fighting to be closer to my father and his beta.

Nobody ever challenged the alpha and lived.

"Ten-hut!" he shouted, and a wave of authoritative power rippled over the group.

Conversations halted mid-word, and people slid into place. Chaz McCarthy wasn't a tall man, but what he lacked in height, he made up for in presence. Everything about him—from the set of his beard-covered jaw to his always-ready stance—projected competence and might. Forest green eyes that mirrored my own slid over his pack approvingly before settling on Daria. His lips spread into a proud, fatherly smile, and she beamed back at him.

Cruel, cunning, and manipulative, Daria exuded all the characteristics an alpha's daughter should have. It took a great deal of effort to school my features into impassivity when I really wanted to gag. Too bad for Dad; he'd gotten stuck with me. My hands drifted down to the daggers sheathed at my thighs, and I ran my fingertips over the notches in the hilt. I knew the design by heart and drew comfort from every dip and rise of the cool metal. As the only pack member unable to shift, these were my teeth and claws.

They were also the only gift my father had ever given me.

He may wish savage, perfect Daria was his daughter, but if it came down to a fair fight, I knew I could take the bitch down.

My gaze shot to the first lieutenant, Rust. My mentor stood just to the right of Hitch, Dad's beta. Rust used to be Beta, but Hitch had supplanted him when I was four. I still believed Rust had thrown the battle, protecting his mate the only way he could. There was no other explanation for my mentor to concede to the two-bit bully.

4

Rust could kick Hitch's ass with one paw tied behind his back, and everyone knew it. But Hitch's volatile temper had earned him a reputation for getting what he wanted one way or another, and he wanted to be my father's Beta.

Rust's gaze met mine, and he tilted his head in a barely perceptible nod, reassuring me I could do this. I returned the gesture, letting his confidence bolster me as I returned my attention to the alpha.

Fighting the urge to fidget with my daggers as the scent of burning ozone tickled my nose, I watched as the alpha's right hand vibrated. Magic crackled the air as bones shifted, dark fur sprouted across tan, leathery skin, and claws extended from elongated fingertips. Sweat beaded at his hairline. Gasps and murmurs bubbled through the pack as the anticipated change stopped at Dad's wrist. He'd somehow managed to contain his shift to his hand. I couldn't even fathom the amount of power and control that must have taken. My father was getting stronger. With a triumphant gleam filling eyes now ringed with gold, he held his hand up for all to see, and several submissive packmates dropped to their knees to grovel and whimper, baring their necks. I was too stunned to even breathe. Judging by the whispers, whines, and astonished looks still cycling through the rest of the pack, nobody else could believe it, either.

My father's voice boomed as he asked, "Are you ready to make your vow, Daria?"

There were two vows in the Bloodrite. The first was made to the alpha as a man, the second was made to his wolf. The crowd hushed in anticipation.

Daria took a tentative step forward. Eyes bright and full of wonder, she nodded. "Is leatsa mo shaol, Alpha."

The Gaelic vow meaning 'my life is yours' made my father nod in acceptance. With one claw from his right hand, he slashed a gash across his left palm. The coppery scent of blood filled the air as he raised his hand for all to see. The cut was deep, and blood flowed over his palm and down his wrist. He nodded at the girl beside me. Daria stepped forward, holding out her trembling left hand. She bit her lip against a whimper as he sliced her palm to mirror his own. Then the alpha claimed her bloody hand with his, their wounds pressed together with fingers intertwined.

Daria straightened her spine and cleared her throat. "Chaz McCarthy, Alpha of the Evergreen Wolf Pack, I choose this day to surrender my personal will and purpose to join the pack. Accept me, and I will pledge my hands, teeth, and claws to your cause. As the moon follows the sun, I shall follow you. Your enemies will be my enemies, your friends, my friends. Become my alpha, and I will offer you the first bite of every hunt and the final beat of my heart."

My father nodded in approval. "I accept your pledge and will be your alpha. With my hands, teeth, and claws, I vow to guide, guard, and train you. As you provide for and protect the pack, so shall we provide for and protect you. The survival of the pack depends on the strength and loyalty of each wolf, after all. You are pack, Daria, from this moment until the final beat of your heart."

The burning scent of ozone increased as magic sealed the vow.

"Thank you, Alpha," Daria said, bowing her head.

"You will leave for training at first light tomorrow," he said. "Are you packed and ready to go?"

"Yes, Alpha. I'm looking forward to it."

He nodded, released her hand, and faced me. Disappointment clouded his eyes as he took in what I was wearing. Everyone else wore T-shirts and sweats that were easy to strip out of so they could shift. Their feet were bare, and they carried no weapons. I, on the other hand, was dressed in my work uniform with my backpack on and my daggers strapped to my thighs. After tonight, I'd officially be an adult in the eyes of my pack, expected to fight for my rank. My stomach clenched with anxiety as I took in the faces sizing me up, wondering who would come at me first. Dominant wolves would want a shot at the alpha's daughter, while submissives would see me as someone they could step on to climb up from the bottom.

But none of them knew I'd been training to fight since I was five. Sure, I couldn't shift, but I was far from helpless. I knew exactly where to stab to incapacitate a person in wolf or human form. The idea of hurting anyone—let alone a packmate—didn't sit well with me, but life hadn't given me many choices.

"Are you ready to make your vow, Grace?" my father asked.

I wasn't, but I nodded anyway. "Is leatsa mo shaol, Alpha."

His wound had already closed, which was fast even for our kind, so he reopened it before slicing my palm. Unlike Daria, I didn't react. The pain was nothing compared to some of my aunt's attempts to release my wolf. Something flickered in my father's eyes as his hand roughly clasped mine. I parroted the same age-old vow Daria had made, only I substituted daggers for claws. After magic sealed the vow, my father stepped back and started to turn away. He hadn't asked me the final question, so I piped up, volunteering my answer.

"I'm also packed and ready for training, Alpha."

He frowned at me. "That's unnecessary. You won't be going to the farm. You will continue your training here."

I gaped at him, wanting to argue but knowing it would do no good. When my father made up his mind, there was no changing it. Ever. So much for seeing Mackiel tomorrow. Disappointment stabbed at me, but I parried by reassuring myself this was okay. Mackiel only had two months left of training. Then he'd be home. I could survive two more months without my friend.

Addressing the entire pack, the alpha said, "It is time for the second half of the Bloodrite. Disrobe."

Everybody stripped but me. I averted my gaze and stared at my feet, trying to ignore the rustling of clothes. I could feel my father's gaze on me, but rather than insist I follow the order, he barked out another command.

"Shift."

Power pulsed through my partially formed pack bond, slamming into me. My entire body trembled with the need to obey.

Bones ground and muscles contracted, sending spikes of agony throughout my body.

This was it. I was finally going to shift!

Closing my eyes, I hunched forward and embraced the magic. I waited on the edge of the shift, desperate to finally topple over and land in my other form, but the change ground to a halt, and I stayed in that in-between state, waiting. Nothing happened.

Eventually, my bones and muscles fell back into place, and the pain subsided.

My father cast a disgusted look in my direction, stripped, and shifted, becoming an enormous brown wolf. I'd never understood the relationship between magic and physics, but the size of the alpha wolf made no sense whatsoever. As a man, he stood barely above five and a half feet. The wolf before me was almost five feet tall on all fours. Stranger still, he'd grown since the last time I'd seen his wolf, I was sure of it. He stood a full head and shoulders taller than any of the other wolves.

My gaze spanned the pack, and a sea of glowing eyes stared back at me. Once again, my hands dropped to the hilts of my daggers as I widened my stance.

Beside me, Daria the wolf crept forward, approaching the alpha with abundant caution. Her human form had been accepted, and now it was up to her wolf. My father watched her progress, his expression impassive. She lowered her head and slowed, inching closer until she cowered directly in front of his muzzle. Dropping fully to her belly, she let out a soft, pleading whine.

The alpha wolf lurched forward with a growl, wrapping his giant maw around her neck.

Daria didn't move. Hell, she probably didn't even breathe. Tense seconds passed as we all waited for the alpha's verdict. I'd seen him kill one recruit, a male born with a deformity that made his rear left leg shorter than the others when in wolf form. The alpha had snapped his neck, then severed his head from his body. It was quick and painless, and the noises had provided a soundtrack for all my nightmares since.

When the alpha released Daria, the entire pack let out a collective breath. Magic hummed between my father and his newest pack member as the bond solidified. Daria had been accepted. Now it was my turn.

The alpha's glowing golden eyes snapped to me, and I dropped to my hands and knees in a bone-rattling thud. Lowering my head, I inched forward like Daria had, trying to make myself as small and non-threatening as possible. I could only imagine how ridiculous I looked to the wolves, but I didn't care. Not when my life was on the line. Rather than dropping to my belly like Daria, I lowered onto my side, facing away from my father. There, I was helpless and completely at his mercy. My nerves hummed as I closed my eyes and prayed he didn't literally stab me in the back.

Air stirred as the alpha struck. Lightning fast, his teeth tore into the soft flesh just above my collarbone. It hurt—holy shit, did it ever—but I clamped my mouth closed and forced myself to hold still. Seconds passed. Soft fur tickled my flesh. Drops of blood dribbled down my neck. His teeth dug in deeper, and I bit the inside of my cheek to keep myself from screaming. The taste of blood filled my mouth, and I wondered if my dad would finally kill me.

Would anyone but Mackiel even care?

Maybe Aunt Sereana or Mackiel's little sister, Tali?

Would my father mourn me after he did the deed?

Finally, the alpha unlocked his jaw and jerked away. A wave of magic hit me, and a cacophony of voices slammed into my head.

"Letting her in?"

"Thought for sure he'd kill her."

"Great. Now we have a freak in the pack."

I recognized the last voice as a guard by the name of Jin. My gaze shot to his wolf form, and he bared his teeth at me.

"I don't know." Someone else said in my head. *"Might not be all bad. I heard omegas make good scapegoats."*

9

"'Bout time she's good for something."

"Look at her watching us. What's wrong little witch? You don't like hearing what everyone really thinks of you?"

"What's wrong? Can't you talk back?"

Mackiel had warned me about the mental connection of the pack. He said I'd have to learn to guard my mind so the packmates in range couldn't pick up on thoughts I didn't want to share. When I'd asked if there was a way to block out the thoughts of others, he admitted he'd never tried. My handsome, loved-by-everyone, perfect friend enjoyed hearing what his people thought of him.

I, on the other hand, was in hell.

Pushing myself off the ground, I slid onto my knees and unsheathed my daggers.

"Why can't we hear her thoughts?" someone thought.

"The bitch probably thinks she's too good to communicate with us."

"Yeah, she doesn't even have to go train."

"Daddy's little princess."

The alpha had to hear their thoughts, too, but he turned his back on me and loped away. My father wouldn't protect me. That was probably for the better since it would only validate their claims of favoritism. Off to my right, Daria snarled, issuing her first challenge. The bitch would probably climb high up the ladder. As an omega, I didn't give two shits about pack rank. All I cared about was surviving.

Wolves closed in around me, forming a snapping, growling semi-circle.

"Come on, little Chipmunk, let's see what you got."

I scrambled to my feet and backed away, hands still clutching my daggers as I considered my options. Fight or submit? I could fight, but these were my people, and the idea of hurting them for a rank I cared nothing about appalled me. It was senseless and cruel and completely against my nature.

Plus, the minute I started fighting, I'd never be able to stop.

There'd always be more challenges, more ranks to climb, but I didn't want to be the type of person who stomped on others to rise. I just wanted to exist and belong. My only real option was to submit and hope they didn't kill me. Decision made, I sheathed my daggers, widened my stance, and braced for the first attack.

"The witch."

"Shit. What's she doing here?"

The wolves snarled and backed away, making room for a more dangerous predator. A hand landed between my shoulder blades. I was saved. Kind of.

"Grace," Aunt Sereana said in my ear. "I hate to interrupt your special night, but I believe I may have found a way to release your wolf. Come with me, child."

I should have felt relief at her invitation to escape the challenges of my packmates, but a shiver of dread crept up my spine. This wasn't the first time she'd tried to release my wolf, and the experience was never pleasant. She might have been rescuing me from multiple beatdowns, but my aunt's methods were their own form of torture.

Welcome to adulthood, Grace. It's gonna hurt.

A lot.

Grace

M y day started upside down.
Literally and figuratively.

Head down, ass up, secured in a harness, I dangled over a twenty-foot drop into darkness while bells tolled and gongs thundered, announcing the midnight hour and the beginning of a new day. I was running out of time.

Again.

As much as I'd like to pretend my days didn't typically begin in an upside-down race against the clock, I was a thief, not a liar. I had standards.

When the echoes of ringing notes dwindled back to silence, I whispered, "How you doin' up there, Rust?"

My mentor, trained muscle, ever watchful babysitter, and talented technology guru, grumbled through my earpiece in response, "Firewall. I'm almost through. Sit tight."

Afraid of botching the heist, I did as he requested. With no windows, only the skylight above kept the tables and shelves crowded into the room from plunging into complete blackness. I blinked, waiting for my vision to adapt. The nocturnal animal within took over my sight, enabling me to make out shapes and silhouettes, but details were difficult to discern. Tonight's job was beyond complicated, but I had the motivation necessary to pull it off. Dad had found the perfect carrot to dangle in front of me, and I was anxious to get busy.

Muscles tense, heart afraid to hope, I took stock of my tools

13

while waiting for my partner's signal. The supplies in my backpack and the daggers strapped to my thighs had seen me through hundreds of jobs in the past, and I was confident they'd get me through this one. Sure, I was further from home than I'd ever been, in the middle of nowhere and with only a single packmate guarding my back, but the job was the same. I could do this. At least, that's what I kept telling myself. Game face on, dressed in my usual black tactical pants, fitted T-shirt, boots, and baseball cap, I sucked down a couple of deep, calming breaths and prepared to make this heist my bitch.

"Almost ready. I'm takin' over the cameras now." Rust said. "There. Footage is on a loop. Yer clear to descend."

"Roger. Goin' in," I said.

Not like I had to tell him. Rust monitored my progress from a small action camera attached to my baseball cap. The cap also carried a light made for mining or spelunking, allowing my hands to remain free. The first time we'd tried out the equipment, we hadn't paid enough respect to gravity. Audio-video equipment was hard to come by, and Dad had lost his shit when we'd returned with mangled gear. Pack alphas don't just yell when they're angry; they roar, and my father had verbally detonated with an eyebrow-melting, knee-buckling, bowel-watering blast-to-the-senses. That had been more than a decade ago, and everything was superglued, sewn, *and* duct-taped onto my cap now, but PTSD reared its ugly head every time my hat wobbled. I'd even duct-taped the cap to my head once. I was eleven at the time and had to cut it off with my daggers. Talk about the worst haircut ever.

I was wiser now. I'd learned. Grown. Evened out the length of my locks. Now I secured the cap to my head with a collection of hairpins and knots that had my long copper-colored hair wrapped around the back hole in a tangled mess it would take me hours to unravel. At least it wouldn't look like a toddler had taken a razor to my hair at night's end.

I hit the button on my harness to begin my slow descent, clicked on the cap lamp, and gasped in surprise. The dim beam from my lamp brightened the area, bouncing off glittering wealth and treasures beyond my wildest dreams. It was like nothing I'd ever seen before. Tables stacked with overflowing containers of gold coins and glittering gems circled a mountain of jewelry boxes. Gaudy rings, watches, and bracelets decorated a splayed mannequin hand perched atop a pedestal. Swords, rapiers, battle axes, and maces—with gem-encrusted hilts—littered an enormous weapon rack stretched along the north wall. A giant-sized medieval suit of gilded armor stood in a corner like a creepy bedazzled sentry with strands of every gem imaginable hanging from its arms. I gaped at it, half expecting the monstrosity to come to life and start flinging necklaces at me.

"Touch nothing but the artifact, or you will die."

The alpha's warning rang in my head, and I almost laughed out loud. My father didn't know me at all if he thought I'd be interested in any of this. I stole for the pack, not myself. And pretty but useless had never been my jam. If I were going to filch a little something on the side, it sure as hell wouldn't be something as impractical as gold, gems, or weapons that looked like they hadn't been wielded in centuries. What use would I have for any of it? Not currency. Only the alpha bought supplies outside the den, and he bartered with essential goods we grew or made, not useless adornments. There wasn't a lot of demand for a pearl necklace that practically glowed in the dark and provided a convenient chokehold for enemies. Here in Terra Fera—the wildlands—survival was key.

Then I saw the books, and my father's warning made sense.

I would give my left arm for something new and exciting to read —well, at least a pinky—and this collection looked ancient and fascinating. Tomes of all shapes and sizes filled dark wooden shelves, some leaning precariously against the wall, others standing like welcome islands of knowledge amidst a sea of glittering crap. Gilded spines thicker than the length of my foot were nestled beside thin, leather-bound journals. One spine appeared to be made of tree bark. I couldn't help but wonder what sort of information and stories I'd find between their covers.

"Hey Rust, you seein' this?" I asked.

"Yep. The selfish bastard's collected 'imself quite the hoard."

Something in my mentor's tone made my senses tingle.

"Do you know the person we're stealing from?" I asked.

"Nope. And I wouldn't throw that 'person' title around too liberally if I was you. We're still on the wild side of the fracture."

Even though he couldn't see me, I rolled my eyes. This was an argument we'd had many times. I should give it up, but descending into a literal treasure trove made me uneasy, and the familiar topic provided a measure of comfort. "Person is not synonymous with human. I'm a person. You're a person. This gaudy disaster could be the collection of another person. You don't know."

"You an' I are half-human. Who knows what this freak is," Rust insisted, clearly exhausted with my unrelenting campaign to open his mind. "Forget all the bullshit terminology. You know what I mean. *Us* an' *them.*" By *us,* he meant packmates. *Them* encompassed everyone else. Typical pack mentality spewed by my father and regurgitated daily by his minions.

"How very uh...." The correct word blinked out of my mind as I hit the button to stop my progression and looked around the room.

"Wise? Mature? Sensible?" he provided helpfully.

I remembered what I was going to say. "Bigoted."

He snorted. "Yer young. Ya still think the world's all rainbows an' stardust."

Funny, since Rust had had a front-row seat to most of my life and could serve as a witness that nothing had ever been easy or safe. "You know me, just out here livin' the dream," I quipped.

"All right, time to stop yappin' and get ta work. You see anythin' interestin' down there?"

Angling the camera on my hat so Rust could get a good look at the thin, broken lines of light moving above the floor, I said, "I see a complication."

"Lasers, huh? You can handle that. What about the target? You got eyes on it yet?"

Jobs always made him anxious, but this one more than most. His pregnant wife was due any day now, and he was champing at the bit to get back to her. He shouldn't even be here. I'd asked my father to send someone else, but Dad was an alpha who demanded no-questions-asked loyalty and ruled the pack with an iron paw. He'd looked Rust in the eye and announced, *"If Janey goes into labor, the bitch can squeeze her legs together and hold that puppy in until you return."* My old man was a good and capable leader, unfettered by silly notions like empathy and compassion, even when the female in question was risking her life by giving birth to a much-needed new packmate. I loved him, but he could be as frustrating as a key broken off in a lock.

"I'm still looking," I said, focusing on the job. Unfortunately, I had no idea what I was looking *for*.

This wasn't my first heist. I'd been enlisted to retrieve other items, but my orders had always included a detailed description and location of the loot. The last job was for an antique gold necklace with an enchanted silver-dollar-sized emerald pendant stored in the master bedroom safe. Dad had provided a picture of the object and everything. This time, my instructions were to search for a relic of unknown size, shape, and substance, rumored to be hidden somewhere in this treasure room. Curiouser still, my father promised I'd find the item because it would call to me.

Call to me?

What the hell did that even mean? I'd asked for clarification, but my old man had nailed me in place with his intimidating alpha stare and said, *"That's all I can tell you. You'll know it when you feel it. This is what you've been training for. Don't let me down."* He'd enforced the order with a low growl that threatened dismemberment if I failed. Talk about spectacular intel and a stress-free work environment.

Then Aunt Sereana had stepped in to give me her version of a pep talk. *"Do you want to shift, child?"*

Biting my tongue so I didn't snap in frustration and point out the stupidity of her question, I replied, *"More than anything."*

So, problem solver that she was, she cast a spell of finding on me. *"Now, when you open your senses and ask the artifact to call to you, it will. And you should have no problem finding it."*

She was wrong. I had a significant problem with finding the artifact. Spells only worked for witches and other Tricari—or magical people—with similar powers, and I had no desire to tap into that side of my family tree. Still, desperate times called for undesirable measures. Opening my mind and senses, I scanned the room, listening.

Nothing called to me.

Unsurprised, I glanced at the bookcases. Books had a lot to say, and I did feel drawn to them. Did that count? *"Touch nothing but the artifact, or you will die"* didn't leave a whole lot of room for misinterpretation. Fearing imminent failure, my stomach sank. Despair knocked on the door to my headspace. I didn't know if I should kick it to the curb or welcome it in and make it a snack.

All right, Grace, that's about enough of that bullshit. You can do this. Figure it out already.

Straightening as much as someone hanging upside down could, I closed my eyes and focused. I wanted to be whole. Complete. Accepted. An invaluable member of my pack and not the team handicap. Therefore, I *needed* to find this artifact.

"Ask the artifact to call to you," my aunt's voice repeated in my head.

Why not? It was worth a shot. "Oh great, mystical artifact, please, in the name of all that is holy and or desperate, call to me," I muttered.

Unfortunately, my mentor had incredible hearing. "Are you... prayin' or pleadin'?" he asked.

"Does it matter?" I fired back. "I'm being creative. Quiet and let me concentrate."

He chuckled. As the sound of his mirth faded, a slight thrumming sound drew my attention. It reminded me of the hum of our old refrigerator on balmy days. But as I listened, the volume increased, morphing into more of a throbbing sound. It stirred something deep within me, drawing my attention to the northeastern corner of the room.

Hope sparked as I concentrated. Nothing moved or waved or spoke, but *something* tugged at my awareness.

"Hey Rust, do you hear or... feel anything weird?"

"Like what?" he asked, sounding genuinely puzzled.

"Like... a heartbeat. But louder." The implication made me pause. My old man had sent me after some shady shit in the past, but a body part?

Please, for the love of all that's holy, don't let the artifact be a body part.

I was desperate, so I'd probably still take an organ, but the thought of carrying around a still-beating heart made me want to hurl. I sniffed the air. Nothing smelled of blood. Hopefully, that meant I was in the clear.

"No," Rust replied after a moment. "I don't hear nuthin' like that. Why?"

He wouldn't hear it if it only called to me. Encouraged, I homed in on the corner emitting the sound, finding a collection of boxes and display cases. The thrumming increased under my scrutiny. I needed to get closer to narrow down the source. "I may have found what we're looking for."

"Can you get to it?"

I hung from the skylight located over the center of the room, and the corner I needed to get to was about twenty feet away. Laser sensors roamed the floor and the three feet above it, turning this task into a complicated game of *the floor is lava*. Unlike when I was a child, this room held no safe sofas to jump from, and touching any of the covered tables or pedestals would start an avalanche of sparkly things sure to trigger an alarm. Not to mention the whole *"Touch anything and die"* warning. I needed to get my ass to that corner without breaking any of the barely visible beams below, using only the items on me.

"Piece of cake," I replied.

"Chip?" Rust asked, sounding worried.

My name was Grace, but everyone called me Chipmunk—or Chip for short. As far as nicknames went, it sucked ass. I'd lobbied for a better one, but crappy handles hung on like a noxious stench. Scrub as I might, I could do nothing to wash it away. In a pack full of rowdy, roughneck shifters, I would forever be dubbed a harmless woodland critter, only considered dangerous if my bite carried a disease.

"I can get to it, but it's gonna take a little longer than planned." I needed an anchor that wouldn't disrupt the lasers. Shifting my weight, I debated swinging toward a nearby bookshelf, but I couldn't tell if it was bolted down and didn't want to take a chance and topple it over. A slightly less risky idea came to me, and I unstrapped a crossbow pistol with an attached electric fishing reel from my backpack. It was a cute little weapon—looked like a child's toy—but it packed a hundred pounds of draw weight, was deadly up to forty feet, and was every bit as accurate as a full-size model. Retrieving a weighted bolt from my pack, I unwound a length of sixty-pound fishing line from the reel, threaded it through the hole in the bolt, and tied it off.

The same gifts that enhanced my vision granted me the strength to cock the crossbow without leverage. I loaded the threaded bolt, aimed at the corner wall, and fired. The bolt sailed through the air with a whirr and bit into the wall with a thump. A small hunk of plaster broke free. Holding my breath, I watched as it tumbled down the wall to shatter against the floor, narrowly missing a laser beam.

"What the hell are you doin' in there?" Rust asked.

I released my breath, relieved the debris hadn't set off an alarm. "Warmin' up," I said in my best Rust impression. "It's time for a little gymnastics."

"Be careful, Chip."

The genuine concern in his voice made me smile. "Always."

He snorted. I had a reputation for being too damn curious for my own good. Pair that with quick healing and that whole hard-to-kill bonus, and it was like I'd been custom crafted to make questionable life choices. At least, that was the excuse I gave whenever I got caught.

Tonight, however, my ass wasn't the only one on the line. Despite my curiosity and debatable sense of self-preservation, I'd never put Rust at risk. Especially not before he'd met his newest pup.

Hitting the button to retract the fishing line, I followed the bolt across the room, simultaneously releasing more of the rope that suspended me from the ceiling to keep my altitude steady. As I neared the corner, the bizarre vibrations intensified. They appeared to be coming from a plain wooden container about the size and shape of a shoebox, the most ordinary, simple item in the room. Curious, I positioned myself above it, then pressed the button to stop my horizontal advancement.

Now, I needed to free up my hands without launching myself back across the room in a counterproductive act of stupidity. With the fishing reel locked so it wouldn't release more line, I secured the crossbow to my backpack. Gravity tugged at my body, ready to turn me into a human pendulum, but the heavy-duty Velcro straps on my bag held, and the fishing line kept me anchored in place. Secure with both hands free, I hovered above the box, suspended between the rope hanging from the skylight and the line connecting my crossbow to the wall.

"This is some next-level skill right here," I said, mentally patting myself on the back. My arms trembled slightly, and my hairline was damp with sweat, but I'd gotten myself to where I needed to be without setting off any alarms or knocking over any freestanding bookcases.

"What?" Rust asked. Shuffling sounds came from the roof. A shadow hung over me as he peered through the skylight. "Ah. I see. Nice work."

"You should snap a picture. Maybe show it around the pack and convince everyone I'm a badass, not a Chipmunk."

Rust chuckled. "Don't count on it, kid. Doesn't matter how skilled ya are, you'll always be a pocket-sized, chubby-cheeked pest. Now get ta work. I see flashlights. You got maybe five minutes."

Sighing, I returned my attention to the box. Weird. I could have sworn it was plain, unremarkable wood, but now, a galaxy of stars covered the top and sides. As I watched, the design stirred to life. Stars twinkled and glowed. Constellations broke apart and reformed, each movement creating deep grooves in the wood, there one moment and gone the next.

"Get a load of that," I said, ducking my head to give the camera a good view.

"The box?" Rust asked.

"Yeah. Well, the design on the box. It's... animated?" That didn't feel like the right word, so I tried again. "Magical?"

"I... uh... What design? You're lookin' at a plain wooden box, Chip."

I blinked. Nope. There was nothing plain about it. I knuckled my eyes, but the glowing galaxy continued to swirl. Maybe it was something technology couldn't pick up, the way mirrors couldn't reflect vampires.

Was that even true? I'd never met a vampire to ask.

"You gonna open it or just stare at it all day?" Rust asked, drawing my attention back to the task at hand.

He was right; we needed to get moving before the patrol made it back. I hesitated, pondering the wisdom of interrupting the star show. Could it open? A thin seam separated the top from the bottom, but it had no visible keyhole or locking device, no tripwires or alarms. Since the box was welded onto a pedestal bolted to the floor, removing it was out of the question. I had no choice but to attempt to crack the container open.

Well, here goes nuthin'.

I slid one gloved hand over the seam and tried to separate the lid from the base. The glove made it impossible to wedge my fingers into the small crack for leverage. Dad had strong opinions against leaving fingerprints behind, but I didn't have time to rifle through my pack and find a pry bar. Especially not when a flick of my bare fingers could do the trick. With plans to wipe away any resulting prints, I removed my glove and tried again. The lip yielded beneath my fingertip, but it pricked my skin instead of opening. Stung, I yanked my hand back and clamped down on a yelp of pain. Too late. The box had extracted its price. I watched in horror as a small trickle of my blood rolled into an etched star. The star swirled and moved, spreading my DNA across the cover and staining the glowing, rotating design red.

Shit!

The entire ordeal had taken maybe five seconds, but the resulting regret promised to follow me for a lifetime. I could deal with fingerprints, but how the hell did one scrub blood out of magical dynamic carvings? Definitely not something covered in training.

"Ru—" My throat was dry, and I choked on the word. Swallowing, I tried again. "Rust?"

"Yeah?"

How could he sound so calm? Shouldn't he be freaking out with me? "Did you... happen to see that?"

"See what?"

Before I could answer, the box popped open to reveal an ornately cast copper goblet cushioned on silky golden fabric.

"I see *that*," Rust said, his tone unimpressed. "Kinda disappointin', don't ya think?"

I laughed. Disappointing? I could barely hear him over the

pounding of my heart. My frayed nerves felt like they were tap-dancing on my bladder. My mentor hadn't heard the thrum of the artifact or seen its creepy blood-drinking magic show. That meant this cup had to be what I was after!

"It's a flashy cup, wrapped in cloth, hidden in a junky ol' box," he said. "I don't see what the big deal is."

The thrumming was louder now, almost like a beacon calling me closer and begging me to take the cup away from this place. Without consciously deciding to do so, I reached out and picked it up with my bare hand. I didn't die. Instead, a warm, tingly sensa-tion seeped into my blood and flowed up my arm. Shocked, I stared at the thing. An unwelcome sense of comfort and assurance swept over me. Caution flared, begging me to drop the artifact and get the hell out of there. According to every book I'd ever read on the subject, sentient objects were not something to be trifled with.

Ever.

But my hand wouldn't release the blasted thing.

"What are ya waitin' for?" Rust asked. "You got maybe a minute and a half before the patrol'll be back around."

His words hit me like a sledgehammer, shattering whatever spell I'd been under. I shoved the cup into my backpack and closed the box. The carvings were gone, along with any sign of my blood. All things considered, taking the time to wipe away my fingerprints seemed pointless, but it was the one problem I could solve, so I did. Flicking off my cap lamp, I plotted my escape route. Getting out of here promised to be tricky. Unsheathing a dagger from my thigh, I blinked until my enhanced vision kicked back in. Bracing myself, I sliced the wire anchoring me to the wall. Gravity finally got its due, sending me rocketing across the room. Dropping in altitude as I threw my weight to one side, I narrowly avoided a table precari-ously piled with riches.

The lasers!

I was falling too quickly. At this rate, I was sure to interrupt the beams and alert the entire estate to my presence. Panicked, I smacked the rapid ascent button on my harness. The contraption whirred to life, sucking in extra slack and shooting me toward the ceiling. Still upside down and swinging like a trapeze artist hopped up on energy potions, I narrowly escaped the laser beams only to find myself on a collision course with the bedazzled suit of armor.

Shit! Shit! Shit!

Throwing my weight to the side, I squeezed my eyes closed, willed myself to be as small and weightless as possible, and crossed my fingers and toes. Metal brushed against my sleeve, but I avoided contact. I would have cheered, but I was too busy swallowing back bile as I ate up the distance to the roof.

If I survived this, I'd have to add upside-down aerial ballerina acrobatics to my training routine because nothing in my life had prepared me for this reckless ride. Stomach roiling, vision blurring, the end of the line came at me like a bad omen. Knowing I couldn't escape my doom, I swung wide, missing the open skylight only to smack my hip against the ceiling. Biting my lip against a cry of pain as momentum hurled me toward the opposite side, I steeled myself for another bone-crunching whack. At the last minute, I came to my senses and threw my weight to slow my progress. I still struck the ceiling, but my teeth hardly rattled this time. Progress. With a few more maneuvers, wild swinging mellowed to a manageable rocking, and my stomach settled enough that I was no longer in danger of tossing my cookies all over the treasure room. Now that would be a humiliating way to set off the alarm. I flipped myself right side up and reached for the skylight.

The dim yellow glow of Rust's eyes greeted me as his hands grabbed mine to hoist me through the narrow opening. The instant my feet hit the roof, he started unhooking my harness. The world rocked back and forth. I couldn't tell if I was swaying or the roof was, but I really wanted everything to hold still.

Rust's gaze locked onto my bare hand, and he froze. "Your glove."

Right. That was a problem. Since he'd missed all the weird shit with the box, it made sense for him to stress about fingerprints, but they were the least of our concerns. The stabby box had my freaking DNA.

"I wiped my prints off," I said. At least I could put his mind at ease about that.

He nodded approvingly. "Good. Ya handled it. Nobody needs to know. It's fine."

Fine? More like screwed six ways to Sunday, but I was willing to play along if he thought we were fine.

"Glove? What glove?" I asked like I was the picture of innocence.

Unfortunately, the question remained, niggling in the back of my mind. Where was my glove? Had it fallen to the floor, somehow missing the laser beams? I must have dropped it when the box pricked my finger. Or was it during my reckless ascent?

The desire to kick my own ass was almost overwhelming. My future was riding on this job, and there was no possible way to screw it up worse than I had.

Then, as Rust stuffed my gear into my pack, the universe decided to prove me wrong.

An alarm screeched.

Grace

With the alarm blaring behind him, Rust dropped into a crouch and gestured for me to do the same. Gazes locked, he held up two fingers and pointed toward the north side of the building, silently letting me know which direction the patrol would come from. Funny, since we were undoubtedly about to be swarmed from all sides. I had no idea what had triggered the alarm, but if we didn't get out of there soon, we'd find ourselves in the crosshairs of the guards.

Obviously thinking the same thing, Rust pointed his finger at me before gesturing toward the south. Hands snapping apart, he pantomimed driving. Finally, he flapped his arms like a chicken. Message received: He wanted me to go south, get to the bikes, and then take off. He would lead the patrol away and then catch up or meet me back at the den.

That last bit—the chicken arms—that was my idea. Long ago, I'd told Rust if he insisted on a gesture that would ensure I fled with no questions asked, that was my price—flapping his arms like an idiot. He could have pulled rank and refused, but I was an anxious little kid on my first heist and worried about the wolf who'd trained me. My safety had mattered more to Rust than his pride. Almost fifteen years later, we still used the signal. And I was only marginally more mature because, despite the severity of the situation, the sight of a muscular five-foot-six, two-hundred-pound bearded man busting into a haphazard version of the chicken dance never ceased to bring a smile to my face.

He scowled and gestured for me to get out of there.

I sobered and mouthed, "Be careful." All kidding aside, I hated that he was putting himself in danger so I could safely escape, but there was no arguing with the stubborn bastard. Best to accept it and be on my way so he could hurry and join me.

Hooking his arm around my neck, he scraped the knuckles of one fist along the top of my head a couple of times, mussing my hair with a noogie. Reconsidering my concern for him escaping unharmed, I shoved him away before taking off. As I scampered away, his gaze burned a hole in the back of my head. Like always, he followed my progress, making sure I made it safely. I reached the edge of the castle roof, waved at him, and jumped.

Yes, castle. More precisely, a secluded stone relic concealed deep in central Washington's overgrown, magical forest.

Anyway, the drop might have broken my legs if I had been fully human, but since I wasn't, I landed in a crouch, froze, and listened. I hadn't seen any patrols, but the estate was rife with scents I'd never smelled before. Rust had picked gargoyles out of the mix and filled me in on the creatures.

Our world was separated into two factions, the magical Tricari and the non-magical Mondeine. Like shifters, gargoyles were Tricari and could transform into three forms. Their forms included: human; a winged creature with sharp talons and flesh-ripping teeth; and stone. It wasn't much information to go on, but Tricari races didn't intermingle. Hell, before the war, our people were too busy pretending to be Mondeine to even acknowledge that other races existed. We'd had twenty-five years of peace to seek out others and form alliances, but my pack had chosen to double down on segregation instead.

It's true what they say, you really can't teach old wolves new tricks.

When nothing came barreling around the corner to rip me limb from limb, I bolted toward the south. The estate was enormous, with multiple buildings and gardens. Darting from one ivy-covered brick archway to the next, I kept my eyes, ears, and nose peeled for any sign of pursuit. Snarls came from somewhere behind me.

As I circled a gazebo, footsteps approached from the opposite direction. Ducking behind a bush, I forced my breathing to slow. Since I'd been running and sweating away the first application, I removed a small spray bottle from my bag and spritzed myself with a concoction my witchy aunt had developed to mask scent. I didn't know if gargoyles had keen noses but decided to play it safe.

Feet pounded the grass on the other side of my hiding spot, drawing near. I drew my daggers, held my breath, and waited in the shadows. The runner passed by and kept going without so much as a sniff in my direction. Releasing my breath, I listened as his footsteps faded. Crisis averted, I re-sheathed my daggers, slipped out of my hiding spot, and continued on my way.

We were about an hour and a half drive southeast of Seattle. I was no expert on isolated residences, but it was easy to surmise that this one didn't roll out the red carpet for visitors. In addition to its remote, hidden location, the estate was surrounded by an eight-foot-tall, barbed wire fence made from a lethal blend of silver and steel. On the way in, Rust and I had cut a small gate in the security fence. Now that I'd put enough distance between myself and the great hunt for my gallant mentor, I altered my course to head toward our entry point. Nearing a familiar copse of trees, I squeezed between two thick shrubs, used my gloved hand to find our hidden makeshift gate, and pushed it open. I slipped through, careful not to let any of my skin touch the lethal wire—I'd been burned by silver once and had no desire to repeat the painful experience. Since Rust would most likely be coming in hot with a pack of guards riding his tail, I left the gate open so he wouldn't have to fiddle with it.

Now that I was off the private property of the estate, nothing but dark forest land stretched out before me. Unlike in the city, there were no overgrown ruins or lingering scents of gasoline and human waste here. I sucked down a deep breath of clean mountain air and stretched into a run, weaving through trees and eating up the distance between the fence and the clearing where we had stashed the bikes.

Growing up in a pack, I'd learned that most shifters didn't distinguish between their halves. Animal and human combined to form one whole person, like two sides of the same coin. My relationship with my wolf was different. I could access her abilities like enhanced sight and smell, but something separated us. It was almost like she was caged within my soul, more of a passenger than an active participant.

Now, however, she unfurled like a bear waking up after months of hibernation. The forest called to her, and her excitement bled over into my senses. I could practically feel her tail wagging. I ran through the dark, soaking up the sights, sounds, and smells like a thirsty sponge. Everything felt intensified. The scent trail of a deer made my mouth water. A cool breeze danced over my skin like soft kisses. My ears perked up at the trickling of a nearby stream, and my feet itched to abandon my path and follow the water wherever it led. My wolf and I had never been on our own in a forest. There was so much to explore I could hardly contain her excitement. She whined, desperate to be let off the leash.

"I'm trying," I muttered, my thoughts drifting to the prize in my backpack. I didn't want to get my hopes up only to be disappointed yet again, but after the trouble I'd gone through to get it, the cup seemed undeniably promising. After almost two decades of suppression, this could finally free my wolf.

Twigs snapped ahead.

I sniffed the air. Something smelled savage and... cold, like a wild beast trapped in ice. Definitely not another gargoyle; this was different. Unease crept up my spine as I drew my daggers and slowed my steps, slipping soundlessly through the night. Rounding a massive tree trunk, I sensed danger and froze. Something sliced the air in front of me, right where I would have been if I hadn't halted. Moonlight glinted off metal. A sword! My heart leaped into my throat as I pivoted, narrowly avoiding a second slash. The attacker was lightning fast. Dropping into a crouch, I parried a third strike. Steel bounced off my daggers, the clash ringing through the silent forest as vibrations rattled my teeth and bones.

Damn! Fast and *strong.*

Surprised my blades didn't crack under the force, I ducked and spun away. Like me, my weapons were built for speed and avoidance, and neither my blades nor my body would survive a vigorous pummeling. My best bet was to bail. Looking side to side, I tried to decide which way to bolt.

"*Leox!*" exclaimed a deep, masculine voice.

Power punched through the ether. The burnt ozone stench of magic tickled my nose as bright light overpowered the darkness. Temporarily blind, I lifted one arm to shield my sensitive eyes so they could adjust. When I could see again, I lowered my arm and watched in fascination as light circled in on itself, growing to about a foot in diameter.

What the...

Since my aunt was a witch, I'd seen some nifty magical creations in my time, but nothing like the blazing blue orb hovering before me. In awe, I prepared to dodge if it came hurtling at my face, but thankfully, the orb didn't move. It did, however, provide enough light to give me a good look at my attacker. He wore only a pair of black sweats, giving me an eyeful of rich walnut skin. I felt my eyes widen at the sight of him, but I couldn't help but gawk. He was huge! He had to be more than six feet tall with broad shoulders, narrow hips, and an athletic physique of mouth-watering, jaw-dropping perfection.

I'd never seen anything like him. Every exposed God-blessed forearm, bicep, pectoral, and abdominal curve screamed for my attention. I didn't know where to look first. My gaze snagged on a dusting of ebony curls that led from his navel downward, disappearing under the waistband of his sweats. The *scandalously low* waistband. How had they even stayed up during our scuffle? It seemed like one wrong move, and every inch of him would be on display. My mind hiccupped on the possibility.

My wolf panted at the sight. Yes, panted. She'd never done that before. I ignored the bitch and continued my perusal of the perfect male specimen before me.

"*You?*" asked a deep, rumbling voice. "You are the beast? How can this be?"

Heat flooded my cheeks as I dragged my gawking gaze upward from his happy trail. Now, I realized he was wearing something besides the sweatpants. A leather strap stretched diagonally from his left shoulder to the right side of his waist before circling around his back. Had to be a baldric for the massive sword still clutched in his right hand. The blade that had tried to kill me. Then again, I wasn't exactly there to plant flowers or lobby for world peace. I was a thief, and people tended to get pissed when I took their shit.

"Me?" I asked, trying to make sense of his words as my gaze finally snapped to his face. All the oxygen vanished from my lungs. "Beast?"

He arched one dark eyebrow at me in question. I'd clearly mystified him with my one-syllable sentences.

Fabulous first impression. You're killin' it, Chipmunk.

Yet the set of his square jaw and frown upon his perfect lips made him seem unimpressed even as his startling silver irises with elongated dark pupils tracked me like a predator stalking prey.

Hoping to save face and break the tension, I tried again. "Hi." I gave him my friendliest, most innocent smile. "I'm not sure what sort of beast you've mistaken me for, but I'm just a girl. Woman, really. I mean, I'm almost twenty, so..." I clamped my mouth shut, appalled by the absolute nonsense I was spewing. What the hell was wrong with me? Sure, the guy was nice to look at, but there were plenty of attractive men in my pack, and none of them made me ramble like an idiot.

His intense, inquiring gaze didn't waver, unnerving me. Fierce determination emanated from my wolf as she locked in on him like he was a destination she was desperate to reach.

Ignoring her bizarre urgency and the odd flutter in my chest, I asked, "Is there something you need?"

"I am the guardian of the chalice you stole." He raised his sword, leveling it at me in challenge. "Prepare to die, beast."

Okay then. The big, scary, hot guy was crazy and determined to kill me. As much as I'd like to pretend that was a new experience, it wasn't. Since becoming an adult, I'd had my ass kicked by nearly every adult member of my pack. But unlike with my packmates, I had no intention of standing there and letting this jerk pummel me.

"I'm not a beast," I snapped before adding, "asshole," under my breath.

His eyes narrowed, and I got the feeling he'd heard that last bit.

"You have to be," he argued. "You stole the Chalice of Power. I can feel it on you. You are the broken beast."

Ouch.

Shocked, I stared up at him. He wasn't wrong—my beast *was* broken—but it was such a cruel truth to voice.

"You can't go around saying shit like that about people you just met," I said.

He drew back at my tone. "Why not?"

"Because it's rude. Obviously." I shifted my stance, preparing to move if he did. "You don't see me tactlessly pointing out your flaws, do you?"

His expression hardened, and every ounce of his attention homed in on me. "I have no flaws."

Was he for real? I snorted. "No flaws? You're a homicidal nut job. I literally just met you, and you want to murder me. That seems like a massive character flaw."

Again, one dark eyebrow shot up. "You stole my artifact."

Okay, he had me there. "It's one cup, and you didn't even ask for it back. You just started swinging. Is violence how you handle all of your problems?" Before he could answer, I forged on. "Besides, why do you even care? You won't miss it. You have a whole trove of shiny crap back there that you probably never even use. Hoarding is a mental disorder, ya know? Some might consider that a flaw as well." Okay, now I was being rude, but he'd brought this upon himself.

Broken beast? Really?

He blinked, opened his mouth, closed it, and blinked again.

Ah-ha! I'd stumped him. Encouraged, I pressed on. "Look, I'm sorry I breached your security and took an old cup you've doubtlessly never used and forgotten about. That was wrong of me, but you didn't exactly handle the situation well either. What do you say we call it even and go our separate ways?" When he didn't immediately object, I bowed. No clue why. It felt right, albeit awkward and unnecessary, but it was too late to take it back now. Straightening, I heaped on another cringeworthy gesture with a finger gun salute of farewell. Because, why not? The urge to smack myself on my stupid forehead was strong, but I resisted, pivoted, and took a side-step away from him. My face blazed with embarrassment, but I responsibly kept the self-proclaimed guardian in my peripheral rather than burying my face in my hands. For one brief, shining moment, I thought I might actually make it to the bikes. They weren't far away, and he seemed dazed by my astonishing display of logic. It was either that or my epic lack of mature elegance.

Turned out I had vastly overestimated my powers of persuasion.

"Congelo!"

I'd only made it two steps before the smell of burnt ozone slammed into me at the exact moment my body froze. I couldn't move. At all. I couldn't even wiggle my fingers or toes. The bastard had trapped me in place with magic. Panic surged through my veins as my wolf whined in my psyche, her confusion bleeding into my fear and outrage.

Closing the distance between us, he circled me until we were face to face again. The glowing orb floated beside him. Now that it was closer, I could make out tiny specks of frost forming on the surface. I tried to focus on that and not the feeling of helplessness building inside me. Trapped was bad. Trapped made me want to jump out of my skin and escape, and I needed to keep my head.

"You are not what I expected," the guardian announced, which was a strange thing to say since there was no way he could have known I was coming to steal the artifact. "But as entertaining as this has been, I am duty-bound to protect the chalice and slay the broken beast who comes for it. I cannot allow you to unravel the thread."

What the ever-loving nonsense was he talking about? What thread? I tried to ask, but my jaw was as immobilized as the rest of me.

"What? Nothing to say now? No quips or accusations?" A condescending smile tugged at his perfect lips, and my vulnerability went up in a poof of indignation.

As he circled me, moving back out of my line of sight, my rage grew. How dare the bastard hold me magically gagged while he hurled barbs at me. Did he plan to keep me immobile when he murdered me? What a bully.

He halted before me once again. "Do you wish to plead for your life, beast?" Tilting his head to the side, he studied my face. I truly hoped my expression conveyed the same emotion as the middle fingers I couldn't raise. "*Loqui*," he said with a flick of his wrist.

My jaw moved, snapping closed before springing open again. The rest of my body remained frozen, but he'd restored my ability to speak. Everything I wanted to say to him came rushing forward at once, but I only gave voice to the two words I couldn't hold back. "Fuck you," I spat.

He laughed in my face.

Appalled, I glared at the bastard. He wasn't pack. He may kill me, but I sure as hell wouldn't kowtow to him. All the anger and frustration I'd suppressed over the years turned to rage that boiled over inside me. The edges of my vision turned crimson as my entire body ached to lunge for him. I had never been a violent person, but this male... this male made me desperate for blood. I wanted to plunge my daggers deep into his throat and slice out his voice box so he could never hurl insults at me again.

"Shut up!" I shouted, surprising both of us.

Laughter cut off, he stared at me like he was finally seeing me for the first time.

"Listen, buddy," I said, putting as much sarcasm as I could behind the term of endearment. "I'm done with this. No more lectures from condescending bullies, no more waiting for a beating, no more unfair fights. I'm not going to stand here and do nothing. Either we have a fair fight, or I'm outta here."

"Intriguing proposal." He eyed me curiously. "But how exactly do you intend to leave? You cannot even move."

"Release me, and we'll fight like adults," I said through gritted teeth. "Unless you're... afraid."

His jaw ticked, and anger flared in his eyes. Closing the distance between us, he growled. The sound resonated in my bones, making me want to drop my gaze and submit, but I didn't.

"Afraid of you?" he spat.

His gaze traveled down my body and back up, leaving an unwelcome trail of fire in its wake. What was it with this asshole? Why was my body responding to every little move and sound he made? Lust danced with the fury coursing through my veins, creating a volatile cocktail of emotions that made me feel deranged and irrational. I wanted to both slam my fist into his gut and lick his face.

What the hell is wrong with me?

"Show me your true form, beast," he said.

It took a moment for his request to pierce the insanity confusing my mind and body. When it finally did, my thoughts stuttered. "My... my true form?"

"Yes. Shift. Show me what you really are, and I will give you the fair fight you desire." His lips quirked to the side. "Well, a fairer fight. I am going to kill you either way."

What?

Had he called me a broken beast without knowing what it meant? Without knowing *how* I was broken? A laugh bubbled up my throat at the absurdity of it.

The frown marring his infuriatingly handsome features deepened. "What is so humorous?"

I would have thrown my head back and screamed in frustration if the jerk hadn't frozen me in place. Looking him square in the eye, I took a deep breath and admitted to the flaw I had assumed he already knew about. "I. Can't. Shift." Then, because he was planning to kill me anyway, I added, "Dumbass."

Faster than I could blink, he pounced, coming so close I could have counted the curly dark hairs on his impressive chest. He smelled like autumn after the first frost, of snuggling under a warm fur on a brisk October day. Cool air radiated off him, chilling my skin and making my internal heater kick on.

"Liar," he spat, dropping his head to the base of my neck.

"What are you—" The question caught in my throat as his cool breath tickled the sensitive area just above my clavicle. He was... sniffing me. The whisper of his breath on my skin made my blood boil but from a different kind of heat. The kind that made it difficult to remember he was essentially one giant red flag. Making a monumental effort, I shouted, "Get away from me, you freak!"

He pulled back like I'd slapped him, which I really wanted to. More than I'd ever wanted to slap anyone in my life. "You have done something to mask your scent," he announced like he was an authority on the matter. "But I can still smell you, wolf. You might as well shift and show me your beast."

"Are you hard of hearing?" I asked. "I *can't* shift."

He rocked back on his heels, eyeing me. "Do not worry, I can make you." The smile that touched his lips made the hair on the back of my neck stand up. "Shift," he commanded.

Magic slammed against me, and my will squished like a grape beneath his will. It tugged at my muscles and bones, trying to force

37

the shift. The bastard wasn't pack, but he pulled rank like an alpha. It hurt a lot, but pain and I were old friends. I gritted my teeth and breathed until the attack passed.

"I said *shift!*" the guardian shouted.

Magic punched me so hard it knocked the air out of me. Blood pounded in my ears as my bones turned and twisted, trying to comply with the compulsion. I gritted my teeth against the pain and prayed it would pass. He eyed me like I was a puzzle he wanted to tear apart. Fitting since that's what his attacks felt like. I sucked down ragged breaths as my body knitted itself back together.

The bastard grabbed my chin, forcing me to meet his gaze. Jaw ticking with barely controlled rage and determination flaring in his cruel silver eyes, he said, "Why do you fight the change? Give in, and this will be easy. I will make your death quick and painless."

"Because. Dumbass. I can't shift," I told him once again. God, it hurt to talk. Or breathe. The healing was every bit as painful as the attempted shift had been. "I'm broken. Defective. Not even my alpha can release my wolf."

He glared at me like *I* was the one wrecking *his* day. "I will not fail in my duty."

"Neat, but I still can't shift, so you're gonna have to find some other broken beast to torture."

"We shall see about that." His eyes hardened, his jaw set, and I knew I was in for a world of hurt before the command rolled off his tongue. "Show. Me. Your. Face. Beast."

Each word was imbued with more power than I'd ever felt before. Everything up to this point had been a tickle. Now, magic gripped my innards and tugged. My flesh swelled and stretched as tissue ripped away from bones and strained against my skin. Blood pounded through my veins as it raced to heal numerous fissures and tears. Agony tore a scream from my raw, mangled throat. My vision swam, and I prayed for death.

Tissue that had been healing was once again ripped apart. Then, everything snapped back into place.

I seethed. "Goddamn you, you sadistic piece of shit."

The stranger's eyebrows rose as he studied my face. Sweat beaded across his forehead, but that was the only evidence of his expended magic while I was spent. His well of power must have been massive.

"You will not refuse me, little wolf," he thundered.

I wanted to laugh but couldn't spare the energy. My body needed it to heal. My knees would have buckled if I hadn't been locked in a supernatural stasis. In the light of the glowing orb, I could make out dark bruises mottling my exposed forearms. No doubt they were everywhere. The overwhelming scent of my blood spoke of extensive internal damage. I'd been told silver and decapitation were the only ways to kill a shifter, but if the guardian continued to break me until I lacked the energy to heal, he wouldn't need his sword to finish me off. Internal bleeding and lack of oxygen would do the trick. That sounded like an excruciating way to go. I had to figure out a way to stop him.

The bastard studied me like I was a malfunctioning science experiment.

"No refusing you, huh? That's a rapey thing to say." I should have kept my mouth shut, but I was pissed and terrified. I didn't want to die like this, caught in some random asshole's magical trap as he tortured me.

"I am attempting to give you your dignity by killing you in your true form. The least you could do is comply."

"You need to get it through your thick skull that this is my true form. My only form." If I was going to die, I refused to go down in a simpering puddle, quaking at his bare feet. Even if my insides felt like goo.

"You are weak," he growled. "A shifter who cannot even shift."

The insult stung far more than it should have. I was a lot of things, but weak wasn't one of them. "*I'm* weak? At least I don't cheat with magic. Release me, and I'll show you just how weak I can be. *Coward.*"

The insult hit home. His eyes flared with rage, and even his nifty little glowing ball flickered. I swallowed, afraid I may have pushed him too far.

"You are a scourge," he spat. "A plague upon this land."

"And you're a self-righteous blowhard with a god complex."

Before the last word tumbled out of my big mouth, the cold steel tip of his blade dug into the soft flesh of my throat. Face to face, he bared his teeth at me. "Enough games. You leave me no choice. SHIFT!" he roared.

It was another command. A compulsion. Power hammered into me as the stench of magic singed my nostrils. Fire shot up and down my nerves like lava flowing through my veins. My body seized and spasmed.

Anger swelled. "Coward!" I managed to wheeze. "You. Goddamn. Coward."

Someone screamed. It had to be me, but it sounded far away. The pressure in my head was too much. Too intense. Tears leaked from my eyes as my insides expanded again.

I had to do something.

Focusing on the man before me, I willed my sight to change. The world blurred, and his physical form faded away, revealing the glowing, three-dimensional ethereal tapestry that hid beneath the skin and bones. His spirit. Luminescent threads of what I suspected to be intellect, emotion, fears, passion, and creativity continuously wove together to create the crux of his life. Like all spirits, the stranger was a fascinating kaleidoscope of shifting colors I could have happily spent hours watching weave and evolve.

But fire seared across my ribs, reminding me I didn't have that kind of time.

I extended my consciousness further, past the shimmering colors to the center of his being, searching for the emotion I'd learned my unique touch could soothe pain. It always manifested as darkened threads that stood out in the colorful fabric of life. Some spirits incorporated the threads of pain, weaving them into the tapestry. There, they pulsed and throbbed until eventually settling down to blend in with the metaphysical canvas. But sometimes, a wound cut the spirit so profoundly it couldn't bear to acknowledge the hurt, let alone absorb the resulting trauma. That pain went elsewhere, buried within the soul. Further wounds would join it, tangling together in a mess of repressed agonies that most people didn't even realize they carried, despite the negative energies leaching into their system.

There.

I caught a glimpse of a black thread as the tapestry continued to weave itself. Following the thread, my subconscious slipped through a curtain of color only to pull up short at what lay beyond.

Holy crap!

It was like nothing I'd ever seen before. A knotted, festering blob of inky black threads expanded. Emotions swelled, pressing in around me. Anger, regret, sorrow... the intensity of it all was overwhelming. It built and built until I thought it would suffocate me. Then, it contracted, lessening for just a moment before expanding again. I gaped, wondering how anyone could function under all that pain. It explained why he was so mean and murderous. I couldn't imagine I'd be all that pleasant if I had this intense hurt hidden inside my soul.

Intuitively, my spirit reached out, wanting to untangle the knots to gently release them like I sometimes did for my pack mates. Untangled threads could weave into the canvas and heal, eventually. But there was no time to ease his spiritual pain. Not when my physical body was still being hammered. Hot moisture rolled over my upper lip and down my earlobes. Blood. The coppery scent overwhelmed my senses as stars danced at the corners of my periphery.

Desperate, I grabbed onto the twisted ball of darkness. It felt grimy and repulsive beneath my touch, sending a shudder down my spine. I fought the impulse to release it and withdraw, but I was in danger of running out of heartbeats and didn't have the luxury of being squeamish. I needed to *do* something. But what? My vision clouded over as my lungs grew too tight.

I tugged on the ball, straining as I dragged it out of its hiding place and to the forefront of the stranger's spirit. That's where I released it, dumping all his dark emotional muck right over his pretty design, putting every festering thread on display.

My consciousness slammed back into my own body. The pressure of magic evaporated as the bite of metal against my throat disappeared. Released, I sagged. A sword clangored against the ground. My hands—still gripping my daggers—smacked my thighs. I blinked slowly, my eyelids scraping against the corneas like sandpaper. My lashes tangled, and I lost myself in how good it felt to close my eyes. I just needed a minute to rest, and then I could deal with the threat.

Oh yeah. That guy.

There could be no rest. Not now. Not while a murderous magic wielder was gunning for me. I had to get away. Forcing my eyes open, I saw the world through a murky haze. Lungs that felt shrunken and depleted struggled to take in enough oxygen. I gulped like a fish stranded on the shore during low tide. The breeze felt startlingly abrasive as it brushed against my skin. My throat burned like I'd taken a shot of gasoline chased by a lit blowtorch.

"What the..." He staggered backward, his eyes wild with fear. Gone was the cocky, overconfident swagger and all-powerful aura. I'd forced his deepest darkest secrets out of hiding, and now he faced decades worth of pain and misery at once. He deserved it. He was a murderous bastard who'd been torturing me, and as soon as he pulled himself together, I was as good as dead.

"How..."

As he struggled to form a sentence, my body busily knitted itself back together. Energy drained from the top of my head to the bottom of my feet, covering my injuries in warmth. Hunger pains gnawed at my stomach as my abused muscles begged for food and sleep. I couldn't even feel my wolf and knew I was dangerously close to slipping into a healing coma.

Shit. I gotta get outta here before that happens.

"I will…" Words gargled in the stranger's throat, but he tried again. "I…."

Something terrible was happening. His skin darkened. Muscles bulged, and power emanated around him. His upper lip raised in a silent promise of retribution.

Determined to vanish before he could make good on that vow, I launched myself into a spin that circled to his back. Momentum carried me through. The world tumbled over itself, and I had to throw out a hand to steady myself. Swaying, I widened my feet, barely managing to stay upright.

"Kill him! Kill him now while he's distracted!" years of my father's methods screamed in my mind.

I plotted my strike. Still stunned by what I had unleashed, the stranger hadn't moved to intercept me, and now I stood at his back. From here, I could puncture his heart, slit his throat, or sever his spinal cord. No matter what he was, if I hit something vital, spilled enough of his blood, or cut off his oxygen, he'd die. No being was immortal.

My attention snagged on the extra skin sprouting out of his back. Wait. Were those… wings? Inky black around the ridges, diaphanous webbing in the center, they stretched and grew, filling me with dread as they expanded. Was he some kind of demon?

Oh, God.

I didn't even want to know. I had a clear shot at his spinal cord. One quick flick of my wrist, and I'd be rid of him. It was my duty, my responsibility, to cut him down so he didn't follow and put my pack at risk. Or get the jump on Rust when my partner stopped playing with the guards and made his way here.

But I didn't aim for the stranger's spinal cord. I couldn't. Everything that made me who I was refused to take the opening.

"Weak. Pathetic." Disgust dripped from my father's voice in my

head. I knew exactly what he'd think of my mercy, but it didn't matter. The stranger was fierce and deadly, fighting past the darkness I'd released within him so he could no doubt deliver me a killing blow. Regardless, I couldn't bring myself to snuff out his volatile, magnificent soul.

So, I did the next best thing.

Dropping low, I lurched forward and struck as quickly as my wobbly arms could manage, running my blade across the back of each of his bare ankles. They slid through the flesh and tendons like butter. Dashing out of his reach, I turned to assess his reaction, ready for anything. Most Tricari could heal, so I assumed he'd bounce back. But how fast?

Brows furrowed, he tried to step forward but must have belatedly realized what I'd done. Pain screwed up his beautiful features as agony poured out of his mouth. Slicing his Achilles tendons should slow him down long enough for me to escape.

"Don't follow me," I spat.

"I will kill you," he vowed, his voice little more than a growl.

Wiping away the blood from beneath my nose, I frowned. I could still feel the pain and anger I'd exposed inside him as he battled to contain it, to shove it back down into its hiding place. I should already be running, getting the hell out of there, but unable to help myself, I opened my other sight. He was a mess inside, and I couldn't leave him to face all that excruciating darkness alone. Imagining my hands dripping with a cooling, healing balm, I quickly untangled the largest knot of darkness, releasing it to heal.

His spirit trembled beneath my touch. Eyes wide as saucers, he gawked at me. "What the fuck are you?"

The confusion splashed across his face was so much better than the hate that had previously been there. I smiled. Maybe he wasn't such a bastard after all. Just a little broken and a lot hurting. We had that in common, as did the rest of the world, apparently, because I dealt with that crap all the time.

"Not a plague," I replied, throwing his accusation back in his face. "And a scourge would have gone for your jugular. I'm certain of it."

His brow furrowed, but his wings had extended past his shoulders and were still growing. Soon, he wouldn't need those injured ankles to follow me.

Definitely, time to go.

Turning, I hobbled toward our stashed motorcycles, each step a testament to my stubbornness and pain tolerance. I shouldn't have soothed him. I was already running on empty, and that futile act had siphoned the last dregs of my energy. So exhausted I could barely see straight, I threw my leg over the seat and tried my earpiece.

"Rust? You in range?"

No response.

I didn't want to leave my partner, but he'd flapped his arms like a chicken, and we had a deal. Kicking my bike to life, I fled down the gravel service road toward the highway. Time to put as much distance as possible between my would-be murderer and me. With a bit of luck, I'd never see him again.

My wolf whimpered at the thought, and I wanted to punch her in the face. I don't know why she'd been so excited to see that psycho, but he clearly wasn't into us.

Shoving thoughts of the mysterious homicidal stranger out of my mind, I focused on staying awake and keeping my bike upright as I got the hell out of Dodge.

Arioch

I was so determined to release the beast and finally face the foe I had spent my entire life preparing to kill that I did not realize the little wolf had gone on the offensive until it was too late. Even if I had suspected her attack, I never would have anticipated the form it took.

Long-buried memories assaulted my mind, crippling me with the sudden influx of all the emotions I had suppressed over the years.

"It's a curse, Arioch. You can't outrun it."

"Hold still and let me get a good look at you, boy. See what sort of little pissant I'm dealing with here. Heh." Crack! "Didn't see that comin' now, did you? Straighten up and quit your blubberin', you little pussy. First lesson: don't trust anyone. Especially not me."

Anger, despair, rage, grief, shame, sorrow, and hopelessness ravaged my psyche. I tried to bottle it all back up, but there was too much. It overwhelmed me. I struggled to remember where and when I was.

"Get the fuck up, boy! Your enemies won't care if you're tired or bleeding. They won't stop until you're dead. Kill them, or they'll kill you. That's the reality of the situation. Accept it, or you might as well give up now and stop wastin' my goddamn time."

"Your mother was ambushed, child. It was a trap. She's not coming home."

"Can't believe you fell for that shit. You're lucky she didn't carve out your fuckin' heart. Nobody loves you, chap. You have no friends; friends are for fools. Only the weak buy into that shit. Anyone who shows an interest in you has an ulterior motive. The sooner you realize that, the

better."

"Think you got what it takes? Let's see how long you can survive down in that hole."

Emotions detonated like explosive arrows, blasting me apart. Physical pain registered, coming from my ankles, but it was nothing compared to the agony slicing through my heart and mind. What had she done?

"You can't go after her killer. If you abandon the chalice, the curse will drive you mad. You know this, child. She would not want you to sacrifice your life in such a way."

"You call that a punch? Put some power behind it, boy. There. That's how you do it. Oh, did it hurt? You pissed? Wanna break my jaw? Good. 'Bout damn time. Maybe you got some fire in you after all. I'll tell you one thing, tap my cheek again, and I'll knock your fuckin' teeth out. Now, hit me like you mean it."

I stood there like an invalid as the little wolf danced in and out of my clouded vision, daggers clutched in her trembling hands.

"Coward! You. Goddamn. Coward!"

Pressure built with the clamoring voices of my past.

"Everything dies eventually, child. You have to let her go."

"Killing me won't change anything. The beast will come for you, and you will fail. The stars have spoken."

No. No! I would not fail. I would pull myself together, and then victory would be mine.

Something flickered in the little wolf's eyes. Guilt? Compassion? Neither emotion made sense. She was the beast, come to steal and destroy. She had deceived me with her innocuous appearance only to destroy me with my own memories.

"Trust is a weapon you should never hand to another," a feminine voice from my past said. *"When will you learn, Arioch?"*

Never, apparently, because another female had made a fool of me. Only this one wasn't gloating. She looked... troubled.

"Don't follow me," the little wolf said.

She stilled, and her gaze locked on me like she was concentrating. The storm raging inside me eased, downgrading from a category five to a three. I could finally breathe. I no longer felt like I was being crushed to death. She should have taken the killing blow, but instead, she had lessened my torture.

Why?

Was she toying with me?

"What the fuck are you?" I wheezed.

She said something about plagues and scourges, but her strained voice could not compete with the screaming inside my head. How was she moving? After what I had done to her, she should lack the strength to stand. The five-foot-nothing, freckle-faced beauty had been knocking on death's door when she had turned the tide and handed me my ass. Was she immortal? She could not be. I doubted any deities suffered from terminal afflictions, and she was limping away in obvious pain and exhaustion.

Not immortal then, just... powerful.

I could catch her if I put my mind and body to the task, but then what? Would she blast me with another dose of her crippling emotional magic? I was not sure I could stomach another drop.

"Calm yourself, child. No need to destroy your home."

"And what do you have to offer me? A golden shackle? My own feather bed next to yours in this luxurious cell? Not interested. Get off your knee. You're humiliating yourself."

In the distance, a motorcycle roared to life. She was getting away. I could not allow that to happen. She had the chalice, and my sanity hinged on staying within a kilometer of that godforsaken artifact.

"Shall I coddle you? Do you wish for me to brush your hair and sing you a lullaby?"

I needed to get to her, but I was frozen in place. And no, the irony was not lost on me. All my training, preparation, and dedication... and I could not fucking move. Frustrated and angry, I wanted to roar—to never stop roaring—but I needed to retreat to safety and piece myself back together.

With a deep, calming breath, I forced myself to focus. I closed my eyes and started to rebuild the mental walls I had erected around my past. Shoving painful memories behind them, I wrestled back control of my emotions and took stock of my physical situation. My Achilles tendons were healing, but walking would be excruciating and would most likely tear the wounds open again. Thankfully, I had another option. Sword still in hand, I extinguished my summoned light.

"You gonna cry for your mama? She's dead, boy, and you will be, too, if you don't learn how to sidestep and block."

Stuffing the memory back where it belonged, I focused on my body. My wings had made an appearance. Great. I had lost control of my magic. It had been at least a decade since that had last happened. Disconcerted, I focused my intention and shoved power behind my will. The air shimmered as ice danced over my skin. A flash of blinding light stole my breath, and magic swept through my body, elongating my torso, hardening my flesh into onyx scales, and extending and widening my wings. Clothes and sword winked out of existence—going to whatever plane they visited when I changed forms—as my arms and legs stretched and thickened, ending in claws tipped with deadly talons. Usually, the change was immediate, but tonight I had to fight for every inch of transformation. I had expelled entirely too much energy trying to bring out the beast. I still couldn't believe the wolf had resisted me.

By the time my wings beat, lifting me into the air, I was spent. Spikes of pain shot up the back of my legs with every movement. Disregarding the icy hot agony, I peered through the trees, marking the motorcycle that raced over the road. I knew the moment she passed the kilometer mark because it triggered an uncomfortable buzzing sensation in the back of my head.

I was oddly overwhelmed and confused by the encounter. I considered going after her, but the relentless barrage of memories and emotions continued to assail me. She was the broken beast. She had to be. The only evidence necessary was the Chalice of

Power in her possession. The artifact had drawn me to her. I had accepted her as my enemy, yet I wavered the instant our gazes met. She should have been a beast, terrifying and deadly. Not an awkward and humorous woman with a curvy body and a nose speckled with freckles.

I had never met anyone like her before.

Of course, I had made the acquaintance of very few people, most of whom I would hunt down like prey if I was ever released from my curse.

Regardless, I needed to kill her, and my conscience rejected the idea of committing the act while she was helpless in human form. Yet her beast was trapped, and not even I could release it. I had no idea how she had summoned my past trauma and used it against me, and I felt ill-prepared to go after her until I found out how to block or counter her unusual attack. But I would see that problematic little wolf again soon.

Guaranteed.

Turning my back on the woman and her escape vehicle, I flew toward home, keeping an eye out for the second intruder, the one who had been tormenting my guards when I shot after the chalice. If I could not put an end to the beast, tearing her companion to shreds would offer some satisfaction at least.

When my grandfather was alive, he had encouraged our land to grow uncultivated, a custom my mother had continued. After the war, magic flares had supercharged the forest growth until it created a canopy of greenery. The natural camouflage helped hide the estate from the outside world but made it frustrating to search through. I flew over my family's sprawling estate, scanning the ground for any sign of the second shifter or the guards chasing him. Finding nothing, I gave up and landed between the two ivy-covered stone pillars that marked the manor's main entrance. The tender flesh of my ankles protested beneath my weight, but I gritted my teeth and ignored it.

The head of my security team came barreling around an overgrown hedge and stopped short when he saw me still in dragon form. Anger iced over my veins at the sight. In response, his pulse skyrocketed, and his gargoyle defenses kicked in, emitting a rancid meat stench that made me want to cover my nose with a wing. No predator in its right mind would want to take a bite out of a frightened gargoyle. I sure as hell did not.

"Tyrin," I snapped, eager to escape the stink. I could not speak aloud in my dragon form but could communicate telepathically. *"Report."*

"Yes, m'lord," he said with a bow. He rose, and his gaze shot to my chin, avoiding my eyes. "We found one intruder west of the manor's treasure wing." The "r" of intruder and manor came out tapped, his Norwegian accent heavier than usual in his distress.

He paused, awaiting my reaction. Tyrin's service was a gift from my father. When my mother was three months pregnant, he had shown up with a letter from the one-night stand who had impregnated her, claiming that the blood debt he owed my sire had been transferred to me, along with my father's curse. The Norseman called himself a húskarl—a household bodyguard—but he had been little more than a worthless shadow so far. Tyrin and I had very different views on what "guarding" entailed. He had placidly stood back and watched as other "gifts" from my father all but murdered me in the name of training. Not only had he failed to protect me, but he had borne witness to my shame and suffering. I could never forgive him for his inaction, and if I ever figured out how to kill the stony bastard, I wouldn't hesitate.

"The intruder ran into the barn, started a fire in the hayloft, and then shifted into a wolf to lead us on a chase."

I snorted, and my cool breath met the mild spring evening with a frosty puff of air. *"A chase? More like a distraction."*

A feminine voice from my past whispered, *"It was fun while it lasted, but nobody wants to snuggle up to an icebox forever, Arioch. Even a rich and powerful one."*

Stuffing the memory back into the corner of my mind with the others, I focused on my useless húskarl.

Tyrin's hand shot out between us, and he offered me a bagged dark cloth. "I found this glove in your hoard."

I could tell the instant my previous statement finally sunk in through his thick skull because his gaze shot up to meet mine for a split second before he found my chin again.

"What do you mean by distraction?"

Not yet ready to reveal the extent of his oversight, I changed the subject. *"I distinctly remember telling you to add shifters to the security team."* Gargoyles were not known for their noses, but shifters would have smelled the wolves and sounded the alarm. Theoretically. Come to think of it, the wolf's scent had eluded me until I was practically standing on top of her, but Tyrin did not need to know that. It was beside the point. I had issued an order, and my húskarl had ignored it. *"I do not see or smell any evidence of your compliance."*

My threatening tone caused his pale skin to darken, hardening to an impenetrable stone that not even my claws could rake. Since I would enjoy nothing more than to take out my frustration on the gargoyle, I found his defenses most inconvenient.

"As I told you before, no shifter will make a blood pact with you," he said. "They only do that with the alpha of their pack, and you're not a pack alpha."

"And I told you to figure it out. Is it too much to ask that you do your fucking job and protect me? Perhaps it is time for you to surprise me by being useful for once." My patience vanished, dropping the temperature around us until ice coated the stone terrace beneath my feet.

Tyrin gulped. My attention snagged on his Adam's apple as it bobbed up and down. It would be so easy to rip the blasted thing out. Just one slash of my claw, and bam. What would it look like? Cartilage? Would it turn to stone the instant I separated it from his body? I had ripped out the jugulars of several different creatures, but never an Adam's apple. Was such a thing even possible?

His practiced excuses brought me back to the present. "Your father had a reason for everything he did, and your trainers—"

Time stopped as my anger swelled into a blizzard, frigid and deadly. The edges of my vision frosted over, and the voices in my head—the memories—finally ceased. Nothing but fury remained. Unable to stomach one more of his goddamn excuses, I roared.

Ice poured from my throat. It coated Tyrin, his mouth hanging open and hands up in a meek, pleading gesture. I did not stop until the blubbering idiot was fully encased. Finally, the night lay blissfully silent. Sighing in relief, I studied my work: thick, solid, it would hold for a while. Could a gargoyle survive a cryogenic freeze? Probably. Regardless, if he said one more word to me, I would bite his head off—rancid stench or not—so his chances of survival were better as an ice sculpture.

Besides, the sight would serve as motivation for my team, reminding them what happened when they failed me. I considered lopping off his head and mounting it on a spike to create a more impressive display, but the security team was made up of Tyrin's clan. The loyal fools would certainly revolt if I killed him, forcing me to end their lives, too. I had a chalice to retrieve and a beast to kill; I did not have time to find a new security team. Disappointed by the necessity of keeping him alive, I used a pulse of magic to shove Tyrin's frozen body out of the way and another to open the twelve-foot-tall wooden double doors. I ducked inside, my claws clicking against the pale marble floor.

My grandfather built the manor in the early 1900s when Washington was a newly formed state, the forest wild and alive. It was approximately twelve-thousand square feet, three floors, and modeled after the European gothic castle keeps of the late 1800s.

I closed the doors behind me and shifted back into my human form. This time, the transition was instantaneous. My clothes and sword flashed into existence precisely as they had been before I transformed. Healing had sapped a significant amount of my strength, but as I strode toward the stairs that led to the second-floor landing, I was careful not to let my exhaustion show.

"Everyone you care for will betray you," the feminine voice from my past whispered in the back of my mind. I almost tripped on the stair but gripped the banister and kept walking. I had forced myself to forget about that section of my curse more than a decade ago. Now that the thought had broken free, it refused to be locked away again.

'Betrayed by all' was the exact wording of the curse, and so far, it had proven true. It was only a matter of time before the last person I cared about betrayed me, and the anticipation had almost driven me mad once.

On the second floor, I ignored the archways that led to the wings and marched straight ahead, throwing open the library doors.

Rows of crowded bookshelves lined the walls and jutted out toward a wide center aisle. I would need research materials later, but I continued on to the mahogany desk at the back of the room for now. Dropping the bagged glove on the desktop, I turned on a nearby light and studied the blood on my blade. I had not sheathed it yet because I had a lot of questions about the little wolf and was hoping her blood would provide answers. Closing my eyes, I blocked out the familiar scents of the library and took a deep breath through my nose.

To a dragon, blood was every bit as important for identifying people and creatures as sight and scent. Having eaten my fair share of hapless trespassers, overly ambitious thieves, and would-be assassins, I understood each race carried its own distinguishable flavor. Trolls had a muddy undertone, while human blood had a metallic aftertaste. My blood held hints of currants and fig, almost like a rich red wine.

Since each race tasted differently, her blood could tell me which race had the power to turn memories into weapons. Drawing the sword to my mouth, I licked the blade's tip, closing my eyes as I rolled her taste over my tongue. The experience was not unpleasant. The woodsy flavor of a wolf shifter was fainter than I had expected, overpowered by warm plums, sweet cherries, a hint of vanilla, citrus undertones, and...

My eyes popped open as I collapsed into the chair and studied the blade, wondering if I had somehow nicked myself because her blood tasted like mine.

Well, not exactly like mine, but close. Could the little larcenist be of the same mysterious race as my father's people?

I had no idea what to do with that possibility. My entire life had been spent seeking answers about my father's people and this goddamn curse. Sure, my investigation had been limited since I was tied to the estate. Therefore, I could not physically search for anything. Still, I had a phone line, internet, Mondeine bank accounts, and safety deposit boxes stocked with enough gold and gems to buy a small country. But none of my vast resources had mattered when it came to finding answers. Finally, someone who could potentially provide a little insight had shown up on my doorstep.

And I had let her escape.

With the Chalice of Power.

The artifact had been locked up in that godforsaken box shortly after my birth when Tyrin showed up with it. Nobody could open the box, so Mother had secured it in the vault to keep it safe. As long as I stayed within a kilometer, the chalice remained silent. But now, the annoying buzz in the back of my mind was already beginning to grate on my nerves. As time passed, the buzzing would only increase in intensity. I had tried to run away from my duty once but had lasted only one hundred and thirty-one hours before the magic had driven me back. The details about my time in the woods were blurry, but my guardian said I was borderline feral when I finally returned. It took her hours to scrub the dirt and blood from my claws and scales.

Losing control like that had terrified me into vowing I would never allow it to happen again. Now a freckle-faced wolf who shared my father's mysterious race had taken the chalice, and if I failed to get it back, I would most likely lose myself for good.

Fuck!

Rage ripped me out of my seat. Lunging forward, I threw my desk across the room. Books and papers rained as the solid mahogany smashed against plaster-covered brick. The destruction was not enough to appease my temper. Scooping up my chair, I raised it above my head and slammed it into the floor. An arm broke off. With another hit, I took off two legs. It hit the floor again and again until my chair was nothing but a pile of kindling.

"Is this what we're doing now?" a feminine musical voice asked as a tall, lithe woman floated into the room like a dancer, her feet barely brushing against the floor. She wore a sleeveless knee-length iridescent green frock that shimmered as she moved. Everything from the dryad's flowing movements and uniquely hued garment to her mottled tawny skin and messy, walnut-colored dreads enabled her to blend in with the forest. Faint crow's feet and laugh lines marked her as middle-aged, but her eyes held the wisdom of centuries. When I was a child, I made the mistake of asking how old she was. In answer, she had awoken a tree to dangle me upside down until I remembered my manners. As my mother's closest friend, Catori had appointed herself as my guardian when my mother's death had made me an orphan. The dryad had been doing everything in her power to keep me from devolving into a boorish little brat ever since. It was a taxing job, but she was the most powerful being I had ever encountered and had yet to let me get away with any of the shit I attempted.

She was also the only person I cared about who had not betrayed me yet.

I glared at her, wondering when she would.

"Do not look at me like that, child. I'm not some blood-bound servant you can freeze in a fit of temper. Get ahold of yourself and mind your face before I mind it for you."

It did not matter if I was twenty-five or two hundred and twenty-five, the dryad would still attempt to turn me over her knee if she decided I required discipline. She took her guardian duties seriously. And, if it ever came down to a fight between us, I was not sure I could take her. Nor would I try. Imminent betrayal aside, she was the closest thing I had to family and the one being I still trusted. Even knowing she would eventually drive a knife into my back—hopefully only figuratively—I could not bring myself to hate her. Not after all she had done for me.

Until she betrays me.

This was why I had to forget about that line of the curse again. Exhausted by the mental acrobatics, I wiped the scowl off my face and dropped the busted back of my chair onto the pile.

Scrutinizing my overturned desk and destroyed chair, she said, "I could not help but notice the frozen gargoyle in front of the manor. Are we having a tantrum?"

As was my way, I got straight to the point. "The chalice is gone."

Her eyes went wild as she glanced toward the door. "The beast was here?"

I nodded, my eyes narrowing. "Where were you? I could have used the help of your plants." Had she been here, the little wolf never would have escaped. Convenient that my guardian had been gone.

"I was precisely where I needed to be," Catori said, her own eyes narrowing to mirror mine. "I am here as a favor because I loved your mother, and I love you. Do not make me withdraw my love and leave you on your own. Now, tell me why you are behaving like a child."

So, I told her about the encounter, careful not to leave out a single detail. If I had any hope of defeating the diabolical little beast, I would require the trove of knowledge in my guardian's ancient brain.

"You remembered the rest of the curse," Catori said.

She did not frame it as a question, but I nodded anyway. "I did."

She sighed, reminding me of a wilting flower. "You had the opportunity to kill her, yet you stayed your hand. Why?"

I thought back to the moment I had seen the female in my summoned light. Black baseball cap, short, curvy body, freckles dusting the bridge of her nose and cheeks, and luscious, full lips, she was... not beautiful, but enchanting. Yet none of that had been the reason I had not killed her. No, her salvation had been her eyes. Irises, the rich, lively green of the meadow after a good night of rain had looked me over with such desire and want it had warmed the icy blood in my veins.

Nobody had ever looked at me like that before.

"I do not know. She was not at all what I expected."

"People rarely are," Catori replied, eyeing me.

"Yes, well, it is a good thing I did not kill her since she may hold answers to the questions I have about my father's people."

I refrained from admitting that the wolf's brilliant green eyes and strangely bewitching freckles had something to do with it. Thankfully, my guardian let the matter drop and moved on.

"How bad is the calling?" she asked.

"Manageable, for now." I focused on the artifact, confirming my earlier guess about her destination. "She is taking it toward Seattle." I had always wanted to visit the Emerald City, and it appeared I would finally get my wish. Hopefully, I would be in control enough to remember the experience.

I felt another roar coming on but breathed through it. There was no need to panic. The little wolf had no idea who she was fucking with. I would crash into her world like a damn hurricane. I could slice off her neck with the element of surprise on my side before she used that emotional witchcraft on me again.

No, that would not do. Not now that I knew what she was. "I must not kill her until I get answers."

"Not a plague. And a scourge would have gone for your jugular. I'm certain of it."

She should have killed me when she had the chance. The existence her theft had condemned me to was far worse than death. I would make her pay for it. Righting my desk, I pulled a rag from the top drawer and ran it across the base of my blade, working toward the tip. Catori crossed the room in a blink. A deceptively strong hand gripped my forearm, stopping me.

"Please tell me that is... *her* blood," my guardian said, laser-focused on the tip of my sword.

"Yes. It is."

A vial appeared in Catori's hand as her razor-thin lips spread into a bone-chilling smile. "Oh, child, we do not waste blood. We use it."

Grace

T he gravel service road was treacherous, but I drove like my ass was on fire. The top speed of my Harley-Davidson Fat Bob was 110 miles per hour, and as soon I turned onto an actual road, I made the speedometer needle bounce. Well, as much as I could. The roads were shit, and the encroaching evergreens did their best to block out the light of the almost full moon. Without my enhanced night vision, I would have been screwed. At least the concentration required to navigate potholes and watch the sky for a tall, dark, and winged guardian kept me from passing out.

A shadow passed above, and my heart about leaped out of my chest. Just an owl. I let out a weak laugh at my overreaction and raced toward home. Then a shallow stream running parallel to the road caught my eye. Crusted blood pulled at the skin below my nose and eyes. I had no idea what I looked like but wanted to avoid uncomfortable questions like "who did this?" and "is he still alive?" I weighed my options, deciding a quick pit stop wouldn't hurt. Worst case scenario, the stranger would dive bomb me from the sky, which could happen on or off my bike. At least if he attacked while I was parked, I could hide or fight back without crashing.

Decision made, I veered into a turnout and parked beside the stream, listening for sounds of pursuit. No ominous flapping of wings, no distant roar of Rust's bike. The stream bubbled, squirrels chittered, and an owl hooted from not far away. It was probably the same asshole who'd tried to give me a heart attack.

A game trail led down to the bank. I followed it, stopping about six feet from the water to watch and listen. I was still deep in Terra Fera—the side of the fracture where magic reigned and supernatural creatures abounded—and there was no telling what sort of monsters hunted these woods. Rust always said patience was the real key to survival, and that old wolf had lived long enough to know. I scanned the trees, sniffing. There was a rabbit den nearby, but I didn't scent any other animals. The moonlight shone off the flowing water. It moved downstream, but nothing appeared to move *within* it. It was difficult to see, though, even with my enhanced sight.

Kneeling on the bank, I kept my eyes and ears open as I lowered my head to the surface and splashed water over my face. The dried blood didn't want to come off, but I scraped at it with my fingernails until my skin was soft. Satisfied, I cupped my hands and bent to get in one last rinse.

A flash of color beneath the surface drew my attention. Three glowing yellow eyes, each about two inches in diameter, appeared just beneath my face. Startled, I froze, hands still cupped and halfway to my face.

What sort of lake monsters have three eyes?

That was a question for another time. For now, my heart pounded in my chest as I slowly balanced my weight on my back foot, preparing to bolt.

The eyeballs lurched forward.

I flung my hands open. Water splashed everywhere as I staggered backward, almost falling on my ass. Three rows of razor-sharp teeth broke the surface, snapping together where my face had been only seconds before. Tentacles whipped out in my direction. Unsheathing my daggers, I leaped to the side. Wet, rubbery flesh slapped against my arm, trying to find purchase. I sliced at it. Green goo spurted everywhere, its stagnant pond stench making me gag. I ducked the spray and darted out of range. Drops of green hit the ground and sizzled. The creature let out a blood-curdling shriek, and the tentacle retracted, disappearing beneath the water as little puffs of steam erupted from the ichor spotting the ground.

"What the hell was that?" I asked the now silent bank.

Nobody answered, but that was for the better since I'd reached my threshold of weird for the night. At least I wasn't tired anymore. Adrenaline pumped through my veins, making me feel like I could sprint for hours. Frantically backpedaling until I reached my bike, I kept one eye on the stream as I hopped on my Harley. Using the spare shirt stashed in my pack, I toweled off my face before gunning the motor to life. The creature didn't reemerge, and I didn't stick around to see if it would.

My heart didn't stop racing until I hit the I5 corridor and made my way north toward Seattle. It had to be close to 2:00 am, and few vehicles dared the road, but I occasionally caught the glow of eyes watching me from the darkness. Of course, that could have been my imagination running away with me. I still couldn't believe I'd escaped with the artifact, the Chalice of Power, as the guardian had called it. Now, that male was an egotistical nut job. Didn't matter how attractive he was, he clearly had a screw loose.

And he'd called *me* a beast? Look who was talking!

He was a savage, raging brute, even more domineering than my alpha. He'd used powerful magic without breaking a sweat, sprouted wings, and who knew what else he was capable of? I'd only survived because I'd surprised him. I wouldn't be that lucky again. Soothing him hadn't been the most brilliant play for me to make... or maybe it was. Perhaps if I had soothed him from the beginning, he wouldn't be so hellbent on ending my life.

But the ragey bastard had attacked me first, and soothing was meant to heal injured spirits, not to redirect people who wanted to kill me.

I should have severed his spinal column. Then I wouldn't have to spend this entire drive looking over my shoulder in anticipation of an attack.

My stomach roiled at the thought. Even the idea of killing made me want to hurl. It was official, I was the worst defective wolf shifter on the planet.

As I reached the city limits, a shimmery blue boundary curtain made of ether came into view. Created by mages at the end of The Eradication, the boundaries separated the land into Terra Victa, where the use of magic was strictly prohibited, and Terra Fera, where magic ran rampant. Translucent and only about an inch thick, the boundary line was anchored by a narrow two-foot-deep fracture and stretched into the sky and east for as far as I could see. On the west side, it butted against the freeway before turning north and running alongside the shoulder.

According to Rust, the nonmagical Mondeine rarely stepped foot in Terra Fera. Since they depended on laws and authorities to keep them safe, most Mondeine couldn't hack it in a land where might made right, and only the fittest survived. As I drove along the barrier, I peeked at the province on the other side, wondering what it was like. Bright streetlights illuminated pristine high-rises. Modern, sleek cars drove along clean, even streets. It looked like a completely different world than the one I'd grown up in.

Probably because it was.

It was also forbidden. Especially for me. My father kept me on a short leash, stuck in the den unless Rust was with me and we were training. I used to sneak out with my best friend, Mackiel, when we were young, but we always stayed within pack territory. I wouldn't have been opposed to venturing further, but not to Seattle-Terra.

I'd learned all about the Mondeine in school and had no interest in a land where officials were elected based on fundraising and promises they never kept. They were a corrupt people who thought only of themselves and amassing wealth, while alphas found their strength in the health and well-being of the pack. Sure, our ways weren't perfect, but our den was always clean, the children were protected, and nobody ever went hungry. Everyone had a job and a purpose.

My thoughts involuntarily drifted back to the guardian who'd attacked me. I wondered if he had ever crossed the fracture. Probably not. Mondeine would take one look at his intense silver eyes— paired with all that dark, dangerous energy—and... something. My brain had drifted back to his thick lips and dark eyebrows, and I'd lost my train of thought. Why the hell were his eyebrows so damn distracting?

"You are the broken beast. I cannot allow you to unravel the thread."

His words haunted me. What if he was right, and in my attempt to release my wolf, I unleashed some sort of apocalypse upon the world? No. That was crazy. If our magical solution to my problem came with doomsday-level potential, my aunt would have mentioned it. Surely.

Most likely.

Okay, that's it. He's the beast, not me. No more letting him mess with my head.

Making the silent pact with myself, I took the Madison Street exit, heading away from the boundary line and into downtown. A lone streetlight flickered, illuminating a spray-painted warning that I was entering pack property and trespassers would be eaten. As much as I'd like to say the last part was a joke, becoming dinner was a strong possibility for those stupid enough to try their luck. The alpha monitored the district through multiple surveillance cameras and pack patrols, and he didn't play when it came to the safety of the pack.

This part of the city had a rough past, and it showed. The photographic travel books I'd scavenged touted the Pioneer District as "richly historical" and known for "Renaissance Revival architecture, thriving restaurants and breweries, and a coffee shop on every corner." But, Seattle-Fera no longer fit that description. During The Eradication, my father assembled an army of shifters and invaded the Emerald City, claiming the downtown districts as pack territory. The humans retaliated with force, launching ballistic missiles packed with explosives and silver dust.

The result had been devastating.

Buildings were demolished, landmarks destroyed, and roads ravaged. Twenty-five years had passed since the war ended, but the wreckage remained. The once famous skyline was now void of the

Space Needle. According to Rust, Seattle's iconic observation deck had crumpled during the first series of blasts. The second attack took out half of the Columbia Center, the art museum, and Smith Tower. Then, when the war ended and the mages fractured the land, a wave of magic flooded Terra Fera, feeding plants and animals an unhealthy dose of arcane Miracle-Gro. Buildings and streets that had survived the bombing were no match for a magically charged Mother Nature.

No longer famous for its architecture and Mondeine comforts, the city's wild side now sported a different shade of beauty. One born of savage brutality.

While the Mondeine province was like a well-groomed house cat, cared for and cherished, the Tricari side was a stray dog, beaten, thrown into a fighting ring, and ripped to shreds. Instead of rolling over and showing its belly, the city fought and survived. It was forever changed but not defeated. Every scar served as an awe-inspiring symbol of its strength and tenacity. I would love to venture into Seattle-Victa someday, but the Ferra side would forever be home.

Navigating my bike around hollow, moss-covered shells of buildings, I slowed my speed to avoid popping a tire on cracks in the uneven pavement. The area teemed with life; nocturnal animals scurried over the ground, chittering and chirping. Lingering scents from the pack's patrols intermingled with game trails. The glowing eyes of a small animal—either a raccoon or an opossum—followed me as I made my way to the giant crater that served as an entrance to my pack's den.

The pack used motorcycles for several reasons: they got an average of fifty miles to a gallon of gas, made for a quick getaway, and were easy to fix. They were a transportation no-brainer. They could also navigate the terrain better than a car, and we could cram everyone's bike into the small lot at the mouth of the den. I rolled into an empty spot at the back of the lot and parked. Sliding off my bike, I stood and stretched.

Everything hurt, but I was safe.

Steadying myself against a concrete pillar, I yawned as the last dregs of adrenaline melted away, leaving behind a bone-deep weariness. Sleep was so close I could almost taste it. I wanted nothing more than to drag my ass to my bed, but I couldn't. Not yet. Not with Rust still out there and in danger. I could text him, but the pack only had two cell phone towers: one close to the den and one at the farm. Cell service elsewhere was shoddy. Besides, he wouldn't hear his phone if he was on the road. Worrying my bottom lip, I listened for the roar of his bike, wondering if I should have broken my word and waited for him.

Too late now.

With nothing to do but wait, I fired off a text to Mackiel.

Me: You up?

No answer. Not surprising since he'd have to get up early to work with the recruits. My friend was still at the farm where new packmates went to train for two years. He'd been there almost four, and instead of bringing him home, the alpha had given him authority over the newbies. I didn't know if he'd ever come home, but at least we still texted daily.

I glanced around, making sure I stood in the blind spot of any surveillance cameras. Careful not to rip my hair out, I untangled my cap and accessed the attached camera. I rewound the footage and watched the scene from the trove. The box didn't change; there was no swirling galaxy or involuntary blood donation. I stared in stunned disbelief as the recorded version of myself opened a plain wooden box. Because of the higher camera angle, I couldn't see my bare hand in the shot when I picked up the chalice. According to the video, my actions were textbook. Fast-forwarding to the attack, I paused on the guardian's handsome, terrifying face, committing it to memory. Not like I was in danger of forgetting him, but still. Something about his eyes drew me in and held me captive, almost as firmly as his freezing spell had. Maybe he was an incubus. I didn't know if the sexual demons existed, but that would explain my instant and senseless attraction to him. I rolled the footage again, pausing when he quirked an eyebrow at me. My wolf whined in response.

Yep. Definitely an incubus.

I rewound the footage, stopping right before the big guy swung at me and hit the button to splice the recording. My thumb hovered over the delete button as I weighed the pros and cons of erasing the encounter. The alpha had a way of turning paranoia into a pack sport. If I so much as muttered phrases like 'took a blood sample,' or 'promised to kill me,' he'd overreact, round up a merry band of pack killers, and they'd march off and attempt to exterminate the threat. *Attempt* being the keyword since my attacker would probably magic the entire team in place and behead them at will with his giant sword.

I didn't want the blood of packmates on my hands. I also wasn't looking forward to the lecture I'd get when the alpha realized I'd had the opportunity to kill the guardian and let him go.

On the other hand, if I kept this encounter from him and my father ever found out, an ear-melting lecture would be the least of my worries. He'd flay my backside. Wouldn't be the first time, but that didn't make me any more eager to be at the receiving end of a beating. Growing up in Ireland in the 1800s, my father was Catholic to his very core. Spare the rod and spoil the child? Not Chaz McCarthy. It had been years since I'd received my last lashing, and although I was technically an adult, there was no way the alpha had forgotten how to wield a belt.

"Chipmunk," a male voice said by way of greeting.

Startled, my cap slipped through my fingers. I fumbled but managed to catch it before it could hit the ground. A notification flashed across the screen, letting me know the spliced footage had been deleted. Whelp, the universe had made the decision for me. Hoping it was the right thing to do, I smacked the cap back onto my head before seeking out the person who'd startled me. Two shifters, obviously out on patrol, stood about ten feet away. Bare-chested, they wore only sweatpants, sneakers, and elastic tactical belts. The sweats and shoes were easy to kick off if they needed to change forms, and the tactical belt would stretch to accommodate any shape. Handheld communicators were clipped onto the belts, keeping the patrol in constant communication with the den. The faces of both shifters were familiar, but I didn't know their names. Not surprising since the alpha strongly discouraged me from fraternizing with the guards after... Well, after one guard had misinterpreted my soothing for something more intimate.

One of the guards met my gaze, unhooked the handheld communicator from his duty belt, and pulled it up to his mouth, all without blinking.

"Stryker here, come in Home Base."

"You got Home Base. Go ahead, Stryker," a female voice replied.

"I got eyes on Chipmunk. She's back and by the bikes."

"Copy that. I saw her arrive on the video feeds and let the alpha know."

Clipping his handheld back into place, he flashed me a condescending sneer that made me grateful I'd figured out how to block the thoughts of my packmates. The bastards seemed to get off on making me feel like a captive—like an outsider and possible flight risk—but they had no idea what I was capable of. Nobody had held a silver-bullet-loaded gun to my head and forced me to come back tonight. I stayed because I wanted to, because this was my pack, too.

Hell, if I wanted to leave right now, I could get on my bike and peel out of there.

But that's what Dad's cronies wanted... a reason to hunt me down and punish me for being different. I refused to give it to them.

Head held high, I marched past them to the jagged concrete hole in the ground that served as the entryway of the den. The patrol continued on, and I let out a breath, relieved that no one had attacked me. The fight for dominance was an ongoing battle within the pack, and since I didn't fight, I made for an easy target whenever some idiot wanted to flex. I tried not to let it get to me, but I avoided most of my packmates whenever I could.

Our pack was housed beneath downtown Seattle, in the original ground level of historic homes and businesses that had been built on filled-in tidelands in the late 1800s. In 1889, a fire raged through the district, destroying the original Pioneer Square and the twenty-five blocks surrounding it. After the fire, officials decided to rebuild at a higher elevation to solve the flooding problem.

Re-grading the streets would take almost a decade to complete, though, and the city was in the middle of an economic boom. Desperate to capitalize on the prosperity of the residents, merchants couldn't afford to wait. They rebuilt storefronts on the muddy land and opened for business. Not to be deterred, the city moved forward with its plans and erected retaining walls at the street-side edge of every sidewalk. Entire blocks were walled off, forcing shoppers to use ladders to climb in and out of blocks to purchase goods and services.

With brick walls enclosing thirty-three blocks of the old downtown, the city moved on to the next step and filled in the old streets. Next, they laid new roads down on top of the landfill, eventually building new sidewalks over the old and turning first-floor display windows and lobbies into basements. The old sidewalks became tunnels that granted underground access to the buildings. The tunnels were used for prostitution and shady dealings until the Bubonic Plague hit, and the city condemned the underground, closing off its passages.

When the Mondeine dropped ballistic missiles on downtown as retribution for the pack evicting their people, my father was away with a small team on a recruiting mission. He and his crew returned to find a ruined city, the air clouded with deadly silver dust, a missing pack, and a crater where Pier 46 used to be that opened to the long-forgotten underground. Needing somewhere safe to lay low, Dad and his team made camp in the basement-level

69

tunnels and waited for the silver to settle. When the air was breathable again, they scoured the district for survivors.

They found no one alive.

Rather than moving on, Dad buried the dead and planted the pack flag underground. He and the dozen or so remaining pack members moved in and started renovating. Most buildings had been restored and received updated electrical in the 1960s when they hit the National Register of Historic Places. The pack was able to focus efforts on reopening the underground entrances, sealing off the upper levels of buildings, hooking up above-ground solar and wind power sources, and turning what had previously been basements of businesses into family homes.

Standing in the den entrance, about a dozen feet separated me from the first row of brick-and-mortar buildings. Old-fashioned gas streetlights rewired for electricity lined the row and lit up arched brick entrances leading to the tunnels that had once been sidewalks.

A Harley rumbled down the street. I turned to watch Rust slide his bike into the open spot next to mine, kill the engine, and stagger off. Relieved, I took my first deep breath in hours.

He approached, and we gave each other the customary once-over. Looking almost as exhausted as I felt, he sniffed the air between us, and a little of the concern eased out of his shoulders. Stopping by the stream to wash had been a smart move, even if I'd nearly had my face bitten off.

"You look like shit," Rust observed aloud.

I chuckled. "You always say the sweetest things. That Janey is one lucky gal."

He gave me a lopsided, weak smile. "I do what I can."

Even his voice sounded rough. He'd changed clothes, but he was in one piece. I couldn't see or smell any blood or wounds, a significant win, all things considered. "You shifted," I observed. He'd never had to go furry on a job before. Of course, I'd never set off an alarm, either. We were covering all sorts of firsts today.

Shifters rarely had time to strip before changing forms, and clothes became casualties. It was the reason every pup learned how to sew.

Rust nodded slowly, watching me like I was an idiot for stating the obvious. "You hit yer head?"

"No, asshole. I'm showing concern. I realize it's a foreign concept to a narcissist like you, but—"

He held up his hand, halting my tirade. Rust was no narcissist, and we both knew it. He cared deeply about every single member of the pack, and even some beings who weren't pack. I'd once seen him give away his rations to a couple of hungry troll kids. He was just a gooey-hearted good guy wrapped in the body of a grouchy old wolf.

"That smart-ass mouth means yer still you," Rust said. "Any skinwalker wearin' your flesh would be better behaved. Ya must be fine. You got anythin' to report?"

Trying not to get caught up in the realization that there were beings who could wear my skin—or his—I shook my head. "Nope." It was a technicality, not a lie. After all, I couldn't very well report on anything we didn't have footage of.

Rust eyed me, but I sidled up next to him before he could get more precise with his questions. He was listing a little to the left. I wanted to duck under his arm and prop him up while he walked, but that would show a level of weakness and vulnerability nobody in the pack would allow. Especially not a badass like Rust. My mentor could be unconscious and bleeding out, and he'd still find a way to walk home under his own power. Without limping. The stubborn was strong with this one.

"Come on, let's get you home to Janey and the kids," I said. As we headed into the den, toward the row of houses, I didn't support him, but I stayed close enough to dive under him if he went down. Breaking his fall with my body was the best plan my tired mind could come up with.

"Why do *you* look so rough?" Rust asked. "Did ya have to fight?"

Technically, there was no fight. All my energy had been spent healing the damage my body had caused itself, but saying that aloud would lead to numerous questions, if not immediate seda- tion and a padded cage, so I shook my head. "I was too stressed about the job to sleep last night. I still have no clue what tripped the alarm, and you took forever to get here. I was worried I'd have to tell Janey her mate wasn't coming home, and she and the kids would gut me. I mean, what the hell, Rust? Did you stop and take a nap along the way?" Between the attack and stopping to wash the blood off, I hadn't arrived much earlier than him, but I was just spouting off nonsense to solidify my story now.

Rust chuckled. "Didn't know ya cared."

"About being gutted? I care very much about that. But yeah, worrying over you took years off my life, but don't you fret about me. I'll go hand the artifact over, pass out for a few hours, and I'll be right as rain." All true. Sure, I'd left out some crucial details, but I still wasn't sold on the idea that lying by omission was still lying. Still, if Rust weren't dead on his feet, he would have scented my deceit and called me on it. Time to change the subject before his senses kicked in. "Why don't you fill me in, and I'll go debrief for both of us while you check on Janey."

He eyed me, slowing his pace. "I should give my own report."

"Yeah, and you will. After you get some rest. You look like death chewed you up, decided you were nothing but gristle and spat you out." He'd changed forms twice before driving home, without food to refuel his system. It was a wonder he hadn't face-planted on the side of the freeway. "Besides, your mate could be in labor. Janey needs you. Nothing fatal happened. We retrieved the artifact and made it home unharmed. Give me the Cliff Notes about your encounter with the guards, and I'll share enough with the alpha to keep him off your back until morning. I already feel bad about taking you from Janey tonight. Let me do this one little thing for you two."

His eyes were full of objections, but I'd offered him a get-out-of- jail-free deal too sweet to pass up. "You're the daughter of the alpha,

Chip," he said, sorrow leaking into his expression. "Kindness shouldn't be your weapon."

My breath caught at his uncanny choice of words. There was no way he knew about my skirmish with the guardian. Rust would have interfered the instant he realized I was in danger. Had he seen me slash my attacker's ankles and leave? No. Rust would have taken advantage of how I'd disabled the man and finished the kill. My chest ached at the thought. The silver-eyed stranger may have scared the common sense out of me, but I didn't want him dead. I opened my mouth to ask about his fate, but Rust cleared his throat and spoke before I could.

"After you left, I got the drop on two guards. I was right about them. Gargoyles," he spat. "I tried ta stab one, but his skin... shimmered and turned light grey. They shifted and sprouted wings. My knife made contact but didn't break the skin. Worse, it... reverberated like trying to stab goddamn stone."

Rust carried a titanium hunting knife spelled to keep the edge sharp. It wasn't necessarily deadly to magical beings with regenerative abilities, but it should have at least bled the guards. My daggers, made of the same metal but without the spell, had sliced right through the guardian's skin and tendons. Thank God he wasn't a gargoyle.

"Those winged freaks are faster than they look," Rust continued. "Gave me a run for my money until I shifted. Then I used my superior endurance to wear 'em out before circling back to the bikes. That's why I'm so late."

"Cardio is key," I said, quoting him. We sometimes missed leg day, but my mentor never let me skip out on a run.

He grinned. "Aww, you do pay attention."

"You are kind of a broken record." I wasn't even sure what a record was but had heard the old wolf use the expression enough times to know it fit. "Are gargoyles in the database?" I asked.

Mondeine liked to intermingle. North America was a melting pot of races and religions, and according to Rust, most non-magical people lived stacked on top of each other in cities. Tricari were different. No laws bound us or kept us from killing one another, so each community stuck to its own territories. Other than recruitment and the occasional heist or hunting party, our pack rarely left Seattle. Limited exposure meant we knew almost nothing about the people and creatures occupying the rest of Terra Fera. Our continued survival depended on collecting information on other Tricari in case we needed to attack or defend ourselves. With this goal in mind, Rust had built the pack a database and populated it with details about the magical beings we encountered.

I'd read every entry, and gargoyles weren't mentioned as far as I could remember. Neither was the creature from the stream. Of course, I hadn't read any entries on breathtakingly beautiful murderous men with silver cat eyes who sprouted wings, created icy balls of light, and froze their opponents in magic, either. There was still so much out there we knew nothing about.

"I'll update the database tonight," Rust said.

"I'm pretty sure you had the entire estate chasing you. I smelled smoke. Did you set something on fire?" If I asked enough questions, he'd be too busy answering to interrogate me.

"The barn. A diversion to keep their attention while I shifted." He continued to watch me. "What about you? Did ya see that monster patrollin' the air?"

Wondering if he was talking about the guardian, my ears perked up even as my heart skipped a beat. I worked to keep my expression neutral as questions cycled through my mind. Had he used those forming wings to take to the sky after I'd bailed? Had he shifted into something else? My curiosity was killing me.

"No. The air was clear," I said, trying not to sound too eager for information. "You saw a... monster?"

"Monster in size, smartass. Should've seen this thing; it was huge. Scales so dark t'was like lookin' into a void. And the power blastin' out of it was like nuthin' I've ever felt. Smelled like blood and magic. It was comin' from the direction of the bikes. Thought for sure he'd gotten ya until I saw yer bike was gone."

Scales? Snakes had elongated pupils. Maybe the guardian shifted into some sort of reptile. "What do you think it was?"

Rust leveled a meaningful look at me. "Think about it, Chip. That room you were in... like a giant treasure chest. The entire estate smelled like a predator. The kind of predator I wouldn't want ta tangle with. I only know of one scaled creature that flies, hoards wealth, and scares the shit out of its enemies."

An answer popped into my mind, but it couldn't be right. Could it? Clinging to my denial, I whispered, "No."

He eyed me. "Why not?"

Glancing around to make sure nobody was in earshot, I lowered my voice. "You really believe you saw a dragon?"

Frowning, he nodded.

"As in a *dragon*. Rust, that's crazy. We don't even know if they exist."

He shrugged. "Doesn't change what I saw. Black scales, thirty-foot-wide wingspan, long-ass tail, claws tipped in talons that could rip a vehicle apart. There was talk of dragons during the war. One guy in my unit claimed to have actually met one. I think they're out there, and we just made an enemy of one."

Jerking my hands to my mouth, I stared at Rust. *Holy shit.* Still, it made sense when I thought about the magic. The light, the way he'd locked me in place, how he'd compelled my body to shift almost to the point of killing me. Here I'd been worried he was an incubus. The prospect of dealing with a sexual demon on the warpath had driven me home at breakneck speeds. The thought of an enraged dragon—*the* apex predator—swooping down to bite off my head made me want to turn into an actual chipmunk so I could hide in a tree trunk for the rest of my life.

"We stole from that monster," I whispered behind my hands as if they could somehow shield me from the repercussions of such stupidity. Real or not, dragons were definitely on the 'Do not steal from' list. Everyone knew that. There were dozens of stories about the repercussions of removing treasures from a dragon's hoard.

Rust nodded, his expression somber.

We'd made it to the row of lampposts, and I felt like we were walking underwater. There wasn't enough oxygen in my lungs. Stars danced in front of my eyes, and bile coated the back of my throat. I bent over, afraid I was about to puke. If Rust was right, I'd squared off with a dragon. He'd been impossibly strong and powerful in human form, and only the element of surprise had enabled me to get away. Now he knew what I was capable of, and he'd vowed to kill me. I couldn't tell anyone because I'd deleted the footage. Even if I hadn't, I wouldn't talk. Dad would send our entire pack to intercept him if I did, and they'd die. The best thing I could do was offer myself up as a sacrifice and hope he'd spare the rest of the pack. I was so dead they'd have to bury me twice.

I'd called a dragon a coward!

Rust was staring at me like I'd grown a second head. "You okay?"

I needed to calm the hell down. No doubt he could hear my racing heart and was about to call bullshit on my story and demand the truth. But really, there was no reason to panic. The guardian hadn't followed me home and couldn't possibly know where I lived. My heart was about to explode for no good reason. I'd gotten away with the chalice. I just needed to lie low until the homicidal dragon found someone else to torment.

No big deal.

I could handle this.

Worst case scenario, he'd show up and kill us all. Then I wouldn't have to deal with anyone's accusations of withholding information and not killing the dragon when I had the chance because we'd all be dead.

What have I done?

I swallowed, got myself under control, and straightened. "Sorry,

I... *we* could have been eaten by a dragon. That's a lot to unpack. Do you think the alpha knows?"

"That he sent us to a dragon trove?" Rust considered me for a moment. "No. The witch told him where the artifact was located. She might've had an inklin' about the dragon and kept the information to herself, but I can't believe Chaz would knowin'ly endanger the pack by sendin' us ta steal from a dragon."

I couldn't believe it either. My father had a lot of faults, but the pack's safety meant the world to him. It was why he was so strict and pushed us so hard. Of course, I didn't like the implications attached to my aunt knowing about the dragon, either. "Maybe neither of them knew they were sending us to a dragon's hoard. And if not, we shouldn't tell them."

Rust eyed me, looking like he wanted to argue.

"Nothing good can come of it," I insisted.

He gave me a curt nod. "I kept watch, but nothin' tailed me. I think we're in the clear."

We reached the first tunnel, and I stopped and eyed my mentor. "And if the alpha asks you?"

"I won't lie to him. I can't. You know that. But I won't volunteer the information, either."

I nodded, expecting as much. "Go home, Rust. You need to be awake and clear-headed when you give your report. I got this," I said.

The side of his mouth quirked up. "When did you start giving me orders, kid?"

"Doesn't matter who says it, you know I'm right. What do you want me to tell the alpha in your absence?"

He gave me his report, and I promised to deliver it word for word. He didn't sigh in relief or anything, but his shoulders did relax a little. "Thanks, Chip."

"Of course. Thanks for having my back out there. And in here."

"Whenever I can, kid." He chucked me on the chin and trudged down the tunnel before I could retaliate.

I walked to the next block and stepped through the reinforced brick archway. A string of white LED lights ran along the retaining wall, lighting the way with a soft glow. Moonlight filtered through small glass squares embedded in the sidewalks above when the streets had been re-graded. They served as beautiful little reminders that life still existed above the dark depths of the den; a life with dragons, tentacled stream creatures, gargoyles, and all manner of bloodthirsty beasts. Maybe it was time to throw in the towel on my dreams of adventure and never leave my house again.

I shook my head as I approached my current and future hidey-hole, a small smile trying to tug its way onto my lips.

Dad and I lived in the remains of an old tourist trap. Before the bombing, our home had been the basement saloon beneath a restaurant. Decorated to celebrate the district's history, it was all red brick walls, exposed pipes, embossed tin ceiling tiles, and hardwood floors. Dad had remodeled the saloon to include a small kitchen and two bedrooms, kept the separate men's and women's bathrooms, and installed a bathtub and shower in each. He also left the old chestnut bar intact. It jutted out from the north wall with a mirror and liquor-packed shelves behind it. The mirror had been cracked in the bombing. Now, it showed a kaleidoscope of reflections like a bizarre, abstract art piece.

I entered, finding the alpha seated on a black leather stool at the bar with a bottle of whiskey in one hand and a three-by-five framed photograph in the other. I didn't have to see the picture to know who was in it. This was how I usually found my old man upon returning from a job.

Dad had been out of town when the Mondeine bombed downtown Seattle, but his family had not. He'd lost his mate, three sons, and two daughters. Twenty-seven years had passed since the bombing, but he'd mourn the woman who wasn't my mother for the rest of his life.

In the shifter world, there were mates, and then there were true mates. Mates logically selected one another in a human-like agreement forged to benefit both parties and the pack. These relationships made strategic sense and lasted until the individuals were no longer compatible. Shifters could live for centuries, and change was inevitable with our long lifespans. Sometimes people grew apart and wanted different things in life. This kind of mating was the shifter equivalent of human marriage, a contract intended to last through life but breakable under the right circumstances.

A true mate bond, however, was something else entirely. It was a primal, carnal reaction to finding the missing half of one's soul. Once a shifter found their true mate, the bond would take hold. No amount of logic could reason it away, and nothing could break the connection, not even death.

Cassandra had been my father's true mate, and when he lost her, he lost a part of his soul.

My sight blurred, and the glowing tapestry of my father's spirit appeared before me. It had been changing over the years, growing darker and more tortured. I wanted to soothe it, but I couldn't, even if I had the energy. I'd tried to soothe him once when I was a child, but he knew immediately and flipped out on me. The next time I tried, it was like slamming into a metal wall. The alpha had found a way to block me. He was the person I wanted to help most in the world, and he wouldn't let me in.

Which pretty much summed up our entire relationship.

Unlike the children from his true mate, born of love and promise, my father must have seen a mistake when he looked at me—the result of a moment of weakness spent in the arms of a woman who never could have replaced the one he lost.

Forcing a smile, I greeted him, "Hello, Alpha." I closed the door behind me.

I'd called him Dad out loud once. I was maybe seven at the time, and one of the other kids had been flicking me shit about referring to my old man as 'Alpha.'

"He's ashamed of her because she can't shift," another kid piped in. "Bet he won't let her call him Dad."

79

"Can you blame him? I wouldn't if she was my kid," a third kid added.

Determined to prove them all wrong, I'd rolled the endearment around in my mouth for a solid month before working up the courage to drop a casual "Goodnight, Dad" on my way to bed one night. Reaching my doorway, I turned to find his face white and a look of absolute horror widening his eyes.

Dad.

He'd probably loved that title once, but from my lips, it brought him pain. Rust called it guilt. He said the alpha blamed himself for my disability. He'd dishonored the memory of his true mate by sleeping with a woman he didn't care for, and I'd paid the price. Regardless, losing his mate and legitimate children had broken something in my old man. His suffering was abysmal, and I wouldn't add to it. Dad was just a word. One I vowed to never speak aloud again. In my heart, he could remain 'Dad,' but 'Alpha' was the only title that would cross my lips. Sure, our lack of father-daughter connection stung, but he gave me what he could. His heart had shattered long ago. I didn't fault him for his inability to piece it back together for me. I was just grateful not to get sliced by the jagged shards left behind.

At my approach, he spun around on his stool. He didn't run to the door and hug me in relief, didn't give me a bright, cheeky smile that said he was happy I'd made it home. That wasn't his way. It hadn't been his way when I was four, and my babysitter accused me of witchcraft and attempted to drown me in the bath. Nor when I was seventeen and had my innocence about men shattered by a guard who was so busy promising to love me forever, he couldn't hear my screams for him to stop.

No, Dad's way was to look me over for damage, get the details, and then fix the problem.

"You're okay," the alpha said, letting his relief show in the softening of his eyes and the relaxing of his shoulders.

"Safe and sound," I confirmed.

"And the artifact?"

"Got it." This time, I beamed. I couldn't help it. I might not be one of the children born of the mate he loved so deeply, but I could still make him proud. Sliding straps down my arms, I took off my backpack and unzipped the pocket I'd stashed the cup in. My fingers wrapped around the chalice, and it seemed to awaken in my hand. A foreign awareness crept over me, making my skin crawl. I couldn't wait to offload the creepy cup. Holding it out toward my father, I approached the bar.

Rather than take it from me, Dad leaped off his stool and backed away. "Stop. Right there is close enough." Was that... fear in his voice? Shocked, I looked from the cup to him. He wasn't afraid of anything, yet he stared at the chalice like it was a wolf-eating plant. "That's it. That's really it."

I nodded. "It... called to me. Like you said it would."

"Good—" His voice cracked. Clearing his throat, he tried again. "Good job. You have no idea what this means to me. What it'll mean for us. This changes everything, Grace."

The way his voice wobbled made my eyes sting and my throat constrict. I'd never heard the alpha sound so vulnerable before. Honestly, I didn't know he cared so much about my wolf being free to run and hunt with the pack. Then again, if I wasn't a shiftless loser anymore, maybe it would reduce the amount of shame he felt over my conception and birth. My heart went out to him. I wanted to wrap my arms around him and reassure him everything would be fine, but the alpha wasn't a hugger. So, I stayed right where I was and soaked up every ounce of victory I could. He seemed proud of me and hopeful for the future. He was right; this little cup had the potential to change everything between us.

But why wasn't he taking it from me?

"Don't you want it?" I asked. He'd never hesitated to take stolen loot off my hands before. The chalice was the most important item I'd ever lifted. He should have snatched it from me and locked it up somewhere safe.

"No. You hang onto it until tomorrow night. Take it to Sereana after sunset. She'll know what to do." When I hesitated, he gestured impatiently toward my bag. "Go ahead now, put it away."

Confused, I slid the cup back into the open pocket and zipped it up. Once it was out of sight, Dad blew out a breath and slid back onto his barstool. I was hoping for an explanation, but he left me hanging and took a long pull from the whiskey bottle.

Questions bounced around my head like rubber balls. I knew better than to ask but ached to understand why my father seemed afraid of the chalice. Was he worried about unraveling some sort of thread if we used it? My previous excitement about finally unleashing my wolf faded, leaving a sour taste in my mouth and an uneasy churning in my stomach.

"Where's Rust?" the alpha asked.

"He was worried about Janey, so I told him I'd handle the debriefing."

Dad ran a finger over the lip of the bottle, studying me. "Think you have that kind of authority?"

"No, sir. But the job was successful, and there wasn't anything to report. Do you know if Janey's in labor yet?"

Rather than answering me, Dad tensed. "This kind of shit is exactly why Rust isn't my second anymore. He needs to get his priorities straight."

Shocked by the flare of vitriol toward his oldest friend, I dropped my gaze in submission. "I'm sorry, Alpha. I shouldn't have sent him home. I messed up. I'm prepared to shoulder whatever punishment you see fit."

He laughed, but the sound was more angry than jovial. "Always so damn willing to be the scapegoat. Rust didn't act on your authority. He knows you don't have any. Well then, out with it. Give me your goddamn report."

I didn't even look up; I didn't want to see the disgust I suspected would be in his eyes. "After we retrieved the artifact, I tripped an alarm; Rust shifted and drew the guards away while I escaped. He followed shortly after. Nobody followed him."

He stared at me as if waiting for more.

I suddenly had the urge to ask if he knew about the dragon. Was he the type of leader who'd send his daughter and his oldest friend into a dragon hoard without warning us what we were up against? Maybe, but not if it put the pack in jeopardy. Especially not to release my wolf. I was one defective person. The payoff wouldn't be worth the risk.

Removing my cap, I set it on the bar so he could check the video.

"Get to bed, Grace."

No punishment, just an order to get out of his sight. The warm and fuzzies resulting from my victory chilled, leaving me feeling cold, exhausted, and hollow. "Is leatsa mo shaol, Alpha. Goodnight."

He held up the bottle in a silent dismissal before taking another swig.

Feeling defeated despite successfully acquiring the artifact, I slipped past him and went to my room with only my pile of questions to keep me company.

Grace

Darkness swirled, condensing and coalescing into a familiar tall, dark, and terrifying male form. Significantly larger than the man I remembered, the guardian towered over me though his starkly beautiful features and hard, chiseled body remained unchanged. Silver eyes flashed as power and seduction crackled in the air between us. He drew closer. His impressive height put the intriguing path of dark curls that had previously seized my attention at eye level, my gaze trailing right down the front of his pants.

The happy trail.

A fitting name since I'd be overjoyed to wander down it. Everything about him directed my thoughts toward intimacy. My instincts told me I should cower and grovel before him, but like in the forest, I couldn't. I stood toe-to-toe with the man, refusing to play small.

I wasn't afraid of him.

I should have been, but his presence had an entirely different effect on me. My fingertips yearned to explore the texture of his skin. To roam over his powerful jaw, trail down his neck and broad shoulders to the firm pectoral and abdominal muscles below. I wanted to memorize every hard contour of his body. My lips ached to brush against his, to taste him and allow him to taste me. Every inch of my body thrummed with desperate anticipation.

Compelled and unthinking, I reached out.

He snatched my wrist out of the air, halting me before I could make contact. "This is what you really want, isn't it, little wolf?"

"This? I don't even know what this is." My words came out breathy and full of longing. Desire pooled in my lower belly, and need pulsed *through my core. I felt strange. Weightless yet heavy. Calm even as my heart raced.*

The side of his lips quirked up in a smirk. "Let me show you. I'll give you what you crave... but first, you must hand over the chalice."

It took a moment for his words to penetrate my lust and register, but when they did, confusion claimed me. He wanted to talk about the artifact? Now? When things were starting to get interesting? Wait. Where was the chalice? My hands were empty, and the familiar weight of my backpack was missing. "I... I don't know where it is." Disturbed by that realization, I scanned the area, seeing nothing but darkness beyond the male. No ceiling, no walls, no forest, nothing but inky blackness for as far as I could see. I sniffed the air but smelled nothing, which alarmed me even more than my missing bag. "Where are we?"

He released my wrist to scoop his hands under my arms and picked me up like I was a child. My feet dangled in the air as our gazes locked. "It doesn't matter. You're with me," he said. "You're mine."

Between the unexpected sweetness of his words and the heat in his eyes, my concerns with the situation vanished. How could I care about anything when he looked at me like I was a gift he couldn't wait to unwrap?

He stalked forward, backing me up until I pressed against something hard. A wall. Before I could wonder where it came from, I was sandwiched between it and him, suspended in the air. Silver eyes held mine as he lowered his head until millimeters separated our lips. Cool air brushed against my heated face, and something in my stomach started fluttering. Lost in the moment, I closed my eyes and willed the guardian to kiss me.

"Look at me, little wolf," he said, his voice a dark caress against my skin.

Lazily lifting my eyelids, I froze, coming face to face with the black-scaled snout of a dragon. Silver eyes laughed at me as he nipped at my lip. Pain registered, and the coppery scent of blood filled the air.

"I'll find you, and I will kill you," he vowed, his voice little more than a growl.

Fear skittered up my spine. I untangled my legs from his waist, wondering when the hell that had happened. Slamming my hands into his chest, I pushed as hard as I could. He staggered backward, dropping me. Landing on my feet, I steadied myself as the muscles of his body contorted. The tips of inky black wings crested his shoulders and continued to grow.

Dozens of warning bells erupted in my head, but I couldn't look away. As he morphed into a beautiful, awe-inspiring monster, my feet finally moved. I broke into a sprint but only made it two steps before a clawed hand grabbed my wrist and whipped me around to face him. Talons bit into my flesh and a scream caught in my throat.

"Oh no, little wolf. Not so fast. You want the man; you get the dragon."

Before I could object and tell him I didn't want either of them, his jaws stretched impossibly wide, and darkness enveloped me.

With a cry, I bolted upright only to realize I was in my bed, tucked safely away in the den. I wasn't being kissed, attacked, or eaten. There was no man, nor dragon, looming over me. My wrists weren't cut up, and my mouth was free of blood. Sniffing the air, I caught the alpha's scent, but it was hours old. I was alone. Relieved, I collapsed back on the bed and stared at the colorful artwork on my ceiling. The discarded drawings and finger paintings created by the pack children always calmed me and made me feel safe.

Safe, but not okay.

No, there was something very wrong with me.

I had the nose of a wolf shifter; therefore, I knew exactly how that dream had affected me. I could smell my arousal.

The guardian had tried to kill me, became enraged when I refused to die, and vowed to see me dead.

And now I was having... *erotic* dreams about him?

My subconscious was stupid.

"You're mine?" I asked out loud, appalled at myself.

'You want the man; you get the dragon,' replayed in my head, making me wonder if I was certifiably insane. I had to be crazy to come up with that level of bullshit. My mind needed to be washed out with soap, soundly beaten, and grounded for a year.

Sure, the man was attractive, but panting over him in my sleep was moronic. Then again, maybe there was something else going on here. Perhaps the asshole was manipulating my dreams. Could dragons resort to succubus-like enthrallment? What if he was seducing me so I'd return with the chalice and he could lop off my head?

Well, it wasn't going to work. If the pervert expected me to give up my one shot at freeing my wolf over a bit of dream lust, he would be disappointed.

"I did not consent," I muttered to myself in reassurance.

Dream me *had* tried to get away. Even while I was being assaulted by the sight of that glorious six-pack and swoon-worthy happy trail, I'd still clung to enough common sense to flee. Good to know my subconscious wasn't a complete sex-crazed animal.

Afflicted by dragon seduction mind mojo or not.

Still exhausted, I tried to roll over, but the sheets clung to my clammy, damp skin. Unable to get comfortable, I gave up and climbed out of bed to stand on wobbly legs. Muscles I didn't even know existed pulled tight, making me feel ninety instead of nineteen. I stretched, folding myself into a series of yoga poses until I could move fluidly once again. The few hours of rest I'd gotten had done wonders for my healing, but I could have slept all day had that stupid dream not awoken me.

I pulled out my phone and checked the screen. No new messages. Mackiel hadn't texted me back yet, which was odd. He usually sent me a message first thing in the morning. Irritated, I fired off a text.

Me: You alive?

No response.

Me: Were you abducted by aliens? Are you being experimented on? Probed in the anus? If not, you better have a damn good reason for not texting me back.

Still no answer.

I needed someone to talk to, but there was no one else. My attention drifted to the backpack propped in the corner. Last night suddenly felt surreal, and I wondered if it had all been some fantasy worked up by my overactive imagination. Needing to reassure myself, I bolted to the bag and unzipped it, finding the copper chalice right where I'd left it. If the cup was real, so was its guardian.

A little thrill skittered up my spine, making me want to throat punch myself.

Needing a distraction, I picked up the cup and turned on the light to better study it. Odd characters were etched around the lip. I'd never seen the writing before, but it felt strangely familiar. Unlike last night, there was no pulsing, thrumming, or arm tingling. And it sure as hell didn't unravel any mysterious threads by being in my possession.

I stuffed the chalice back into my pack and stood to go shower. By the time I dressed, made my bed, and brushed my teeth and hair, my stomach was growling like a cornered raccoon protecting its kits. Finding sustenance vaulted to the top of the priority list, sending me to the kitchen where our mini refrigerator lay empty as usual. I didn't know how to cook and didn't have the necessary equipment even if I did. Like most other homes in the den, our house lacked a stove. It was an unnecessary luxury since the pack's head cook provided all our meals, enabling him to monitor food stores and utilize surpluses. Besides, we lived in basements that had been closed off to the above-ground levels. The ventilation was shit. A glance at the kitchen clock told me I could still make breakfast if I hurried.

Decision made, I retrieved my backpack from my room and raced out the door.

The mess hall was located in the basement of a hotel toward the center of the den. It was two blocks from our house, but the minute I stepped into the tunnels, I knew what we were having: sausage, eggs, potatoes, and freshly baked bread. The aroma made my mouth water as I jogged the short distance. I was so focused on getting there and filling my rumbling tummy I didn't see the attack until it was too late.

One minute I was running, and the next, my face was slammed into the brick wall separating the underground walkway from the old filled-in street. Pain registered, and my ears rang as I struggled to make sense of what was happening. For one heart-stopping moment, I feared the guardian had somehow found me and was here to make good on his promise to kill me.

But no, my assailant was female. She spun me around and her hands gripped the front of my shirt as she tugged me to her. A long, hooked nose poked out at me from a thin face surrounded by curls so dark they looked blue in the low light.

Calista, a submissive who'd recently returned from her two-year training at the farm, glared at me, trying to look tough, but the slight tremble in her hands betrayed her. "Let's... let's do this, Chipmunk."

I sighed. Man, I didn't want to deal with pack politics today. There were only two reasons for a submissive to attack me. Either nobody had bothered to tell her I was at the bottom of the pack ladder and nothing could be gained by beating me, or she'd lost all her other challenges and planned to rough me up to boost her ego. My bet was on the latter.

"You don't want to fight me, Calista."

Her thin, black eyebrows drew together. "Yes, I do. I need to."

Before I could explain why she actually didn't, she balled up her fist, drew back, and slammed a punch into my gut, just below my left rib. I'd seen the hit coming and had braced my core for impact, but shifter strength was no joke. Even though her form was sloppy. I doubled over, trying to protect my midsection, but the bitch punched me again.

Trying to block out the pain, I opened my other sight and analyzed her spirit. The tapestry was a mess, with dark threads sticking out everywhere. I reached out with my ethereal hands to soothe her, thinking if I took some of that pain away, I could talk some sense into her. Get her to see how ridiculous this was.

"Hey!" a familiar young feminine voice called.

"Shit," I muttered, shaking my head.

"What?" Calista asked. Still gripping my shirt in a hold I could easily break free of, she turned her head to face the newcomer.

"Never take your eyes off your opponent," I chided. "Geez. This is why you're losing your challenges."

Her head whipped back around to face me. "What did you say to me?"

I held up my hands in surrender. "No offense. Just trying to help you out. Also, you step before you punch. Step with the punch—not before—and it'll help you build momentum without broad-casting what you're about to do."

Sneakers padded against the concrete, and an indignant-looking twelve-year-old joined us. Tali, Mackiel's little sister, crossed her arms and narrowed her big brown eyes at Calista. Envi-ably thick lashes cast long shadows across her chubby cheeks, and the corners of her bow-shaped lips dropped into a frown.

"What's going on here?" Tali asked, looking down her nose at the older packmate. Quite the feat considering Calista was about a foot taller.

"Stay out of it, pup; it's no concern of yours," Calista said, keeping her attention on me.

I pleaded with my eyes for Tali to stay out of it, but the sparkle in her eyes told me I was out of luck. With her brother gone, I tried to keep the girl out of trouble; it was like trying to teach a hare to run without hopping.

"I don't know," Tali said. "I feel all sorts of concern for you."

Calista scoffed. "For *me*?"

Tali nodded. "How weak do you have to be to pick on an omega who won't fight back? Be honest, is Grace the only packmate you can beat?"

Even in the dim light, I could see red creeping up Calista's neck and cheeks. "You're lucky you're not an adult, or I'd beat *you*," she fired back.

Over the past two years that Calista had been gone, Tali's dominance had shot off the charts. The girl looked like a four-and-a-half-foot blonde cherub, but she had the presence of a battle-hardened, blood-smeared giant. Calista must have sucked at reading people, or she would have picked up on how Tali held herself. Power coursed over the girl as she drew dominance from her wolf.

"I think *you're* the lucky one," Tali said, head high as she marched right up to my attacker. "But I'll be an adult soon, and my memory is solid."

Fear flickered in Calista's eyes as Tali's presence enveloped her. The older packmate wilted and faced me, again taking her attention off the more significant threat. "Fine, but if anyone asks, I bested you."

She'd learn that wasn't the brag she thought it was.

"Congratulations," I deadpanned.

She released me and backed into the tunnel that crossed the old street. Once she was far enough away, she turned and ran toward the mess hall.

Tali looked me over. "You okay?"

I listened and sniffed the air, ensuring we were alone before grabbing her by the arm and tugging her to a spot where light filtered in through the faded stained-glass squares built into the sidewalk above. Between that and the LED lights at our feet, I could get a good look at her, which meant she could see the anger rolling off me.

"Why did you do that?" I asked.

"Because if you're not going to stand up for yourself, someone has to."

I gaped at the girl. "And you think having a twelve-year-old fight my battles will help me?"

She blew out a frustrated breath, sending her blonde bangs fluttering. "What am I supposed to do? Stand back and watch them pulverize you?"

"Yes. I can take it."

"That's lame."

A twinge of pain shot through my skull. I massaged my right temple to keep the budding headache at bay. "Yeah, but it's my choice to make." It was my rebellion against the system. "I've got the situation under control now, but the moment I start fighting, I won't be able to stop. Everyone will come for me."

"As they should." She leaned against the brick wall. "You're a badass, and you can take most of them. You shouldn't have to submit to pathetic bitches like Calista."

Aww. Her faith in my fighting skills warmed my belly. "I don't have to; I choose to. You know I don't give a damn about rank."

"I know you *say* you don't, but everyone cares about rank. It's what brings stability and order to the pack."

"No, rank brings dominant and submissive shifters stability and order. I am neither."

"You're a weirdo," she said, a mischievous smile softening her words.

"I am," I admitted. "But you are, too. And you need to stop dominating the adults, or they're going to team up and destroy you after your Bloodrite. Trust me, Tali, you need to make allies and play nice."

"It's not like it'll matter," she muttered.

As much as I hated to admit it, the girl was right. She had the dominance of a budding alpha, which would be a problem regardless of how many friends she made. When Tali turned eighteen and went through the Bloodrite, her wolf would have to submit to my father. And at the rate her power was growing, I didn't know if Tali would be able to submit to anyone by then.

Like me, once she started fighting, she wouldn't be able to stop. Her wolf would demand the top rung on the ladder, a position my father would never relinquish. But we had years to worry about that.

My stomach growled, and Tali laughed.

"I'm starving. You eat yet?" I asked, grateful to my stomach for the topic change.

She shook her head. "Nope. Let's go."

Looping my arm through hers, I turned us toward the mess hall and started walking. "You still struggling with the locks I gave you to practice on?"

"Nope." She beamed a smile at me. "You should see how fast I can pick them now."

"Dammit, now I'll have to find a new way to keep you out of trouble."

6

Grace

I had to knock three times before Rust answered the door. Skin disturbingly pale, he studied me through bloodshot, heavy-lidded eyes.

"You look good," I snarked. "Like the dark circles around your eyes, but don't you think you're a little old to go goth?"

I expected a sarcastic retort, but my mentor didn't appear to have the energy required to trade quips with me.

"Janey's been in labor all night," he said, confirming what I'd heard at the mess hall. Everyone was on edge, waiting for the arrival of the new pup. "You smell like food." He sniffed the air, and the slightest bit of hope brightened his eyes. "Did you happen to uh..."

"Bring you something?" He hadn't shown up for breakfast, so I'd snagged him a plate that was now hidden behind my back. Since shifter noses made food surprises impossible, I brandished the plate with a flourish and said, "Yeah, I did."

A golden sheen rolled over his eyes as he fought his wolf for control. Snatching the plate out of my hands, he grabbed a sausage link and popped it into his mouth with a snarl.

"Close the door," I chided. "Janey's probably as hungry as you are, and she can't eat right now. Doc said so. I saw him at the mess hall."

Reaching behind him to shut the door, he plopped down cross-legged on the stoop and balanced the plate in his lap. The LED lights flashed off his canines, making him look feral as he tore into the meal.

"Grandmother dear, what big teeth you have," I said, quoting the *Little Red Riding Hood*.

He grunted and continued to eat.

Sobering, I asked, "How is she?"

He held up a finger, requesting a moment to finish, then mopped up the drippings with the last bite of bread before stuffing it into his mouth. Mere seconds had passed, and the plate was spotless. Now he was eyeing it like he was about to lick it clean.

"You better give that back to me," I said, reaching out to take the hard plastic. "Hash will kick both our asses if you eat it." Hash was a crotchety old wolf who ran the kitchen with an iron spatula. I didn't even want to think about what he'd do to me if I didn't return the plate as promised.

"Thanks, Chip. I needed that."

"I don't think 'needed' is a strong enough word." I'd never seen him so hungry, but now that I'd fed the beast, I was worried about his mate. "Is everything okay with Janey?"

Standing, he opened the door. "Come in, and we'll chat."

That sounded ominous. I peeped past him, trying to get a look at the inside of his place. I'd never been inside his home before. Hell, I could count on one hand the number of times I'd even approached his door. Rust and I typically spent about four hours a day together training or working, but we always met up at the gym, or he grabbed me from my house. He was my mentor, not my buddy.

"You want *me* to come *in*?" I asked.

The look he gave me questioned my intelligence. "That's what I said, isn't it?"

Before I could come up with a smartass reply, he turned and walked down the entry hallway, leaving the door open. I had no idea what to do with the dirty plate that still smelled of food, so I set it beside the door before following him inside. Framed black and white pictures of people holding musical instruments hung on the walls. I recognized some of the faces from book covers.

"Who's that?" I asked, pointing at a photograph of a shaggy, light-haired man playing guitar and singing into a microphone.

"Kurt Cobain, the lead singer of a local nineties band. The restaurant above used to host all the musicians you see here." His arms swept around to include the entire house.

Interesting. I had follow-up questions, but Rust gestured me forward. The hall ended, opening into a living room centered around a sleek baby grand piano and two red leather sofas. More framed black and white photos covered the walls, and a shiny brass saxophone hung from a hook. Shocked, I gaped at my mentor. "Do you—"

He held a finger to his lips, silencing me, then pointed to a spot on the floor. I stepped around him to see a big, three-inch-thick round cushion situated between the sofas. A coyote pup, with the same coloring as her mother, slept atop the cushion, her soft belly up and tiny paws twitching as she dreamed.

My hands flew to my mouth as my insides went all gooey at the view. My curiosity over Rust's musical prowess forgotten, I lowered my voice and whispered, "Ohmigod, I think my ovaries just exploded."

His face scrunched up in disgust. "Really, Chip?"

"Sorry. I can't help it. Look at little miss Aidy. I've never seen anything so adorable in my life. How old is she now?" I should have known the answer, but Rust was always too busy barking orders at me to chat about his family.

"She just turned two last week. You don't have to whisper. Just keep your voice down."

"And Cohen?" I asked in a slightly softer version of my usual tone.

"That one's eight goin' on twenty. Went to school early to work on a project." Rust plopped down on the piano bench and gestured at the sofa across from him. "Please, have a seat."

I perched more than sat, not letting myself get too comfortable. A million questions cycled through my mind, but I already felt like

I was invading my mentor's personal space. Janey's scent was everywhere but strongest behind a closed door on the north side of the room. Someone was in there with her, and my nose told me it was her sister.

Lowering my voice so I wouldn't be heard by the two women, I asked, "So, how is she?"

Rust's brows pinched together in thought as he eyed me. Women my age were expected to mate and pop out as many pups as possible to pad the pack numbers. My mentor wouldn't want to scare me away from my duty, but he had to know men weren't exactly breaking down my door. Most of the pack treated me like I had an infectious, incurable disease and stayed away. Even if any guys were interested, nobody knew if my condition was hereditary, and I was in no hurry to find out.

"The contractions started about an hour before we got back, and they're about ten minutes apart now. It's been a rough night, but it shouldn't last much longer."

The worry in his eyes made it clear there was more to the story. "I'm not a child. I know how dangerous childbirth can be, Rust." Every year we lost shifters to birthing. Mothers and babies couldn't shift during pregnancy, making the coma used for deep healing unattainable. Shifter newborns tended to weigh around ten pounds, and with limited access to medical supplies, Doc didn't have a lot of options.

"The labor seems to get worse with every pregnancy." Rust dropped his head into his hands like he couldn't bear the weight of it any longer. Poor guy. He had to be exhausted. My mentor had shifted twice last night, and judging by the dark circles around his eyes, he hadn't gotten a wink of sleep.

My heart went out to him. "Well, you look like shit. You should try to get in a power nap while Elise is with Janey."

He gave me a lopsided smile. "I've faced much tougher enemies than a sleepless night, kid. Don't you worry about me."

Stubborn, condescending bastard.

"We're not training today. You'd probably pass out and cut yourself on my daggers, and that's not an injury I'm willing to explain to your mate."

His grin widened. "I could have one foot in the grave, and you still couldn't take m—." Rust's face contorted in agony, and his body curled in on itself, feet rising off the floor to bring his knees to his chest. Behind the door, Janey cried out in pain. Rust squeezed his eyes closed and gritted his teeth so hard I thought his jaw might crack.

A... contraction? Holy shit! It had to be.

Rust and Janey were true mates. He was a wolf, and she was a coyote, but their souls had melded all the same. They shared strong emotions like joy and anger, but what he was doing now was something more. Rust was using their bond to siphon a portion of Janey's pain onto himself. I'd heard rumors that pain mitigation was possible through the bond but doubted any guy would be brave or selfless enough to try it, especially during childbirth.

But leave it to Rust to try. It was the sweetest and most masochistic act of love I'd ever witnessed. True mates were a hell of a thing. I knew I should look away but couldn't. His pain was a palpable, tangible force in the room, and looking away from such a beautiful, selfless sacrifice seemed downright disrespectful.

Finally, the contraction ended. Murmurs came from the other room, Elise comforting her sister. Rust sucked down a deep breath, unfurled his body, lowered his feet to the floor, and opened his eyes. His gaze locked with mine, and all the oxygen vanished from the room. I'd witnessed an intimate, sacred act between him and his mate, and now here we were, drowning in awkwardness.

Moments ticked by. I didn't want to suffocate here with him. Panicking, I blurted out the first thing that came to mind. "Tell me how you met Janey!" The words came out a little louder and more aggressive than necessary, but at least they shattered the disturbing silence.

Rust blinked. His face and shoulders relaxed, and his eyebrows rose. "You wanna know how I met Janey?"

"Yeah." I gave a self-deprecating shrug. "Why not?"

Leaning forward in my seat, I concentrated on his spirit. I'd done this almost daily since discovering I could, so I knew his glowing tapestry well. Not like Rust required much soothing. The man was an icebox, all cool and functional. But today was different. Dark threads of worry and fear were tangled up all over the place. Focusing, I loosened one and settled it where it could heal. I couldn't do anything for Janey, but I could help her mate carry the burden.

Rust steepled his hands. "Pretty sure I already told you that story."

"No, you didn't. I was barely more than a pup when I asked. We were in the gym, and Janey stopped by to watch us train. She kept giving you side-eye every time the story started to get interesting. You mentioned something about an ogre, and she practically had a seizure signaling you to shut up." I'd immediately sought out the database to fill in the blanks for myself. Ogres were enormous hunched, bipedal creatures with a taste for flesh. "You gave me the watered-down child-appropriate version."

I ran my ethereal hand over a particularly stubborn knot in his spirit, willing it to loosen up. The knot tightened and then relaxed just a smidge, allowing me to work another thread free.

Rust frowned. "That's right. I remember now." He tilted his head to the side and eyed me. There was no way he couldn't feel the internal changes. He had to know I was doing something to him.

But he didn't tell me to stop.

"Stop stalling and give me the real story," I prodded. "You can even embellish a little like you do when you're bragging to the men."

"I do not embellish or brag. I merely add color to liven shit up."

"My mistake. Feel free to paint in or outside the lines; just give me the scoop already."

"Fine. But I gotta start off with a little background."

Of course, he did. I bit back a smile and continued to soothe away his worry and frustration.

"Janey and her sister grew up in the mountains of southeastern Oregon with their parents. Just four coyotes, no pack. One day, not long after the war ended, a vampire was travelin' through their territory, caught their scent, and decided to stop in for a snack."

His mention of the creatures triggered a question about something I'd read. "According to the database, vampires can feed without killing. Is that true?"

He nodded. "Vamps can feed off *humans* without killin' 'em. That's how they've existed for centuries without gettin' caught. But shifter blood is like crack for blood drinkin' races of the Tricari. Tastes good, makes 'em strong and powerful, and it's addictive as hell. Once they start drinkin', most *can't* stop. Blood lust is real, and if you ever come across one of those dirty bloodsuckers, you need to run." Eyes narrowing, he pinned me in place with a glare. "I mean it, Chip. Don't try to fight one. Just get the hell out of there."

I threw up my hands in surrender. "All right, all right. I promise to flee like a spineless coward. Please continue."

"Janey and Elise were out huntin' when the vamp attacked and killed their parents."

"A single vampire took down two shifters?" I leaned toward him and plucked another thread free. His shoulders loosened, and a smidgeon of worry ebbed from his eyes.

"Vamps are strong and smart. They have no heartbeat, and their scent... they smell like death. Janey said the deer carcass dryin' not far from the house probably masked the vamp's scent." He shrugged. "Who knows what really went down? Doesn't matter. The females returned home from their hunt to find their parents drained dry."

I tried to imagine how that must have felt but couldn't. If something happened to my father and the rest of the pack turned on me, Rust and Mackiel would have my back. Well, maybe not Rust, since he had a mate and pups to consider, but Mackiel for sure. Assuming I could get to the farm and find him. Without the protection of my father, the pack would turn on Aunt Sereana, so I couldn't count on her. Yeah, Mackiel would be my only hope for survival. He and I should really come up with a plan… a meeting place or something. I really wanted to check my phone and see if he'd messaged me back, but Rust was still talking, and I needed to focus on his spirit and his story. Where were we? Oh yeah. Janey and Elise were utterly alone, with a murderous vampire on the loose.

"What did they do?" I asked.

"Hunted his ass down." Pride shone in Rust's eyes as he glanced toward the closed bedroom door. "They were about your age. Too damn young to go chasin' after some shifter blood-boosted vamp, but grief can make a person lose their mind and do stupid shit. The two of 'em were hell-bent on revenge at any cost. They tracked that bastard back to his lair and ripped him to shreds. Beheaded the son-of-a-bitch."

The database claimed vampires had robust regeneration, but few creatures could survive the removal of their noggin. Still, something didn't track. "I thought you saved Janey from an ogre."

"Patience." He chuckled. "I'm gettin' there. The vamp didn't go down without a fight. He tore them both up, but Elise got the brunt of his attack. Once the threat was gone, her body shifted out of battle form and into her coyote, shut down, and started healin'."

Shifters had three forms—human, animal, and a battle form that looked like a hideous blend of both. As far as I knew, only my father could partially transform, a skill he'd been improving since my Bloodrite. Shifters within a pack spent most of their time in human form for day-to-day life since features like opposable thumbs and speech were handy. The animal form was for hunting, healing, and running long distances. I didn't know what battle form looked like for different shifters, but for wolves and coyotes, it resembled what humans called werewolves: extended claws; dense bones; sharp, elongated teeth; keen eyesight; and rugged, hair-covered hides—like a savage, bloodthirsty nightmare that could slash and bite on two feet or chase down prey on four.

Regardless of the form, shifting was magic and cost energy. The first shift was no big deal, but the second one usually required a protein-rich meal and a nap. Changing forms a third time without sleep and food was dangerous. It wouldn't kill a shifter, but it ran the risk of knocking them out, usually at the most inconvenient time. Healing also required energy. Whenever a shifter's wounds drew close to fatal, the body would automatically force a shift into animal form and induce a coma-like healing state.

"An ogre smelled the blood and came runnin' like someone had rung the damn dinner bell. Ogres will eat raw meat in a pinch, but they prefer their meals cooked. With Janey weakened and refusin' to leave her sister, he easily collected the two and hauled them back to his camp. Janey was barely holdin' onto her human form. She'd already shifted twice and was afraid if she let her beast take over, she'd lose consciousness and the chance to get away."

Rust's body tensed with the pain of another contraction. Suddenly, his spirit pulsed around me. I stilled, unsure of what to do. I wanted to flee back into my own body, but instead, I reached out, soothing the pain as he took it into himself.

He stared at me, his eyes full of wonder.

I didn't like that look. It made me feel different. Strange. Like some kind of freak. This was Rust, and I needed him to remember that this was just omega mojo, and I was only its vessel. As soon as the contraction passed, I gave him my best okay-old-wolf-get-on-with-it look. "The ogre took them back to his camp..." I prompted.

Rust's expression blanked. He nodded and cleared his throat. "Yes. I was in the area. Your father had sent me out with a recruitin' team, tryin' to build our pack numbers back up. We saw smoke and decided to investigate." A shadow fell over Rust's eyes, and he looked away. "The smell of burnin' flesh hit me first. Then once we were in range...." He ran a hand through his hair. "Shit, Chip. The minute I heard her screamin' over the rumble of my bike, I knew I had to get to her. I cut the engine and ran faster than I'd ever run. When we came upon that fire, Janey was...." He blanched. "I barely made it in time. A couple more minutes and no amount of healin' would have saved her."

His words sunk in, and my stomach churned. "He was roasting her alive?" That big breakfast I'd eaten no longer seemed like such a great idea.

Glowing eyes met mine, giving me a peek at the wolf beneath the skin. "There's a lot of bad shit out there, Chip. Ogres are sadistic motherfuckers, and vampires can barely control their bloodlust, but they're far from the worst. We are nuthin' but food to a lot of creatures. But I'll tell you one thing, roastin' Janey was the last bad decision that bloated son-of-a-bitch ever made. Let me assure you, he regretted it in the end." Rust sank a world of meaning into that sentence and punctuated it with a growl. His fierce and predatory smile made me want to lean back and drop my gaze.

"I..." I grappled with words until I found the only one that seemed fitting. "Wow."

"Yeah. Wow is right. I know you don't feel the call of the pack like the rest of us, and you're too damn curious for your own good. You train hard, and you're smart as a goddamn whip, but there's shit out there you can't face alone. Shit you need a pack for."

But before I could reply, his body tensed again. This contraction was even more potent than the last, and my chest squeezed as I watched him share this moment with the mate he'd rescued from the fire of an ogre. Being in the presence of such a breathtakingly beautiful bond made me ache. I couldn't help but wonder if there was a true mate out there somewhere for me. Rust was my father's oldest friend. Thick as thieves, they'd grown up dirt poor in Ireland during the potato famine of the 1800s, migrating to America just in time to join the 69th Irish Brigade in the Civil War. Both were wounded and left for dead on the battlefield, but a sympathetic shifter rescued them and turned them into shifters to save their lives.

My father didn't meet Cassandra until the end of World War II. She was a nurse who'd been turned by one of the soldiers taking advantage of her submissive nature. Dad put an end to her abuser and brought her home after the war. Rust didn't meet Janey until after The Eradication. Both males had waited an awfully long time to find their true mate.

Then Cassandra had died so young, leaving Dad with half a soul for the rest of his life. Dad and Cassandra's story made me question whether true mates were worth the trouble, but Rust and Janey's relationship made me want to believe they could be.

If a person was lucky enough to find their true mate. Most never did.

Aidy stirred from her spot on the doggy bed. She rolled to her feet, wobbled and stood, looking from me to her father. Rust's eyes were closed as he suffered through the contraction. I thought she'd go to him, but she sleepily tottered toward me instead. At my feet, she went up on her hind legs and rested her front paws against my knees, letting out a pleading whimper.

I didn't know what to do. Aidy clearly wanted to be picked up, but I didn't want to upset her parents.

"You just gonna ignore her?" my mentor asked.

My gaze shot to him. His eyes were open, and he appeared to be coming out of the contraction.

"You want me to pick her up?" I asked.

"That's usually what people do when a pup whines like that."

"Are you sure it's okay?" I repeated, excited about the idea but not entirely convinced he meant it.

Rust snorted. "I don't know why you can't shift, but if it was communicable, someone would've caught it by now. You're protective of the pack, Chip, and I respect that. But sometimes you need to relax and enjoy your people. Pick her up."

"Are you sure?" I asked.

In answer, he stood, scooped up his daughter, and deposited her into my arms. She was so adorable and fluffy that I couldn't help but smile. Aidy rolled in my arms, giving me access to her belly. I gently rubbed the soft fur, grinning like an idiot. "She's amazing."

He nodded. "Yeah, she is. And she's into everythin'. Our little heart attack waitin' to happen."

I laughed. "So, you're the one turning your daddy grey," I cooed to the baby, brushing the fur back from her eyes. She settled in my arms, and I stroked her head until her eyelids drooped and closed. As she drifted back to sleep, I refocused on Rust and asked, "When did you know Janey was your true mate?"

"The instant I touched her." A flicker of a smile chased away the last of his pain. "After we killed the ogre, I released her from the bonds, and there was just this... spark. This understandin'. I was hers, she was mine, and nothin' else mattered. She stood there, naked, burned, and bloody, and I started shoutin' at my team to look the fuck away before I ripped their eyeballs out."

"Ah, the mating craze," I laughed. Any shifter lucky enough to find their true mate became a possessive, uncontrollable, paranoid psychopath for a few months until the bond settled. The rest of the pack gave mating couples a wide berth and plenty of grace during the craze.

"Yeah." Rust grimaced. "That was not a fun trip back to the den. Janey was wounded and vulnerable. She rode bitch on my bike because I needed to feel her at my back. I was supposed to be leadin' the team, but I couldn't let them see her weak and injured. I'd dressed her from head to toe in my clothes, and she was so wrapped in my scent everyone knew she was mine and under my protection, but I couldn't keep myself reined in. Whenever anyone got close to us, I'd lose my shit. Had we been ten minutes later, she would have been dead. Shifter magic can't do shit to restart a heart that's been cooked. It's been fourteen years, and I still have nightmares about her tied to that damn spit, hearin' her scream and smellin' her burned flesh." He shuddered, shaking his head. "No one should ever have to see their mate like that. Especially not a true mate."

"But she lived," I reminded him. "Killed a vampire, survived an ogre, you got yourself a badass."

He glanced past me to the bedroom door as if he could see beyond it and smiled. "The baddest of asses. Wasn't easy, bringin' her back here after your father had lost Cassandra. Especially since Janey's not a wolf, and the alpha... well, it wasn't easy on any of us."

I couldn't even imagine. "Has he stopped by to check on her yet?" I didn't scent him, which was odd. He'd been present during Cohen's birth. Afterward, Dad and Rust had celebrated the birth at our house. I remembered it well because it had taken months for the stench of cigars to fade.

Rust shook his head. "No. I'm sure he's just busy. How'd the debriefin' go last night?"

I didn't want to add to Rust's stress, but I couldn't exactly lie to him. "The alpha wasn't happy about your absence. I'm sorry. I probably shouldn't have sent you home." I didn't regret my actions, but I had been out of line. The last thing I wanted to do was drive a wedge between my father and his oldest friend.

The side of Rust's lips quirked up. "You don't have that kind of authority, kid. I was thinkin' about headin' straight home long before you suggested it. I know you get tired of hearin' me say it, but your father is a good alpha. Complicated as hell, but good. It's not easy bein' the king, but he wears the crown well."

Darkness rolled over Rust's face. He dropped his head, gritted his teeth, and braced as another contraction hit him. I instinctively started to soothe it, but stars danced in my vision. *Dammit!* I'd used too much magic, and my well had run dry. I broke our connection, slamming back into my own essence. Janey cried out, and Rust gritted his teeth against the pain.

I waited for the contraction to pass before asking, "Is she okay?"

His eyes darkened with worry as he looked toward the door. "I don't know. I should get in there."

I felt bad for my mentor and his mate and wanted to help. "Once you guys get through this, there are herbs to keep her from conc—"

Rust held up a hand, silencing me. "Stop. Don't ask me to defy my alpha, Chip."

My heart sunk, but I refused to give up. "This is your third child, Rust. Surely you and Janey have taken enough chances with her life."

"I'd follow your father off a cliff," Rust said. "He's the kind of leader who weighs all the options and makes the best decision for his pack. He's buildin' up the pack numbers for a reason. And before you ask, no, I don't know what that reason is, but I trust the alpha. You should, too."

He was so damn frustrating I wanted to shake him.

"You should go," he said.

Feeling defeated and exhausted, I stood on wobbly legs and handed Aidy to her father. "Want me to find Doc?"

Someone knocked on the door. Rust sniffed the air. "No need."

"I'll let him in." I headed for the door.

"Chip," Rust said, stopping me. "Thanks. For breakfast and... everythin' else. You're a good kid."

I didn't know how to respond, so I nodded and went to the door to let Doc in before stumbling home.

Arioch

"You must eat."

The barked order startled me. Reflexively, I slammed closed the book I was reading and reached for my sword. The voice registered as Catori's at the exact moment her scent hit me. Relaxing my hand, I eyed my guardian, who was rolling a cart toward my desk.

A smile tugged at her lips. "I did not think I was capable of startling you anymore."

Decades of training had honed my senses and should have made such a thing impossible, but I was clearly exhausted and distracted. Mid-morning sun streamed in from the window, alerting me to the hour and adding another layer of fatigue. I had spent all night and most of the morning researching but had little to show for it. The annoying buzz in the back of my head mocked me for gambling away so much time when I should abandon the fruitless texts and hunt down the chalice before it was too late. But I was not desperate enough to pitch myself into a possible trap unprepared. At least, not yet.

Weariness sunk into my bones and made my joints ache. A glance at the clock told me it had been about nine hours since the little wolf had stolen the chalice, and I still had no idea what she planned to do with it, what she had done to me, or how I could combat her remarkable magic. My gaze dropped to the giant tome sitting on top of my desk. Finding where I had left off would be a pain in the ass, and I was not sure it was worth the trouble. I knuckled my bleary eyes, trying to rub a few more hours of life back into them.

Catori stopped the cart on the other side of my desk. "Good morning, child. I figured you'd be in here brooding."

Her chipper tone grated on my nerves. "I am not brooding, I am researching."

She angled herself to peer at my notepad. "Have you found anything interesting?"

Embarrassed by my lack of progress, I flipped the pad over. "Not a blasted thing."

And, ancestors help me, I had tried. My desk bisected the back of the library floor. Piled on the left were the many books that made no reference at all to the chalice, the box that had held it, or shifters. The small stack on the right held vague riddles and obscure prophesies that may or may not refer to the chalice, its box, or the goddamn meaning of life. Those books made me want to hunt down their authors and burn them alive in a pyre fueled by their own ambiguous pages. Why did every being with an ounce of paranormal blood feel the need to be so damn cryptic? Was it a requirement? A perk of being Tricari? At some point, I had given up on my original quest and devoted myself to reading everything I could on wolf shifters, searching for answers about what the little wolf had done so I could protect myself against it in our next encounter. But so far, I had found nothing that even hinted at an ability that enabled shifters to attack with memories and emotions.

It had to come from whatever else she was. From whatever mysterious race my father had been. Great. The beast had been gifted with advantageous combat abilities, while all I had inherited from our people was a curse. Fucking wonderful.

Catori put a hand on her hip, looking pointedly at the book. "Something in there had you so enthralled you did not even hear me approach. What was it?"

My hand roamed over the dark leather cover of the book I had found in my trove. Ancient and smelling of power, it had all but drawn me to it the minute I had entered the room. "I was researching shifters."

Catori's expression turned thoughtful as she spun toward the cart and began unloading dishes. The scent of warm food tugged at my attention, making my stomach growl. Catori tsked at the noise, setting a cup of leaves in front of me and retrieving a teapot. She poured hot water over the leaves, and the spiced earthy scent of her reinvigorating tea blend tickled my senses. The dryad had a tea for everything, but this one was my favorite. Not for the spiced dirt taste—ancestors, it was awful—but for the effects. I would gag down every disgusting drop for an energy boost.

She prepared a second cup for herself. "But you have found nothing of interest?"

Wishing I could plug my nose without offending her, I sipped. Bitter and chalky, it tasted like grated tree bark mixed with mud and pond water, but I made myself swallow. "What I did not find is what interests me."

"Great Arborvitae, help me. Am I going to have to drag every detail out of you today, you vexing boy?"

I hid my smile behind my cup. Usually, *she* was the ambiguous one. It was nice to turn the tables for once. With my free hand, I thumped the book. "This is the diary of an alpha wolf shifter who migrated to Peru from Spain, where he started a pack in 1502. It was part of Grandfather's collection. I do not know how it came into his possession, but the entries span hundreds of years, thousands of pack members, and provide a detailed picture of the struggles and intricacies of pack life."

Catori set a bowl of oatmeal with fruit and nuts in front of me. Dryads were vegetarians. I preferred meat and eggs but was hungry enough to eat anything. I now regretted my standing orders restricting the house staff from interrupting my work, even to break my fast. Thanking my guardian, I picked up the spoon and stirred the hot cereal. Steam rose, the scent mingling with the tea leaves and making me want to wrinkle my nose in distaste. I ate it anyway.

"And this book on pack life... it has been illuminating?" she asked.

"Fascinating, really." Dragons were solitary creatures, so the pack mindset was a whole new concept for me. Wolf shifters needed one another on a level I could not begin to comprehend. In the wild, wolves primarily existed in family groups. Shifters, however, formed codependent communities under the sovereign rule of an alpha. And the loyalty a strong leader evoked was unfathomable. I could understand the draw of safety in numbers, but the instant an alpha with a God complex tried to tell me what to do, I would be forced to rip out his throat. Wolves appeared to need someone to order them around.

"You are trying to drive me insane, are you not?" The look on Catori's face told me she was seconds away from throttling me.

Time to speak plainly. "According to these records, shifters are either made or born. Those born of shifter parents come out of the womb in their human form and change into their animal by age two." I paused, letting that sink in. "The only adult shifters who cannot shift are with child."

"You think the thief was pregnant?" Catori asked.

"No." The word came out sharper than intended, but I was too wound up to hold back. Something about that possibility made me want to toss my desk again.

Catori's dark, pupilless eyes looked me over with a measure of curiosity, making me want to shield myself. "Are you certain?" she asked.

"I only heard one heartbeat. Besides, the book says wolves have trouble carrying a child to term. Childbirth is especially perilous for them. Pregnant females are protected and revered, not sent to steal artifacts from dragon hoards."

Catori cocked her head to the side, eyeing me. "Do wolves only breed within their species?"

The peculiar question made me pause. "Why do you ask?"

"Perhaps her inability to shift is the result of interbreeding."

I shook my head. "Doubtful. The shifters in this diary mated with Mondeine and various mammal shifters such as bears and jaguars, and I even found one mention of a manatee shifter. The offspring take on the animal form of one of their shifter parents, even if one parent is fully human."

"Perhaps the ability to attack your emotions is what has suppressed her animal," Catori said.

"Interesting theory."

Catori leaned forward, setting her teacup down. "Do you think this unusual ability of hers comes from the other side of her lineage? The race of people she shares with you?"

I nodded. "I do. Yet I cannot do what she did. Nor is my dragon suppressed. In fact, you said my magic is much stronger than my mother's, even though she was over a century old. The thief's wolf felt... caged somehow. Like something physically restricted her from manifesting."

"We could sit here and speculate all day, or we can finish eating and then get answers."

The spoon was halfway to my mouth when Catori's words sunk in. "How?" I asked, focusing on the location of the artifact. It was still to the northwest. "The wolf and the chalice are long gone."

My life was bound to the chalice, but Catori was connected to this land. Somewhere, not far from my estate, grew the ancient tree that had birthed the dryad. She protected the tree, and in turn, it sustained her with its magic. I did not know what would happen if she traveled too far away from the ancient tree because she never did. I had always assumed she could not.

Catori gestured toward my bowl. "Eat, child."

She had baited the hook, dangled it in front of me, and now she was reeling me in. Whenever I forgot how sadistic dryads could be, my guardian was quick to remind me.

"Everyone you care for will betray you."

I pushed that memory to the back of my mind and devoured my meal and every drop of my tea. As soon as I finished, she scooped up our dishes and exchanged them for a hemp bag sitting on the cart. I reached for the bag, but she slapped my hand away.

"Meddlesome child. You should have grown out of that behavior by now." Before I could respond, she opened the bag, reached inside, and retrieved a dark glass ball about a foot in diameter. Gently placing the ball in the center of the desk, she steadied it before removing her hand.

My brain immediately went into overdrive, working to connect the prospect of getting answers with the sphere. "Is that a crystal ball?"

"Crystal balls are the tools of witches." Catori spat in disgust. "This is a scrying orb." My guardian had experienced a few run-ins with spell casters, and each had left a foul taste in her mouth.

Okay. "What is the difference?"

"Intent."

I stared at her, waiting for more of an explanation, but it quickly became apparent that was all she planned to give me. "And you call *me* vexing," I grumbled.

"I am not vexing; I am mysterious and mystical. I only speak the truth." She pulled out another hemp bag, drew open the tie, and peered inside. "You might want to move your book."

I picked up the pack diary and set it aside. Catori upended the bag, and a mixture of potent-smelling herbs slid over the orb, creating a ring around it on my desktop. Before I could ask any questions like 'what is that?' and 'why does it smell so awful?' her eyes snapped closed, and she started mumbling. Magic thrummed from the depths of the earth, answering her call. She splayed out her fingers and drew the power into herself as the volume of her chant increased. I recognized the musical language of the ancient fae, but my knowledge was limited, making it impossible to discern meaning from her words.

Catori's tone deepened, and she began to sway in steps choreographed from centuries of wisdom and instinct. As she danced and chanted, magic built, charging the air until it prickled my skin and made the hair on my arms stand up. Pages of my overturned notepad fluttered. The woven tapestries depicting my family history smacked against the wall behind me. Catori threw her arms out toward the open window, and a gust of wind blew in, billowing the curtains and adding disembodied voices to her chant. The orb pulsed with weak bursts of light in response. She reached into a pocket and produced the vial of blood collected from my sword. Still chanting and stomping, she tipped the vial above the desk until one fat drop left the rim to splatter against the top of the orb. The pulses of light intensified as the orb raised a good six inches above my desk and started spinning clockwise. After several rotations, Catori clapped her hands three times and froze. Instantly, the spinning and pulsing stopped, and the orb lay dark, still hovering in the air.

Silence settled over us, a stark contrast to the chaos of mere seconds ago. Minutes ticked by, and nothing changed.

I looked to my guardian, but her attention was locked on the orb. The ends of her dreads had risen, shooting out from her head like branches of a tree. Magic gathered and pressure built against my chest and forehead.

With the rest of her body stiff and still, Catori's head swiveled until she faced me. The whites had vanished from her round, pupilless eyes, turning them into bottomless pools of darkness. Her focus appeared to be beyond the physical realm, but I was ensnared the moment her gaze met mine. Images flashed in the depths of her eyes, changing with every rapid beat of my heart. As I watched, time passed, seasons changed, wars raged, and forests withered. My life was but a speck of dust within it all, insignificant and small. Fleeting.

No! I am dragon! I wanted to roar, but I had no voice in this frozen place and time.

"What are you waiting for, child?" Catori asked, her voice deep and hollow as her eyes went still again.

Released, I staggered, gasping for air. The dark orb between us beckoned for my attention, but I resisted the impulse to face it.

"Do not fight the power; use it. Come closer. Pour your intention into the scrying orb and make your request," Catori said.

Her instructions caught me off guard. It would have been helpful had she prepared me for this ahead of time, but I had a feeling I was not dealing with my guardian anymore. At least, not entirely. There was something else inside her, something older and more fearsome. I instinctively knew to be respectful and obey without question. As for my request, I knew what I needed the orb to show me. Stepping forward, I focused my energy into the darkness and said, "Show me the owner of the blood."

Catori cocked her head to the side in an unnerving gesture that reminded me of a bird. "Be more precise."

Okay. What else did I need to see? The little wolf's surroundings. If I planned to swoop onto her location and retrieve the chalice, I needed to know what I would be up against. I needed information on the terrain, her pack numbers, and their defenses. I needed a complete reconnaissance. Opening my desk drawer, I retrieved the glove she had abandoned in my trove. Clutching the thin fabric, I focused on my memory of the thief, recalling the compassion flickering in her eyes.

"Not a plague," she said. *"And a scourge would have gone for your jugular. I'm certain of it."*

I pushed that part of the memory aside, refusing to allow her confusing show of compassion to dissuade me. This was my destiny. My duty. I spread my awareness to the orb.

"Like a hummingbird hovering above the broken little wolf, let us watch her from above, going where she goes and seeing what she sees until we break the connection."

Catori focused back on the orb, chanting once again. Palms open, she reached toward me, closed her hands around an invisible rope, and tugged. Power ripped out of me in an agonizing gush. I had expended a great deal of magic to transform and heal myself mere hours ago, so the sudden, unexpected loss stole my breath and buckled my knees. My pulse pounded in my ears as the room swam. Dropping the glove, I grappled until I caught the edge of the desktop. Hands latched on, I locked my arms and struggled to keep myself upright as I found my feet. The drain of magic ebbed.

The orb iced over.

"Interesting," Catori said, studying it. My guardian was back to herself. The endless blackness had receded from her eyes, and gravity had reclaimed her dreads.

"What is?" I asked, my voice worn and raspy.

Catori's gaze swung toward me, and concern creased her brow. "When your mother and grandfather scried, the orb would fill with smoke. I should have expected yours to freeze."

How long had she owned the orb?

Why was I only now learning about it?

Could we have used it to find my mother's killer?

Questions formed on my tongue, but condensation dripped onto my desktop before I could decide which one to ask first. The frosty casing around the orb was melting, revealing the thief. Like the first time I saw her, she was dressed in a black T-shirt and black pants. The straps of her backpack were still over her shoulders, but her hat was gone. Her hair was the color of fire, blazing shades of reds and oranges that hung in loose waves. Intelligent green eyes practically glowed with joy as she smiled down at the little ball of fur in her arms. It moved, and I realized it was a pup. Something twisted inside of me, sending sharp pains through my chest.

"Is she a... a mother?" The question slipped out before I could even consider the implications. I felt the pressure of Catori's gaze but could not drag my attention away from the orb. Who was that male with her? Her mate? I would rip the motherfucker apart. No, I would gut him and strangle him with his own intestines, leaving him somewhere public for all to see. My chest tightened as I imagined all the ways I could make him pay for daring to put a single paw on her.

"Breathe, Arioch," Catori commanded.

Power punched through the haze of rage.

What the...

I shook myself. My lungs filled with air, and I held it for a count of four before exhaling as my mind spun. I had no idea what had just happened. Why was I so furious?

"Good," Catori crooned. "Now open your fists and unlock your jaw."

Every inch of my body felt tense and ready to pounce. Forcing my hands to unfurl and my shoulders to drop, I attempted to relax but still felt coiled as tight as a bowstring. I had no idea how long the orb had held my attention, nor did I understand why the sight of the thief with another male had evoked such a bizarre reaction. Befuddled, I looked to my guardian for help.

Catori met my gaze with a knowing look that made me want to defend myself.

"Oh, child, you have been keeping things from me," she said.

"I have told you everything," I insisted.

"There is a spark between the two of you."

Leave it to the dryad to pick up on the one thing I had not wanted to admit, not even to myself.

"She is a thief," I said. "The broken beast come to steal and destroy. I *will* kill her, Catori."

My guardian chuckled. "Ah, to be young and foolish again."

Before I could argue, sound came from the orb, drawing my attention.

"Once you guys get through this, there are herbs to keep her from conc—"

The man silenced her with a hand. "Stop. Don't ask me to defy my alpha, Chip."

Chip? Her name was Chip?

"This is your third child, Rust. Surely you and Janey have taken enough chances with her life."

"You should go."

Chip stood unsteadily and handed the pup to the male. "Want me to find Doc?"

"No need."

Her head tilted as if she picked up a scent or sound. "I'll let him in." The orb tracked Chip as she navigated a brightly lit, sparsely furnished living area and down a narrow hallway. The space was clean and comfortable, the furniture modest but cozy.

"Chip," Rust called out. When she stopped and turned, he said, "Thanks. For breakfast and everythin' else. You're a good kid."

"You mean a good thief," I said to the orb.

"A courageous, compassionate thief," Catori added. "Willing to risk her alpha's wrath to suggest herbs to prevent pregnancy."

I did not know what to say to that, so I kept my mouth shut and watched Chip greet an older male before exiting the house into a narrow tunnel illuminated by a strand of lights. A brick wall ran along her left side, and brick buildings along the right. A large, cracked window gave me a peek at the inside of another brightly lit home. This one had a young boy seated at a small table, writing on a piece of paper, a textbook open in front of him.

After reading the journal, I had expected the pack to occupy a rudimentary village nestled beside a freshwater stream, where they could hunt and thrive in the wild. Possibly even a cave in the side of the mountain.

"Where did they find an underground city?" I muttered to myself as frustration and despair dug under my skin.

The answer did not matter. Chip and the chalice were beyond my reach as long as she stayed put. Dragons, in general, were not fond of underground places since there was no room to fight or shift. Unlucky bastard that I was, my aversion to tight spaces was due to reasons more personal. Memories of the two weeks I had endured being buried in a pine box, courtesy of one of my many sadistic trainers, invoked a visceral reaction I could not control. My hands felt clammy, and my stomach roiled at the mere thought of once again submitting myself to the helplessness I had experienced while trapped underground.

I collapsed in my chair. "Shit."

"If we are patient, an answer will present itself," Catori said.

As if in answer, the buzzing in the back of my head kicked up a notch. Time was not on our side.

My guardian retrieved another cup from the tray behind her, pouring hot water over more leaves before handing it to me. Exhausted, frustrated, and desperate for another energy boost, I breathed into the cup, cooling the contents so I could gulp down the brew. As soon as I set down the empty teacup, I realized my mistake. A familiar, bitter flavor lingered on my tastebuds. I glared at my guardian.

"That was dirty," I growled.

"No, that was necessary."

The dryad had slipped me a sleeping concoction. "Dammit, Catori, I do not have time to nap."

"You are drained and useless in this state. Directing the orb required the last of your energy, and you need your rest. I will keep an eye on the girl and take note of anything important."

"What if she handed off the chalice?" I asked.

"Focus, child. You should be able to answer that question."

Studying the orb, I realized my guardian was correct. I could pinpoint the exact location of the artifact, even through the orb. "In her backpack," I grumbled.

"I will watch her and it. Now go to bed before you lose consciousness. I do not wish to carry you."

I wanted to argue, but the damn tea was already dragging me under. "I need numbers. Details. Weaknesses. Whatever you can give me to help me penetrate their den."

"Do not confuse me for a sapling. You are not the first troublesome child I have taken under my branches. You've finished your tea, now find your bed."

Since arguing with the dryad never ended in success, I stood and stumbled out of the library toward my bedchamber wing, cursing the distance with every step. Ambling through the door of my suite, I collapsed on my bed. The last thing I saw before sleep

AMARA MAE

claimed me was Chip's smiling face as she watched the pup in her arms. Heat bloomed in my gut, but I assured myself it was a byproduct of the sleeping drought.

Catori was wrong; there was no spark. There simply could not be.

Yet Chip's smile when she looked at that pup had transfixed me. The female was beyond beautiful. She was captivating.

Too bad I still had to kill her.

Grace

S weat stung my eyes and blurred my vision. I used the bottom
of my tank top to mop at my face, but the fabric was too damp
to do much good. Resigned to suffer through the discomfort, I
rolled my shoulders and struck out at the punching bag with
another jab-hook-cross combo.

Smack, smack, smack.

This morning, after taking Rust breakfast, I'd stumbled home
and fell into bed fully clothed. My sleep was restless, an incessant
stream of bizarre nightmares about beasts, chalices, and giant,
bleeding tapestries. I awoke to the premonition I'd massively
screwed up, and everyone I knew and loved would die because of
my transgressions. Then reality filtered through the fog of nightmares, spotlighting the fact that I was one defective wolf, safe in my
den and surrounded by my pack. In the colossal scheme of life,
how much damage could I really do?

I shook off the dreams, climbed out of bed, and checked my
phone. There was still no response from Mackiel. I felt the weight
of someone's gaze and spun around, scanning the room for an
intruder. Nobody was there. Still, my wolf's hackles were up,
causing the hair on the back of my neck to stand. My nose assured
me I was alone, but I searched the house anyway. I found nothing
—not a single scent or footprint that didn't belong—but it didn't
put me at ease.

Had to be the dreams. Or the uncertainty of what tonight would
bring. My father's reaction to the chalice still bugged me, and I
couldn't put my finger on why.

"You hang onto it until tomorrow night. Take it to Sereana after sunset. She'll know what to do."

Uneasy, concerned my instincts were going haywire, and with hours to kill before I needed to head to Aunt Sereana's, I made my way through the tunnels to the little gym in the back of the den where Rust and I trained. I'd been pummeling a punching bag ever since, attempting to exhaust myself into some semblance of serenity. So far, all I had to show for my efforts was a good sweat and a set of rubbery arms.

Pain sprouted across my knuckles as my skin split again. Fresh dark blotches speckled the faded grey vinyl, adding to the layers of spots from years of bouts with the bag. My hands itched as flesh tugged and knitted itself back together, healing. Once upon a time, I'd mistakenly asked Rust why we didn't use boxing gloves to train. The next day, he showed up with a pair, tossed them to me, and gave me a sound thrashing in the moments it took me to put them on.

"We don't train for a boxin' ring; we train for survival," he said. *"Gotta learn to embrace pain, so it's not a distraction in a real fight."*

Now, the sting in my hands served a different purpose, distracting me from the unease I couldn't seem to shake. The tingling between my shoulder blades intensified, and I spun around, expecting to catch someone watching me from the door. Nobody was there. Wondering if I was on the verge of a mental breakdown, I swore, my chest a tight ball of anxiety wrapped in self-doubt as I turned back to the bag. Uppercut, cross, jab.

Smack, smack, smack.

Biceps trembling in fatigue, common sense moved over and let frustration into the driver's seat, and that bitch was determined to ride me into the ground. Sweat soaked through my clothes, adding to the stench of the training room. With no ventilation to speak of, I kept both doors open, trying to get air to flow, but the stink of sweat had seeped into the walls, permeating down to the studs. This was one of those times when having an enhanced sense of smell wasn't all it was cracked up to be. I rubbed a damp hand across my wet brow and laid into the bag with another combo.

"Daaaamn," a familiar male voice said from the doorway, interrupting me mid-cross.

Barely tapping the bag with the last hit, I whipped around and froze in shock.

It was like seeing a ghost. But unlike the dead, Mackiel Denael had aged in the four years since I'd last seen him. Hints of the beautiful child I'd grown up with remained, but the silky chestnut curls were longer now, just this side of shaggy. Once pale chubby cheeks were now lean and sun-kissed. Heavy stubble covered his jaw and upper lip, giving him a rugged, unrefined vibe. Big brown eyes framed by an enviable curtain of long, dark lashes once made the boy look innocent. Now, he looked like trouble as he stepped toward me, muscle rippling beneath his fitted T-shirt.

My adorable childhood friend had been converted into a devastatingly handsome man.

He gave me a lopsided smirk, and the years of separation melted away. He was still the boy who'd once held me down and farted on me for taking one of his toys. The jerk who'd stopped talking to me for a week because I wouldn't write his tenth-grade report on agriculture for him. The protective fool who'd knocked out two of Thomas Henderson's teeth for telling the entire third-grade class I'd cast a spell on him and made him kiss Regina Meyers.

My partner-in-crime, my headache, my best bud.

"Hey, Chipmunk," he said. His smirk stretched into a grin that put the dimple in his left cheek on full display. "You miss me?"

I couldn't believe he was actually here, asking the stupidest question in the history of questions. I would have told him as much if I could get any words past the giant lump in my throat.

Concern flickered in his eyes as he stalked forward. "You okay?"

I still couldn't talk, so I did the only thing I could; I tackled him. Well, that was the goal, but in reality, I launched myself at him like a spider monkey. He caught me, and I wrapped both arms and legs around him like a human backpack attached to his front. Laughing, he staggered back against the wall and steadied us. I unwrapped my legs and dropped, settling my head against his shoulder to breathe in his familiar woodsy scent. A tear or two even leaked from my eyes as I squeezed him for all I was worth. I didn't even care that I was getting him all sweaty and gross. I was too preoccupied with making sure he didn't disappear, turning this moment into one massive heartbreaking dream.

His firm, warm palm landed between my shoulder blades and stroked up and down my back, soothing me. The familiar gesture obliterated the last of my composure. His presence had always anchored me with comfort and safety, and I'd felt so isolated and adrift without it. Without *him*.

Then, I composed myself, wiped my eyes on his shirt, and punched him in the gut.

He caved in on himself, laughing. "Ouch! Damn, what was that for?"

I pushed away from him. "Not returning my texts and making me worry. That was a dick move, Mack."

Throwing up his hands in defense, "I wanted to surprise you." He flashed me a crooked smile that would probably melt the common sense out of most females. Luckily, I was immune.

"My last text literally asked if you were alive. That one you have to answer, otherwise, I will believe you're dead, and that's not cool."

"Yeah, but how cool would it be if dead people texted?"

I narrowed my eyes at him. "Don't make me punch you again."

"Fine. I'm sorry I didn't text you."

"Forgiven. But only because I'm happy to see you. Do not let it happen again." I brushed invisible lint from my clothing because I needed something physical to focus on. "I can't believe you're finally home."

"Yeah. It's wild."

Our gazes met.

"For good?" I asked, afraid to hope.

"I think so. He told me to bring my shit."

"Why now?" I asked. His smile fell, making me realize how that came out, so I shook my head and tried again. "I mean, I'm super glad you're home, obviously, but why now? I thought you said the alpha was keeping you at the farm indefinitely."

Mackiel shrugged. "I thought he was, then last night, out of the blue, Luc showed up with instructions for me to bring him up to speed on my duties and head home first thing this morning. I arrived about an hour ago and checked in with the alpha. He said something big is happening tonight, and he wanted me to be here for you."

My world flipped on its head. I gaped at my best friend, certain I must have misunderstood him. "Come again?"

"Uh..." His eyebrows shot up in confusion. "I know you heard me. What's going on tonight?"

"Nothing he'd bring you home for."

"Except he did," Mackiel said, sounding exasperated. "So, spill. What have you been keeping from me, Chip?"

"Nothing. I planned to tell you all about it, but you didn't answer your texts."

He spread out his hands in acknowledgment. "Point. But I'm here now, so start talking."

There was only one task on my agenda for the evening, and I couldn't imagine Dad bringing Mackiel back for it. "I... I stole an artifact, a chalice, and the alpha is having me take it to Aunt Sereana after nightfall. She's going to use it to try to release my wolf."

Mackiel's eyes narrowed. "Like the other times?"

Okay, so I'd drunk potions, had spells cast on me, and uh... come dangerously close to death all at the hands of my aunt. Mackiel didn't know the half of it because I'd stopped telling him about my aunt's experiments long ago. He didn't trust the witch and couldn't seem to understand that she was trying to help me.

I shrugged off his concern. "I don't know what to expect, but the bigger question here is why did the alpha really call you home?"

Even in my own ears, it sounded like a deflection, but I desperately needed the answer. Dad couldn't have brought Mackiel home to support me. The alpha never did anything *for me*. Every command he made and word he uttered was for the pack. He didn't play favorites, and he certainly didn't rearrange plans and move his pack around because of me. There had to be another reason.

"He sounded worried about you."

"My father?"

"Yes." Mackiel nodded solemnly. "He loves you, Chip. I know you never thought so when we were kids, but he does."

What in the upside-down world was happening? "*I* never thought...? You were there and saw what he was like. What he's still like. You didn't think he loved me either."

"Yeah, but that was before the Bloodrite."

Understanding dawned on me. "Right. The packmind."

He sighed. "Can you not make the connection sound so... cultish?"

"You all chat inside each other's heads. It *is* cultish. And creepy." And even though I'd learned how to block out the hateful voices in my head, I was jealous of the connection the pack shared. They bit and clawed their way through the ranks, but at the end of the day, they knew and related to each other on a level I could never hope to reach.

No matter how many spirits I soothed on the sly.

"If you would have given it a little more time, you would have seen how useful the connection is. I know how deeply the alpha cares about you because I feel it when he mentions you. You are important to him, Chip."

I desperately wanted to believe my father loved me, so I clung to that hope. "Mack, if the alpha called you home to be there for me tonight, he must actually believe the chalice will work."

Or, whispered my cynical internal voice, *the alpha knows the chalice will turn you into a broken beast and plans to use your best friend to rein you in.*

No. That was crazy. I banished the thought to the furthest reaches of my subconscious, along with any and all thoughts of a certain psychotic guardian who'd spewed nonsense about me unraveling threads. I didn't unravel threads, I soothed them. Remembering who I was and what I was about, I opened my other sight and studied my friend's tapestry.

Mackiel was the happiest person I knew, all crooked smiles and snappy jokes.

At least, it appeared that way on the outside.

On the inside, however, he had this bone-deep melancholy that manifested in a tangled, dark mess of threads. Growing up, I'd worked on it almost every day, soothing the threads and unraveling them one by one. My efforts reduced the density of his depression, but no matter how long I'd worked at it, I could never take it away completely.

Now, his mass of sadness was all-consuming. Dark knots rubbed against the threads of his tapestry, irritating the entire design, and even rubbing it bare in places. I'd never seen anything like it.

Trying to keep my expression neutral, I grabbed his hand and sat cross-legged, pulling him down beside me.

"What are you doing?" he asked with a chuckle.

"Telling you about my adventure since you didn't bother to respond to my text. Now hush and listen."

As I soothed threads and gently tugged on knots, I recounted the events of last night, detailing all the gilded wonders of the treasure room and my ridiculous acrobatics. I glossed over the part about the box taking a blood sample and the missing glove. As much as I hated to admit it, Mackiel was my father's creature now. I had to be careful what I told him because, like the others who'd participated in the Bloodrite, he could no longer lie to my father. If

Dad asked him what I'd said, my friend would have no choice but to tell him everything.

I, on the other hand, was an enigma. I wasn't sure if it was because of my mother's witch blood, a perk of being an omega, a side effect of not being able to shift, or a combination of all three, but the Bloodrite didn't make me subservient to my father. I could still lie to him. Hell, I occasionally disobeyed his orders just to prove I could. Nothing major, of course. I only committed small, meaningless acts of rebellion that would hopefully never be discovered.

Like deleting the footage of the guardian.

I was careful to leave out any mention of that guy—or dragon or whatever—as I continued to work Mackiel's knots of sadness free.

"But Rust made it out," he said when I finally finished my tale.

"Yeah. He's fine." Realizing Mackiel hadn't phrased it as a question, I asked, "How'd you know?"

"We felt it in the pack connection while I was with the alpha. Rust and Janey welcomed another baby boy. Named him Rhett."

Okay, the packmind clearly had its benefits. "Janey's okay?" I asked.

"Yeah. She and the baby are both doing well."

"Thank God," I said, relaxing.

He eyed me curiously. "Back to this thing you're doing tonight. You think it'll work, Grace?"

He hadn't called me by my real name in... well, forever. He'd given me the nickname Chipmunk before I could walk and had somehow convinced almost everyone in the pack to use it.

I shrugged. "I don't know." I released another knot of Mackiel's sadness.

He watched me with a level of scrutiny that made my skin itch. I'd left out a lot of details, and he knew me well. He'd always been the one person in the pack I could confide in without fear of judgment or condemnation. Now, I could only share the tip of the iceberg with him, and I could sink several ships with the information hiding beneath the surface.

There could be an honest-to-God dragon after me, and I couldn't tell my best friend about it for fear that his thoughts would be overheard or he'd have to tell my father.

He sat close to me, but my heart hurt at the distance forced between us by the stupid Bloodrite. The one person I'd always depended on to be my rock was now just another of my father's soldiers. He couldn't be my sounding board anymore. Rather than come clean about all the details I couldn't safely tell him, I opened up to him about how I felt.

"The alpha and Aunt Sereana worked hard to find this artifact, and Janey went into labor while Rust and I were retrieving it. Now the alpha's brought you home. Everyone's sacrificed to get me to this point, and I'm terrified it'll all be for nothing. What if Sereana does her magical mojo thing tonight, and nothing happens?" Worse, what if I freed my wolf only to unravel some mystical thread that kept the planets from spinning out of control? As much as I wanted to disregard the guardian's crazy ramblings, they might as well have had a catchy tune for the earworm they'd become, repeatedly playing in my mind. "I've already disappointed the alpha so much. I don't want this to fail. I'm so damn sick of being the weak link in this pack."

"Come here." He held out an arm.

I slid closer, tucking myself against his hard body. Dropping his arm, he ensconced me in a warm, protective cocoon that smelled of childhood memories all grown up and matured. Tali sometimes hugged me, but nobody held me the way Mackiel did. Heat stung my eyes, and that damn lump lodged in my throat again. This time, I breathed through it, borrowing strength from my friend to combat my weakness as I continued working out the knots in his spirit. Minutes passed in silence, with only the sound of his heart beating beneath my ear. Weariness tugged at me, so I withdrew from his spirit. For now. With Mackiel home for good, I could work more of it out later.

"You're not a weak link," he said finally.

"Right," I grunted. "Just a shifter who can't shift."

He squeezed me and then planted a kiss on my forehead. I stilled, unsure of what to think of the gesture. My friend had never kissed me anywhere before. Sure, this was just a friendly forehead kiss that I was doubtlessly reading too much into, but it felt intimate somehow.

"Hey, remember that time you saved my ass?" he asked.

Tilting my head, I looked up at him. "Which time?"

He grinned, unable to dispute the truth of my statement. "The time I got shocked and burned for breaking into that tunnel we were supposed to stay out of."

During Mackiel's childhood 'girls are gross' phase, he used to sometimes ditch me to hang out with a group of like-minded boys. One time, Rust challenged me to see how long I could follow the boys before getting caught. I'd been trailing Mackiel and his merry band of miscreants for two days when a series of bad choices and ridiculous dares ended in him disobeying a handwritten 'DO NOT ENTER' notice from my father and triggering a magical trap.

There was an explosion, and the boys fled, leaving my fear-shifted friend in a heap of scorched flesh and bloody fur. I stayed behind, cleaned up the mess, and got him out of there before the trap's caster—which had to be my aunt—arrived.

"You were eight," Mackiel said. "But you were clear-headed enough to take charge of the situation, set my leg, and cover our tracks. You didn't tattle. You didn't try to hold it over me; you just saved the day."

"I'd been training with Rust for three years when that happened. I followed protocol."

"And we didn't get caught. The alpha knew it was us, of course. He asked me about it, you know. After the Bloodrite. He thought you were the one who tripped the alarm."

It was just like my father to wait until Mackiel couldn't lie to him to get the scoop. Forcing my jaw to unclench, I asked, "What did you tell him?"

"The truth." Mackiel frowned. "Not like I had much choice. I admitted I'd tripped the alarm. He wanted to know about you, asked if you went down the tunnel and if you saw anything. I told him you cleaned up the mess and collected me, and then we got the hell out of there."

A memory tickled the back of my mind. There was something about that door... something I'd intended to go back and investigate, but I'd forgotten all about it. Even now, I couldn't remember where it was. As I tried to focus, pressure built behind my temples. Wincing, I gave up, and the strange tension vanished.

"Why didn't you tell me when the alpha cornered you?" I asked.

"He didn't corner me, he just asked," Mackiel said. "And I don't know. I was embarrassed. It was the first thing he asked me after the ceremony, and I discovered I couldn't lie to him. To be honest, I felt a little... violated. Don't get me wrong, I know the alpha does what he does to protect us, but the way he pulled that secret out of me like it was nothing... it was a wake-up call. And I couldn't tell you how he'd pulled the secret from me without admitting the ceremony took away my ability to keep things from him, and you know we're not allowed to talk about what happens after the Blood-rite with anyone who hasn't gone through it. Also, I knew things would change between us the minute I told you. That you wouldn't be able to trust me anymore." He paused as the truth of his comment hung in the air, a dark cloud I couldn't soothe away. "I should have told you, but I didn't want to send it in a text."

"I get it," I said.

He watched me for a minute before standing and offering me his hand. "Come on."

I eyed the outstretched appendage. "Where?"

Chuckling, he said, "Trust issues, much? You need a distraction, and I have an idea."

Since his ideas usually led to bad decisions and a boatload of trouble, I let him help me up. Oddly enough, he didn't release my hand. Tugging me behind him, he marched past the balance beam, the weight bench, and a mismatched set of free weights to stop in front of the water table in the corner. Still not releasing my hand, he poured two cups of water and handed me one.

"Hydrate first." Lifting his cup to toast mine, he added, "Bottoms up."

We slammed back the drinks like pilfered vodka from his parents' stash. When we finished, he led me to the weapon rack mounted on the north wall. Pausing in front of wooden practice swords, daggers, maces, and a set of pugil sticks, he cracked that crooked smile again.

"I have been waiting four years to kick your ass again." He plucked a pugil stick off the rack and tossed it to me.

Unamused, I glared at him. "The word *again* implies you've kicked my ass at least once before, and we both know that's not the case."

The stick flew above my head, forcing me to jump and snatch it out of the air.

"Sorry," he said, but his grin had reached his eyes. "I forget how tiny you are."

"Yeah, well, no matter how much taller you are than me, I'm sure you still fight like a little bitch."

Unleashing his stick, he spun it around to warm up his wrists. "What a sexist thing to say, Chip. I see you've learned no manners while I was gone." He threw his head back to look up at the ceiling. "Thank God."

Laughing, I lunged backward, creating space between us so he couldn't get in any cheap shots before I was ready. "You gonna flap your jaw all night, or are you gonna step up and show me what you learned on the farm?"

"Little girl, always trying to antagonize the big bad wolves."

I rolled my shoulders and bounced on the balls of my feet.

"Since it's just the two of us, level with me. That is the only book in the library you can read, isn't it?"

He gasped. "Mean. That would hurt if book worms didn't have such weak swings."

"Oh yeah? Speaking of weakness, there's something I've been meaning to ask you about that day I saved your ass."

He eyed me, no doubt sensing a trap. "What's that?"

"Was that... urine I smelled? Did you really piss yourself?"

He squared his shoulders, and all traces of amusement vanished. "I was ten and had just been nuked by a witch's spell."

Unable to help myself, I laughed.

"Low blow. Even for you, shorty. I can't believe you brought that up."

"Why? Your big, bad ego can't handle it?"

He leaped across the room onto the balance beam in one fluid motion and steadied himself, his expression full of challenge. "Why don't you get your ass over here, and I'll show you what my big, bad ego can handle."

The side of his lips curled up in a smirk that I planned to wipe the floor with.

Springing onto the beam, I grinned maniacally and swung my weapon in wide arcs to the left and right, warming up. Rust had introduced me to pugil stick fighting when I was six. He'd tossed me a two-foot-long wooden bar heavily padded with foam at both ends, explaining that the military used the sticks to teach young soldiers how to fight with a musket or bayonet. Yes, musket. I was young, but we'd already gone over weapons. Extensively. Recalling that muskets were muzzle-loaded long guns replaced by rifles in the 1800s, I'd stared at him in shock until I could finally form the question I was dying to ask.

Just how old are you?

In answer, my mentor had promptly thwapped me upside the head with his pugil stick, sending me flying off the balance beam. *Old enough to block, smartass.*

Now, our pugil sticks were about six feet long, and the dense foam padding on either side was worn and lumpy with age. As Mackiel and I squared off, he aimed his weapon at me accusingly. "No shots in the junk. I mean it."

Fighting back my grin, I nodded. "Okay, fine. Boobs are off-limits, too."

His gaze predictably went to my chest, and I attacked. Sliding in under his outstretched stick, I whacked his front leg and jumped back. He managed to counter in time to barely graze my shoulder. When I straightened, he winced.

I glanced at my shoulder. "Was that supposed to hurt?"

"Not nearly as much as your face hurts me." He launched himself at me. I threw up my stick in time to deflect. The instant his downward motion halted, I jabbed, nailing him in the arm. With no momentum, my attack didn't have enough force behind it. He countered, and I took a blow to the hip. *Ouch.* That one hurt. Time to stop messing around. He swung his stick around, but this time, I blocked. Reverberations jarred my arms.

"Really?" I asked, surprised by how much of his weight he'd put behind the strike. "That's how you're gonna play it?"

He grinned. "If you can't handle the heat, feel free to step out of my kitchen."

His kitchen? Not today. I threw a stiff jab toward his stomach. He blocked, knocking my stick away and testing my balance. As I wobbled, he attacked again, but I recovered and ducked. He overextended, and I swung upward, grazing his chin.

We continued trading strikes and insults until the alarm went off on my watch. It was time to clean up and get ready for tonight. I jumped off the balance beam, and he landed beside me.

"I gotta go shower and get ready," I said, too tired and sore to be anxious about tonight.

He draped an arm around my neck and tugged me against him, kissing my forehead again. Apparently, this was something he did now. "'Kay. I'm gonna go spend some time with Tali, but I'll pick you up in a couple of hours."

"Thanks." I still couldn't believe my father had brought Mackiel back to help me, but I wouldn't look that gift wolf in the mouth. "And thanks for this," I said, racking my pugil stick. "I needed it."

"I know. I'm here now, and I got you, Chip. We'll get through this."

I didn't feel nearly as confident, but I grabbed my backpack and headed out. It was time to get ready to try and free my wolf.

Grace

Before The Eradication, Aunt Sereana lived on the east side of I5, in what was now Seattle-Victa. When the land was fractured, she had to choose to either leave her home for good or stay and travel outside the boundary whenever she wanted to access her magic. Without the continued use of magic to sustain her, Sereana would age, wither, and die. So, she left her home on the Mondeine side of the fracture and struck a bargain with my father. She would neutralize and remove the silver from the area, and in turn, the pack would allow her to select a home and live in the district under their protection. Ignoring the countless still-standing houses and condos available, my aunt chose the Pike Place Market as her home.

The Market once served as a downtown storefront for local farmers, craftspeople, and merchants and had numerous restaurant kitchens for her concoctions, a workable rooftop garden, and access to the crystals, books, and random witchy materials left behind in the Market's stalls. It also had a breathtaking view of the Sound, but the property wasn't exactly cozy.

"This place *still* creeps me out," Mackiel grumbled as the cluster of buildings came into view. His body was coiled so tight I wouldn't have been surprised if he started bouncing like a spring. "Thought that since I'm older and bigger now, it'd be different, but nope. Still makes my skin crawl."

"It's even worse on the inside," I assured him. "You don't have to do this, you know." He should be out celebrating the full moon with the rest of the pack. "Your family has barely gotten to see you since you arrived, and I can do this on my own."

Full moon runs were a sacred tradition. The pack would meet up at the den's entrance to initiate the run, and every able-bodied shifter would go furry. Then, they'd follow the alpha around the district, marking the territory and letting any intruders know our people were numerous, healthy, and prepared to defend. Since I couldn't sprout fur and run around peeing on things, I waited with the pregnant females and pups at the park. When the wolves returned, filthy and exhausted, everyone would hunker down in the park for the night. It was the one night a month we all slept above ground.

Before Mackiel had moved out to the ranch, he'd return from his run and seek me out, crashing on my bedroll with me. My friend was a snuggler. I'd wake up sweltering beside a massive brown wolf, usually with a paw in my face or a snout in my armpit. His complete and total disregard for personal boundaries used to drive me crazy, but then he left, and nobody invaded my space anymore. That's when I discovered what loneliness truly felt like.

But I also learned I was perfectly capable of doing hard shit on my own.

"I know you're used to going solo, but you shouldn't have to. You're pack. Besides, friends don't let friends venture into witch's lairs alone."

Now he was being dramatic. "I'll be perfectly safe in my aunt's *home*. She won't hurt me." Okay, that was a lie. Her attempts to bring out my wolf had caused me a great deal of physical pain over the years, so I amended my statement. "She won't kill me."

Mackiel didn't look convinced. "Really reassuring, Chip."

I rolled my eyes. "If she wanted me dead, she's had plenty of opportunities to take me out."

"Not makin' me feel any better. You realize this isn't how normal people talk about their family, right?"

"Yay, me. One more reason I'm a freak."

"You're not a freak. You just have... a shady aunt. Literally, I mean, look at this place." He gestured at the Market. "Why is it so

137

dark? There's a full moon for Chrissake. And not a cloud in the sky."

He was right. Even if the moon was hidden, I should be able to make out the recesses of doorways and windows with my enhanced sight, but I couldn't see jack. Unnatural shadows shrouded the entire property. Squinting, I could barely discern the outline of the iconic 'Public Market' lettering and clock erected over the main entrance. The sign's lights had burned out long ago, and the 'M' of 'Market' now hung askew. Every time a breeze blew, it sent an eerie whistling sound through the metal, making me want to turn tail and skedaddle.

"And it's so... dead. Nothing living gets close. Not even the plants."

We were in the Emerald City, nicknamed for its year-round greenery even before the influx of magic from fracturing gave it a boost. Now the entire district looked more like verdant ruins than an abandoned city.

Except Pike Place Market.

To an outsider, it must look like the building was wrapped in an invisible forcefield that neither animals nor plants dared breach.

"Seriously, why does she keep it so damn creepy?" Gold flickered in Mackiel's dark eyes as he fought his wolf for control.

"She doesn't like company," I said.

"I get that, but why keep the plants and animals away?"

Witch magic was... unnatural. Unlike shifters who drew on internal energy to shift and heal, witches siphoned vitality from external sources. *Living* sources. She extracted the life forces of plants and animals alike. As a result, animals intuitively stayed away. Any plants she didn't want in her bubble wouldn't live long enough to grow roots.

Honestly, witch magic scared the shit out of me.

"You don't want to know," I replied. When he started arguing, I threw up a hand to stop him. "Trust me. The less you know, the better you'll sleep at night."

I wished someone had given me the option of ignorance. My thoughts drifted back to the first time I'd seen my aunt drain the life from a rat. I was a child, no more than seven or eight, and we were in her rooftop garden, where she was teaching me about the plants she allowed to grow.

Leaving me by one of the raised beds, Aunt Sereana carried a small cage and a mortar and pestle to the space she'd cleared for spell casting. Curious, I climbed up on the bronze pig by the raised beds and watched as she flitted around the garden, collecting herbs and flowers. After using the mortar and pestle to grind them into a paste, she drew a chalk circle around herself and the cage. She began to cast, chanting in the musical, unfamiliar language of magic. As the volume and speed of her words increased, she opened the cage and removed a rat, cradling it in one hand. Her spell reached a crescendo, and she flipped the rat over on its back in her hand. With a flick of her wrist, metal glinted. The rat squeaked, and a thin red line stretched across its belly. The line darkened, and I watched in horror as blood pooled across the wound.

Flipping the rodent back onto its belly, Sereana leaned over the pestle and wrung the blood out of the critter like it was a sponge. But that wasn't all she took. As she chanted, a gossamer current streamed from the rodent, swirling around the bowl like an ethereal spoon, mixing the blood with the herb and flower paste. I gaped, frozen and unable to avert my gaze as the empty rat corpse caved in on itself like a popped balloon before its texture changed entirely. Holding her hand up, Sereana spread her fingers to reveal a pile of dark grey dust. It caught the breeze and fluttered away. When her hands were empty, she dusted them off, faced me, and smiled.

I passed out.

When I came to, I was lying on the floor at the feet of the bronze pig, and Sereana hovered over me, concern filling her eyes.

"What happened?" I asked, my head aching from the fall as what I'd witnessed came back to me. "You... you killed that rat and turned it to dust." Indignation filled my veins. She'd taken a life. That had to be wrong.

"Sometimes, I forget how young and immature you are."

Her disappointed tone stung, and I tried to dial back my emotions. I enjoyed hanging out in the garden and learning about plants, and I didn't want to let her down.

"I... I don't understand," I said. "It was alive, and now it's gone. It doesn't even have a body anymore. Where did it go?"

The harshness eased from her expression. "That's the wrong question, my curious little angel."

Encouraged, I asked, "What's the right question?"

"What is the purpose of a rat?"

I'd heard Hash complain about rats getting into food supplies, but I'd never heard anyone talk about why rats were a necessary part of the circle of life. "I don't know."

"They feed a number of predators, but other than that, they're pests. I caught that rat chewing a hole in a bag of rice. He was planning to eat my food. Rather than release him outside to become some beast's dinner, I took his pathetic little life and turned it into something greater. The worthless pest is now a useful potion. Think of it like cutting down a tree to make a wooden chair or a table. Sacrifices must often be made before life, magic, or even technology can advance. When the pack hunters kill game, you eat the meat, turning it into energy for your body. It's the same thing."

"Oh." I was still uncomfortable with what I'd witnessed, but I couldn't argue with her logic. "What's the potion for?"

An odd expression drifted over her features, making my wolf stir and setting off warning bells in my head. "Secrets," she said. "It's a potion that will help me learn more secrets." I didn't understand her answer, but before I could ask for clarification, she straightened, looking toward the chalk circle she'd drawn on the ground. "Go home, girl. I have work to do."

"Chip?" Mackiel asked, pulling me out of the memory. Worry stretched across his forehead before settling in the line of his frown.

"What?" I realized I'd stopped walking, frozen in the middle of the uneven street in front of the market.

"Are you okay?" he asked.

"Sorry. Yeah." I shook myself. "I was just remembering something my aunt once said."

He stared at me for a beat. "Are you gonna tell me or leave me hangin'?"

"She was making a potion, and I asked her what it was for. She said it would help her learn more secrets."

Mackiel's eyebrows rose. "What do you think she meant by that?"

I shrugged. "I have no idea. Come on. Let's go."

Mackiel closed the distance between us. His right hand landed on my shoulder, he squeezed, and then his fingers feathered down my arm and slid into my hand, intertwining with mine.

He was... holding my hand.

At the gym, he'd helped me up and didn't release me, but this was different. More intentional. A strange sensation pinged between us, causing my pulse to spike and my mind to race. The gesture wasn't unpleasant; it was just... unexpected. I thought about asking him why he'd done it but realized how lame that would sound and snapped my mouth closed.

"It's not too late to back out," he said.

I stared up at him, still trying to make sense of our joined hands. "To back out of what?"

He nodded toward the Market. "Of this. Magical artifacts are nothing to fuck with, and I'm sure if you tell the alpha you're not comfortable with using witch magic to access it...." His words trailed off.

I snorted. "You're wrong, Mack. It's far too late to back out of anything. The alpha sent me after the chalice because he wants me to shift. *I* want to shift. I want to be part of this pack."

"You are," he argued. "An important part."

"A damaged part," I amended.

The alpha's words from last night kept ringing through my

head. *"You have no idea what this means to me. What it'll mean for us. This changes everything, Grace."*

God, I wanted that. I ached for his approval, for the pack's acceptance and inclusion. I'd do anything to belong with my people. To no longer see shame and regret in my father's eyes whenever his gaze met mine. It had been all I'd wanted for as long as I could remember. If Mackiel knew the lengths I was willing to go—the details I'd kept from him about my aunt's experiments— he'd be shocked and disgusted.

"I don't fit," I said.

"Maybe you're not supposed to," he argued.

"Easy for you to say since everyone loves you. You don't know what it's like to be an outsider. I know you're only trying to help, but you're misreading my emotions. I'm not hesitating because I'm afraid of using the chalice. I'm dragging my feet because all our previous attempts have failed. This time, the alpha is involved, and it feels..." I swallowed back the lump of emotion threatening to strangle me. "It feels like a last-ditch effort. Like, if this doesn't work, I'll have to admit that I'm never gonna shift. Ever. And that... that terrifies me."

Tonight, I'd either leave this place whole, with my wolf free, or I'd accept my abnormality as untreatable and move on with my life. The continuous hope and disappointment cycle was becoming too much for me to take.

"I have to see this through, but you don't. You should be with the rest of the pack." I looked up, finding the moon. It called to my wolf, and she whimpered in response. She was miserable, and I couldn't blame her. We didn't get many cloudless nights here in Seattle, especially not in the spring. It was a perfect evening for a run. "You should be out there enjoying your first night back, not stuck here listening to my insecurities. And definitely not going with me to try another of my aunt's experiments."

He shook his head. "Not gonna happen. This is a big deal, and I wanna be here for you regardless of the outcome."

"It probably won't work," I muttered, preparing us both for the possibility of failure.

"Probably not," Mackiel said, surprising me.

I looked up at him, ready to rail him for agreeing with me, but his lopsided, dimpled smile disarmed my attack.

"But you're determined to try," he continued. "And the alpha's behind it, so who knows? Anything's possible, right?"

"That's the rumor."

"Well, either way, we'll get through it. Together."

As usual, my friend's words were exactly what I needed to hear. Releasing his hand, I threw my arms around him and squeezed for all I was worth. He grunted, let out a low chuckle, and then patted me on the back. When I pulled away, my resolve was strengthened. I sucked down a deep breath and got myself under control. "Thank you."

"Just stating the obvious." His dimple made another appearance. "You good now?"

I nodded. "I'm ready." It was a lie, but I'd latched onto the mantra of *fake it 'till you make it* and was determined to ride that baby into the ground. Or into insanity. Whichever destination we reached first.

His hand found mine again. It still felt odd, but it was less surprising this time. We slipped through the shadows and into the entrance. As soon as we crossed the threshold, the unnatural darkness engulfed us. Despite the many windows, I couldn't see a thing; the security lights had burned out long ago. I'd offered to replace them once, and Sereana stared at me aghast like I'd offered to dip her spell book in acid. *"I do not fear the darkness, child. Some truths can only be found in its inky embrace,"* she'd said. Sometimes it felt like my aunt was messing with me, but I'd never mentioned the lights again.

I didn't fear the darkness, either, but being unable to see was still disconcerting. I took a deep breath through my nose, sniffing out dust, rot, damp wood, and hints of my aunt's tangy scent.

Nothing out of the normal. Fumbling along the wall, I located the light switch and flipped it on. My aunt may enjoy the dark, but even she needs to see what she's doing sometimes. Electricity hummed through the old building, and a spattering of lights broke up the gloom. Three rows of bulbs ran along the ceiling, but only one bulb worked every ten feet or so. The place must have been well-lit before the war, but now the fixtures provided just enough light to keep the shadows from closing in completely.

We followed the center aisle toward the stairs, eyeing the stalls we passed along the way. Mackiel's head was on a swivel as he took in the sights. Trying to put myself in the shoes of someone seeing my aunt's domain for the first time, I did the same. Faded wood and metal signs depicting images of fruit, flowers, and fish hung here and there, providing shop names. Broken furniture cluttered the entrance of a store. A row of dust-dulled jewelry displays stood across the hall. Further down, rows of Seattle-themed coffee mugs and various souvenirs rested between racks of moth-eaten T-shirts and tie-dyed dresses. All in all, the bottom floor of the Market was a dingy, dank mess.

"Is it what you expected?" I asked.

"Nah. I mean, don't get me wrong, it's creepy as fuck, but I'm kind of disappointed I haven't seen any black cats or half-eaten children." He grinned. "Where do you think she keeps her cauldron?"

Chuckling, I shook my head. "Dork."

"That's fair," he said with a shrug. "Are all the floors like this one?"

It was my turn to shrug. "I'm only allowed on this level and on the roof. That's where Aunt Sereana's garden is. She spends most of her time up there." At least, that's where I found her whenever I was here.

"Don't you want to... explore it?" he asked, lowering his voice. "Aren't you curious?"

"Of course." Who wouldn't be? Even though she was family,

everything about my aunt was shrouded in mystery. I would love to see where she slept, ate, and read. She'd fled Seattle-Victa with only the clothes on her back and a handful of spell books, and I couldn't help but wonder what all she'd collected over the years. I wanted to know what was important to her, but not enough to risk her wrath. "But I'm not suicidal, Mack."

He shuddered. "Point taken."

"That reminds me, don't touch anything in the garden. Aunt Sereana has a close, personal relationship with her plants. If you kill one, she'll probably turn you into a frog."

He chuckled, but I did not.

Laughter dying on his lips, he asked, "You're kidding, right?"

"I've seen her do worse. Do not piss her off."

He blanched.

"It's not too late for *you* to back out," I said.

Drawing in a deep breath, he visibly rallied. "Nope. I'm in. I'll keep my hands to myself and be on my best behavior."

I squeezed his hand. "Thank you."

Without another word, I led him up the stairs to the rooftop garden, where we found my aunt hunched over a raised garden bed. After more than a decade under her tutelage, my gaze immediately shot to the plant she was trimming. The green stems and bulbous yellow flowers identified it as wormwood. Countless pop quizzes sent my brain whirling to pull up all pertinent information; I could recite it if prompted. Wormwood flowers could be used to treat digestion problems, fever, and various other illnesses. Next to the wormwood grew Jack-in-the-pulpit with an upright spadix arched over by a striped purplish-brown spathe. I still wasn't sure why I had to call it a spadix and spathe rather than flower, but in her home, Aunt Sereana was God. And not some graceful goddess of love and light who accepted imperfections and practiced forgiveness. No, she was all about fire, brimstone, and smiting those stupid enough to question her.

Anyway, Jack-in-the-pulpit was toxic when ingested raw but

could be ground to make a poultice that cured ringworm, numerous rashes, some abscesses, and several other skin infections. Not like I had to worry about any of that since shifters didn't get sick, and we certainly didn't get rashes from anything other than silver exposure. Still, medicinal knowledge could come in handy someday. Besides, it made my aunt smile when I learned, and like one of her plants, I thrived under her attention, greedily drinking up every ounce of affection she was willing to bestow on me.

Unlike the rest of her residence, the garden wasn't dark and scary. It was a magical place that held shadows at bay. Strings of colorful lights were draped from pole to pole like a canopy. Beyond the lights and lattices, stars twinkled, surrounding the rising moon. The sight took my breath away and stirred up that mournful yearning in my wolf again. I glanced over to Mackiel, finding him taking in the scenery, too. In the distance, someone howled. It sounded like Hitch, my father's beta.

Mackiel's usually brown eyes glowed with gold as his wolf fought to break free and join the pack. A shudder ripped through his body, and fur ghosted his arms. My friend held his animal side back, clenching his fists and jaw until fur melded back into skin. His chest rose and fell with deep breaths, but his eyes were brown again when his gaze met mine. Tiny specks of gold still danced in the irises, and his hairline had developed a sheen, but he appeared to be under control.

"You good?" I asked.

He nodded.

We turned to find my aunt watching us. She was a beautiful woman with caramel-colored hair that hung in a shiny, straight curtain down to the middle of her back. Her lips were thin and glossy, and her cheekbones were high. Most Tricari aged slowly— the universe's balance to our low birth rates—but my aunt appeared to be somewhere around my age. Of course, her appearance had remained unchanged for as long as I could remember, so

I had no idea how old she was. She bore no wrinkles, no grey hair, and her skin wasn't marked with a single age spot. She looked too perfect, like a queen in the fairytales I used to read as a child.

Despite her being my mother's half-sister, we looked nothing alike.

She studied me, seeming to bore past my skin and bones and into my soul. My aunt wasn't a shifter, but her mannerisms marked her as dominant. She didn't drop her gaze to anyone, not even my father. A long yellow dress with white flowers hugged her slender figure, ending about an inch above her sandaled feet. Cinched around her waist was a dingy white fanny pack screen-printed with the silhouette of the Seattle skyline. A leather strap hung below the fanny pack, weighted down by her sheathed eighteen-inch machete. I'd only ever seen her use it like a tool to slice open plants, animals, and me during her experiments, but I had no doubt she could wield it as a weapon.

"Hello, Auntie," I said.

She didn't smile—smiles were rare, treasured gifts earned only through parroting her teachings back to her—but her grey, stormy eyes did light up at my presence.

"Hello, niece." Her gaze drifted to Mackiel, and her expression flattened. "You've brought company."

Feeling like a child who'd been caught doing something wrong, I yanked my hand free of my friend's. His gaze burned a hole in the side of my face, but I kept my attention on my aunt.

"That was my doing," my father said, stepping out of the shadows. I hadn't scented him over the flowers, and his appearance took me by surprise. He should have been leading the pack run, keeping them safe, and ensuring everyone made it to the park at the end of the night. There was no reason for him to be on the rooftop with us. Either the chalice worked, or it didn't. The alpha's presence wouldn't affect the outcome. "Having her friend here will help Grace get through this."

The confirmation he'd brought Mackiel back for me hit me

right in the feels. Sometimes my father still managed to surprise me. "Thank you, Alpha."

He nodded.

"The boy's presence is of no consequence to me," Sereana said, thoroughly dismissing Mackiel. "You have the artifact with you, Grace?"

Still feeling like my world had been tipped sideways, I nodded. Then my manners kicked in, and I replied, "Yes, ma'am."

"Good." Gliding across the floor, she closed the distance between us. Clasping my shoulders, she dropped her face to my neck and inhaled through her nose. Unsurprised by her behavior, I stayed still and let her sniff me over. Her sense of smell was much weaker than a shifter's, so she had to be close to detect what she was looking for.

"I'm clean," I assured her. "I used what you left for me."

After this afternoon's sparring session, I'd returned home, where I found handcrafted bathing supplies and instructions. I'd practically melted the flesh off my bones and scrubbed myself raw, but my body and aura were now clean.

"Good, good," she repeated. "That couldn't have been a pleasant experience, but it was necessary. We must take every precaution possible to assure the best outcome." She grabbed my hand and led me away from the raised garden boxes to the open spellcasting area. Releasing me, she gestured at my backpack. "Let me see the artifact."

I slid my bag down my arms, unzipped the pocket, and removed the cup. Like this morning, it lay silent in my hand. Feeling underwhelmed and hoping I hadn't made a colossal mistake, I asked, "This is it, right?"

My aunt ogled the cup like it held the answers to all her problems. Unblinking, she nodded. "Yes. Power radiates from it. Can't you feel it?"

Oddly enough, I felt nothing at all. "No, ma'am." I extended the cup toward her. Rather than taking it, her face contorted into horror, and she leaped out of range. "What do you think you're doing?" she snapped. "Keep that away from me."

I was stunned. Her reaction—like my father's—made no sense. The chalice wasn't deadly. At least it hadn't hurt me. Yet the two most powerful people I'd ever known had treated the artifact like it was a hive of murder hornets. "What's wrong with it?" I asked. "Is it dangerous? Should I... put it down?" I started lowering it to the ground.

She held up a hand to stop me. "No." Tension eased from her shoulders, and her expression relaxed. Even so, she stayed well out of my reach. "It's not dangerous; it's... interactive. It called to you, correct?"

"I think so. It made a... a thrumming sound. Like a heartbeat."

"Well, it chose you. It's bonded to you now. That bond is tenuous, and if someone like your father or I—or even your friend there —were to touch the artifact, we could unintentionally sway it to bond with us. We wouldn't want to interfere with your intention for the chalice."

She made it sound like the lamp of a Djinn or something. Did I rub it and get three wishes? I wanted to believe my aunt was trying to protect my interests, but all of my instincts told me she was lying. The question was, why?

"What do you want me to do with it?" I asked.

She looked me over, taking in my clothes, daggers, and the backpack still dangling from one arm. "Set it on the ground gently, and remove your bag, weapons, and clothing."

I lowered the cup and stood, the rest of her instructions sinking in. My gaze swept to the alpha and Mackiel before settling back on my aunt. "You want me to undress?" *In front of them?* went unsaid. For most shifters, nudity was no big deal. Customarily, everyone else shed their clothes lest they destroy them during the change. Since I couldn't shift, there was no reason for me to ever get naked in front of anyone. I'd never told my aunt I was insecure about my body, but she had to know I didn't run around stripping like the rest of the shifters.

"Is that really necessary?" the alpha asked, and at that moment, I could have hugged him.

I didn't—I wouldn't—but I could have.

The look she gave my father made the hair on the back of my neck stand up. Some sort of non-verbal communication passed between them, and the anger rolled off the alpha.

"We don't want anything hindering her wolf from breaking free now, do we, Chaz?" Sereana asked.

My father's jaw ticked as he continued to stare her down. Tension built until the air around us crackled with it. Mackiel's gaze met mine, and his eyes widened with concern. This was insane. If my father and aunt fought, I wasn't sure any of us would survive. Guarding my stupid body insecurities wasn't worth a magical death match. Setting my backpack aside, I toed off my shoes and said, "It's fine, Alpha, I can do this. If Aunt Sereana's concerned that clothing might restrict my wolf, I'll remove it. I don't want to screw anything up."

Dad looked like he wanted to argue, but I was already undressing.

Sereana tilted her head toward me. "Thank you, Grace. That's very mature of you."

"And unnecessary," the alpha added, barely loud enough for me to hear. Mouth tightening into a hard line, he took a giant step back and settled in, folding his arms across his chest. Mackiel joined him. Turning my back on the males, I faced the Sound and removed my socks.

At least the view was lovely. A Ferris wheel once stood on Pier 57, but it had toppled over when I was a child, causing one hell of a ruckus. Beyond the piers, moonlight reflected off rolling water like a pale, glimmering line that led to the dark silhouette of Bainbridge Island. Tugging off my shirt and sports bra, I tossed both aside and let my mind wander about the sort of people or creatures that lived on the island. It was easier than focusing on my increasing discomfort with this situation. I unzipped my pants and tugged them and my underwear down, adding both to the growing pile of clothing. Cool, salty air brushed over my exposed flesh, and I suppressed a shudder while forcing myself to stand tall and not fidget. Sereana's gaze swept over my body, and I wanted to cross my arms over my breasts and hide. But I didn't. I was a shifter, dammit, and determined to be comfortable in my nudity. Hopefully, tonight we'd release my wolf. Then I'd spend a lot more time naked in front of pack mates. Might as well get used to it now.

She plucked a small spray bottle from the fanny pack around her waist, dropped into a squat, and started spritzing my feet. The unexpected bite of icy liquid made me wince, but I held still. My body adjusted to the cold, drawing heat from my wolf. Sereana sprayed her way up my legs. The scent was an odd mixture of chamomile, peppermint, and cannabis. Probably meant to calm me to aid the transition. Interesting. Once my entire body was dewy, she exchanged the spray bottle for a vial and extended it toward me.

"Take this," she said. When I did, she stepped back. "Good. I'll give you directions as soon as I finish."

I had so many questions, but I managed to swallow them back and watch as Sereana pulled a thick stick of chalk out of her fanny pack and drew a circle around me. It was large, giving me about four feet of space in each direction. Outside the circle, she added a pentagram with a few loops and embellishments I'd never seen her use before. Pricking her finger on the edge of her machete, she sealed the complicated design with blood. My eardrums popped, and the calming scents she'd sprayed over my body intensified. I could no longer smell the alpha or Mackiel, so I turned to ensure they were still there. My friend looked worried, but my father did not.

Finished, Sereana stood and eyed her work. "Can you hear me?" she asked.

"Yes, ma'am."

"Good. Uncork the potion and pour every drop into the Chalice of Power."

I froze, staring at my aunt. She wasn't the first person I'd heard use that title. The guardian had called it the Chalice of Power. Had Sereana known it was a cup all along? If so, why hadn't she told me when she'd sent me after it? More importantly, if the guardian was right about the title, what else was he right about?

"You are the broken beast. I cannot allow you to unravel the thread."

What did that even mean? Why the hell couldn't people be more specific with their warnings? Frustration made me want to tear my hair out, but my hands were tied. I couldn't ask questions about my interaction with the guardian. Especially not with the alpha watching me with the merest hint of pride in his eyes.

So, I did as I was told. Careful to stay well away from the chalk circle, I kneeled on the ground and uncorked the vial. The coppery scent of blood made my stomach sink. Had she drained another rat to make this? Ugh. I didn't want to think about that. And I shouldn't. I was a wolf. A predator. I'd be expected to tear prey apart with my bare teeth once I shifted. A little rodent blood shouldn't make me want to vomit. Still, bile rose in my throat as I poured the blood into the cup. I tried to ignore it and focus on the other scents coming from the potion. Hounds-tongue tangled with the earthy odor of mushrooms, the tangy bite of blackberries, and something else I couldn't place. The consistency was thicker than milk but thinner than yogurt. At least I wouldn't have to chew it.

Gross.

Determined to stop psyching myself out and focus on the task at hand, I set aside the empty vial, scooped up the chalice, and stood, watching my aunt. She owned several spell books, but I'd never seen her use one for a casting. Today was no different. She needed no visual instructions as she broke into the ancient tongue of the Tricari, chanting and waving her arms in exaggerated circles as if bringing ether into her. The storm in her grey eyes broke, and they glowed silver. Carmel-colored locks whipped around her face in a gust of wind that only seemed to affect her immediate area. None of the surrounding plants stirred. My father and Mackiel stood precisely as they had before, watching us.

Sereana's magic crested, and she jerked forward, falling to her knees with a bone-rattling thud. It had to hurt, but she didn't cry out. Instead, her hands flew to the spot she'd sealed with blood, and she resumed chanting. At first, nothing happened. I stared at my aunt, waiting as she channeled ether. The scent of burnt ozone hit me at the same time my feet began to tingle. Looking down, I was surprised I couldn't see the magic because it felt condensed and concentrated as it circled up my ankles, over my calves and shins, to my knees. Pulsing with power, it slid over my exposed flesh. More magic than I'd ever felt before swept up my thighs and hamstrings to my groin, butt, hips, and waist. The pulsing deepened, turning to constant pressure as magic consumed me. Hands, arms, back, breasts, it climbed, overwhelming my essence with ether. I could no longer feel where I ended, and the magic began. We were one. A heart that no longer felt familiar hammered in a chest that had grown too tight.

"Drink!" Sereana's voice thundered through the chaos, sounding miles away. "Drink, Grace!"

The chalice was at my lips before I even registered her command. Liquid sloshed and lukewarm blood and herbs filled my mouth. My gorge rose, but I forced myself to gag every ounce down. The potion served as a catalyst, altering the magic that had consumed me. No, activating it. It swirled and stormed within me, making my entire body swell and contract with its power.

Hands still settled over the chalk outline, Sereana chanted again. More magic swelled around and in me until I felt like a teapot about to blow. It was too much. Too intense. I needed to let it out, but I couldn't. Not until I freed my wolf. I gasped for breath and swallowed back bile. My stomach churned. I was going to be sick.

No matter how I tried to hold it in, the tickle at the back of my throat intensified until I had no choice but to open my mouth.

I didn't vomit.

Instead, words came out.

"Look past the old land out to the sea and find the island of paradise, gifted by God but seized from sinful man. Follow the canyon of stone that burns to lime. There, you will find what you seek at the heart of life birthed from the blood of two brothers."

My mouth slammed shut, finally obeying me as all remaining energy fled from my body. The ground tumbled over itself, and everything went black.

10

Arioch

I stared at the scrying orb, unable to take my eyes off the little wolf. She was nude, and it was a struggle to keep my gaze on her face and not the swell of her breasts, the perfect curves of her hips, or the inviting patch of curls between her thighs. The man she called Mack watched her backside with a combination of concern and interest, making me want to rip every bone from his body. The bastard had been flirting with her all day, and while Chip's romantic life should not concern me, it did. It very much did.

Not Chip, Grace, I corrected myself. Such an absurd name for a malevolent beast.

Her eyes glowed like the sun as magic filled her. I braced, wondering what to expect. I had been given little information about the artifact, but *'You must destroy the broken beast before it unravels the curtain between life and death'* had a decidedly ominous ring.

Only when Grace used the Chalice of Power nothing happened.

At least nothing happened to me. She rambled off some sort of riddled directions and collapsed.

"Chip!" Mack shouted, lunging forward. His concern grated on my nerves as I watched her chest to make sure it still rose and fell.

The alpha threw out an arm to stop the lovesick little puppy. "Do not interfere."

"Is she okay?" the younger male asked.

She had to be. The little wolf had survived an encounter with me; a mere spell would not take her out. Still, I leaned forward, awaiting the alpha's response. Not because I cared whether Grace

AMARA MAE

lived or died, but because I needed answers only she could provide. And then I needed to kill her to break the curse.

Ironic, yes, but nothing about this situation was forthright.

"She lives," the witch announced.

Tension eased from my shoulders, and I cracked my neck.

"But she didn't shift," Mack said, sounding confused. "I thought she was supposed to shift."

"No." The alpha's gaze flickered to the witch. "There appears to be another step."

"The chalice demands a price." Sereana bent and smudged a line of the chalk pentagram before wiping it away completely. Then she started on the next line. "Grace will need to retrieve something."

Understanding shone in Mack's eyes. "The heart of life birthed from the blood of two brothers. What is that?"

I glanced at Catori, wondering if my guardian knew the answer, but her attention remained focused on the orb. Not wanting her to miss any crucial details, I kept my thoughts to myself. I was still struggling to understand how Grace had used the artifact without any real consequences. Nothing had noticeably changed, and the chalice kept buzzing in the back of my head. It all felt so damn anti-climactic.

"I don't know," the alpha said.

With the pentagram broken, the witch started on the circle. "Nor do I, but I will find out." She paused long enough to eye the alpha. Those two were up to something. I would bet my sword arm on it. "This was good, Chaz. We're making progress. How soon can you assemble a team and supplies to accompany Grace on her quest?"

"How soon can you figure out where we need to go?" the alpha fired back.

"She's not even conscious!" Mack complained, gesturing wildly at Grace's prone form and growing increasingly distraught. "You want to send her out on some quest? Won't she need to rest? To recover from whatever this was?"

"Watch your tone, boy." The witch's eyes hardened. "I am not in the habit of explaining myself." To the alpha, she added, "Control your wolf before I do."

The challenge in her tone made the predator within me stir. If she had used that tone on me, she would be frozen next to my gargoyle doorstop. The alpha didn't seem inclined to react, however. Instead, he gripped Mack's shoulders, turning the younger male until the two were eye to eye. "You need to chill the feck out, Mackiel."

Now I knew another true name. Mackiel wilted under the scrutiny of his alpha.

"Grace is my responsibility, not yours. Not yet, and not ever if you don't remember your place. You really wanna help her, take her home, and put her to bed." The alpha removed a key from the ring attached to his belt and tossed it to Mackiel.

Confusion filled Mackiel's eyes as he accepted the key. "Your... house key?"

The alpha shook his head. "The house is unlocked. That key will get you into the mess hall. Hash is running with the pack tonight, and I don't want to wait until morning to prepare for our trip. Go into the pantry and bag up the jerky on the third shelf to the left. All of it."

Mackiel started to say something, but the alpha interrupted him. "You think I can't damn well handle Hash?" The younger wolf's jaw snapped shut as the leader's glare dared him to respond. "Drop the jerky off at my house—leave it on the bar—then go home and pack a few changes of clothes."

Mackiel snapped to attention. "Is leatsa mo shaol, Alpha."

"After you pack, get a good night's sleep. Be prepared to leave first thing in the morning. We'll be traveling light and moving quickly."

"I'll be ready, Alpha."

Chaz clapped the younger wolf on the shoulder in a physical show of affection not mirrored by his expression and released him. "Now get Grace to bed."

This alpha was a piece of work. Clearly, he knew how to manipulate his pack with hints of loyalty and affection, strictly to fulfill his own desires and goals. I could almost respect that if not for his naked, crumpled daughter, for whom he had shown no concern whatsoever.

Then again, my own father had saddled me with a curse and sent sadists to break me under the guise of training, so what did I know about fatherly love?

The witch had stepped away from the circle. As the boy approached, she cautioned, "Take care not to touch the chalice."

My attention shifted to the artifact. Grace had dropped it when she collapsed, and it now rested beside her head. Even though I bore the responsibility of guarding the chalice, I had never laid eyes on it before today. The artifact had arrived in a wooden box that neither my mother nor I had been able to open, despite our most creative efforts. Grace had somehow managed to not only open the box, but also to remove the chalice from my hoard. That chafed.

I glared at the artifact, wondering why it had refused me. The copper chalice was underwhelming in appearance, not nearly as fancy as the custom crystal glassware or China teacups I used daily.

"What should we do with the chalice?" Chaz asked.

"Leave it there. Grace will have to return for it in the morning," Serena replied. "See that she keeps it on her at all times."

Chaz's eyes hardened, but he gave her a brisk nod. I could not help but wonder why the alpha was putting up with the witch's orders. According to the shifter journal I had read, shifters were bigoted against anyone who was not pack. Yet this alpha was working with a witch. Grace had called her Auntie.

Had Chaz mated with a witch?

Mackiel knelt on the opposite side of Grace, away from both the witch and the chalice. He moved to touch her but seemed to think better of it. "She's naked," he pointed out.

"Are you just now realizing that?" the witch asked.

Something about her answer made *me* want to cover Grace. It was such a bizarre instinct that I had to drag my gaze from Grace and focus on Mackiel, who was looking to the alpha for directions.

"Do what you must. Just get her out of here," Chaz said.

Mackiel reached for Grace's clothes, opened her backpack, and stuffed everything in. Removing his own T-shirt, he gently tugged it over Grace's head, sliding her arms into the holes and pulling it down to her knees. He was wrapping her in his scent. Claiming her while she was unconscious.

"Arioch, you are growling," Catori said.

I started to argue but realized my guardian was right. As Mackiel scooped Grace into his arms, cradling her against his chest, I forced my fists to unclench, flattening them against the desktop. He stood, and the concern and affection on his face made me want to toss my desk again.

Catori tapped her chin with a finger. "The girl thinks this is about her wolf, but the witch and the alpha clearly have a different motive. I wish I knew what it was."

I frowned, watching Mackiel exit the building with Grace. The curse required me to retrieve the chalice and kill the broken beast, but now the situation was growing complicated. As the broken beast, Grace should be the villain, not a pawn in some scheme cooked up by her family.

But what if I was wrong and she was not the enemy I had to kill?

No. It was absurd and dangerous to even consider sparing her life when my freedom depended on fulfilling my duty. The note my father had left me was sorely lacking in details, but that one order had been abundantly clear.

'The broken beast will come for the chalice. To break the curse, you must slay the beast before it unravels the thread between life and death.'

Grace was still unconscious. Mackiel kept muttering reassurances and promising to protect her. Concern etched lines across his forehead as he watched her like she was the center of his universe.

He had no right to look at her like that.

"Now that is quite interesting," Catori said, sounding amused.

I spared her a glance before focusing back on the orb. Did the bastard have to hold her so tightly? Was he trying to crush her? The thin material of his T-shirt covered very little of her flesh, and it kept sliding up her thighs. Grace's reaction when the witch told her to disrobe made it clear she did not like being exposed, and here her friend was, practically showing off her ass he carried her.

Catori's words sunk in, and I dragged my attention away from the orb to figure out what she was talking about. "What is interesting?"

"You. I have never seen you so enthralled before. Not even with Fleur."

I stiffened, feeling my blood pressure rise with my temper. "We do not mention that name in this house, Catori. Ever. And I am not enthralled. I am... keeping an eye on my enemy."

"Hm." Her gaze drifted back to the orb. "Grace and Mackiel seem close. Do you think they will become lovers?"

Her question dug in beneath my skin, but I relaxed my jaw enough to grind out, "Not my concern."

"Are you certain? You seem bothered by the sight of them so... intimate."

She was fishing for information, but I refused to take the bait. Stabbing a finger toward the orb, I replied, "They have the fucking chalice, Catori. *That is* bothering me."

My guardian appeared unruffled. "I am aware of the situation with the artifact."

"Then why would you ask such a ridiculous question?"

"Because there seems to be something else on your mind. Something a little more feminine."

I squeezed the back of my neck, wincing at the tightness. "How can anything be on my mind with this constant goddamn buzzing? I cannot think straight."

The sleeping concoction Catori had slipped me had knocked me out cold, providing a few hours of much-needed silence. But then the buzzing grew until it woke me and had only intensified since. It would continue to worsen until I once more had the artifact in my possession. Which would not happen until...

I froze as realization hit me. "It is no longer underground."

"What?" Catori asked.

"The chalice. They left it on the rooftop, where it will remain until Grace picks it up in the morning. I can fly there right now and retrieve it."

Grace would be back in the den long before I made it to Seattle, so she would be out of my reach, but at least I could retrieve the artifact and end this incessant buzzing before it drove me out of my mind. I could worry about questioning and killing the beast later.

"No," Catori said, her tone brooking no argument.

Surprised, I stared at my guardian. "What? Why not?" It would take me no time at all to reach the city in dragon form. Through the orb, I had seen enough of the building's surroundings to locate it. All I had to do was look for the unnatural shadows. "This is the perfect opportunity. I can reclaim the chalice and be back within hours."

"You cannot let your judgment be compromised by your discomfort."

Stung by the harsh rebuke, I snapped, "There is nothing wrong with my judgment." Did she not trust me to make a single goddamn decision? "An unexpected opportunity has presented itself, and I would be a fool not to capitalize on it."

"Nonsense. You would be a fool to rush in there and get yourself killed. You are not looking at the big picture."

"Everyone you care for will betray you," whispered a voice in the back of my mind.

Gritting my teeth against it, I shoved the concern away. I had long ago decided to trust Catori, and she had never steered me wrong. Blowing out a breath, I collapsed back in my chair and stared at the ceiling. If she was advising caution, I should at least hear her out. If her argument was unreasonable, I could take off for Seattle as soon as she finished talking.

"Enlighten me," I said, spreading my hands out. "What am I missing?"

"Grace is onto us. Either your wolf is paranoid, or she has felt us watching her all day."

"She is not *my* wolf," I snapped, sitting up so I could glare at my guardian. "I only want two things from her: information and her death." The words tasted like lies, but I spat them out anyway.

Catori blinked. "As I was saying, she should not be aware of our surveillance, but she is. She appears to have empathic abilities, which might explain why she can sense us. But it does not matter. If Grace can sense us, we must assume the witch can, as well. What if she left the chalice on that rooftop as a trap?"

"Then I will kill her."

Catori stared at me, her expression incredulous.

I resisted the urge to squirm under her gaze. "What?" I asked. "I will."

"Great Arborvitae, save me from the arrogance of youth."

"I *will* kill her," I repeated.

"Do I need to remind you that the Peace Council found traces of witch magic at the scene of your mother's death?"

My mother had been away on business for the Peace Council, the group formed to end The Eradication, when she was murdered. The Council claimed ignorance as to the nature and attendees of the meeting, but they had provided Catori with a report that included their crime scene evaluation.

"Trust me, I have forgotten nothing about my mother's murder," I gritted out.

I was a child when she was taken from me, but I had wanted to hunt down her killer and avenge her. Unfortunately, being away from the chalice for any length of time had been out of the question. Mom had secured the box with fire and magic, and since I could not open the box, I was confined to the estate while her murderer walked free. The Council had launched an investigation, but it was nothing more than a formality so they could pretend they took care of their own.

"Your mother was both powerful and wise, yet she fell. Sereana is unpredictable, child. Do not underestimate her."

"Mackiel," a male voice said in the orb.

I looked up to see another shifter nod a greeting to the wolf. A sentry, perhaps. They were back underground, and Mackiel still carried an unconscious Grace. I considered Catori's warning as the wolf adjusted her weight before ducking into a tunnel.

"Besides," Catori continued, "I am not certain you could even touch the chalice."

That got my attention. My gaze swiveled back to her. Her attention was on the scene in the orb. "What do you mean?" I asked.

"Did you not see the way the witch reacted? She reacted out of fear, and you cannot for a moment believe the lie she told Grace."

No, it was clear the witch had lied. I had spent more time around the artifact than anyone, and it had not even allowed me to lay eyes on it. "But I am the chalice's guardian. It is my curse."

Catori inclined her head. "Are you not curious why the box never opened for you?"

I wasn't curious; I was enraged. I had tried everything I could think of to get that damn box to open. Magic, pry bars, fire, ice, swords, maces, hammers, nothing had even made a dent. In moments, the little wolf managed to do what had eluded me for years.

As time passed and I accepted the box would not open, I built up my tolerance to the curse. Once a month, I would fly until the buzzing started, and then I would see how long I could stay away. Although my threshold had increased, I had never made it past five days.

"It does not matter why the box opened for her," I replied. "I have to get the chalice back."

I felt Catori's gaze burning a hole into the side of my head, but I refused to look at her. Instead, I watched Mackiel open a door and awkwardly carry Grace through. I recognized her house as he passed the bar and entered her room, bending to deposit her on the bed. Once she was settled, he pulled a thin, worn blanket over her and knelt on the floor beside her.

"Oh, Chipmunk," he murmured, shaking his head fondly. "What have you gotten yourself into?"

She did not stir.

"Doesn't matter. You've always had my back, and now I got yours. I'll protect you. I promise." He swept a lock of hair away from her face and then bent to kiss her forehead.

"You are growling again, Arioch," Catori said.

I snapped my mouth closed.

Mackiel stood, set Grace's backpack beside her bed, and walked out.

"Have you considered the possibility that she is a pawn in all of this? Like you?" Catori asked.

"I am no pawn," I snapped, offended that she would even suggest such a role for me. Dragons were not pawns. We flew above the chessboard, ready to swoop down and gobble up the chessmen as they fought amongst each other.

"Oh?" Her eyebrows shot up. "Please remind me what you did to deserve this curse." When I neglected to answer, she continued, "Would you prefer the term victim?"

"Would you prefer to be a block of ice?"

She eyed me. "I will let your impertinence slide because you are distraught."

I set my elbows on the desktop and dropped my head into my hands. "A beast can still be a pawn."

"Indeed."

The directions Grace had uttered under the witch's spell tugged at my thoughts. "*Look past the old land out to the sea and find the island of paradise, gifted by God but seized from sinful man. Follow the canyon of stone that burns to lime. There, you will find what you seek at the heart of life birthed from the blood of two brothers.*" I quoted. "Do you know what that means?"

Catori turned her gaze on the sleeping female. "No, but we do not need to know. The girl will be going with them, and they will have to reveal their destination sooner or later. When they do, you will follow. You have always wanted to travel, Arioch. Here is your chance."

"Once I retrieve the chalice, then question and slay the beast, I will be able to travel all I want."

"Careful, child. Do not become a beast yourself in order to slay one. Vengeance always requires a price. Make sure you are willing to pay it." A shiver passed over my skin as her warning resonated. "Go get some rest."

"I do not require rest; I require the artifact."

"Then go brood elsewhere. I need a break from your presence. I will watch her and alert you the moment your wolf awakes."

"She is not *my* wolf, Catori."

My guardian sighed. "So you say."

Grace

I woke up a failure.

The instant my eyes opened, the events of last night crashed into me. I'd drunk from the chalice, and then... nothing. Focusing internally, I could feel my wolf, but she was still locked away. I hadn't released her.

It was over.

Time to accept that I'd never be a real shifter. Despair crippled my will to get up, and I rolled over, pulling the blanket over my head. My nose twitched as it registered that something was off. I smelled like Mackiel. Flinging off the covers, I sat up and looked down at myself. I was wearing his shirt. What had happened after I'd drunk from the chalice? I couldn't remember anything.

"Mornin', sleepy head," Mackiel said. My gaze sprung to my doorway to find my friend dressed in a different T-shirt and sweats and smiling down at me. "I was about to pounce on that bed and wake you up."

His cheerful demeanor only made me feel worse. "I didn't shift," I groaned. Heat stung the backs of my eyes, but I blinked it away. Tears had never fixed anything, and they'd do nothing to improve my situation. I was never going to shift, and I needed to accept that reality. Resigned, I collapsed back on the bed.

"No, you didn't shift." Mackiel's voice was softer now. "But it's not all bad."

"I failed. I don't see how it can get any worse."

"There's still hope." He stalked forward, pausing at the foot of my bed. "Apparently, the chalice demands a payment. It... I don't know, possessed you last night, and you rattled off some riddle about where to find what it wants. Sereana decoded the riddle, and you, me, Rust, and the alpha will be heading to an island in the Middle East in about a half-hour. I brought you breakfast, and you need to get up, pack, and get ready to go."

I sat back up and frowned at him. He'd provided a good deal of information, and I was still half asleep. "Wait. What? The Middle East? How are we getting there? Are we... flying? In an airplane?" I'd read about those, but I'd never seen one. I wasn't even sure they still existed.

"No. The alpha said we're taking a portal."

I had to still be dreaming because nothing my friend said made sense. "As in teleporting? Like in a science fiction or fantasy novel?"

He chuckled. "I'm pretty sure they intend for us to teleport in real life, but I could be wrong."

"I have so many questions."

"Same, so don't direct them at me. I'm here to get your ass up and out the door so we can meet the others at the bikes. If you want answers, try the alpha."

I stood and remembered I wore nothing but Mackiel's T-shirt. It was so big it almost reached my knees, but the thin cotton material made me feel exposed, which was weird since my friend had seen me naked last night.

"Did you dress me?" I asked, heading for my dresser.

"Yeah." The slightest hint of pink colored his cheeks. "Sorry. I had to. You were out cold. Most everyone was out on the run, but a few security guards were still roaming around, and I didn't think you'd want them to see you naked."

He was right, awkward naked moment or not, and I was touched by his thoughtfulness. Selecting clothes from my drawers, I said, "Thank you."

"Of course. I'll step out so you can change."

Mackiel left, closing my bedroom door behind him, and I

shucked his shirt, dressing in my usual dark tactical pants and T-shirt. Stuffing my daggers into the sewn-in thigh holsters of my pants, I straightened and opened the door. Mackiel stood by the bar where a plate of food waited. The scent and sight of biscuits and sausage gravy made me ravenous.

"Did the alpha say how many days I'd need to pack for?" I asked, darting to the food.

"No. He said pack light, we'll be moving quickly. Might want to bring your bedroll. I'm sure we'll be camping, and I don't know how comfortable the desert ground will be."

Reaching my breakfast, I shoveled food into my mouth and let my mind wander free. We would be teleporting to the Middle East. The prospect of going somewhere new and exciting was insane enough, but the reason behind our travels... I couldn't wrap my mind around it. Swallowing, I said, "We're going to this island on the other side of the world to retrieve something for the chalice so it will release my wolf?"

"Yeah." Mackiel grinned, showing off his dimple. "Crazy, right?"

Crazy didn't begin to describe the plan. "But we don't know what all's out there. Is this island even in Terra Fera? Or will we have to go into a Mondeine territory?"

My friend shrugged. "No clue."

"All to free *my* wolf." That was the part I had the most trouble with. I knew Dad would go to the ends of the earth for the pack, but for me...? I hadn't seen that coming. I took another bite, chewed, and swallowed. "How are you doing with all this?"

"I'm fine, Chip. In fact, I feel better than I have in years. I forgot how good it feels to be around you."

Because I eased his sadness. He may not realize why he felt better around me, but I knew the reason. No point in reading more into it. With all this focus on releasing my wolf, I'd slacked in my duties and felt a tad bit guilty. Opening my other sight, I reached for my friend's darkness and started soothing it. "But you just got home. Your family—"

"Will be fine for a few more days without me." He stepped closer, his face lighting up. "We used to always talk about getting out of the rain and gloom of Seattle and seeing the world. I never thought it would happen, but this is... legit. There is no way in hell I'd let you go without me."

Sliding another dark thread from the knot of sorrow inside him, I soothed and released it to settle against his tapestry before finishing off the last of my breakfast. Then, I stood and hugged him. "Thank you. For everything." I withdrew from his spirit. I wanted to unravel more of his sadness, but I was still tired from last night and needed to get ready.

He patted my back and held me close. "My pleasure."

A knock sounded on the front door.

"I'll get it," Mackiel said. "Go pack."

I hurried into my bedroom and grabbed my backpack. Sereana had supplied me with containers filled with my most frequently used herbs. I refilled the labeled baggies in my pack before checking my other necessities. Lockpicks, check. Rope, check. Canteen, check. Tali's voice drifted from the living room. Assuming she was here to say goodbye to her brother, I kept at my task, adding clothes to my bag. Finished, I turned to head out and found the girl standing in my doorway.

"Hi Grace," she said, her big brown eyes bright and her hair messy. "Mom and Dad said you and Mackiel are leaving today, so I wanted to stop by and say goodbye."

Guilt tugged at me. "I'm sorry to be taking him away right after he got home."

The knowing look Tali gave me didn't belong on someone so young. "We know how the pack works. You're not responsible."

"Tali," Mackiel said, her name a warning to watch her words and tone.

"I didn't even say anything bad." The girl rolled her eyes. "Anyway, I wanted to give you this." She held out a small brown and white paw toward me.

169

"Your lucky rabbit's foot?" I asked, eyeing the gift Mackiel and I had given Tali for her fifth birthday. We'd found it in a surface store during one of our clandestine adventures. Mackiel hadn't wanted to give it to his little sister because he was afraid someone would see it and she'd rat us out. I had more faith in the girl. Even then, I knew she was stronger and more intelligent than anyone gave her credit for. "But that's to keep you safe and protected."

"I'll be here where I have nothing to worry about." She frowned. "Not for a few more years, at least. You're the one who needs protection now. You can give it back to me when you come home."

Touched by her concern and generosity, I accepted the rabbit's foot, affixing it to the strap of my backpack.

She watched me with a curious expression. "Aren't you afraid the alpha will see it and ask where it came from?"

I shrugged. "Nope. I'll tell him I stole it. That's what he trained me for, isn't it? Anyway, what's he gonna do? Send me home?"

She grinned.

I hugged her, reveling in her familiar sweet scent and warm embrace. "Thank you. Stay safe while we're gone."

"You too. Make good choices."

I laughed at the advice I always gave her. "I will."

At least, I hoped my choices would be good.

Mackiel and I retrieved the chalice from Aunt Sereana's rooftop garden and met Rust and the alpha by the bikes. We then drove north on I5, exited onto Lakeview Blvd East, and made a couple of turns, staying just this side of the fracture as we parked in a large, mostly empty lot. The alpha was already off his Harley and marching toward a historic building with giant stained-glass windows and embellishments that made it look like an old-fashioned gothic church. It rested on the fracture, the blue border cradling the building. I wondered if the portal station also had an entrance on the Mondeine side.

Rust shook rainwater out of his hair. The past two days had been sunny, but Seattle had a reputation to uphold. The sky had clouded up early this morning, and we'd emerged from the den into a downpour. It was only drizzling now, but the damage was done. Our waterproof jackets only covered our torsos and arms. Everything else was soaked through.

My mentor leaned against his bike and folded his arms like he'd be there a while. Curious, I joined Rust as Mackiel parked beside my bike.

"What are we waiting for?" I asked.

"The alpha has to get some information about the portal station nearest to our destination," he said.

"We're really teleporting?"

He nodded.

My mind still required clarification. "Making our bodies, molecules, atoms, or whatever disappear from one location to appear in another? That's what we'll be doing?" I asked.

This time his nod came with the hint of a smile. "Somethin' like that."

"Don't laugh at me with your eyes," I snapped. "It's a perfectly reasonable question for someone who's just learning that teleportation is a travel option." Mackiel joined us, and I turned my attention to him. "You didn't know about porting either, did you?"

"No. I would have told you if I did."

"Which is why nobody told him," Rust said. "The trouble you two would have gotten into had you known...." He shook his head. "Nobody wanted to go traipsin' around the globe tryin' to find you two."

I gave him my best innocent look before facing Mackiel. "He makes us sound like hellions."

Rust snorted. "Do you know how long it took us to find and dispose of all those damn shavin' cream balloons?"

Mackiel and I weren't demons, but we weren't exactly angels either. We weren't trying to disobey the alpha's orders; it was a matter of survival, really. But, the prospect of spending every day of our childhood stuck in the den threatened to snuff out our souls with boredom, so we'd occasionally snuck out. We'd found a corner store stocked with random treasures I'd only read about, and the various packages and products were fascinating. After eating our body weight in expired candy, we discovered balloons, and our lives changed forever. Or at least for that summer.

The first time a balloon popped, we realized how much more fun it would be if they were full of something other than air. Something that exploded into a goopy mess. One experiment led to another, and the next thing I knew, we were sneaking balloons and shaving cream into the den. Since all the adults had duties and children were sequestered in the safe space, our supervision was minimal, leaving us plenty of time to fill the balloons and stash them around the den.

Shifters were clean freaks. Something about the stigma of being half-animal made my people physically unable to leave filled balloons lying around. They had to pop them to dispose of them, and, well, chaos ensued. Dad and Rust had to know Mackiel and I were responsible, but since I used herbs to mask our scents, they couldn't prove a damn thing. We didn't entirely get away with it since the alpha had security cameras installed inside the den shortly after the fiasco, making it almost impossible for us to sneak out again. Almost, but we'd still managed.

"Do you have any idea what he's talking about?" I asked Mackiel, my tone sugary-sweet innocence.

Mackiel shook his head, but a smile played on his lips. "No clue."

"Rust is really old," I told Mackiel. "Ancient, even. His geriatric mind confuses details sometimes."

Rust's eyes narrowed on me. "As I was sayin', nobody told you about the portals because I had no desire to drag your asses back from China."

Wait, China was an option? Okay. Yeah, we would have attempted to use a portal. At least before Mackiel took the Blood-rite. Now, I'd be on my own if I left. That sucked, but at least my friend and I would have this adventure together.

"Why are we taking a portal?" I asked.

The look Rust gave me questioned my intelligence. "Why not? How else would we cross the ocean?"

Trekking across the globe wasn't my forte since I'd never been allowed further than an hour and a half drive away from the den, but I'd read books that mentioned other methods of travel. "I don't know. Airplane? Ship? Submarine? Why did the alpha choose to travel by teleportation?"

"A ship would take months and be both dangerous and expensive, and nobody travels by plane anymore."

"Why not?" Mackiel asked, chiming in before I could.

"Well, fracturin' the land complicated shit. Some airports ended up in Terra Fera, and some landed in Terra Victa. Made a mess of the whole system. Even if they hadn't, could you imagine Mondeine and Tricari trapped together in a metal flying box? Someone would spout off, and it'd turn into a feckin' blood bath. But that's not the only reason. You know how magic isn't only channeled through people and creatures?" Rust asked.

I nodded while Mackiel asked, "What do you mean?"

"Places and things can hold traces of magic. Take the artifact Chip stole, for example. Places like Loch Ness in Scotland also hold magic," Rust explained.

"Because of Nessie?" I asked. Mackiel didn't seem to know what I was talking about, so I added, "The Lock Ness Monster." At his continued blank expression, I sighed. "You really need to read more books."

"Visited Loch Ness once when I was younger," Rust continued, ignoring us. "Didn't see Nessie, but I smelled her. The magic was so thick in parts of that lake that I felt... charged. Had to hold my wolf side back."

"What does that have to do with airplanes?" I asked, confused.

"When the mages fractured the land to separate the people, they pulled magic from items and places in Terra Victa. Some of that magic went into erectin' the border, but the rest shot into Terra Fera, makin' pockets of concentrated, unstable magic. Right after the war, an airplane packed with Mondeine flyin' from Vegas to Chicago hit one of those pockets, and... well, nobody wanted to fly after that."

In true Rust fashion, he'd glossed over the best part, treating me like I was too young to hear the details. "Oh, come on," I complained. "You can't leave us hangin' like that. What happened to the plane?"

"Some things you don't need to know," he replied.

"We're not kids anymore," I shot back.

"That may be true, but you're a long way from grown."

Exasperated, I threw my head back. "That doesn't even make sense."

"Give it fifty years. It will."

"We don't have fifty years, Rust. We're traveling *now*. Don't you think we should know what's out there?"

He considered the question for a moment before nodding. "I suppose preparin' you is more important than protectin' you at this point. Fine. Don't say I didn't warn ya. And don't come cryin' to me if you have nightmares. When that plane hit the pocket of magic, it mutated the travelers on board."

"Mutated?" The term caught me off guard. I understood the definition—changed in form or nature—but I couldn't visualize how anyone could instantly be altered. Shifters were born or made through a bite. The process wasn't instant, and it was painful from what I'd heard. But people who were bitten were infected with the animal DNA strain of their biter. Their animal sides were related like a parent and child. For a pocket of concentrated magic to alter a human... "Mutated how?"

"They were transformed into hideous, deformed monsters. They grew fangs and claws, sprouted fur and scales, and grew additional arms and legs. Their humanity was stripped away. They lost all control and attacked each other like they were infected with rabies or some shit like that."

Okay. Now I couldn't turn off the disturbing visuals. "How is that even possible?"

Rust scratched at the whiskers covering his chin. "Who the hell knows? Change always carries consequences, sometimes good, sometimes bad. Those mages may have saved us from killin' one another off by separatin' us, but they broke somethin' in the process."

Mackiel's brow furrowed in thought. He opened and closed his mouth a few times before asking, "But how do you know what the people mutated into? Didn't the plane crash?"

"Oddly enough, no." Rust leaned forward. "At the time, everyone speculated about why, but accordin' to the flight recorder, auto-land kicked on."

"How do you know all of this?" I asked.

"Happened right after the war ended, and we were still keepin' an eye on shit, makin' sure the Mondeine didn't change their tune and attack. It was all over the news."

"And nobody thought to tell us?" Mackiel asked.

Rust shrugged. "To what end? To scare you? There's not shit you can do about it, and nobody in the pack has been affected. Why talk about it? Anyway, the travelers that survived the flight ripped apart the first responders who came to help them. The Peace Council had to send bounty hunters to take the monsters out. Whole situation was a nightmare."

"That's awful," I said on a breath.

"A tragedy," he agreed. "And not an isolated one. Two other planes hit magic pockets in different parts of the world, but they both crashed. Didn't take long for the officials to figure out the pockets didn't show up on radar and couldn't be avoided. It was a mess. The Mondeine don't like bein' grounded. They blamed the mages who'd created the fractures, claimin' they intended for this to happen. Almost restarted the war until a handful of scientists and mages teamed up and created the portals."

"Are the portals safe?" Mackiel asked.

Rust chuckled. "Safer than flyin'."

"That answer does *not* instill confidence," I pointed out.

"Sure doesn't." Rust stared me down. "Tell me what you want here. Assurance or truth?"

"Both."

He met my gaze. "You wanna be an adult, you gotta accept that you don't get both."

My mentor's answering grin didn't quite reach his eyes. I looked him over, noting the bags under his eyes and worry lines across his forehead. In my excitement over the prospect of traveling, I hadn't even considered how difficult this must be on him. Just yesterday afternoon, Janey had given birth to a healthy baby boy. Both mother and pup were doing well, but the delivery had been difficult. Janey had lost a lot of blood and required stitches since she wouldn't be able to shift and heal for a few days yet.

And, of course, Rust had carried as much of her pain load as he could through the process. He had to be as wiped out as she was, but no way in hell would he ever admit it.

"I'm sorry, Rust," I said, my excitement draining away.

He eyed me curiously. "For what?"

"For all of this. You shouldn't be here. You should be at home with your mate and baby."

His shoulders straightened. "I don't question the orders of my alpha, kid. You shouldn't either."

But I did have questions. Lots of them. And I was sick to death of being left in the dark. "But why now?" I asked. "I've waited nineteen years to shift, and suddenly the alpha's all about making it happen. Why?"

"I'm sure he has his reasons."

That answer made me want to scream in frustration. I understood that none of my packmates could defy my father, but did they have to follow him with such blind devotion? Loyalty was one thing, but this? This was so much more.

"Yeah, but I'm sure his reasons could have allowed you to spend at least a few days with your new pup."

His jaw ticked, and his eyes hardened. "That's enough, Chip. Barkin' up that tree won't catch you anythin'. Let it go."

I wanted to rage and demand to know why Rust and the rest of the pack had placed my father on such a high pedestal they couldn't even ask him questions, but I knew better than to push my mentor further than I already had.

Mackiel's strong hand landed on my shoulder, drawing my attention. When our gazes met, he gave me a slight shake of his head, silently telling me to drop it. My friend was only looking out for me, but his interference kind of made me want to punch him in the throat. Despite what he, Rust, or any of my father's other minions thought, my point was valid, but I knew when to shut my mouth. I didn't need to be shushed.

"The alpha's ready for us." Rust hiked his pack over his shoulders. "Come on. Socotra awaits."

Mackiel must have sensed my irritation because he tried to catch my eye, but I ignored him and followed Rust to line up behind the alpha. In front of the line, an oak door swung open. An older gentleman leaned heavily on his cane and climbed the single step. As he moved, his human disguise distorted, revealing glimpses of tawny skin and pointed ears. What was he? Some sort of elf or tree folk? Washington's wild, lush forests had to be full of people who thrived in nature.

An elbow nudged me in the side. "You okay?" Mackiel whispered.

AMARA MAE

The concern on my friend's face made me realize how ridiculous I was being. Mackiel had always treated me like a little sister he needed to protect. After four years apart, I'd hoped he'd grown out of that behavior, but he was a dominant wolf. Protection was part of who he was, ingrained in his DNA, and intertwined with every fiber of his being. I wasn't even sure he *could* grow out of it.

"I'm fine," I said, and I was. "Just anxious. And a little worried."

Rust and my father had their heads together and were speaking in Irish. I'd picked up a few words over the years, but not nearly enough to follow their conversation. I wondered what they were discussing that they didn't want us to overhear.

"Worried?" Mackiel followed my gaze to Rust. "About him? Come on, Chip, you know better. *You* told me how he got his name."

Not exactly. I'd told Mackiel why Rust's name was a perfect fit for the corrosive son-of-a-bitch whose sole purpose in life was to break me down. In my defense, that epiphany came after a particularly grueling training session. I'd been certain Rust was trying to kill me at the time.

"He'll be fine," Mackiel assured me. "We all will. And I can do without this weather for a while. Rust said Socotra, but I haven't the foggiest idea where that is. The Middle East is desert, though, right?" He held up a hand, allowing it to fill with raindrops. "Desert weather works for me."

"Still hate the rain, huh?" I asked.

"Even more now that my days are usually spent out in it. Never thought I'd say this, but underground was better."

The line moved forward, and I realized there were only two people in front of our group now. A slight female who stood no higher than half my father's height waited beside a blond boy who barely came to her hips. I tugged on Mackiel's sleeve and discretely gestured toward the diminutive duo. "What do you think? Halflings?" I whispered.

My friend looked at me like I was speaking a different language. "Uh... sure?"

178

I sighed. "I thought you were studying the database."

"The animal section. I'm a hunter, Chip. All I need to know is which meat is edible and where to wound 'em without ruining any of the tasty parts."

"But don't you want to know about the other people out there?" I asked.

"Why?" He shrugged. "It's not like we're gonna invite them over for a party or anything. All the people I need to know live in the den or at the farm."

"You sound like them." I nodded toward Rust and my father.

"Like I enjoy the company of my pack and don't plan on needing anyone else?"

"But there could be really cool people out there that you'll never know."

He frowned. "Still workin' through that fear of missing out, huh?"

"The world is massive. I will never understand why the pack is content to stay in our little corner of it."

Turning back to face forward, I focused on the boy. A bag strap slipped down his arm. As he adjusted it, his gaze snagged on my father, and his eyes grew wide as saucers. Whipping around to fully face the alpha, his mouth gaped open like a dead fish. Dad wasn't tall, but he was built like a brick shithouse, broad, muscular, and immovable. Regardless, he must have seemed like a giant in the eyes of the miniature child. Something tumbled out of the boy's hand, hitting the ground with a loud thwack, but he didn't so much as blink.

Hearing the sound, the woman spun around to find the boy's attention locked on the alpha. Her cheeks flamed red, and concern flooded her eyes. "Sorry. Sorry," she muttered, keeping her gaze lowered. Bowing at the waist, she picked up a wooden car and handed it to the boy. When he didn't take it, she smacked it into his open hand and forced his fingers closed around it before spinning him around to face forward. "Stop staring, Kipp, and mind your own business."

The boy tried to peek over his shoulder, but the woman flicked his ear.

"Ow! Mom," he whined.

"Do as you're told," she snapped.

The oak door creaked open again. The woman grabbed her son's arm and towed him up the step, their little bodies wobbling as they made the climb. They disappeared into the building and the doors closed with a thud. Unable to control my excitement, I grinned at Mackiel. "We're next."

When it was our turn, the four of us entered the building together, stepping into a spacious foyer. An armed guard pointed us toward a knee-high conveyor belt that ran along the wall, stretching as far as I could see. My father led the way. An automated voice came out of the overhead speakers as he approached the belt.

"You have entered a neutral zone," the disembodied voice said. "By declaration of the Peace Council, no fighting is allowed on the premises. Violators will be eliminated or contained by the Wardens for prosecution and sentencing by the Peace Council. Deposit all weapons, bags, and belongings onto the belt."

The alpha did as he was instructed.

A machine next to the conveyer belt whirred to life and a yellow paper ticket popped out.

"Take your ticket," the voice continued. "The ticket will be required to retrieve your gear at your destination. Please proceed to the automatic walkway."

Dad pocketed the ticket and stepped onto a conveyer belt for people. It carried him between two giant metal bars. The belt stopped. A soft beeping noise came from the metal bars, then a green light flashed as the belt started moving again.

Mackiel went next, and the recording started over.

I lingered beside Rust. "Wardens are bounty hunters for the Peace Council, right?" I asked.

"Sure are."

I eyed the wardens in question. "Doesn't it seem odd to you that a group formed to keep peace employs bounty hunters? Kind of off message, isn't it?"

My mentor shrugged. "Peace is a fickle bitch. We've courted her since the beginnin' of time, but she plays hard to get. This last time she really worked us over."

Sometimes I got lost in Rust's metaphors, but I found my way through that one easily enough. "You mean the war?" I asked.

"Not the war itself, but the cause."

I'd learned about that in school, so I said, "The end of the cloaking."

The cloaking was a spell that disguised the Tricari to appear Mondeine. Nobody knew when it started, but one day the spell shattered, and the Mondeine came face to face with creatures of myths, fairytales, and nightmares. The two factions had coexisted peacefully for millennia, but with knowledge of one another came war.

He nodded. "Someone sure as hell didn't want peace."

I stared at him, gob-smacked. "You think someone intentionally removed the cloaking?" Over half the population—both Mondeine and Tricari—had died in The Eradication. Nobody knew why the cloaking had ended, but it couldn't have been intentional. Nobody could be that evil.

"I been around long enough to know when bad shit happens, there's usually a shitstain of a person responsible. The wardens are scary sons-of-bitches, and sometimes that's just what you need to keep the peace. You're up, kid." He gestured for me to approach the conveyor belt.

My mind whirring, I ambled forward, removing the daggers from my thigh sheaths, and storing them in my backpack before setting it and my bedroll on the belt. My ticket popped out, and I saw a barcode imprinted on the paper. Stuffing it into my pocket, I stepped onto the automatic walkway and took in my surroundings.

The foyer opened to a giant room. Massive white pillars supported a high wood-raftered ceiling, and stained-glass windows let in the gloomy daylight.

The conveyer belt with our gear ran parallel to the automatic walkway, bisecting the room. Another conveyer belt and automatic walkway ran in the opposite direction on the other side. That must have been the Mondeine side. Curious, I watched for people but didn't see anyone.

My ride came to an end, depositing me beside Mackiel. My father stood in front of a computer a few feet away, selecting options on a touchscreen monitor. He slipped a thin gold bar and a handful of bills into a slot beneath the monitor.

Rust joined us, and I leaned toward my mentor. "What's the alpha doing?" I asked.

"Payin' for our tickets. Well, part of 'em, anyway. You'll have to pay for the other half on your own."

Confident I must have misheard him, I cocked an eyebrow at Rust. "I don't have anything of value on me." Looking at Mackiel, I asked, "Do you?"

He shook his head.

"You have the payment *in* you," Rust said. "The alpha's payin' for the technology, but the magic will also require its due."

"Energy?" I asked.

Rust nodded. "Yep. Yemen is a long way away. Probably around thirteen thousand kilometers."

"In miles?" being born and raised in Seattle, I had no idea how far a kilometer was. All the signs were in miles, and the mile markers along the road helped me understand how far that distance was, but I'd never seen such a measurement for kilometers. I didn't know how it compared.

Rust shook his head at my American ignorance. "More than eight thousand miles. A direct flight would take around twenty hours, but even when planes were flyin', you couldn't have gotten a direct flight.

There'd be plane changes and layovers and shit. I believe Yemen's eleven hours ahead of Seattle." He glanced at his watch, and his eyes sparkled with mischief. "Let's see how smart the two of you are. It's about nine-thirty here, so what time do you think it is in Yemen?"

"Twenty-thirty?" Mackiel asked.

Changing his calculations to am/pm, I said, "Eight-thirty... tonight? How is that possible? What happens to the eleven hours we lose?"

"Just the way time zones work."

"Because the earth is round," Mackiel added. "And spinning on an axis as it orbits the sun. So different sections of the planet have direct sunlight at different times."

"Good," Rust sounded surprised. "Glad to know they're teachin' somethin' in that school."

"The alpha dictates the school curriculum," I reminded my mentor with a smile. "He could improve upon what we're taught at any time."

Rust's frown carried a whole heap of disappointment. Like I was the one holding our education system back. "Anyway, you'd be pure shit if you had to fly twenty hours only to land thirty-one hours ahead of the time you left. It'd leave ya so damn confused you wouldn't know day from night. Used to call that jet lag. Now, the travel time is instant, but magic still zaps that energy from your body to transport you. Once we teleport, you'll feel like shit for a while, but it'll pass."

"So, if the fatigue that comes from jets is called jet lag, is this... portal lag?" I asked.

Rust's lips quirked up into a half-smile. "I think people just call it travel fatigue, but that's a fittin' name."

"How long will it last?" Mackiel asked.

Rust shrugged and then nodded toward my father. "Looks like you're about to find out. The alpha needs you to go accept the charges with a fingerprint."

Mackiel joined my father, and I moved closer to overhear the two.

"Go ahead and put your index finger right there," Dad said.

Without even taking a moment to read the screen, Mackiel did as he was told and then joined us.

"How long will the fatigue last?" I asked.

He shrugged. "The alpha didn't say."

His answer made me want to bash my head against the wall. "Why didn't you read the screen?"

Another shrug. "Won't change anything. I still would have agreed to the terms."

"It would be nice to know what to expect." Couldn't he see that some questions were necessary?

"Grace," the alpha said, gesturing me over. "You're up."

I joined him at the computer but, unlike my friend, I quickly scanned the screen. 'Traveler agrees to the charge of approximately twenty-six hours of fatigue. Uninterrupted sleep will cut the duration in half. If traveler chooses not to sleep during fatigue, we recommend practicing extreme caution when participating in any and all physical activity and—'

"Grace," the alpha growled, packing a world of frustration into the word. "You're holding us up. Don't you trust your alpha?"

Not wanting to push him, I pressed my index finger against the box and accepted the charge. Once Rust added his fingerprint, the four of us stepped onto another belt.

"But I don't wanna go poof!" A young male voice shouted ahead.

Stepping to the side, I angled myself to take in the scene. Two giant, round platforms stood side by side. One held the bag of the small blond boy I'd seen earlier. The child stood on the other platform clutching his mother's dress as she methodically pried each of his fingers free. One hand popped off, but before she could start on the other, he tangled his now free fingers in her dress once again.

"Stop it!" she shouted. "You're being ridiculous. I told you, you won't go poof. You pop out of this spot and pop up at the portal by Nana's house. It's... it's like a game."

"Nana don't like it when I poof. That's a bad game."

The woman's gaze snagged on us, and her posture stiffened. "I'm so sorry for the delay. I'm... I'm trying."

"I can restrain him if you'd like," the silver-haired man standing beside the portal said.

A look of horror flickered across the woman's face before she schooled her features. "Thank you, but that won't be necessary. Can I... Am I allowed to port with him?"

"We recommend one person per portal."

"I understand, but is it possible?"

The man acted like she'd asked him to pluck the moon from the sky and hand it to her. Settling his hands on his hips, his shoulders spasmed with an erratic shrug as he gave her a dramatic eye roll. "Yes, I can do it. This one time. Do not let him make a habit of teleporting with you. I will do this as a kindness, but other mages will not allow such a breach of protocol."

Nothing about his tone sounded kind, and I wondered what the big deal was. The mother and child together didn't make up the body mass of my father. Surely the mage could teleport them together.

"Thank you," she said. Her relief was almost palpable as she picked up the child and settled him on her hip before moving toward the center of the portal.

The boy hid his face in his mother's chest as an emerald-skinned female with small tusks protruding from either side of her upper lip joined them. She used a handheld device to scan the mother's tag, causing the luggage conveyer belt to jerk forward, and another bag was deposited onto the second portal. The tusked female stepped off the transport pad, and the mage moved to the computer. He pushed a button and then waved his hand in the air, muttering a spell. Blue light shot up from both portals as a faint whirring sound grew louder.

"No!" the child shouted, panicking as he must have realized what was really happening. "I don't wanna poof!"

His mother tightened her hold around him, and then just like that, the two disappeared. The blue light faded, and both portals stood empty.

As excited as I'd previously been to travel, I suddenly didn't want to poof, either.

Arioch

Fifty-seven hours had passed since Grace had stolen the chalice, and I felt every minute of it as I watched her step onto a portal platform and prepare to teleport. "Where the hell is Socotra?" I asked, my patience waning as the buzzing in the back of my head continued to intensify.

After my mother's death, Catori and Tyrin shared the responsibility for my education. Catori was an expert in science, math, and language, but bound to her tree as she was, she knew nothing about the outside world. Tyrin had handled subjects like geography, world history, and government. The mention of Yemen sparked memories of his teachings, but I was finding it increasingly difficult to focus on anything, much less old lessons of places I had no hope of ever visiting.

Catori unrolled a world map across my desk. Using books to secure the edges, she zeroed in on the country south of Saudi Arabia with her fingertip. "There is Yemen." Her fingertip hovered over the sea as she leaned closer to the map. She stabbed a speck of land east of Somalia. "There. That is Socotra."

The orb went black. A heartbeat later, Grace reappeared on a different portal platform. She staggered once, twice, and then collapsed.

Like before, watching her crumple had an odd effect on me. I felt restless and angry as I eyed her chest, making sure it rose and fell with breath. Good. Still alive. "What happened to her?" I asked.

"Poor thing must be exhausted," Catori replied. "She expended a lot of magic last night, and traveling so soon afterward must have sapped the last of her strength."

187

The shifter journal I had read made it sound like an alpha's number one priority was to protect his pack, but Grace's alpha—her father—seemed to have no trouble putting her in danger. Instead of voicing my concerns about her mistreatment, I said, "Kindly refrain from referring to my sworn enemy as 'poor thing.' I find it... unsettling."

Catori did not respond. Mackiel appeared on the platform, scooping up the woman like he had the last time she had passed out. This time, he struggled under her weight. Travel fatigue was affecting him, too. Interesting.

"There. What does that sign say?" Catori asked, pointing at the orb where a prominent welcome sign hung on the wall. "Al Mukalla. That is where you must go. I will have Fred pack your bag." Catori's eyes darkened as she communicated with my house-keeper telepathically.

I retrieved a sheathed dagger from the bottom drawer of my desk and strapped it around my ankle. Tugging at the sheath that crossed my torso, I found comfort in the weight of my sword against my back.

Mackiel carried Grace down a hallway. Bright red arrows led past advertisements for local food, clothing, and fishing tours. Warnings were also tacked onto the walls. Mackiel slowed to study a drawing of a man wearing a long white dress. The left half of the drawing's body looked normal, but the right was a skeleton. Beneath the illustration was the word 'Nesna.' Next to the Nesna was another drawing, a snake so massive it looped over the page multiple times without showing a tail. The name beneath the snake was 'Falak.' There were additional warnings for something that looked like a zombie and a giant bird with a ridiculously long neck.

"Are those creatures real?" I asked Catori.

She studied the flyers. "I do not know, but there have been horrors in these woods I would not have believed had I not seen them with my own eyes. You must be cautious."

"What sort of horrors?" I asked, wondering why this was the first time I was hearing about them.

"The kind you do not need to concern yourself with. I am perfectly capable of protecting my forest."

I would never dream of questioning her abilities; I merely wanted the opportunity to test my own. It had been years since my last trainer had left, and sparring with the gargoyles provided no challenge whatsoever.

"What happened to her?" the alpha asked Mackiel, his tone more annoyed than concerned.

"She passed out."

"Didn't she eat breakfast?"

"Yes, Alpha."

Chaz frowned.

Rust joined the trio. They exchanged tickets for their gear and exited the building into darkness. The alpha stopped beside the building, setting his leather duffle bag on a bench. Grace stirred, and Mackiel lowered her to sit beside the bag. Her eyes popped open, and she glanced around, confused.

"Where are we?" she asked.

"Al Mukalla," the alpha said.

Rust's attention snapped to the alpha. "East or west side of the channel?"

"East. West side is Terra Victa now." The alpha rifled through the contents of his bag. "We need to travel south to get to the shore. Grace, put on your daggers."

Catori studied the map. "According to the key, Socotra is about five hundred kilometers from Al Mukalla."

Unlike Grace, I had been trained in both the metric and imperial measurement systems and could convert kilometers to miles. The practical application of the distance was another story since I had never been able to travel far from home. "How long do you think it will take me to fly the distance?"

"You have never stretched your wings in such a way, but

dragons can easily cover five hundred kilometers within a day. My concern lies with the portal fatigue they mentioned. You do not know how it will affect you."

"But I am a dragon," I reminded her. "Unlike shifters, it does not tire me to take my true form. And like you and your tree, I can pull energy from sunshine."

"Yes. I have faith you will be fine." Catori steepled her long, narrow fingers, and her gaze grew distant. "Your mother could fly across the Pacific Ocean without rest. She found it peaceful and refreshing and would often escape to the sky when she fought with her father."

Catori rarely spoke about my mother, so I leaned in and gave her my full attention.

Sadness flickered in her eyes, and her attention settled back on the orb. "Fly high and catch the wind currents. Soar as often as possible to preserve your strength."

Disappointed she had not shared more, I followed her gaze. In the orb, Grace slid her daggers into thigh sheaths. Chaz removed a bundle from his bag and passed it to her.

She unwrapped a shoulder harness, pistol, and a box of ammo, setting each on her lap. "You think guns are necessary?" she asked.

The alpha's expression hardened. It appeared he did not appreciate being questioned. "We won't be able to safely shift until the fatigue wears off. Rust tells me you've been keeping up on your target practice and prefer the Glock."

She nodded. "Yes, Alpha. Thank you." She slid the shoulder harness on over her T-shirt and holstered the gun before removing a light jacket from her bag.

Chaz shook his head before she could put the jacket on. "Keep it visible. People will be less likely to mess with you if they know you're packing."

Grace stuffed the jacket into her bag. Worry filled her eyes as Chaz handed two pistols, a box of ammo, and a spear to Mackiel. Rust received an AR15, enough ammo to start a war, and a long sword. The alpha equipped himself with the same. Questions danced in Grace's eyes, but she wisely kept her mouth closed.

Finished, the alpha zipped his bag and swung it over the shoulder opposite his rifle as his gaze swept the area. "Before the war, Al Mukalla was a beautiful city. The residents had reclaimed their port from Al Qaeda and survived the country's civil war. Since the port is on this side of the fracture, we won't have to deal with any Mondeine bastards, but the Tricari here can be a little... tricky to deal with. You saw the posters in the hall?"

Everyone but Grace nodded. "What posters?" she asked.

Mackiel nudged her leg with his. "I'll explain later."

"Keep your eyes and ears open," Chaz continued. "And if you don't like the scent of anyone or anything approaching, shoot or slice first. Ask questions later. Understood?"

"Is leatsa mo shaol, Alpha," the three said in unison.

"Good. I'm gonna try to get us a lift to the coast. Stick close to me."

Something plopped down at my feet, taking my attention from the orb. I looked down to find a worn leather satchel. There was no sign of Fred, but that did not surprise me. My peculiar little housekeeper liked to stay out of sight. Wondering what Catori had instructed him to pack, I picked up the satchel and placed it on my desk. The front pocket held a thick stack of bills. I pulled it out and thumbed through what had to be at least five thousand dollars.

Arching an eyebrow at my guardian, I asked, "You anticipate such expenses?"

"It is better to be overprepared than under. The cash came from your mother's old safe. If you require more, Fred hid a bank card in the inside pocket." She leaned over and pointed at the zipper. "You can use it to pull money from Mondeine banks. The pin number is zero-nine-two-zero."

"My birthday." Figured. Before my mother's murder, she had transferred all her accounts to me, with Catori listed as my legal guardian. Mom must have suspected her life was in danger, but she had gone to the meeting anyway. I only wished I knew why.

"I'll be back before you know it," my mother's voice said in my mind.

Ever since Grace had released the memories, they popped up at the most inconvenient times. I stuffed this one back with the others and put the cash away. Opening the main flap of the satchel, I found a few pairs of sweatpants surrounding a waterproof bag. The bag held a handgun and two boxes of ammunition. They were unnecessary and unwelcome travel companions, so I removed the waterproof bag and set it on my desk.

"What are you doing?" Catori asked.

"Leaving this here where it belongs."

She folded her arms across her chest, and I could almost see her heels digging in as she prepared for battle. "I realize Commander Rivera's unorthodox training methods were—"

"Barbaric?" I suggested. "Abusive? Torturous? Traumatizing?"

"Yes. But his methods do not negate the reason your father sent him to train you."

I snorted. "My father was a sadistic bastard."

Her eyes narrowed, and her lips drew into a disapproving frown.

"What? That could very well be the reason behind my father's selection of trainers."

"Perhaps," she admitted. "But since we never met your father, we cannot assume cruelty was his motivation."

"Fair. But let us examine what we do know. My sperm donor had a multi-generational curse hanging over his head. Knowing that, the coward impregnated my mother and then fell on his sword, leaving the responsibility of the curse to me. I think we can safely assume he was not a man of honor or integrity."

"Your mother—"

"Had sex with a stranger," I said, cutting in again. "I do not fault her for it." Catori always tried to sugarcoat their story, but I knew better. For a long time, I had wanted to believe my father was something better than a piece of shit, but the evidence suggested otherwise. Not even Commander Rivera—a man who had beaten me and buried me alive —was evil enough to be cursed. The actions of my father must have been truly vile. It was past time for us to admit as much. "My mother was not the first lonely female to fall for the lies of an asshole at a bar."

"You are making a lot of assumptions."

"I am only stating the obvious. The most reasonable explanation is usually the truth, Catori. You have taught me that."

"And as usual, you have taken my wisdom out of context and used it against me." She unfolded her arms, dropping them to her hips, where she smoothed away imaginary wrinkles in her skirt. "There is no point in arguing about two souls that have passed beyond this world. What matters now is ensuring you are properly prepared for what you are about to face. The wolves will have a head start in their recovery from this travel fatigue."

"Yes, but they are not dragons," I said. "And as you pointed out, Grace expended a good deal of energy last night."

"And Seattle is further away than you have ever flown before. You may be winded before you take the portal as well."

She had a point. "There will be snacks along the way." Maybe I would find myself a nice juicy deer or a fat grazing cow.

"Do not be stubborn, child. You saw the alpha distribute firearms, even equipping himself. Are you afraid you have forgotten how to shoot a gun?"

I bristled. "I remember everything that bastard taught me."

"Then what is the problem? As I said before, it is better to be overprepared. If you do not need the weapon, you do not have to use it, but I would feel much better knowing you have every available resource with you."

As much as I hated touching anything that reminded me of Commander Rivera, Catori's logic was sound. And surprising since

Dryads loathed guns almost as much as they loathed chain saws. Yet she was essentially begging me to take one.

"What are the chances of you dropping the matter?" I asked.

"You are not leaving without a firearm, Arioch. I will die on this hill if I must. Please do not make me."

"Fine. I will take the gun." I relented.

"And the appropriate ammunition."

Despite my annoyance, a smile tugged at my lips. The relentless woman never let anything slide. "And silver bullets." Picking up the waterproof bag, I tucked it back into my satchel.

"And Tyrin," Catori added.

We had already had this argument, and my stance had not changed. "He will only slow me down."

"His flight speed may not be as fast as yours, but his skill with weapons makes up for it. The portal will leave you exhausted, and you will require someone capable to watch your back. Tyrin is sworn to protect you."

If only that were true, it would have saved me years of pain and misery in my youth. "No, he is sworn to keep me breathing. There is a difference."

Catori frowned but did not argue. There were long stretches of my life when she had hibernated while Tyrin had remained to oversee the training my father had ordered. The gargoyle may not have been an active participant in my more... distressing lessons, but his unwillingness to shield me from them made him every bit as guilty as my trainers.

"Regardless, you cannot deny his skill," Catori said.

I glanced at the orb where Mackiel was helping Grace into the back of a beat-up truck. The rest of the shifters climbed in beside her. The alpha tapped on the back window, and the vehicle started moving. Grace hunkered down, and Mackiel draped an arm over her shoulders. Confusion wrinkled her forehead, but she did not fight it when he tugged her against him. Laying her head against his chest, she closed her eyes. The sight of them together like that made something menacing and possessive stir within me. I wanted to yank her out of his arms and... and.... I refused to consider what I wanted to do to her, so I focused on the matter at hand.

"On Tyrin's watch, she stole the chalice," I reminded Catori.

She inclined her head. "Grace bested both of you individually. Perhaps you will have better luck fighting her together."

The simple truth infuriated me. "I do not have time to wait for him to thaw."

"Which is why I thawed him out last night. Other than some healing frostbite, he is well."

I gritted my teeth. "That useless gargoyle will only get in my way."

"That *useless gargoyle* would take a bullet for you."

"Good. Perhaps I shall throw him in front of one."

Catori took a deep breath as her temper raged in her eyes. "Do not be petulant now, child. You were doing so well. We were compromising."

"Compromising?" I snorted. "You do not know the meaning of the word. If we were compromising, I would get to leave Tyrin here since I gave in and packed the gun." But she was right; I did sound petulant and childish. Everything was getting out of hand, and I needed to feel in control of something.

"You misunderstand. The compromise here is that you do what I tell you, and you get to live. If you do not take him along, Tyrin will follow you anyway."

Reading between the lines, I replied, "You will tell him to follow me, you mean."

"I will do what is necessary to ensure your safety. As I always have."

Apparently, there were multiple hills my guardian was prepared to die on today. I honestly did not believe I would be any safer with Tyrin than without, but I would relent if it made her feel better. "All right." I blew out a breath. "I will take the damn gargoyle."

The smile she blessed me with almost made it worth the hassle. Almost. "Good. He is prepared and waiting by the front door."

Of course, he was. I ran a hand through my hair. I should have just given in from the start and saved us both the headache. My guardian always got her way in the end. "You know, your methods could be seen as manipulative," I told her.

Reaching forward, she patted me on the shoulder and said, "It is not manipulation when it is for your own good."

Her disturbing logic did not even bother me anymore. It was a good thing she was on my side because Catori would make a terrifying enemy. "Thanks."

She held my gaze. "Reclaim the chalice and come home safely. That is all the thanks I require."

Touched by her concern, I nodded. "And bring back the beast, so I can question her, kill her, and end the curse."

My guardian frowned, her expression thoughtful. "Prophesies rarely turn out as expected. Be careful with your assumptions, child. Your little wolf is broken, but she may not be the beast you need to slay. I want you to make me a promise."

I eyed her, wondering what she was up to. "I am listening."

"Promise me you will not kill Grace until you bring her here."

"Why?"

"I wish to speak to the girl."

I considered her request and felt strangely relieved by the prospect. I did not want to kill Grace. She had shown me mercy when she could have ended my life, and it would be cruel to return her compassion with bloodshed. But she was dangerous. What she had done to me ... I could never allow her to do that again. And there was the curse to consider.

The truck stopped, and the group climbed out of the bed. Chaz paid the driver. The truck drove off, and the wolves walked through the sand until they reached a cliff.

"Wow," Grace said, her entire face lighting up at the sight. "It's beautiful."

She was beautiful. Spending any time at all with her would be a mistake, but I would not refuse to honor Catori's request. "Okay," I said. "I promise to bring Grace back alive."

Catori smiled at me. "Good. Thank you. Now, be on your way, child. You must catch up with the wolves."

13

Grace

Portal lag was no joke. I felt like death as I stretched out on my sleeping roll, but my internal clock seemed to know it was still the middle of the day back home and refused to let the Sandman drag me under. I tossed and turned most of the night, but I wasn't the only one. It was well before dawn when we gave up on sleep and broke camp.

"I called for a ride last night," the alpha informed us as he handed out rations of jerky.

Wondering how and when he called, I tugged my cell phone out. It was just as I suspected. I had no bars. I glanced at Mackiel, and he gave me a slight shrug.

"It should be at the port by now," the alpha continued. "No use sticking around here when we can get started."

"Is that the port over there?" Rust asked, gesturing to the east.

There was a small peninsula about a half-mile away from our vantage point. But that wasn't what he was talking about. No, he was pointing beyond the peninsula. Squinting, I could barely make out what might be ships at a dock. But I was still more interested in how the alpha had called for a ride.

Had it been when we'd first made camp? He'd walked down to the water, and moments later, there'd been a deep, resonant rumbling sound, almost like someone was blowing a horn. It wasn't loud but had echoed long into the night. Neither Rust nor Mackiel knew what it was, and when my father rejoined us, he was throwing off some pretty strong don't talk to me vibes, so I hadn't asked him about it.

"Yes." Dad shouldered his bag and adjusted the rifle sling

around his neck and opposite shoulder. "It's about a four-mile walk. Let's head out."

Following the road along the coast, we avoided the peninsula, which was abandoned and super creepy. About a half-mile beyond it, we came upon a peculiar translucent material flitting in the wind on the side of the road. The alpha held up a hand for the rest of us to stay back and proceeded alone to investigate. With weapons drawn, we monitored the area and watched his back. As my father approached, it struck me how enormous the gauzy material had to be. It dwarfed my old man.

I studied the material. Tinted orange and black, it was a cross between plastic and mesh. The sight tickled my memories, but it took me a moment to realize where I'd seen the substance before.

"That's not... shed snakeskin, is it?" I asked Rust and Mackiel.

It couldn't possibly be. The snake that had shed it would have to be enormous.

Fear skittered up my backbone, and every ounce of my consciousness went on high alert. Last night, Mackiel told me about the warning posters he'd seen in the portal station, filling my head with all sorts of disturbing images.

"I hope not," Mackiel replied.

Rust made the sign of the cross and muttered a Hail Mary.

Dad approached the film, and I held my breath, waiting. He examined it, frowned, and then waved us forward. As soon as we were within range, he said, "The good news is the snake that shed this has to be about eight feet wide and at least a hundred feet long."

"That's the good news?" I asked.

He gave a curt nod. "Yeah. We'll see it comin'."

I fought the urge to suggest we go home and give up on this crazy quest. Releasing my wolf wasn't worth getting eaten by Snakezilla. A breeze lifted the stench of sea brine and sunbaked fish off the skin and smacked me in the face with it. Bile rose in the back of my throat, and I held my breath, trying not to throw up.

"How fresh do you think it is?" Mackiel asked.

"Hard to tell," the alpha replied.

Drawing closer to the skin, Rust sniffed and then wrinkled his nose. "Never seen anythin' like it."

"You okay, Grace?" Mackiel asked. "You look a little pale."

"How can you guys handle the smell?" I asked.

"Breathe through your mouth," Rust said.

I tried, but that was worse. "Gah! I can taste it."

"We need to get goin'," Dad said. "We don't want to be here if this thing returns."

No, we sure the hell did not. I hooked my arm in Mackiel's and started walking, dragging him right along with me. Snakes had never frightened me before, but the reptiles back home were considerate enough not to reach bus size. Coexisting with reptiles I could step on was no sweat. Living in a world with snakes large enough to swallow a small town... I wasn't down with that.

"How are you okay right now?" I asked Mackiel as we walked. "You saw the size of that thing, didn't you?"

"Yeah. It was big."

"Big?" Never in the history of language had anyone used such an inadequate word to describe something. "*Big*?"

"I'm tryin' really hard not to think about it, Chip." Mackiel had a pistol in his right hand and a spear in his left, and I realized both weapons were trembling slightly in his grip.

Satisfied I wasn't the only one freaking out, I muttered, "There's no reason for anything that big to exist."

Mackiel grunted in agreement. "Stay close to me."

Duh. He was out of his mind if he thought I'd go wandering off now that I knew what was roaming around the desert. I doubted I'd ever sleep again. At least not until we got home. I planned to be attached to Mackiel's hip for the foreseeable future, keeping both the alpha and Rust in view.

We continued along the coastline, skirting the city of Al Mukalla.

In addition to colossal snakes, I watched for zombies, creepy half-skeleton people, and giant murder birds. The posters in the portal station had been candid about one inconceivable monster, which meant the others probably existed as well. Comforting thought, that. It made me want to simultaneously curl up in the fetal position and sprint away from this giant sandbox as fast as I could. My weapons felt grossly inadequate, and I was ill-prepared. What could a Glock do against monsters? Bullets would probably only piss off the snake. We should have brought C-4. A truckload of it might do the trick.

The further we marched from the fracture, the more dilapidated the buildings and landscape became. Sand had attacked and overwhelmed the district from the backside while the sea brutalized and demolished it from the front. Still, despite its disturbing monsters and an ongoing battle against nature, people called Al Mukalla-Ferra home. The occasional flicker of a ratty curtain or waft of pungent cooking spices made that much clear. Thankfully, the residents kept to themselves.

Stacks of shipping containers came into view.

"That's the port up ahead," Dad said, his tone back to business. "Keep your eyes open."

I leaned closer to Mackiel and whispered, "When I used to fantasize about adventure and travel, this was not what I envisioned."

He snorted. "Yeah, me neither."

We wove in and out of rusted shipping containers, and Dad stopped short. I almost planted my face in his back but managed to dodge to the side just in time. Wondering what had so thoroughly captured his attention, I followed his gaze. A galleon was docked at the port, and not just any galleon, either. This thing had to be centuries old. Fully rigged, the weathered monstrosity was coal-black with three enormous masts, their sails furled. A spiked iron ribcage encircled the hull, protecting the entrails of the ship and leaving only the gunports unobstructed. Someone must have dredged it up from the ocean floor, resurrected it through elbow grease, and powered it through nightmares.

My wolf stirred to life and insisted we wanted nothing to do with the ship.

"The Gibil Anzû," Dad said, his voice full of reverence.

"The what?" I asked.

"Gibil Anzû," he repeated. "Sumerian for Fiery Stormbird. That's our ride."

The alpha resumed his course before I could voice any of my dozen or so concerns, no doubt saving me from getting swatted across the dock for questioning him. I threw Mackiel and Rust a questioning look, but they both shrugged, and Rust gestured for me to follow my father.

The ship was docked facing inland, giving us a decent view of the bow as we approached. The figurehead was a birdlike beast with blazing eyes that followed our progress, causing my skin to prickle with wariness. Iron protruded from its forehead, twisting into a narrow, elongated lance that reminded me of the tusk of a narwhal. Its monstrous beaked maw gaped open, revealing a mouth of fire. The Fiery Stormbird. Fitting name. It was a wonder the entire vessel hadn't gone up in flames. The ship felt like a living, breathing entity, so I opened my other sight to check for a spirit. Only the crew and the fire inside the figurehead's mouth possessed glowing tapestries. Interesting.

Mackiel stuck so close to me that I worried I might trip over him. We marched up the gangway to board the ship with the alpha in the lead and Rust pulling up the rear, silently marking Mackiel and me as weak, protected members of our little pack. Or, at least, that was the message other shifters would have gotten from our lineup. But judging by the cerulean skin of the crew working the rigging and littering the deck, we weren't dealing with shifters. At least not any I'd heard of. Chests and webbed feet bare, the sailors wore faded short pants. Colorful bandanas whipped around their heads and cheeks like flags in the wind. All male, they each wore a cutlass at their waist and a short-necked primitive stringed instrument strapped around their torso. As we neared, I realized their head coverings actually ended at their temples, and what hung below were brightly colored fins that fanned out from their cheeks and jaws. The thin slits of fish gills marred the darker blue skin of their necks, and additional fins hung from their forearms and distended from their calves.

One of the sailors caught me staring and winked. I startled, and he grinned, revealing rows of serrated teeth. Suppressing a shudder, I pressed against Mackiel's side, leeching comfort from my friend's presence.

"You sure there wasn't a warning poster in the portal station for these guys?" I whispered.

"Probably should be," Mackiel replied.

The captain approached, distinguished by his tricorn hat embellished with barnacles, iron bars, and a small iron key. Like the ship, the hat seemed sentient and evil and smelled like rotten fish. Or maybe that godawful stench was coming from the captain. I couldn't tell.

He extended a hand to my father and introduced himself. "Captain Oannes." His whimsical baritone carried a heavy accent, sounding somewhat like the man who'd given us a ride last night. "Welcome aboard the Gibil Anzû."

The alpha shook the captain's hand. "Alpha McCarthy of the Evergreen Wolf Pack."

"You have our conch?" Captain Oannes asked.

The alpha opened his bag and pulled out an ornate iron seashell, smaller than the palm of his hand. Holding it out for inspection, he waited. I stared, wondering if that was what he'd used to call for our ride. I'd read somewhere that blowing on a conch could sound somewhat like a horn. Was that what I'd heard last night?

The attention of every sailor on the ship homed in on the shell.

Eyes full of reverence, the captain reached for it, but my father closed his fingers and brought the shell to his chest.

"*After* we reach our destination," the alpha said, placing heavy emphasis on the 'after.'

The captain scowled at him. "There is no need to behave in such a fashion. The sons of Oannes do not go back on our word, wolf. Regardless of when you hand it over, the deal has been struck. The conch in exchange for one sea passage to anywhere in the Red Sea, as promised."

The alpha held the captain's glare. "Including the Gulf of Aden."

The captain inclined his head. "It is as you say."

"And what about the return voyage?"

"As we told the witch, the conch is a one-way ticket. You will have to secure your own return passage."

"I have gold and iron to offer," the alpha said.

"Passage on the Gibil Anzû cannot be purchased," the captain scoffed, seemingly offended. "It is dangerous for us to tarry in this water. Sea voyage must be earned."

But the conch seemed like payment. What was the difference? And how had Sereana earned passage from the creepy fish people? Assuming my aunt was the witch he spoke of.

The alpha slid the iron conch back into his bag. "Then I'll go ahead and hold onto this until we safely reach our destination."

"Do not think to double-cross us, Alpha McCarthy. Gods have tried and failed. They now sleep at the bottom of the briny deep."

I hoped he didn't mean literal gods. Dumping deities into an ocean seemed like a horrible idea. Especially if we were about to cross part of that ocean.

Dad didn't so much as blink at the threat. "Noted."

Appeased, the captain waved over the creep who'd winked at me. "Lakhmu will take you to your quarters. We shall set sail within the hour. You are free to roam about the ship but do practice caution. If you or any of your crew falls overboard, we will not stop to fish you out."

Dad's nod was curt. "Understood. If one of my people is intentionally injured while on your ship, know that I will not hesitate to burn this motherfecker down."

Tension charged the air as the two males squared off, locked in a silent snarling contest of testosterone and machismo. Rust pressed in, assault rifle still in hand. Mackiel tightened his grip on his spear and pistol as I watched the sailors surrounding us, prepared to react if a single fishy bastard went for his cutlass.

Captain Oannes's gaze cut to our guide in a silent order.

Lakhmu stepped in and said, "Follow me."

Turning on his heel, he headed toward the front end of the boat. With one final glare at the captain, my father gestured for us to follow and trailed after the leering fishman. We slipped through a doorway that put us beneath the foredeck, where circular glass windows let in enough daylight to see the cramped space. Wooden barrels were stacked and wedged between the wall and the railing, forming a narrow walkway to a hatch in the floor. Without so much as a glance to ensure we were still behind him, Lakhmu disappeared down the hole. Shifting the weight of his bag, the alpha gestured for us to stay back. Rifle in hand, he followed Lakhmu, slowly taking each ladder's rung as if anticipating an attack.

When he hit bottom, the alpha shouted, "Clear."

I went next down the narrow, steep ladder into darkness, my footsteps echoing ominously. The alpha was waiting, gaze affixed to the shadows beside him when I reached the bottom. As my sight adjusted to the lower light, I made out the form of Lakhmu; his lips split into another toothy leer as he glided forward and reached for me.

I turned my Glock on him.

Or, I would have had Dad not lunged between us. There was a blur of movement as the alpha grabbed the fishman by the wrist and twisted it behind his back, shoving his face into a wooden pillar. With a flash of metal, the alpha's sword pressed against the side of the fishman's neck, in position to decapitate the male. "You will not lay a fecking hand on my daughter. You got that?"

I could see the side of Lakhmu's face, smushed against the pillar as it was. His grin widened like he enjoyed the altercation.

"I was only trying to move her so she did not block the way for the others."

"I don't care." The alpha tightened his grip. "You touch her, you die. That goes for the rest of your crew, too. Spread the word."

"As you say." The malicious gleam in Lakhmu's eyes promised he'd welcome violence. "Now release me so I can show you to your quarters. We cannot set sail until I am above deck with my brothers."

The alpha withdrew his sword, re-sheathing it. Pulling Lakhmu away from the pillar, he shoved him in the direction opposite of me. The fishman stumbled, then reestablished his footing, releasing an eerie chuckle as he strode down a passageway. My father threw me a worried glance over his shoulder before following the fishman.

Stunned, I stared after them. The alpha had called me his daughter. Sure, that familial title shouldn't be a big deal, but I'd never heard the words leave his mouth before.

My daughter.

It hit hard, sucker-punching me in the gut. To my father, I was Grace. There were no nicknames and no terms of endearment, not even when I was little. Just Grace. My mind kept trying to normalize my feelings, insisting that the alpha's words meant nothing, but my heart said otherwise. This felt like progress. It had taken a trip halfway around the world and a run-in with creepy fishmen, but Dad had finally called me his daughter. I knew I should be worried about the sinister ship and its menacing crew, but I was so damn happy I couldn't suppress the smile tugging at my lips.

The look Mackiel gave me questioned my sanity as he nudged me to follow Dad. We didn't go far before Lakhmu opened a door and gestured us inside with a ridiculous flourish. As we passed, Mackiel put himself between me and the fishman, earning us another guttural chuckle. We amused the asshole. Good to know.

The musty scent of the room hit me as I took in its triangular shape. We had to be against the bow, right in the front of the ship. Fragmented light drifted in from two portholes so covered in grime I couldn't see out of them. Dad's steps stirred up dust, the motes dancing in the faint rays of sunlight as they tickled my nose and made my eyes water. I fought back a sneeze, afraid I wouldn't be able to stop if I started. Beneath each porthole stood a large wooden trunk bolted to the floor. Four worn, grey linen hammocks hung from the ceiling. A thick layer of dust and grime covered every available surface.

"The sick bay?" the alpha asked, sounding outraged. "You expect us to sleep in the infirmary?"

Slipping into the room behind us, Lakhmu sneered. "It is none of my concern what you do in here, but unless you want to bed down with the crew," his gaze drifted to me, and wicked humor glinted in his eyes, "this is all we have to offer. Forgive me, Alpha of the Evergreen Pack. We do not often take on passengers. At least, not willing ones." With that eerie revelation, he turned to leave.

"Can we at least get a broom?" I asked, stopping him by the door. "Maybe some washrags and a bucket of clean water?"

One long finger tapped out a little tune on the wooden frame before he peered at me over his shoulder. "And what would I get in exchange?"

My father growled at the obvious insinuation.

"A clean sick bay," I replied.

He inclined his head. "As you say."

I had no clue if that meant yes or no, but I wasn't about to ask. Either he brought the supplies, or he didn't. Only time would tell. Dad and Rust stowed their bags in one of the wooden storage boxes, but they kept their rifles on their persons, attached to slings. I holstered my Glock and rushed to the nearest porthole, prying it open so we could get some fresh air. The salty sea breeze had never smelled so good. The view of never-ending ocean waves, on the other hand, was disconcerting. Crossing the room, I threw open the other porthole and was relieved to see the pier right where we'd left it. Shouts came from the deck, and the ship gave a little jerk before pushing away from the dock.

Wood creaked, and I glanced down to find Mackiel stowing his spear and bag in the wooden box beneath the porthole. "Hand me your bag," he said.

Lowering it from my shoulders, I passed it to him. "Thank you."

Watching me like I was some mystery he couldn't solve, he asked, "You okay?"

"Fine." I shrugged off his concern. "Why?"

"The hallway."

I frowned. "Nothing happened. The creep didn't even reach me before the alpha intercepted him." My gaze snagged on my father, who had retreated into the passageway where he and Rust spoke in hushed tones. In Irish, of course. They returned to their private conversation, keeping secrets from Mackiel and me. So much for progress.

Mackiel shifted uncomfortably. "Don't talk to that guy again."

Confused, I stared at him. "What guy?"

"The fish pervert. In fact, you should probably stay down here away from all those bastards. I don't like the way they stare at you."

I knew he was only looking out for me, but my wolf's hackles rose at his overbearing tone. I hadn't done anything wrong, and I'd be damned if he planned to keep me in this room for the entire trip. The smell alone would drive me crazy. "You know I can defend myself, right?" I asked.

"Normally, yeah, but we have no idea what these guys are capable of, Chip. Just be smart and stay away from them."

I stared at my best friend, completely floored.

I knew I was a weirdo. If life was a radio, all my packmates were tuned into a station I could never seem to find. Their way of thinking just wasn't available to me. Although Mackiel wasn't on my wavelength, he used to understand my frequency. But now... did he think I was stupid? I had more than two brain cells to rub together, which meant I had no intention of interacting with the fishmen, a fact he should damn well know.

"Be smart?" I asked. "Really, Mack? Who do you think you're talking to right now?"

His jaw tensed. "I saw the way you smiled at his attention."

Baffled, I gaped at him, shocked at how grossly he'd misread me. "Are you seriously accusing me of flirting with the fish creep?"

Doubt softened his expression, but rather than backing down, he shoved his foot even further into his mouth. "I get it. Females like it when males fight over them, but these guys are bad news. Don't tempt them."

"I'm gonna need you to stop talking," I said, anger spiking as I shook my head in disgust. This couldn't be happening. Not with Mackiel. He was the one ally I'd always been able to count on.

Frowning, he opened his mouth to continue, but I narrowed my eyes.

"Seriously. Stop." Lowering my voice so only he could hear, I said, "I smiled because the alpha called me his daughter. He's never done that before, and I...." The backs of my eyes stung. Blinking, I swallowed past the lump in my throat and tried to get my emotions under control.

Mackiel's brow furrowed, and again he opened his mouth to speak.

But I wasn't finished. "And I only asked for cleaning supplies because none of us will be able to sleep in this filth. He was about to leave, and you guys didn't ask. Did the thought even cross your mind?"

His frown deepened. "The alpha is in charge."

"So, nobody else can think or speak for themselves?"

His gaze flickered nervously toward the alpha, and he lowered his voice, "Stop saying shit like that. You're gonna get in trouble."

Yes, because how dare I make the alpha's authoritarian methods sound bad. I was so frustrated I could scream. "Mack, you and I used to be a team. We had each other's backs. When you didn't think of something, I did, and vice versa. Now, it feels like you don't remember who I am. What I'm capable of. I'm still the girl who got you out of that tunnel when you set off my aunt's magical booby trap. I'm the one who broke into the security room to locate the cameras so we could continue to sneak out of the den after the balloon incident." I turned my gaze back to the receding shoreline. "I've never been the girl who wanted the alpha—or anyone else—to fight for me. I just want my pack to accept me. You used to know that."

Silence stretched between us as I listened to sailors above shout in a language I couldn't understand. The ship was turning away from the port. We'd be on our way soon. We were so far from home, and I felt more alone and misunderstood than ever. Gently rocking waves soothed away my anger, leaving me with a bone-deep sadness and yearning for the friendship Mackiel and I had once shared. Was it gone now? Nothing more than childhood memories?

He sighed and settled a hand between my shoulder blades. "Hey. Come here." Sliding his hand over my back, he turned me around. When we were face-to-face, he tugged me to him and hugged me. His warmth and scent wrapped me in comforting nostalgia, and I held on for all I was worth.

"You're right. I'm sorry. Things are so damn complicated now, and this whole trip has me on edge. I want to do everything I can to protect you."

I pulled back to meet his gaze. "I don't need a protector. I need my friend."

Determination flickered in his eyes. His gaze dipped to my lips, and then the most unexpected thing happened. He kissed me. Warm lips met mine, and I... had no idea what to do. It happened so fast, and I didn't think I'd encouraged it. Had I sent him some sort of signal that we should kiss? I didn't mean to. Mackiel was amazing, but he wasn't...

An image of a man popped into my mind. His rich walnut skin and icy silver eyes called to me, and guilt stabbed me in the chest. I pulled away. Confusion contorted Mackiel's eyebrows as his gaze met mine. I wanted to hide under a rug and die.

Why?

The question formed on my tongue, but a shrill shout sounded from above before I could ask. Seconds later, it was joined by more sounds of alarm. Heart still pounding, I was grateful for the distraction as I returned my attention to the porthole. Scanning the horizon, I looked for anything that could save me from this awkward moment and keep me from turning around to face my friend.

I didn't have to look hard. Something enormous was in the water, and it was shooting toward our ship like a missile.

14

Arioch

Catori was rarely wrong about anything, and as much as I hated to admit it, the dryad had been spot-on in her concern about how portal fatigue would affect me. I had expected the magical fee of teleporting to Al Mukalla to do little more than wind me, but as I stepped off the portal platform, my body felt cumbersome and clunky, and someone was hammering nails into the back of my head. I was not even sure I could shift into my dragon form.

The gun had been a good idea.

I was still unsure about the gargoyle, but I let him trail after me as I made my way out of the portal station. A shock of warm, humid air made me gasp for breath. It felt like walking into a steamy shower. A sheen of perspiration instantly coated my skin as I looked around and tried to figure out my next move. The wolves had somehow gotten a ride, so I stepped toward the street and gestured for passing vehicles to stop. The drivers took one look at me and sped away.

"It's your scowl," Tyrin said.

My expression was the least of my worries because my head felt like it was about to shatter. My stomach churned from the pain, and bile rose in the back of my throat. I had not considered how the energy drain would affect the curse, an oversight I now paid mightily for.

"People won't pick you up if they think you're gonna eat them and steal their car," he said.

I had not yet considered taking a more violent approach, but I was not against the idea. "That might prove to be a more expedient option. If I dispose of the driver, can you take their place behind the wheel?" I asked.

Tyrin gaped at me. "Dispose of the driver? You mean kill them?"

"You suggested I eat them," I reminded him.

"Uh... that wasn't a suggestion. That was..." He shook his head. "Never mind. Why don't you hang back and let me flag us down a ride?"

Too tired and prickly to argue, I gestured for him to take my place. "Be my guest."

Backing into the shadows, I watched Tyrin wave down an approaching car. I thought for sure they would drive right past him, but at the last minute, they slowed and addressed him through the open window. Tyrin spoke to the driver in a language I vaguely recognized. Then he waved me forward and opened the back door.

I had never been in a car before, and the metal box was even smaller than expected. I hesitated and looked toward the empty front seat. It seemed slightly roomier than the back. I was about to insist I ride up there when Tyrin leaned toward me.

"Fares ride in the back," he whispered.

"Fares?" Was he insulting me?

"That's what paying passengers are called," he clarified.

There was no way I could have known that, but the lapse in my education still rankled as I slid onto the seat and adjusted my bag on my lap. My knees pressed against the back of the front seat, my head inches from the roof. I felt like a grasshopper caught in a matchbox. There was barely any room to move. How did anyone travel like this?

Think you got what it takes? Let's see how long you can survive down in that hole.

The memory of Commander Rivera's raspy words sent me spiraling back in time.

Panic seized me as he tightened the harpy net around me and shoved me back into the coffin. The lid slammed shut, followed by the pounding of his hammer as he nailed it shut.

The coffin moved. I flexed against my bonds, but the more I struggled, the more the magical net dug into my skin, siphoning my magic.

I could still smell pine and dirt.

It filled my senses, threatening to drive me mad.

I was vaguely aware that Tyrin now sat beside me and that we were in a vehicle, not a casket, but my heart raced all the same. Sweat rolled down my back. The damn car was sweltering. Why was it so hot in this goddamn desert?

Tyrin watched me with concern in his eyes, but I could not take in enough air to tell him to mind his own business.

"The driver needs directions," he said.

Of course. I tried to focus on the artifact, but the sound of my own heartbeat was too loud, the blood rushing through my veins too distracting. My tongue had dried up like a sponge, and my hands would not stop shaking. The car shrunk around me, and I pawed at the door, desperate to get out.

"Here," Tyrin said.

His arm crossed in front of me, and the door creaked open.

Blessed air poured in, and I stumbled toward it, greedily sucking in a lungful. One ankle caught on the interior, and I had to catch myself to avoid taking a tumble.

Tyrin joined me on the street, waving the car off. I expected him to poke fun at my incapacity, but he hefted his bag over his shoulder and simply said, "We'll walk."

Grateful for his discretion, I started walking. We headed out of the populated area, away from the fracture. By the time we reached the coastline, my heart rate and breathing were back to normal, and my well of magic no longer felt bone dry. I was recovering.

About a mile down the coast, the ringing and pressure in my head vanished, and the remaining tension drained from my body. I stopped. I had almost forgotten what it felt like when the chalice was silent. Bliss... absolute bliss. I closed my eyes and basked in it for a moment.

"I take it they're close," Tyrin said.

Grace's sweet, soft scent filled my nostrils, and I leaned into it. The little thief's scent was disturbingly calming, but I refused to let myself wonder why.

"Just down by the water," I replied.

I wondered what would happen if we rushed them. They could not shift, but their weapons were formidable, and Chaz and Rust carried themselves like seasoned soldiers.

"Can you shift yet?" I asked Tyrin.

"I can try, but it would probably knock me out. I might be able to harden my skin for a time, but I'm not sure how long I can keep it up. What about you?"

With the chalice silent, I was able to focus. I reached for my magic and felt it respond. I was recovering quickly but was still nowhere near full strength. "Yes." But I did not know what shape I would be in afterward, a fact I was unwilling to admit aloud. Shifting usually did not tire me, but I had not felt this magically drained since my training days. We continued on.

We were still within a kilometer of the chalice when we reached a crossroad. We needed to find shelter for the night, and the road to the right led to a peninsula that looked promising since it would keep us close to the water and within the chalice's range. We took the turnoff, but as we approached the first building, I saw it was missing a majority of its northern wall. Beyond it, other buildings stood in various stages of neglect, seemingly abandoned.

The peninsula was alarmingly silent. Other than Tyrin's footfalls and the sounds of the crashing surf, I could not hear a damn thing. No scurrying rodents, muted conversations, or children crying in the night. I took a deep breath through my nose and scented rot and sea.

Tyrin halted, tilting his head to the side. "Something about this place feels wrong, m'lord. Perhaps we should make camp inland, instead."

I understood his concern, and the warning posters I had seen back in the portal station did give me pause, but I was exhausted, and we were still hours from sunrise. Being within range of the arti-fact had provided a measure of relief, and I was unwilling to give that up. We were far enough downwind from the shifters that there was no risk of discovery, and without the constant buzzing in my head, I would be able to rest. I focused on my magic and realized I could now safely shift. If I could restore enough energy to grab Grace and the chalice before they left for Socotra, the wolves would still be suffering from portal fatigue, and I would have an advantage.

"Surely, this cannot be the first abandoned hovel you have stayed in," I said, strolling past him toward the coast.

Tyrin followed. "No. In fact, I've stayed in enough of these places to know there's usually a reason they're abandoned."

"Keep an eye out for monsters, then," I replied drolly. "I shall find a place to bed down."

We walked along the road that encircled the peninsula, and the eerie absence of life struck me again. Had I not been so goddamn exhausted, I would have considered following my húskarl's advice, but as it was, I could barely keep moving. A sandstone wall sepa-rated the road from the buildings, so we walked until we came to a flight of stairs that allowed us access to the area. I stopped in the mouth of an alley between two mostly standing buildings and decided it would suffice.

"We shall rest here until sunrise," I announced.

Tyrin scanned the area. "I really don't like the looks of this place."

"Try spending a week trapped underground in a coffin, draining your own magic to keep yourself from dying of thirst," I shot back. "I think you shall find this most pleasant by comparison."

The bastard had nothing to say to that, so he shuffled to a pale brick wall, kicking trash out of the way to clear himself a spot. Then he sat on the hard ground with his back against the wall and his bag on his lap. I studied the gargoyle, waiting for him to shift. Instead, he leaned his head back and closed his eyes.

"Are you not going to shift?" I asked, setting my bag on a broken wooden box.

"No," he said.

"You plan to be useless tomorrow then?" I asked.

Gargoyles had three forms: human, flight, and stone. They looked like winged demons with horns, fangs, and clawed hands and feet in flight form. Their stone form was a nearly indestructible shell that allowed them to enter a hibernation-like sleep they could not awaken from until they were fully recharged.

Eyes still closed, he said, "I'm not leaving you alone here."

I laughed. Hard. That was the most absurd claim I had ever heard. "*Now* you wish to protect me? Do you not think it is a bit late to pretend like you care about my wellbeing, *húskarl*?" I spat, sobering as anger iced over my veins. "*Trusted bodyguard*? You do not even know the meaning of the term. When I needed you most, you did nothing to guard me."

"I had no choice," he said, his tone resigned. "I made a vow."

He was a broken record, stuck on a tune I was sick to death of hearing.

"You always have a fucking choice! You *chose* to stand back and watch me suffer. But never fear. Your inaction taught me that I can endure on my own. I do not need your assistance tonight or ever, so please turn yourself to stone and sleep. After all, standing by and watching as I fight for my life is what you do best."

He glared at me in a silent refusal to shift, but I would not waste one more breath arguing with the bastard. Instead, I dropped my bag by his feet and tugged on my magic, wrapping it around me. Fueled by my anger, it flowed unhindered, transforming me into my dragon form.

Wings unfurling, I breathed easier and took in our surroundings. In dragon form, I was tall enough to see into the second-story windows of the buildings on either side of us, but ahead, a building blocked off the alleyway. Turning, I backed myself into the narrow space in front of Tyrin and sat, completely blocking his view of anything but the alley and my backside.

Despite my anger, sleep tugged at my eyelids. I was so damn exhausted, not even my desire to ice the bastard could keep me awake. I made myself comfortable, resting my head under a wing before letting myself drift off.

I had no idea how much time had passed before the sound of footsteps startled me awake. Whipping my head from beneath my wing, I shook off the dregs of sleep and scanned the area, remembering where I was and why. Movement drew my attention. A man ambled down the road, his motions jerky and awkward. He halted at the top of the stairs, his shaggy dark hair flinging forward to cover his face. Raising his head, he sniffed the air like a dog before spinning to face me head-on.

He only had half of a face.

Moonlight glinted off bone where the other half should be. One eye watched me unblinking while the other was nothing but a dark socket.

"By Thor's hammer, what is that thing?" Tyrin swore.

He was trying to peer around me, so I scooted to the side to make room.

"Nesna," I told him telepathically. "Remember the posters in the portal station?"

"Well, it's an abomination." Tyrin drew his gun. "One I intend to put an end to."

I swung my wing around to block his shot.

"Dammit, bairn," he grumbled. "Get out of my way."

"If you start shooting, the wolves will know we are here."

Another step and the nesna was descending stairs leading from the road.

Tyrin's eyes widened comically as he pointed toward the thing. "Would you rather lose your life? To that?"

So goddamn dramatic. "Surely you can kill one slow-moving

skeleton man. *Just slice its head off with your sword."* Really, how difficult could it be?

"Fine."

Tyrin slammed his gun into his holster and drew his sword. I
dropped my wing, and he advanced, sliding past me to approach
the nesna as it reached the bottom of the stairs. The breeze blew,
and the stench of carrion almost knocked me on my ass. Tyrin
flinched, ducking his head. Even his weak gargoyle nose had taken
that hit. He threw me a scowl over his shoulder before creeping
forward with his sword at the ready.

The nesna's robe was in rags with dark blotches staining the
fabric. As it came closer, I could discern more details of its face and
body. It literally had a line down the center separating flesh from
bone.

How the fuck?

It lurched, both hands—skin and skeletal—jutting out to reach
for the gargoyle. In one fluid motion, Tyrin swung his sword. Steel
sliced through flesh, and the nesna's head slid to the side and then
rolled off its body. Rather than toppling like the decapitated body
should have, it stood perfectly still. The head smacked against
debris with a wet thud and stopped. One eye blinked at Tyrin.

"That... What in Helheim is that thing?" he asked.

The nesna's body lurched forward, and both hands latched on
to Tyrin's shirt. Jerking backward, he swung his sword twice more,
lopping off one arm and then the next. They joined the head on the
ground. Released, the gargoyle backed up a step. There was no
spray of blood, but the stench of rotten meat made me gag. Tyrin's
gargoyle defenses were kicking in, adding to the stink.

The skeletal arm landed with the hand facing up. Fingers
squeezed and released as it rocked back and forth, trying to turn
itself over. The fingers of the flesh hand crept toward Tyrin, dragging its attached forearm behind. The body took a step.

"Son of Odin," Tyrin cursed.

His sword was not working, which meant I would have to handle the situation.

"*Move,*" I said to the gargoyle's mind.

He backed up, and I sprung forward, landing on the body with a splat. It wriggled under me, and I dug my talons in. The arms that had been creeping toward Tyrin now inched toward me. I filled my lungs with ice, opened my mouth, and froze the arms and head. My magic was still recovering, so only a thin layer of ice coated them.

The legs kicked and the body bucked. Despite my impressive dragon weight, I had to hold on so as not to go flying across the walkway. I ripped the torso in half, and the stench of decaying innards made me gag. I held my breath and batted both halves away with my tail. They flew through the air and smacked against the stone wall separating the street from the buildings.

And then the legs stood and ambled toward me.

"*It refuses to die!*" I said, frustrated.

"I noticed." Tyrin pointed toward the frozen arms and head. Most of the ice had melted, and the fingers were working to break free of what remained.

I stared in disbelief, wondering what to do. We had tried slicing, squashing, and freezing the nesna. The only option left in my arsenal was to eat it, and there was no way in hell that thing was going into my mouth. Exhaustion weighed on me. I just wanted a few goddamn hours of rest. Was that too much to ask?

"*I do not know what to do.*"

"Can you take it somewhere else?" Tyrin asked. "Somewhere it can't get to us?"

Yes. That I could do. Gathering up squirming arms, body, and head, I flapped my wings and rose into the air. I flew about a half-mile over the ocean and dropped the nesna into the sea. Or, at least, most of it. One adamant hand clung to my claw and refused to let go. I had to balance mid-air and use my other claw to rake it free. It hit the water with a splash, and I spat after it before heading back.

By the time I reached Tyrin, he had another nesna hacked into pieces.

"What the hell?" I asked as I landed. *"Where did this one come from?"*

"I don't know. They're like undead cockroaches."

As I collected the writhing body parts that were trying to scratch and bite off my legs, I said, *"This would be easier if you would keep them in one piece."*

"They're trying to kill me, m'lord. I'm doing the best I can. Fuck. There's another one."

He pointed down the road, and I groaned. Rising with nesna parts in my clutches, I attempted to scoop up the approaching undead abomination on my way back out to sea. But when I opened my talons, a leg fell, and a set of fingernails dug under one of my scales. It felt like being stabbed by a bone shard. I shook the damn thing, barely resisting the urge to roar. If I could have strummed up the energy, I would have turned the entire peninsula into ice. Instead, I gathered up all the pieces that were once again attacking me and flew them out to sea.

We rid the peninsula of five more nesnas before I finally got some rest. My last thought before losing consciousness was that, in hindsight, we probably should have avoided the peninsula. Not even being near the chalice was worth fighting those wretched monsters.

Morning came early. Feeling the chalice as it passed by the peninsula and continued east, I woke Tyrin, and we followed the water until we faced the pier. It was still quite a ways out, but I could see a ship docked and waiting. Tyrin pulled out an antique nautical spyglass and pressed it against his eye.

"There," he pointed.

Following his finger, movement drew my eye to the wolves. They boarded a foreboding ship crewed by blue-skinned men. The ship pushed out to sea, and with it, my opportunity to grab Grace on this side of the Gulf of Aden. We would be heading to the island after all.

Still in my dragon form, I spread my wings so the sun could beat down on my glossy black scales and rejuvenate me. Minutes ticked by as exhaustion eased from my bones and muscles, and magic hummed in my veins.

Tyrin collapsed his spyglass and stuffed it into his bag, his expression hardening like he was bracing for a fight. "You're going to have to carry me."

The bastard thought he could command me? *"Should have turned to stone like I suggested."*

"And leave you to fight the nesnas alone?" he asked.

"Like you were much help. All you did was slice them into more pieces for me to pick up."

He snorted. "Taking them somewhere else was my idea. If I hadn't suggested that, you'd probably still be trying to flatten them."

Our argument was cut short when a shout of alarm came from the ship.

Grace

I barely had time to shout for everyone to brace before the enormous creature barreling through the water rammed us. The Fiery Stormbird pitched to the port side, flinging me away from the starboard porthole. I caught myself on one of the hammocks and held on tight as water splashed in. The starboard porthole that was supposed to be at a ninety-degree angle was now at forty-five-degrees. I whipped my head around to the port side at the sound of rushing water. That porthole was almost entirely submerged. We hadn't tipped over, but all it would take was a strong breeze to get us there.

"You okay?" Mackiel asked from the hammock beside mine.

I nodded, lying with every inch of the gesture. My best friend had kissed me, we were being attacked by something my mind refused to admit existed, and I was fantasizing about an asshole who'd tried to kill me. I wasn't even sure okay existed anymore.

"Alpha? Rust?" I shouted. The hallway they'd been in stood empty.

The ship groaned and then rolled again. It slammed back down, righting itself with a bone-shaking splash. Had I not been hanging onto the hammock for dear life, I would have gone sliding across the room. I tasted blood and felt a hole in my tongue.

A meaty hand smacked against the doorway, and the alpha wobbled into view. "We're fine. Just a little banged up." Keeping one hand on the doorjamb, he lurched into the room, making way for Rust to follow. "What the feck is going on? Can you see anything?"

The starboard porthole darkened. Orange and black scales

223

slithered past it, blotting out the light. Snakeskin grated against iron and wood, continuing around the ship until the port side window was also covered. Water stopped pouring in, and we were left in an unnatural darkness, all outside sounds muted.

I looked to Mackiel. My vision adjusted to the darkness, enabling me to make out my friend's outline and the whites of his eyes as he clung to his hammock.

"It's the snake, Alpha," he said.

"The one f-from the shore," I added lamely, then shook myself. "I mean the one that lost its skin. Obviously."

As the ship groaned and rocked again, the alpha and Rust fought to keep their footing. Staggering to the starboard porthole, Dad raised his rifle, took aim out the window, and squeezed the trigger, unloading a three-shot burst into the creature. An ear-piercing hiss bounced off the walls, followed by more rocking of the galleon. More shots. One ricocheted off the iron bars and whizzed back into the cabin. My stomach lurched as I looked around our small team, but nobody was hit. He released his rifle to hang from its sling again and staggered backward, hands shooting out to steady himself.

Rust—who'd been on his way to the opposite window—dove for a hammock. Reaching for my father, I clutched his hand and pulled him to me. He let me draw him close enough to launch himself to the foot of my hammock. There, he held on.

I'd saved him. Probably from nothing more than a bruise or two, and we still had the massive snake to worry about, but I accepted that minor win like a freaking medal.

A high-pitched screech sounded from the front of the galleon. Wondering what fresh hell this was, I recalled the glowing tapestry of a spirit located within the fiery mouth of the ship's figurehead. Opening my other sight, I focused on the bow. The tapestry that had been so calm and placid when we'd boarded now raged, blazing with fire. My spirit instinctively jerked away from it.

Another ear-splitting screech accompanied a hissing bellow as the ship lurched. The scales blocking the porthole shuddered and writhed, letting in glimpses of light. On deck, the fishmen shouted what sounded like a rallying cry in their strange language.

A third screech made my ears ring. The ship rocked so hard I thought for sure we'd capsize. Scales continued to slide over the portholes. Fire lit up the port side window. There was a loud splash, and when the flames flickered out, the monster was gone. Slowly, the ship's rocking began to ebb while water splashed into our cabin. I scanned my team, assessing the damage. Rust had a cut over his left eyebrow that was already stitching itself shut, and Mackiel's face had turned green.

"Don't throw up in here," I told my friend. I would follow suit if he blew chunks, and the cabin already smelled rotten enough.

He swallowed and nodded. "I'm good."

He didn't look good, but I didn't blame him one bit. The jerky I'd had for breakfast was creeping up my throat, too, but we'd survived. Something had fought off the gargantuan snake, and now we just needed to cross an ocean possibly full of angry gods.

Piece of cake.

Something was happening above us. Feet pounded against the deck in a rhythmic thumping.

"What are they doing?" I asked.

The alpha's expression soured. "Preparing to get us on our way, I imagine." He kept a hold on his side of the hammock, so I followed suit. Rust and Mackiel also continued to hold on.

Moments later, instruments joined the stomping. I listened, surprised by how much lutes sounded like guitars, only brighter and with more twang. The tempo increased, and the fishmen added their voices. The song, soft and reverent at first, quickly grew in volume and speed until it was so fast it felt like the ship was trying to keep up. Rattled, I glanced out the porthole and saw it wasn't some strange musical illusion.

We were racing across the water!

Our speed continued to increase, and I clutched my

hammock for dear life once again. This time, inertia forced me toward the back of the ship, plastering my innards against my backbone. The netting dug into my hands, gouging deep grooves into my fingers, but if I let go, I would fly into my old man and send us both crashing against the back wall, so I held on. The crew above continued to dance and sing, and I feared they'd never stop.

Exactly how far away was that freaking island?

My arms trembled from the strain, and blood dripped down my arms. Darkness clouded the edges of my vision, and my heart threatened to pound out of my chest. Swallowing back bile, I wondered how long I could hold out.

Then, the chanting and pounding feet above us died down. The unnatural speed slowed, and the g-force released me to slump forward, exhausted. Finally able to stand freely, I peeled my bloody fingers from the hammock and stumbled toward the porthole. My three companions bolted out the door, their footsteps echoing in the hallway and up the stairs. Gripping the iron bars outside the ship, I yanked myself forward to lean out over the water and emptied my stomach into the deep.

The rest of the team returned, looking slightly less green. To my surprise, Lakhmu followed shortly thereafter with cleaning supplies. He entered the room and made a beeline for me, but the alpha intercepted the fishman, taking the bucket and rag. Dad folded his arms across his chest and widened his stance, turning himself into a human wall. Casting me a leer that made my skin crawl, the fishman chuckled and left.

Dad set the supplies at my feet. "This should keep you busy for a while. I don't want you leaving the cabin, Grace, you hear me?"

What was I, Cinderella? I opened my mouth to argue, but the alpha held up a hand, silencing me.

"There is only one response I want to hear from you right now," he said in a tone I knew all too well.

Accepting my fate, I lowered my gaze and parroted him. "Is leatsa mo shaol, Alpha."

"Your life *is* mine. Remember that, pup. Someone'll be in here with you at all times." Dad's gaze took in our companions, making the order clear. "Rust, you have the first shift. Mack, you're with me."

Great. Not only was I stuck below deck, but I would also be saddled with a babysitter. My father's sudden protective streak was growing increasingly suffocating. Wolves were meant to be free. Even children restricted to the den were allowed to roam and explore. We had a jail cell made with silver bars, but the alpha only ever used it when someone had really messed up. Usually, when they'd done something to put the pack at risk. I'd done nothing wrong, yet I was being locked up as if I had.

Every time I started to think Dad and I were making progress, he found a way to shut me out again.

As Mackiel followed my father, he threw me a look over his shoulder that promised one hell of a conversation later. I worried my bottom lip, wondering what to make of our unexpected kiss. The entire time we were growing up, he'd never shown the slightest hint of romantic interest in me, so why now? Had something changed between us that I didn't know about? I needed to corner my friend and find out what was going on with him.

And then there was the chalice's guardian to consider. I was no expert on romantic relationships, but I knew I shouldn't be thinking about one guy while kissing another. Why couldn't I get the tall, dark, and terrifying man—and most likely dragon—out of my head?

My mind wouldn't stop spinning, and I felt helpless and caged. The water that had spilled in when the giant snake was rocking the ship had only soaked the dust and grime, turning the floor into a slippery mess. Desperate for something to do, I grabbed the bucket of somewhat clean water and wrung out the rag. Then I started washing down the hammocks.

Rust ambled over and held out his hand.

"What?" I asked.

"Give me the rag."

When I handed it over, he ripped it into two and gave me back half. Before I could ask what he was up to, he dunked his half of the rag into the bucket, wrung it out, and started on the next hammock.

"Thank you," I said.

"We're all stayin' here. You shouldn't have to clean it alone."

"You're a good guy, Rust." Then, because I couldn't resist the urge to mess with him, I added, "I don't care what Janey says."

He chuckled at that. "Always tryin' to make trouble."

"Gotta keep you on your toes."

It felt like the walls were closing around me by the time we finished. I needed to break out of this stuffy room and breathe some fresh air. So, I played the only card I could think of playing.

"I-have-to-go-to-the-bathroom!" The announcement came out as one word squished together with way more enthusiasm than it deserved.

Rust blinked at me.

"What? I have to use the facilities."

He snorted. "You think this ship has facilities?"

Every building in the den had facilities. As had every above-ground building Mackiel and I had raided. A bathroom seemed like a necessity for all... even creepy fishmen. "Why wouldn't it?"

Rust picked up the cleaning bucket and offered it to me. "Here's your facilities, Chip."

I eyed the bucket but didn't take it. "That's disgusting."

He nodded. "It's also true."

I'd started this conversation to get out of the cabin, but now I was super concerned. "Surely, the bucket can't be the only option."

He scratched at the whiskers on his chin. "Nope." He pointed a finger above us and said, "Up there, you'll find two holes carved out of the planks that lead to the figurehead. Sailors just piss off the deck, but when they need to take a shit, they climb up on that plank, drop trou, and pop a squat in front of God and everyone."

I stared at him, waiting for the punchline. "Please tell me you're joking."

"Not at all. And now you know why people say they're goin' to *the head* to take a piss."

"I could have gone my whole life without knowing that."

Leaning forward, he chucked me on the chin. "Knowledge is power, kid." He wiggled the bucket. "Still need to use the facilities?"

"Nope."

Between the portal fatigue, our restless night, the excitement of today's attacks, and my little cleaning spree, I was too spent to even consider something as stressful as using a bucket for a toilet. I climbed into my hammock and closed my eyes, determined to ignore the promptings of my bladder. I never should have set my mind on that path because now it was all I could think about.

Before I could drift off, the scent of cooked fish and potatoes wafted into the room, making me sit up and look around.

Footsteps echoed down the passageway, and then Mackiel opened the door and strode into the cabin carrying two plates of steaming food.

"I got her," he said to Rust. "There's food in the galley."

Rust nodded and slipped out, closing the door behind him.

Reminding myself that my mentor and best friend were only following the alpha's orders, I resisted the urge to pop off about not being a child they had to babysit and climbed out of the hammock. I hadn't eaten since the jerky Dad had divvied up this morning, and I was starving.

Mackiel sat on the portside wooden box beneath the porthole. Settling one plate in his lap, he held the other out toward me. Gliding forward, I accepted the proffered plate and froze, eyeing the thing. It wasn't a plate but a large sea scallop shell. It was worn with a chip on one side and a small crack on the other.

"Interesting dish," I said, sitting beside him.

"Yeah, and they don't believe in flatware, so you have to eat with your hands."

"How... quaint." I broke off a bite of flaky white meat and popped it into my mouth. It was delicious. Suddenly ravenous, I attacked the meal with gusto.

"Careful, there's bones," Mackiel warned.

A smile tugged at his lips as he watched me, but I didn't care. I needed all the food in my belly right then.

"How ya holdin' up?" he asked.

Swallowing, I asked, "Are we there yet?"

"Soon. Captain Oannes said we'll reach the island tomorrow morning. Eat, then you can sleep, and we'll be there when you wake up."

That sounded like a plan to me, but he was missing an important step. "After we talk."

He nodded. "Yeah. We should probably do that."

Yet he sounded like he didn't want to, which was odd. Regardless, I finished off my meal, set my plate aside, and got right down to business.

"Why did you kiss me?" I asked.

Mackiel was still eating, and he choked on his bite. Coughing, he cleared his airway and set his own plate beside mine.

"You should finish that," I said, eyeing his remaining food. If he didn't eat it, I would.

"I will, but I want to answer you first."

I watched him, waiting.

He took a deep breath, turned to face me, and asked, "Why not?"

That was not what I'd been expecting, but my answer came immediately. "Because we're friends, not mates."

"My parents started out as friends, too, and they've been mated a long-ass time." He dropped his elbows to his thighs and leaned forward. "Mom says friendship is the key to mating. That it's a far sight better than searching for a true mate and losing your mind."

"And what do your parents think about me becoming your mate?" I asked.

Mackiel looked away. "They respect the alpha and will honor his will."

In other words, they weren't happy about it, but my father wanted Mackiel and me together. I wondered why he hadn't mentioned it to me.

"And what about you?" I asked. "What do you want?"

He rubbed at a spot on his leg, just above his knee. "You and I make sense, Chip. You're gorgeous and funny, and I like being around you. I hope you feel the same way about me."

His gaze met mine then, and the pleading look in his eyes made me realize it wasn't just my father; Mackiel wanted us mated, too. I had no idea how to process that. Having never considered there being anything more than friendship between the two of us, I felt blindsided. Sure, my friend was one of the most attractive guys I'd ever met, and I could hang out with him every day for the rest of my life and be perfectly happy, but he didn't make my stomach flutter or my heart race like... like the guardian had.

The guardian who'd tried to kill me and promised to track me down and finish the job.

The murderous nutjob I'd hopefully never see again.

The tall, dark, and terrifying stranger I couldn't stop thinking about.

Man, I was a mess.

"Say something, Chip," Mackiel said.

How long had I been staring at him, trying to make sense of it all? Shaking myself, I said, "Right. Sorry. I... Wow. This is a lot to take in."

His expression fell.

"I'm not saying no," I hurried to add. "I just need a little time." I wasn't even sure I could say no if the alpha supported our mating.

He forced a smile, but it didn't reach his eyes. "I understand."

I threw my arms around him and gave him a hug. "Thanks, Mack."

And then, because I suddenly felt awkward as hell and had no idea what else to do, I stood and climbed back into my hammock.

Grace

Despite my racing mind, I must have passed out because I awoke surrounded by a chorus of snoring. The cabin was dark, and all three of my packmates were out cold, catching up on sleep and getting rid of the last of their portal lag. Surprised the alpha didn't have anyone awake keeping watch, I sat up and glanced at the door. Someone had used Mackiel's spear to wedge the door shut.

Smart.

I relaxed back in my hammock as remnants of my dream tugged at my subconscious. Silvery eyes, walnut skin, and an undeniable sense of rightness invaded my senses. It had been three days since my encounter with the guardian, and the asshole was still mucking up my dreams.

Annoyed, I stared at the ceiling and tried to think about something else—*anything* else—but the man was relentless. Every time I closed my eyes, he was there, infuriatingly handsome, his spirit all dark and twisted. I wondered what he was up to and immediately wanted to slap myself across the face.

What was wrong with me?

Despite my cleaning efforts and the fact both portholes were wide open, the room still stank. Someone farted in their sleep, and I groaned. Sharing a cramped sick bay with three grown male shifters was the definition of funky.

Feeling well-rested and desperate for clean air, I climbed out of my hammock and crept to the porthole. The waning moon was high in the sky above us. I'd slept all afternoon and halfway through the night. No wonder I was so wide awake. Stepping onto the wooden storage box, I leaned out of the window and took a deep breath of sea air. The night was silent, aside from the snoring behind me and the low conversation of two fishmen on deck above. For the moment, at least.

Then, there was music. It wasn't like before with the pounding feet, plucking lute, and baritone voices. This was light, high-pitched, tinkly, and barely audible over the waves crashing against the ship. Someone was singing. I couldn't understand the lyrics, but the voice was beautiful and sweet. Feminine and sad. As I listened, entranced, the music wrapped me in sorrow. Longing for the green fields of a home I'd never seen and the loving arms of a family I'd never known made my heart ache for the singer. She'd lost so much. Everything. All she had left was this life—this duty—she did not want. A sense of hopelessness tugged at me, making me wish I could throw myself into the ocean and end my torture.

Only I wasn't the one enduring this pain; she was.

Diving deeper with my spiritual sight, I focused on the front of the ship. The tiny tapestry that had raged with fire yesterday was now calm and forlorn, rife with the type of overwhelming sorrow and pain I usually only saw in Mackiel. But unlike my friend, this little being wasn't hiding her emotions away. Her darkness was there for the world to see, like a festering mass that threatened to overwhelm her tapestry.

Kind of like the chalice's guardian.

I'd used his unrelenting torment against him to save myself, but now I couldn't help but wonder what would have happened had I handled the situation differently. Maybe if I'd thought to soothe him from the beginning, he wouldn't have tried to kill me.

I pushed the pointless thought aside. It was too late to help him, but I could still do something for this suffering soul. I'd never tried to soothe someone through a wall before, but instinct and necessity sent my spirit into action. Her spirit shuddered beneath my ethereal fingertips, and her song halted.

"*Who touches me?*" Her tinkling, high-pitched voice sounded in my mind rather than in my ears.

It was too much like the pack bond for comfort, and memories of that experience sent my spirit hurling back into my own body. Before I had time to slam a mental block between us, she spoke again.

"*Wait. Please do not go.*"

She sounded so lonely and desperate that I hesitated.

"*Are you a prisoner, too?*" she asked.

How do I communicate with her? I thought to myself.

Laughter tinkled in my mind. "*You just did, silly.*"

"*You can hear me?*" I asked. It was a stupid question since the answer was obvious, but my pack hadn't been able to hear me, so communicating with a complete stranger seemed surreal.

"*I can.*"

It was also terrifying.

What if I accidentally shared thoughts I didn't want to share?

More tinkling laughter answered my unvoiced question. "*You must learn to guard your thoughts, sharing only those you wish to share.*"

"*How?*" I asked.

"*As with all things, intention is key.*"

I had no idea what that meant, so I circled back to the previous subject. "*You're a prisoner?*"

"*I am,*" she confirmed, sadness creeping back into her voice. "*The Sons of Oannes stole me from my field when I was but a child.*"

"*You mean Captain Oannes?*"

"*All of the sailors were born of Ea's emissary.*"

"*I'm sorry, but I don't know who Ea is.*"

"*No. You would not,*" she replied. "*You are not of the old land. Your language is foreign. Ea is the Mesopotamian god of water and wisdom. His emissary, Oannes, would often come ashore and teach the Babylonians science, arts, and writing. Unfortunately, he was an amorous being who spread his seed amongst many Babylonian women.*"

"*Creating his own crew of pervy fishmen,*" I said, understanding where she was going with this little story.

"*They are not his crew,*" she corrected. "*This is not even their ship. They stole it from their father. Despite his indiscretions, Oannes did much good in the world.*" Her tone took on an edge. "*His sons, however, are vengeful rogues that hired a witch to help them trap his spirit inside Falak.*"

Unfamiliar with the term, I asked, *Falak?*

"*The snake god.*"

"*That was a god?*" My blood chilled as more pieces of the puzzle began to fit into place. Something tugged at the back of my mind, and as much as I wanted to disregard it, I couldn't. Captain Oannes had made a deal with a witch, and my father had cashed in on a deal made with a witch. The captain had also mentioned that the ship's passage couldn't be purchased, only earned. Had Sereana acquired passage by trapping Oannes for his sons?

"*What did the witch look like?*" I asked, hoping beyond hope that my theory was wrong. My aunt was no saint, but I didn't want her to be the type of witch who trapped gods for their terrible children. Of course, if the god was a better father, maybe his children wouldn't have turned out to be vengeful rogues, but I was trying not to judge.

"*I never saw the witch. That was long before my time. At least a century ago.*"

I had no idea how old Aunt Sereana was. It was almost impossible to tell with Tricari, who could magic themselves to never age. The question was, could I see my aunt trapping the spirit of a sea god's emissary in the body of a snake god?

Yes. Yes, I could.

"*Will you kill me?*" the female asked.

"*W-what?*" I stammered, stunned by her question. "*No. Why would you even think that? I'm not here to kill you. We are passengers. The ship is taking us to the island of Socotra. I am not a murderer.*"

"*It would not be murder, but a kindness.*" Sadness streamed through our connection, tugging at my heartstrings. *"An end to my torture."*

"You're being tortured?" I asked, feeling strangely protective of the girl. She was so small and disheartened, and sadness had all but threaded itself over her tapestry. Suffocating sorrow overwhelmed her tiny spirit. She was a person, a sentient consciousness, and it enraged me that someone had done this to her.

"My cage is made of iron," she replied. *"Every time the waves toss me, I smash against the bars, and they burn my flesh. The iron will not kill me, but it melts my skin until I fight off Oannes."*

The fiery rage I'd felt from her last night now made sense. Her captors were forcing her to defend them from their father. *"How long have you been their prisoner?"*

"I do not know." More sorrow pinged between us. *"I lost count of the seasons long ago. Are you sure you will not kill me? I would take my life myself, but the iron bars cannot pierce, only burn."*

Judging by her tone, she'd tried. Many times. There had to be a better way to help her. *"Is it possible to free you?"*

She hesitated. *"But the iron...."*

"Iron doesn't hurt me." Silver was the only metal I couldn't touch. I wondered what would hurt the fishmen since they clearly had no fear of iron.

"There is a lock, but the captain carries the key on his hat. You cannot get to it. I do not wish to put your life in peril."

I almost laughed out loud but managed to smack my jaw closed in time to cut off the sound. The last thing I needed was my pack-mates to wake up in the middle of my scheming.

"A lock is not a problem," I assured her. Scanning the area, I formulated a plan to get to the figurehead before lowering myself back into the room and climbing down from the wooden storage box. I started opening the chest but froze when the old wood creaked.

Someone's snore cut off. I waited, listening. When Rust's heavy breathing started up again, I slipped my backpack out—careful to steady Mackiel's bag before it could topple over—and closed the box. This time, the lid was silent.

"What can you tell me about their patrols?" I asked.

"What do you mean?"

"How often do they come to the front of the ship and check on you?"

"Never." She sounded almost amused by the notion. *"They know I cannot escape, and they are arrogant. They only come to the front of the ship to use the head."*

"Don't they feed you?"

"No. I do not need to eat." She giggled, sounding so young it hurt my heart.

That made me pause. *"What... what are you? I'm sorry if that's a rude question, but I've never met someone who doesn't need to eat before."*

"I am a fire sprite," she replied with the brightest tinkle of pride.

A fire sprite? That was something new and not listed in the pack database. It also sounded dangerous. Especially considering what she'd done to the giant snake. *"If I come out to free you, will you hurt me?"* I asked, watching her tapestry for any sign of trickery.

"You... you intend to free me?" she asked, her voice quivering with disbelief. *"Truly?"*

I glanced back at my companions. They were all still sound asleep. If I wanted to free her, it was now or never. *"As long as you don't intend to hurt me."*

"I will not hurt you," she assured me. *"I swear it on the flames of my people."*

The vows of the Tricari were binding, and that particular vow sounded sincere. Besides, I really wanted to see what a fire sprite looked like. I took a steadying breath and climbed out of the porthole, gripping the iron ribcage. We were only two nights past the full moon, and the sky was clear, so there was plenty of light to see by. It took a bit of finagling, but I squeezed my hips through the bars. Body plastered against the iron, I listened and sniffed the air, ensuring nobody was nearby. I had no desire whatsoever to catch one of the fishmen using the head. Confirming that the coast was clear, I crept toward the ship's bow.

The night was warm, but the bars were wet from the waves. As the ship rocked, water splashed my bare feet, dampening my pant legs, and it hit me that skulking over slippery bars above the ocean, alone, in the middle of the night, wasn't my best decision. Throw in a vengeful snake god and no telling what else—a bloodthirsty shark, a giant octopus, or even a freaking sea monster—and I was questioning my life choices. If I lost my grip and landed in the water, my packmates would never even know what happened to me. What was I thinking? I couldn't even swim!

I probably should have woken Mackiel, but my friend's loyalties were clear. If he didn't immediately wake the alpha and nark on me, I could see him doing something stupid like tying me to my hammock to keep me safe until morning. But I didn't want to be safe and secure in my bed. I finally had a chance to be useful and help someone, and I needed to take it.

"*Hey, what's your name?*" I asked the sprite.

There was a beat of silence, then she said, "*Are you really coming to free me?*"

"*Yes.*" Hand over hand, foot over foot, I crept closer. The area around the figurehead's mouth brightened with a fiery glow, leading me to it. "*Nobody should have to spend their life in a cage.*"

"*Please be careful,*" she said, her voice trembling. "*The Sons of Oannes will be angry if they discover what you are attempting.*"

"*I'm not afraid of creepy fishmen,*" I replied with way more bravado than I felt. "*Besides, you said they never check on you, so how will they know?*"

"*They will not until they dock. Then they will surely notice. Or if the ship is attacked and I do not defend it. When you free me, I will seek out Oannes and tell him not to make a move until you reach your destination. He will listen to me, and I will help him take his revenge when the time comes.*"

Now that sounded like a plan I could endorse. I reached the

mouth of the figurehead and swung my leg over to climb inside, careful not to scrape my back on the sharp iron upper beak. Turning, I came face to face with the fire sprite and froze. She couldn't have been any larger than my hand, and everything from her toes to her head glowed with flames. Elongated ears, pointed at the tips, wiggled in greeting. When I looked into her eyes, I saw the heart of an inferno. She wasn't made of flames; she *was* fire. Odd markings covered her exposed skin, and it took me a moment to realize they weren't tattoos but scars from the iron bars encasing her.

A beautiful smile lit up her tiny face. "Why hello there," she said aloud. "My name is Anunit."

"You speak English," I said, surprised. I'd heard the language in my mind, but I still wasn't sure how that skill worked. Telepathy was magic, so it could have a built-in translator for all I knew.

"Fire knows no boundaries," she said. "It is not confined to any language."

With no clue what to say to that, I started to introduce myself, but her bizarre eyes grew comically large as she waved her hands and said, "No. Do not tell me."

"You don't want to know my name?" I asked, pulling my backpack off and extracting my lockpicks from their pocket.

"No." She let out a relieved breath, her shoulders sagging with the effort. "Names have power. You should tell yours only to those you trust not to misuse it."

I was confused. "You gave me your name."

She nodded, and the flames that made up her hair flickered with the movement. "I did, but you are here to free me at significant risk to yourself. I offer my name as a favor for your kindness. If you speak into a fire, I will come to your aid. As long as I am free and able to do so."

I studied the rudimentary iron padlock that had kept Anunit locked up for longer than she could remember. "That's not necessary. I'm not freeing you to earn a favor. I'm freeing you because enslaving and torturing people is wrong."

She studied me, her eyes warm with affection. Or maybe that was just the fire. It was difficult to tell. "You have a kind soul."

It wasn't kindness; it was common decency. But rather than argue, I went to work on the lock, surprised by how clean it was.

"Shouldn't this be rusted?" I asked.

"The Sons of Oannes spell the iron to keep it free of corrosion," Anunit said. "Otherwise, the entire ship casing would be nothing but rust."

"Why iron?"

"It burns Falak. Oannes and the snake god are old enemies. When the ship was his, Oannes embraced the ship in iron to keep the snake away. Now that they share a body, Oannes protects the snake from the metal, but it still hurts him."

Within seconds the familiar click of release sounded. Before I swung the door open, I met Anunit's gaze. "I have packmates on this ship. Do you promise not to hurt them or do anything to damage the ship until we reach land?"

She nodded, her expression solemn. "On the flames of my people, I will protect this ship and its passengers with my life until you are safely on land," she said, her language more actively binding than mine. "That is an easy promise to make," she continued, "for I am not the only one the Sons of Oannes have wronged. Vengeance should not be mine alone."

I didn't feel bad for the fishmen, but I sure as hell didn't envy them either. With the giant snake and the fire sprite teamed up, they were in for one massive beatdown.

"Some people call me Chip," I said, heeding her advice but also giving her a name to call me.

She grinned. "It is a pleasure to meet you, Chip."

Then I opened the door and watched as the fire sprite shot out of her cage and into the sky like a shooting star. As she winked out of sight, I really hoped my actions wouldn't come back to burn me in the ass.

17

Arioch

Lugging Tyrin across the goddamn ocean was a chore. It mattered not how high I flew nor how many times I glided; he was a heavy son-of-a-bitch. I was still battling portal fatigue, and although the hot desert sun had restored a portion of my energy, the influx was far from the massive boost I had anticipated. Halfway through the flight, I was ready to chuck the gargoyle into the ocean as if he were a walking corpse nesna that refused to die. By the time we made land, my entire body was stiff, my right leg was asleep, and the base of my left wing would not stop twitching.

I had expected Socotra to consist of more of the same nature-ravaged desert we had seen in Yemen, but as we approached the island, it was clear my assumptions were wrong. The slug-shaped island looked more like a tropical paradise mentioned in one of the science fiction books in my library than a desert wasteland. Inviting sandy white beaches backed up to narrow coastal plains overgrown with unfamiliar flora. Bizarre umbrella-shaped trees and white shrubs with pink flowers littered cliffs and what must pass for mountains here. Having grown up with a view of Mt. Rainier, it looked more like a collection of hills to me. Turquoise pools dotted a limestone plateau and snaked up a brightly colored canyon.

Even the birds were bizarre. I had to do a double-take as we passed a flock of yellow-faced flying freaks that appeared to be spawned from the regrettable encounter of a seagull and a vulture. At least they were smart enough to get out of my way.

Camels and livestock grazed near the few small, sparsely popu-lated villages dotting the coastline. I did a quick sweep of the island

and then landed on the north end beside the only pier I found. Due to the size of the galleon, it would have to dock there if it docked at all. I focused on the chalice, but it was still a considerable distance away, which meant we had plenty of time to rest up, investigate the area, and find somewhere to hide before the wolves arrived.

Tyrin staggered off my back, still grumbling about the bumpy ride. I smiled to myself. The aerial acrobatics were admittedly uncalled for, but the sound of him squealing like a pig had almost made up for the trouble of carrying his stony ass. The bastard was lucky to be alive and therefore had nothing to complain about. He dropped our bags on the beach, opening his to rifle through it. Positioning myself to watch both the sea and the narrow coastline, I sunk into the warm white sand and made myself comfortable. Between the rhythmic roar of the surf, the muted glare of the setting sun, and the temperate breeze coming off the sea, my overtaxed muscles relaxed, and my eyelids started to droop.

"How far out is the ship?" Tyrin asked.

I cracked an eyelid and focused on the chalice, considering the distance. *"They are about two-thirds of the way here,"* I replied telepathically. *"They appear to be moving slowly now, and I do not anticipate their arrival until sometime tomorrow."*

"Good. Then we've got time, then."

Time for what, he did not say, and I did not care enough to ask. I planned to spend my time napping, and then maybe I would hunt down a camel since I was curious about the taste.

"Have you ever eaten camel meat?" I asked Tyrin.

"Yes, and I wouldn't recommend it. It's like beef but leaner. Tougher. And more gamey." He grimaced. "Not enough fat to flavor it."

Well, that was disappointing.

Hands full, Tyrin marched to the pier and unrolled about twelve feet of netting material.

My eyelids drifted closed, but the sound of tin scraping against glass tugged at my attention. I watched as he unscrewed the lid off a jar and smeared a goopy substance over the flattened net. A putrid fishy stench declared an act of war on my nostrils. I snorted in disgust and tucked my muzzle under my wing, keeping one eye out so I could spy on the gargoyle. He gathered driftwood and stones, arranging the supplies on the pier. Scooping up the net, he slipped into the water with a splash before stretching his net from the dock outward. Making multiple trips back to the pier for the driftwood and stones, he kept disappearing beneath the surface to secure the net.

Finished and dripping wet, he emerged from the water and scurried around the beach, collecting more driftwood and tossing it into a pile. I was trying to sleep, and the bastard was making enough noise to wake the dead.

"Do you mind?" I asked.

"Do you want to eat or not?" he shot back.

Now that he mentioned it, I was hungry. If he planned to feed me, I would not complain.

The gargoyle lit a fire. Driftwood crackled and popped as he coaxed the flame to life. Once it was soundly roaring, he waded back out to his net. The tide was coming in, and the water was higher now, almost over his head. He disappeared beneath the surface. Seconds ticked by, and I feared I would have to go in after the idiot. Not because I cared about his wellbeing, of course, but because Catori would never let me hear the end of it if I let him drown or get eaten by a sea creature. I scanned the water. No sign of a struggle, no flailing Norseman, nothing but silence.

I was about to get up and investigate when a mop of brown hair crested the waves. Tyrin popped his head up. His breathing was labored, but determination had etched itself into the hard lines of his face. He swore and wrestled with something as it splashed about. Emerging with a sizable rose-colored fish, he produced a switchblade, flicked it open, and gutted the fish. Dumping the entrails back into the sea, he rinsed off both blade and fish before scooping up a couple of thin, long sticks and heading toward the fire.

He stopped in front of me. "Unless you want to eat this snapper raw, I suggest you grow a pair of thumbs so you can roast it."

I considered having him toss it to me raw, but there was an insinuation of laziness in his statement I did not care for. Begrudgingly, I called on my magic to transform me into a human. Sand enveloped my feet, an oddly pleasant sensation. I wiggled my toes, sinking deeper, and accepted half of the fish and a stick from Tyrin.

Snapper had a clean, light flavor with the barest hint of nutty aftertaste. The smoke added a complexity that danced over my tastebuds. The fish would be perfect with some light seasoning and paired with rice pilaf or scalloped potatoes. Perhaps I could freeze a fillet and take it home to see what my cook could do with it.

How many delicious wonders had I missed out on?

Once the curse was broken, I would finally be able to find out.

After the snapper, we gobbled down grouper, coral trout, and a teal-colored fish Tyrin had never seen before. The scenery was idyllic, the temperature was pleasant, and the beach was peaceful. We ate in relaxed silence, watching the flames flicker. I was dangerously close to enjoying myself before Tyrin had to open his mouth and ruin the moment.

"Here, the ocean is full of fish," he said with a wistful look in his eyes. "Back home, my people would have had to fish for days to catch what we just consumed."

I stared at him, somewhat shocked he had the balls to attempt a casual conversation with me. There was a time when my húskarl's words had mattered to me. When I was a child, he used to take me hunting and camping on our property. In the evenings, I would sit at his feet and listen to stories about his people and his childhood home. He taught me how to ride a horse—much to the equine's horror—and how to climb trees. Together, we built forts, repaired fences, dug ditches, and played tricks on Tyrin's men.

He was the closest thing I had had to a father, once.

But that was before Mom had died, and the trainers had started cycling through my life. Another memory surfaced.

Fire licked at my back, the stench of my own burnt flesh and blood thick in my nostrils. Tyrin looked on, his face a mask of stone as I screamed for him to save me.

He had said and done nothing, yet that was the most painful memory of my childhood.

More memories trickled in as I stared into the dying embers.

"And what do you have to offer me? A golden shackle? My own feather bed next to yours in this luxurious cell? Not interested. Get off your knee. You're humiliating yourself."

Despite the heat of the island, a chill slithered up my spine.

"If you were smart, you'd want to be alone," a voice from my past whispered. *"Everyone you care for will betray you."*

I hadn't wanted to believe her, but she'd been right.

Sitting beside one of my betrayers now, contentedly sharing a meal, felt like yet another stab in the back to the boy I had once been. Tyrin had not done a damn thing to deserve my forgiveness, and the idea of swapping stories with him lit a fire under my temper.

"Save your tales, Tyrin," I snapped. "We are not friends. You are only here at the insistence of Catori. I would still kill you if she would allow it."

He looked like he was about to argue, so, staying in my human form, I wrapped myself in magic, pushing and pulling the air currents to lift myself atop a nearby cliff. There, I kept watch on the pier while staying out of range of Tyrin's ceaseless clamor.

I did not see where the gargoyle slept, nor did I care.

———

Grace's ship arrived around noon. As soon as it was in range, the buzzing in my head vanished, and I nodded to Tyrin, letting him know the chalice was still on the ship. Hopefully, the girl was as well. I had woken up still pissed at the gargoyle, but the fish break-fast he had prepared for us took the edge off both my anger and my hunger. With stomachs full, I had lifted us both up to the cliff to watch for the ship. Now he stood beside me with his spyglass to his eye.

Rather than docking, the galleon dropped anchor off the coast and lowered a dinghy into the sea. Two sailors rowed the wolves in and dropped them off at the end of the pier. There was a tense exchange, and then Chaz handed one of the sailors something I could not see from my position on the cliff.

Chaz and his team headed for the shore while the sailors rowed back toward the ship. As the wolves stepped onto the beach, one rower in the dinghy stood, waving his arms at the bow of the galleon and shouting in a language that sounded ancient. Two sailors scurried over the deck, their steps full of purpose.

Chaz spun around to watch the commotion, questions etched into the lines of his face.

Grace's gaze flickered to the ship, and her posture stiffened.

"Hey, remember that peculiar fire in the galleon's figurehead?" Tyrin asked from his spot beside me.

"Yes, why?" I followed his gaze and saw the answer for myself. "Shit."

"Yep. And judging by the guilty look on her face, your little thief found something else to steal."

My gaze shot back to the shore. Grace tugged on the alpha's arm. I could not hear her words from where I hid, but her pleading, desperate expression spoke volumes.

The alpha swore. Even the deaf would have heard him. Shaking my head at the surprising turn of events, I chuckled as Grace removed a spray bottle from the side pocket of her backpack and spritzed the wolves.

"What do you suppose that is?" Tyrin asked.

I thought about it for a beat. "That day she stole the chalice, I could not smell her until I was practically standing on her." That night, when I had flown over the estate looking for her cohort, I could not get a single whiff of either of them. It had bugged me ever since, but now I knew why. Even if I had an entire pack of shifters working guard duty that night, she still would have gotten away with the chalice. I would have to devise an extremely creative defense system to keep her out of anywhere I did not wish her to be. "I bet it is something to mask their scents."

"She wants them to escape and hide," Tyrin said, his tone impressed. "Clever girl."

I had to admit, he was right, and, for some strange reason, I felt a swell of pride in her actions.

The wolves sprinted inland. Chaos erupted on the ship. Four sailors dove off the deck straight into the water, swimming for shore. Oars flashed as the dinghy, halfway to the galleon, turned and raced back to the dock. The wolves crested a hill and disappeared from view.

Tyrin chuckled. "That dirty little thief."

It was nice to know I was not the only sucker she had ripped off. There was less shame in getting robbed by a professional. Marginally.

"How long do you think fish people can survive on land?" I asked.

"Not as long as the wolves, that's for sure." Tyrin grinned. "And the fish people are already struggling."

I followed his gaze to find the dinghy smacking against the dock as the rowers jumped out and sprinted after the wolves without tying up their ride. It drifted, smashing into one of the sailors swimming in from the ship. He shoved the dinghy away but not before it got in his way and slowed him down. Two more got tangled up in Tyrin's net.

The wolves were long gone by the time the blue-skinned sailors reached the shore. Within seconds, the buzzing in my head started back up as the chalice once again slipped out of range. We could not let the wolves escape. As entertaining as the sailors were to watch, we needed to hunt them down. Again. Maybe we could reach the troublesome wolf before she got herself killed by someone else.

Lowering his spyglass, Tyrin grinned. "She certainly keeps things interesting."

18

Grace

"Dammit, Grace, what the hell did you do?" the alpha shouted as we ran.

"I..." Feet pounding against the ground, I tried to conjure up the best possible defense, but my motive was unimportant. I knew my father, and nothing I said or did would justify my actions in his eyes. Not when my actions had led to us being chased by creepy fish people who outnumbered us and didn't seem at all reasonable or forgiving. Still, I had to try to plead my case.

"They were torturing her!" I blurted out. It wasn't an eloquent defense, but it was honest and to the point.

By the fury raging in his irises, you'd think I'd just admitted to selling pack secrets or giving away our food supply. He looked like he wanted to strangle me. If we escaped the Sons of Oannes, I was in for the punishment of my life.

"They can't track us now," I said, having masked our scents. "All we have to do is hide until they return to their ship. They can't stay on land forever."

"We don't have time to hide," the alpha shouted. "Shift!" he commanded.

The order wasn't meant for me, but the compulsion still made my wolf fight to obey. Pain erupted in my stomach, but I squeezed my core tight and kept sprinting. The alpha, Mackiel, and Rust lurched forward, sprouting fur and shredding clothing. Instead of hands, paws hit the ground. Bags fell from shoulders as their bodies contorted and changed. With one smooth drop of their heads, they scooped up their discarded bags between their teeth and kicked their speed into high gear. I pushed myself hard, pulling energy from my wolf to keep up as best as I could.

We circled a small village, giving it a wide birth. A woman must have seen us because she shouted a warning, no doubt wondering why three giant wolves were racing alongside a human. My sniffer picked up some intriguing animal scents, but I didn't smell any other wolves. I wondered if my companions were the first the woman had seen.

Despite my best efforts to keep up, I started lagging behind. The stitch in my side was killing me, but I was trying to ignore it. Mackiel slowed his speed to match mine and nudged me with his muzzle. I knew what he wanted me to do, but I didn't want to be a burden, so I pushed myself harder.

The alpha turned and snarled at me, ears flat against his head in warning. Since I was already skating on thin ice, I gave in, leaping onto my friend's back without breaking stride. I tried to distribute my weight evenly, but I threw him off balance, and he had to pump his brakes to avoid taking a tumble.

"Sorry," I said, burying my hands in his fur and holding on for all I was worth.

I'd ridden on his back dozens of times, and he always assured me it didn't hurt. But that was leisurely running; now, we were trying to match the speed of sound. Despite my attempts to be gentle, with every lurch, I tugged on his pelt. No matter what he claimed, that had to be painful.

Wind stung my face as the bizarre landscape of Socotra zipped by in a blur of shapes and colors. We darted over hills, and I clung to my friend while trying not to fixate on my inevitable confrontation with the alpha. About twenty-four hours ago, he'd called me his daughter, giving me hope we might actually have a relationship someday. Now, his wolf looked at me like he understood why some parents ate their young.

I wished we could go back to that moment on the ship. I wouldn't change anything that had happened since, but I wanted to feel his acceptance one more time. Just for a moment. I had no idea what kind of reckoning was in store for me, but I'd consider myself lucky if he didn't banish me from the pack for my insubordination. Here he was, going through all this trouble to free my wolf so I could be a normal member of the pack, and I'd put him and his team in danger.

I should have woken him and asked if I could free Anunit.

He probably would have said no since Anunit wasn't pack. But she was a sentient being, dammit, with hopes and dreams and a family. She didn't deserve to be enslaved and tortured. Hell, nobody deserved that sort of treatment. Leaving her trapped in an iron cage, collecting new scars every time the waves got too rocky, hadn't been an option. Not if I ever wanted to look myself in the mirror again.

I didn't expect my father, pack loyalist that he was, to understand my convictions. What was done was done, and I'd have to live with the consequences.

We skirted a low mountain range before dipping into a narrow ravine. Single file, we loped over pale limestone through an area where the walls connected about a foot over Dad's head to close in a cramped passageway. As the team slowed to a walk, my eyes adjusted to the darkness. Our collective breathing sounded heavy and labored, and our footsteps echoed as we marched toward the light ahead. The narrow tunnel opened to an equally narrow canyon, and Mackiel slowed, following the alpha's lead. A shallow pool of radiant orange water ringed with matching rocks stood before us.

All three wolves came to a halt. The alpha must have sent a command through the pack bond because power streamed from him. Mackiel dropped the bag hanging from his mouth, and the fur on his back began to melt away. I leaped off him, putting as much space between us as possible. The kiss we'd shared on the Fiery Stormbird had been uncomfortable enough; straddling his naked human form would be a whole new level of awkward.

Spinning so I didn't have to see Dad or Rust naked either, I took in my surroundings. The pale limestone canyon floor felt solid beneath my feet. Spongy, moss-covered walls led beyond the shallow orange pool and veered sharply to the left.

"What is this place?" I asked. Power vibrated from the rocks and echoed off the walls. It felt magical and sacred.

"Wadi Dirhur Canyon," the alpha said, his words clipped with barely suppressed anger as he adjusted the rifle, still on its sling, around his shoulder and picked up his bag.

He and Rust must have had their weapons strapped on for the entire run. Talk about one uncomfortable dash. Mackiel's staff was nowhere in sight, and the handle of his Glock was sticking out of a side pocket of his bag.

"According to Sereana, it's *'The canyon of stone that burns to lime,'*" the alpha added.

Recognition lifted my head. "We're there? Already?" This was it?

"No thanks to you," the alpha spat. Didn't sound like he'd be referring to me as his daughter again any time soon. Shocker. "Come on. We have to find the tree."

He started walking. Avoiding my gaze, Rust followed. Mackiel shook his head at me and did the same. All three of my packmates looked exhausted. They'd slept off the portal lag, but they'd shifted twice over a short period of time with a sprint in between. I felt awful, but it didn't matter. I could apologize until I was blue in the face, and nothing I said would fix what I'd done. Any attempts to explain my behavior would be seen as making excuses. My only chance at redemption was to find *'the heart of life birthed from the blood of two brothers'* and offer it to the alpha on a platter made from any metal but silver.

Hurrying to catch up with my companions, I asked, "We're looking for a tree?"

The alpha ignored me.

Okay, I'd screwed up, but come on. We needed to work together

AMARA MAE

to find this thing so we could get out of there. I took a few deep breaths and tried again. "I'm trying to help, Alpha. Please tell me what we're looking for."

He rounded on me, his golden glare pinning me in place. My father, the man, tolerated me. Sometimes, I could even fool myself into believing he liked me. Maybe he would have loved me had the circumstances of my conception and birth been different.

However, my father, the wolf, was a pragmatic beast who weighed pros and cons, making emotionless decisions that benefitted the pack. The wolf saw me as a liability. A weakness. He'd almost taken my life during my Bloodrite, and my shenanigans since had no doubt only driven down my value. As the wolf's gaze held me captive, he took my measure and weighed my usefulness. When he leaned forward—invading my personal space—it took every ounce of courage I had not to cower.

"Every goddamn time I start to believe you might turn out to be something other than a fecking disappointment, you prove me wrong, Grace."

After nineteen years, I should be immune to his insults, but they were like arrows that never failed to hit their mark. I wanted to rage at him, to tell him I was doing the best I could under the circumstances and had no idea what more he wanted from me. I longed to apologize for being born and remind him I'd never asked for any of this.

But I wasn't ready to die quite yet, so I kept my mouth shut.

"How many times do I have to tell you that the pack always comes first?" he asked.

It was a rhetorical question, but when I didn't answer, he clenched his fists. I got the distinct impression it required all his willpower not to pummel me.

"You think this is a game?" he asked. "That those assholes from the ship won't gut us if they get the chance?"

"No, Alpha. I don't think it's a game," I insisted.

"Then why the feck would you put us all in danger like this?" he roared.

His rage ricocheted off the cavern walls, battering me again and again. He was my alpha—my protector—and he wanted to kill me. I could see it in his eyes. My wolf whimpered, desperate to appease him. To make him happy and proud of us. She didn't understand why that seemed impossible. Why nothing I ever did made him love us. A deep, menacing growl came from the alpha's throat. Instincts kicked in, and I took a step back before I could stop myself.

Rust stepped forward. "Alpha..."

The alpha spun on him. "This is your fault. I entrusted you with her training. You were supposed to hone her into a weapon for the pack. Instead, you let her grow into a disobedient bitch who puts us at risk. You were too lenient and now look at her. She's useless to me."

When Rust didn't respond, the alpha spun back to me, his index finger pointed in my face. "This will be the last time you put my pack in danger. You hear me?"

Useless to me.

Those three little words wouldn't stop echoing in my head. I swallowed the ball of emotion clogging my throat as my wolf whined. She wanted to be one with the pack and didn't understand why I kept messing it up. Frustrated and misunderstood, I dropped my gaze and leaned my head to the side, showing the alpha my neck. "Is leatsa mo shaol, Alpha."

He accepted my submission, and the gold drained from his eyes until they were once again the same forest green as mine. The pressure on my chest eased. Behind me, Mackiel released an audible breath.

The alpha turned and started walking again. I didn't expect him to actually answer the question I had asked, so I was surprised when he said, "Sereana said it will be a tree. One of those umbrella-looking ones we saw along the way."

"Dragon blood trees," Rust clarified.

The alpha nodded. "Their Arabic name means 'the blood of the two brothers.' They only grow on this island, and the original tree should be somewhere in this canyon. Sereana seems to think we'll know it when we see it."

I wondered if it would call to me like the chalice had. Hopefully not, since that kind of creeped me out. The canyon opened up, revealing what could only be described as a mythical fairyland.

"Holy shit," Mackiel breathed.

I had to agree. It was like nothing I could have imagined. In vivid shades of greens, yellows, reds, and blues, pools danced around the umbrella-shaped trees Dad had mentioned. But unlike the dragon blood trees above, these trees were speckled in vibrant rainbow shades, looking more like enormous magic mushrooms than umbrellas. Multicolored butterflies and moths flitted around a collection of teal rocks. A strange, elongated lizard dove for a treat, but the moth rose out of range at the last instant.

The soft earthen smell of the canyon carried a hint of natural sweetness, like the tea with honey I sometimes drank with Aunt Sereana. I breathed in deeply and let the familiarity center me in this bizarre land. We had to be getting close to the tree, and with it, my one shot at redemption.

One heart, delivered on a non-silver platter coming up.

Steering clear of the moss-covered walls, we wove through the pools to another bend in the canyon. This one led to the right. We continued through the narrow canyon until it widened, and we got our first look at what had to be *the* original dragon blood tree. It was the most magnificent tree I'd ever laid eyes on. It stood smack dab in the canyon's center, the base of its shimmery, silver trunk elevated at least thirty feet off the ground by dozens of enormous, exposed roots that led up to it like ramps.

The alpha led us to the base of one root and held up a hand for us to hold back. He tentatively took one step and then another. When the root didn't immediately snap to life and buck him off, he strode forward, gesturing for us to follow. I went next, with Mackiel on my heels and Rust watching our six.

The tree itself wasn't very tall—maybe thirty feet or so—but its presence was unlike anything I'd ever felt. I opened my spiritual sight and saw a tapestry so rich and majestic that all I could do was gape at it. I'd never seen a sentient tree before. Judging by the details on its tapestry, it had to be centuries old.

"The flowers are the color of blood," Rust pointed out.

I blinked, returning my vision to normal to study the canopy of elongated green leaves. Sure enough, Rust was right. Unlike the barely visible white and green flower clusters on the other trees, these were deep crimson.

"We approach with caution," the alpha said, adjusting his rifle in his hands.

I wasn't sure when he'd drawn the weapon from its sling, but the tension rolling off him made me reevaluate the scene. I pulled my Glock as we crept forward, watching all directions at once. I'd seen nothing but a sentient tree and oddly colored bugs and lizards since we entered the canyon, but anything could be hiding in the mossy shadows between exposed roots.

We were only a few feet from the trunk when a whimsical voice said, *"Come closer, Daughter of Light."*

Startled, I looked to my companions. "Did you hear that?"

The alpha froze. "What'd you hear, Grace?"

"A voice. It told me to come closer and called me Daughter of Light? What does that mean?"

My father's eyes widened a fraction of an inch before his expression hardened. "Doesn't matter. You think it's the tree?"

There was something he wasn't telling me. That was no surprise since my old man rarely told me anything, but this had to do with me. My hackles rose as I watched him, but before I could answer, the voice spoke again.

"There is something I wish to show you."

Was it the tree? The fire sprite's voice had tinkled melodiously, but this one made me think of wind rushing through leaves. But maybe it could hear my thoughts like the sprite had.

"Who are you?" I thought back.

The trunk of the dragon blood tree moved.

Spooked, I rocketed back, but the alpha snatched my arm and tugged me to his side. Wood and bark splintered with thunderous creaks and pops, forcing outward and re-forming into the semblance of a person trying to escape the tree, its upper body leaning away from the trunk. Then it thrust a hand toward me, palm up.

It wasn't escaping; it was... inviting.

The being's lips were neither smiling nor frowning, and as I looked into its round eyes, a deep sense of sadness wrapped around me. I studied its tapestry again, only to realize heartbreak was woven into its spirit. Sadness wasn't something it needed to deal with; it was part of who it was.

I couldn't help but glance at Mackiel, wondering if this was what the evolution of my friend's depression would look like. How was the tree functioning? And how could it be so sad surrounded by all the magical wonder of the canyon? If I lived here, I'd feel safe and... lonely. God, it was so very lonely.

"What does it want?" my father asked.

My attention was still locked on the tapestry. It was beautifully tragic, and I couldn't look away. "To show me something."

He spun me to face him, breaking the spell. He gave me a firm shake that made my teeth rattle. "Focus, Grace. You need to get the tree's heart."

"How?" More importantly, why? Its heart was already broken. It had suffered enough.

"I don't know. It's a magical being, so find out what it wants and see if you can make a deal."

He wanted me to negotiate for its heart? That was the craziest thing I'd ever heard, but the fervor in my father's eyes told me there'd be no arguing.

"Okay," I said. Remembering who I was talking to, I hurried to add, "Yes, Alpha."

He squeezed my arms. "Agree to whatever it wants, you hear me? *Whatever* it wants."

I stared at him in shock. He was willing to pay any price to release my wolf? Even after I'd set the fire sprite free and pissed off the Sons of Oannes? Hell, *I* wasn't willing to pay any price for my life. If this tree asked for my firstborn or something equally monstrous, I was out. But I couldn't tell Dad that. Not when his eyes were rimmed in glowing gold and fur ghosted his arms.

Uncertainty felt like a lump of silver in my gut, poisoning me from the inside out, but I nodded. "Yes, Alpha."

"I'm counting on you. Don't let me down."

Something was going on here, and I had a bad feeling about it. Were we still talking about retrieving an item to release *my* wolf? A chill skittered up my spine as I held his gaze. "I won't."

He released me.

I looked to Rust and Mackiel, but neither said anything. With no other options, I holstered my Glock, approached the tree, and slid my hand on top of its upturned wooden palm.

19

Grace

The dragon tree's wooden hand turned sideways, wrapping its fingers around mine and trapping me. I let out a startled squeak and looked to the alpha, but the disapproval written on his face turned me back around. Agree to whatever it wants. Right. I blew out a shaky breath.

"Okay, I'm here," I said aloud so my father could hear my compliance. "What do you wish to show me?"

"Watch closely," the whimsical voice said in my head.

Then, everything went black.

Bright, scintillating shapes and colors pierced the darkness, flashing and swirling until I could no longer tell up from down. Then, as suddenly as it had begun, the chaos around me settled, and I once again stood in the canyon. Only Dad, Rust, Mackiel, and the ancient dragon blood tree were gone.

A six-foot-tall monolith sprung up in the center of the canyon floor. As I watched, a young couple materialized and approached the monolith arm-in-arm, the man carrying a basket of flowers in his free hand. Both were clothed in rudimentary strips of leather, and the woman was sporting a massive baby bump that turned her walk into more of a waddle. They spoke quietly in a language I couldn't understand, and after depositing the flower basket in front of the monolith, the two shared a long look and an even longer kiss.

I was beginning to feel like a peeping tom, but a second man appeared, and—plot twist—he had to be the first man's identical twin brother. He stormed onto the scene, his face a mask of rage as he pointed and shouted at the first twin. Confusion flashed in the woman's eyes as she looked from one man to the next before pushing away from the first

260

twin. *Twin Two was carrying an iron-tipped spear, and he raised it and charged the first twin with a cry.*

Twin One spoke, and roots shot out of the limestone ground, entangling the second twin's feet. Twin Two threw his spear at Twin One, who lurched to the side, fast enough to keep the weapon from nailing anything vital but too slow to avoid it altogether. A red streak formed across his arm, and the scent of blood overwhelmed the burnt ozone stench of magic. Blood gushed from the wound, and the skin around it turned grey. The man screamed, slapping a hand over the wound to stanch the blood flow.

With one hand protectively cradling her swollen belly, the woman shouted at the brothers. I couldn't understand her words, but her intention was clear. She wanted them to knock that shit off before someone got seriously injured. Neither paid her any mind.

Twin Two squatted, plucked a stone from the canyon floor, and slashed at the roots clinging to his ankles. I didn't think a rock would do much, but with Twin One distracted by his injury, Twin Two freed himself within seconds. He dove for the spear with the grace of a trained thief, rising with the weapon in hand. With murder in his eyes, he stalked toward Twin One, who summoned another root. It shot out of the ground and straight toward Twin Two like a nature missile, striking him in the chest with a wet thump before shooting out his back. At the same time, Twin Two buried his blade into his brother's chest.

Both men fell, blood pooling around them.

The woman screamed.

Lightning split the sky, and a woman so gorgeous she had to be a goddess stepped through a portal, hovering above the ground. She wore a sheer white dress, her long, dark tresses hung past her waist, and her almond-shaped sky-blue eyes were charged with power.

The pregnant woman fell to her knees before the goddess, dropping her head to the ground in a bow of reverence. She muttered, "Sikotar Mata."

Only a few feet away, the twins were dying. Their breaths came in labored pants as their mahogany skin greyed. The goddess frowned at them before closing her eyes and whispering something I couldn't make out. The hard ground cracked between the twins' bodies, and green fronds shot through the newly formed hole in the limestone. Dripping in the blood of the brothers, they rose, crumbling the ground and absorbing the bodies and the stone monolith. Within seconds, the umbrella-shaped tree stood as tall as the goddess, its roots raising the ground as they tunneled through it.

When the tree settled, the goddess smiled fondly at her creation. "Bear witness, my pet," she said in perfect English. "I warned the brothers their war would bring nothing but death, but they refused to listen. Now, they will pay."

They were dead. I figured that was payment enough, but she turned and pointed at the woman's swollen belly.

"For spilling blood on my sacred ground, I curse their descendants. Like their fathers before them, one line shall be born iron, the other of ether, and they will clash until one eradicates the other."

Then, she vanished, leaving the pregnant woman sobbing beside the blood tree.

My mind stuttered as I realized what I was witnessing. Was that how the animosity between the Mondeine and the Tricari had begun? Brothers cursed to wipe one another out?

The woman and the bodies faded as days and nights cycled past. The tree's roots stretched across the island, and my subconscious followed. Warm breezes tickled my skin, and the innocent laughter of children rang through my ears. I followed the sound to find water sprites dancing over the white, sandy beaches. Their tiny bodies shimmered, and they suddenly appeared human. That was the cloaking? It was incredible!

"Where did the cloaking come from?" I asked, but nobody answered.

Nymphs galloped over grassy hills, playing tricks on lion creatures with humanoid upper bodies. Seemingly oblivious to the Tricari living among them, the Mondeine thrived in their villages, building, growing, and expanding.

Life was happy. Peaceful.

I wondered why the two factions weren't trying to kill one another.

Then a male with skin the color of honey and short, spiky hair in all the shades of sunset appeared. His clothes were so pale and delicate that they looked like woven spider webs, and when he turned his kind, whiskey-colored eyes on the tree, his entire being brightened. The tree's heart soared at the sight of him.

He was love and light. Companionship.

He was Everything.

Then darkness shrouded the island. Fear clouded the male's eyes as bombs exploded and magic raged. Something had changed, and Mondeine and Tricari were at war. I rode the shoulders of the honey-skinned Everything as he fled in fear. Heart pounding, he raced for his tree. Shots rang out. Struck from behind, he jerked forward. His knees buckled, pitching him forward. Fire erupted in his torso as the iron bullets burned the sap in his veins.

The tree ached to save Everything, but he was too far away. All it could do was watch, powerless, as life leaked from his body and love drained from his eyes.

A chasm of hopelessness opened before me and I leaned toward it, but something held me back.

"No." The whimsical voice in my head said. "That is my path, not yours."

The scene faded into darkness, and a person stood before me. It had silvery wooden skin, hair of spiky green fronds, and blood-colored eyes full of sorrow. It watched me as I studied it. Something precious was cupped in its wooden hands. The treasure called to me, offering the slightest sliver of... hope. I couldn't take my eyes off the being's hands as it extended them toward me and opened its palms. A round, red seed glowed. It was cracked and bruised but still glowing.

The heart!

This was what my father was after; I could feel it in my wolf. I reached for it but hesitated because I didn't know what it would cost me.

"What do you want for it?" I asked.

It tilted its head to the side like it didn't understand my question. "Is this not what you came for, Daughter of Light?"

That name again. "Why do you call me that?"

A sad smile stretched across its cracked lips. "Because that is what you are. Take the seed. You will need it for the path ahead."

Before I could ask any more questions, the being deposited the heart in my hands and shoved me back. Suddenly untethered, I flipped and slammed back into my body.

I stood on the root of the giant dragon blood tree with my father on my right and Rust and Mackiel on my left. The seed pulsed in my hand, but my companions were too distracted to realize what I held. I immediately saw why. The trunk had shifted back into its original form, and mini crimson flowers fluttered around us like bloody dandelion fluff.

"What's happenin'?" Rust asked, holding his hand out to catch one.

Before anyone could respond, a spiky black leaf spiraled down inches in front of my face. I looked up and watched in horror as the densely packed crown of stiff, green leaves blackened and followed suit. Disturbed by the sight, I opened my spiritual vision and focused on the tree's tapestry. It was... unraveling. Rapidly. Rows were already undone, and more stitches pulled free with every second that passed.

"Fall back!" the alpha shouted.

The others obeyed, but I couldn't. The tree had given me its heart, and now it was dying! I had to do something. Shoving the seed in my pocket, I fell to my knees and placed my hands on the root to strengthen the connection.

"Goddammit, Grace!" the alpha shouted.

But over half of the tree's tapestry was already gone. I reached for the thread, but it slid between my spiritual fingers. Cursing, I tried again. I caught the string this time, but I had no idea what to do with it. Stitches kept unraveling. I looped it around a stitch, attempting to knot it, but the thread was so slippery I lost my grip. A leaf pelted my back. Another hit my head. I knew I needed to get out of there, but I couldn't just let it die. Color leached from the silvery trunk beneath me, turning the tree a lifeless gray.

"No. Please don't do this," I muttered. My anxiety and grief grew with each lost strand. As I desperately grasped for threads to stop the unraveling, tears filled my eyes, blurring my vision. I blinked them away and kept at it, determined.

A beast roared above us, echoing off the canyon walls.

"Take cover!" my father shouted.

A dark shadow blotted out the sunlight, but I was so close. If I could just loop the thread and tie it off...

"Chip!" Mackiel shouted.

Wind beat against me as I tugged the thread around itself and secured a knot before slumping down where I knelt. There was only one little stitch remaining. One. My head ached and my entire body felt drained, but I'd saved one stitch.

Something solid smacked into me, and I slammed against the root so hard stars danced before my eyes.

Mackiel screamed.

I struggled to find my feet as my gaze sought out the source of the sound. My best friend hung about a dozen feet above me, dangling from the claws of a massive black dragon flying away. The batlike wingspan was at least twenty-five feet wide, supporting a lizard-shaped body about half that length. Every inch of the beast was covered in thick, inky black scales that I knew my Glock and daggers would be useless against. I opened my spiritual sight and immediately recognized the disjointed tapestry of the guardian.

The bastard must have come for me, and Mackiel had shoved me out of the way. The guardian probably didn't even realize he had the wrong person. Well, I knew how to remedy that.

"Hey, asshole!" I shouted.

"Chip, no!" Rust said.

But I couldn't let Mackiel take the fall for my thievery. Besides, my shouting worked. The dragon's head whipped around and silver eyes burning with rage met mine. He roared again, flipping a mid-air U-turn, and released Mackiel. My friend plummeted to the ground below, and I closed my eyes, bracing against the pain the guardian's sharp claws would bring.

Someone shoved me from behind.

I toppled off the root as gunfire erupted. Bouncing off one root, I thwacked against another before landing on my ass with a bone-rattling thud. The mossy floor had done little to break my thirty-foot fall. I pitched myself back and stared at the sky long enough to take stock of my body. My left hand felt broken, my tailbone had to be bruised, and my left ankle hurt like hell, but I could move it. I'd heal eventually, but I was magically spent. Every inch of my body ached. Still, I pushed myself off the ground and tried to get my bearings.

Above, the rifles continued to bark. Something screeched; the sound was so different from the dragon that I looked up to see what new monster we faced. A giant stone-skinned bat swooped into the fray.

A gargoyle.

But there was nothing I could do about it, so I focused on finding Mackiel. Following the scent of blood, I limped toward my fallen friend. Thankfully, I only had to climb over a couple of small roots to reach him. Mackiel's prone form sprawled on the ground, facing away from me, his shirt shredded and bloody, and his right leg at an odd angle. I called out his name, but he didn't respond. Ignoring the pain in my healing ankle, I bolted to his side, kneeling to check for a pulse.

My friend was still alive.

Blowing out a breath, I rocked back on my heels and took in the scene. Blood was everywhere, and I had to clear away moss and blackened leaves to assess the damage. Grabbing the canteen from my backpack, I poured the last of my water on his back and stomach. The gouges were so deep I could see meat and bone. Wondering why he was still in human form, I opened my other sight and checked his tapestry.

His fear was suffocating. Determined to ease it so he could shift,

I imagined dipping my hands into a calming balm and slid them down his dark threads.

My head felt like it was about to split, and stars danced before my eyes. I was spent, but he needed to shift and heal. Grabbing one of his hands to anchor myself, I took one more restorative pass at his darkness.

Fur sprouted along Mackiel's skin. Muscle and bone shifted, shredding what remained of his clothing as a familiar brown wolf appeared before me.

"Thank you, universe," I whispered, releasing his spirit.

With my friend taken care of, I eyed the massive root, wondering if I could somehow climb it and get back to Dad and Rust. It was all I could do to keep my eyes open, but we were all still in danger. Who had shoved me off it and why? The dragon wanted me and his stupid, worthless cup. Had they let him take me, they wouldn't be up there battling for their lives right now.

There was a shriek of pain above. The dragon swooped toward the gargoyle, and then both winged beasts vanished from sight. The gunfire stopped, but I didn't see anyone else fall. Had the winged beasts retreated? I stared up, looking for some sign of Dad and Rust. Minutes passed as I sat beside Mackiel, stroking the fur of his paw and wondering what to do. Finally, twigs snapped nearby, and Rust swore.

"Over here!" I shouted, unable to hide my relief at hearing my mentor's voice.

Feet pounded against the ground, and released Mackiel's paw and stood. Rust and the alpha cleared the root, and I was so grateful to see them uninjured that a rush of heat stung the back of my eyes. Dad didn't even spare a glance in Mackiel's direction before homing in on me.

Barely controlled rage rolled off the alpha as he stopped in front of me and asked, "Did you get the heart?"

Confused, I glanced at our injured packmate, wondering why he wasn't the priority.

"Answer me, Grace."

The low alpha command demanded my undivided attention. I reached into my pocket and pulled out the cracked, glowing red seed. He snatched it out of my hand and examined it before running a pocketknife along the crack. The action seemed super disrespectful, and I had to look away, turning my gaze on the dragon blood tree that had given it to me. Blood red sap rolled down the trunk like fat teardrops. The leaves and flowers had all fallen and littered the moss-covered ground. I opened my spiritual sight and peered at the tapestry.

The one little stitch remained.

I could see what the pattern had been, an impressive design formed of hatred that found love and peace only to die in sorrow. I reached for it, wondering if I could somehow re-stitch it and revive the odd wooden being. But I had no energy left to give. Besides, I'd never learned to knit, crochet, cross-stitch, or whatever skill would enable me to repair the tapestry of a person's spirit.

Guilt stabbed me in the chest as I realized the tree wasn't the only thing dying. It must have been magically powering this entire canyon because all around us, the unusual, bright colors drained from the vegetation as it wilted away. This place that had been magical and sacred was rapidly becoming a wasteland.

Why did you give me your heart? I thought toward the tree, but there was no answer.

The alpha folded up his pocketknife and put it away before plucking an inch-long glass vial from the seed. He popped off the cork and dumped a rolled parchment into his hand. I caught a glimpse of foreign writing as he turned the page over and studied it.

"Alpha, Mack is injured," I pointed out, unable to keep the bite from my tone. I wanted to snatch that little paper from my father's hands and shred it. I was sick to death of this idiotic quest. I didn't know what the alpha was really up to, but nothing was worth killing sentient beings and sending my best friend into a healing coma with a dragon and a gargoyle trying to murder us all.

The alpha's eyes narrowed as he met my gaze. "I'm fully aware of Mackiel's condition." He rolled the paper up, stuffed it back into the glass vial, and pocketed it. "The dumbass risked his life to save yours." His gaze slid to Rust, and I knew who'd shoved me off the root.

"We need to move," the alpha said. "That overgrown lizard won't be gone long, and we're too exposed here."

I wondered why the dragon had left, but now didn't seem like the time to ask. Rust started to remove his rifle, presumably to hand it to me so he could carry Mackiel, but my father stopped him.

"No. Grace'll carry him," the alpha said.

I was so exhausted I could barely carry myself, but I drew strength from my wolf and bent to pick up my friend. At least one bone in my left hand was broken because agony shot up my arm the moment I put pressure on it. Stars danced before my eyes and my gorge rose, but I swallowed back bile and gently slung Mackiel over my shoulder. He was so heavy, I had to distribute his weight so we wouldn't topple sideways. I took a step forward and almost tripped over his back paws. His soft fur tickled my cheek and slid into my mouth as I adjusted him again. I spat and cursed, but my friend didn't so much as stir.

"Let's move out," the alpha said, rifle at the ready. Some silent communication passed between him and Rust, and my mentor moved to walk beside Dad rather than taking up the rear.

My ankle was healing, but the strain on my body was intense. The alpha set a pace that made my short legs scream in protest. It was all I could do to keep putting one foot in front of the other and keep up as we headed back the way we'd come. My mind raced, wondering what the hell was on that tiny parchment. Another riddle? Our next dangerous quest? Would I have to take a kidney or a brain from the next sentient being?

This was bullshit, and I was finished.

As soon as we got home, I'd tell Dad I was out. I didn't care how disappointed or angry he got with me. Hell, I no longer cared if he killed me or threw me out of the pack. I wouldn't do this. I couldn't.

My wolf would just have to stay locked within me forever.

Not like I believed that was what this journey was about anymore.

We passed a sheet of melting ice. I would have asked about it, but keeping up with Dad and Rust required all my breath. We made our way back to the cramped, closed-in passageway we'd arrived through. Rather than leading us back out the canyon entrance, the alpha veered right, taking us to a spot where the limestone wall recessed into a short, narrow cave. He and Rust had to duck to enter it. I slid in behind them and, at Dad's direction, laid Mackiel down on the ground. The alpha immediately pulled Rust aside and started speaking in Gaelic.

I had no idea what my father said, but the worried glances Rust kept throwing me spoke volumes. He appeared to argue for a moment before dropping his gaze and submitting with a clipped, "Yes, Alpha."

Seemingly appeased, the alpha faced me. "Stay with Mackiel. The dragon can't fit in here, so the two of you should be safe."

I opened my mouth to inform my father of the dragon's human form but decided against it. Admitting I'd kept valuable information from the alpha wouldn't do anyone any favors.

"Are you leaving us behind?" I asked instead, trying to keep my tone matter of fact and free of judgment.

"That depends on what we find," my father answered honestly. "If we can avoid the dragon, the gargoyle, the fishmen you pissed off, secure passage on a boat, *and* safely return to retrieve the two of you, we will. But I have to do what is best for the pack, Grace. I will not die and leave my people without an alpha to save you."

Rust's jaw ticked, but he said nothing.

"Is leatsa mo shaol, Alpha," I said, feeling the full weight of my vow. "I understand. And for what it's worth, I'm sorry. For... everything."

My father nodded once, turned, and ducked out of the cramped cave.

Rust moved to follow but paused, clenching his fists. Clearly, he wasn't happy with my father's decision, and I was terrified he'd say something in anger and torch the last of their friendship and put himself in danger. I couldn't let him do that.

"Give Janey and the kids my love," I said. The words tumbled from my mouth in a desperate rush. I needed to remind him of what was on the line. My life wasn't worth his wife and kids losing him.

His eyes softened as he swallowed back whatever he was going to say. "Goodbye, Chip."

The concern in his eyes made my stomach clench. I knew my father had no intention of returning for Mackiel and me, but I gave my mentor a reassuring smile.

"Be safe, Rust."

They left.

I told my father I understood, and I did. I fully supported his decision to abandon me on a foreign island, surrounded by blood-thirsty enemies. I almost convinced myself that the hollowness in my chest wasn't for my life but for Mackiel's. He'd been nothing but faithful to my father, and he didn't deserve to be left in this cave with me. This felt like his punishment for trying to save my life.

Now I had to try to save his.

Knowing I had limited time before the dragon returned for me and his goddamn chalice, I came up with an idea. Leaving Mackiel asleep where he was, I ran back out of the cave and gathered up as many dead plants and fallen branches as I could carry. My subconscious kept trying to remind me that I was responsible for the death of the canyon's lush, unique vegetation, but I didn't have time to wallow in regret and self-loathing. I had shit to do.

But if I lived, I fully intended to schedule a well-deserved mental breakdown.

My left hand still hurt like hell, but I fought through the pain and arranged my dead foliage into a pile. God, I hoped this worked. Pulling a lighter from my bag, I bent and set a leaf ablaze. It burned for approximately two seconds before sputtering out without catching anything else on fire.

Damn.

I wouldn't have much time and had been given no useful instructions on summoning the sprite. Determined, I tried again, this time blowing gently on the fire to coax it onto the other dead leaves. The flame took off, engulfing the vegetation in its blaze.

"Anunit," I said into the flame. Then, because there was power in the number three, I repeated the name twice more.

Nothing happened.

The flames incinerated my meager offering, turning my hopes of saving Mackiel to ash. There was nothing left to do but reflect on all that had happened. I'd accomplished the task the alpha had set before me, but at what cost? This didn't feel like a win; it felt like... we'd committed an atrocity, and Mackiel was paying for it.

Well, Mackiel and the tree.

The tree had to know it would die, yet it had handed over its heart without hesitation. I thought of the bone-deep hopelessness and loneliness I'd felt when the tree lost its honey-skinned Everything. The call of that gaping chasm of sorrow had been so powerful.

'That is my path, not yours.'

Had the tree fallen into its depression? Was that why it had given me its seed?

My thoughts and emotions were all over the place. I wanted to scream and cry and flip out. By accepting that seed, I'd destroyed something ancient and harmless, a being that had witnessed the very beginning of the Tricari and Mondeine animosity.

Had I unraveled the thread between life and death?

Maybe I was the cursed broken beast.

My father was right; the Chalice of Power would change everything, but not for the better.

He'd really left me to die.

I understood and supported his decision, but holy shit, did it ever sting. Tears burned the backs of my eyes, and I really wanted to have that breakdown, but I needed to keep a clear head in case I came up with another idea.

My hand throbbed, redirecting my scattered and depressed thoughts. Worse, it looked... lumpy. The bones were fusing back together wrong. I probably needed to rebreak it and set the bone, but I had no clue how to do that.

Glancing at my unconscious friend, I wished Mackiel was awake so I could tell him how sorry I was.

Then I'd chew his ass out for putting himself between me and the dragon. What the hell had he been thinking? It was a dragon, for Chrissake! What did he hope to accomplish with that foolish, albeit brave, move?

He was such an amazing friend. Why in the world did he want to punish himself by becoming my mate?

I had to find a way to save him.

If the fire sprite would just show the fuck up...

Was she okay? Had the Sons of Oannes recaptured her?

The lingering smoke from the fire took on a distinctly burnt ozone stench. Expecting the dragon, I drew my daggers and spun around.

No one was there.

Something brightened, drawing my attention. An ember from the burned-out fire glowed. Daring to hope, I stalked forward to investigate. The pile of ash cracked, and out popped a familiar being.

"Anunit," I said on a breath, unable to stop my voice from trembling.

"Chip," she replied, taking in the scene. "What do you need?"

Before I could answer, heavy footsteps echoed off the canyon walls, coming from the direction of the blood tree.

Once again, I found myself in a race against the clock, but this time, my whole life was upside-down, and I'd run out of time to right it.

Arioch

I dropped Tyrin off on the shelf overlooking the canyon, not far from the bags we had stashed before attacking the wolves. He flapped his uninjured wing once before landing hard. Gargoyles could turn most of their bodies to stone, all but the sensitive membranes of the inner wings. It was their one weak spot, and the wolves had managed to find it, shredding the inside of Tyrin's right wing with bullets.

As the gargoyle shifted into his human form, I banked and landed, doing the same. By the time I joined him, he was pulling on a pair of pants, wincing at the pain in his back where his wings had retracted to heal.

"You saved me," he said, his tone stunned.

"No," I snapped, still reeling from the horror I had just witnessed. "I made a strategic retreat, and you happened to fall in my way."

Grace had killed the Ancient.

I had seen her do so with my own eyes, yet I still could not wrap my mind around the atrocity she had committed. I should not be surprised since the little thief had declared herself as the broken beast when she stole the Chalice of Power, but watching her through the orb had made me second guess the prophecy. She seemed kind and thoughtful, courageous, and... good.

Had it all been an act? Some sort of ploy to gain my trust? She had suspected she was being watched. Perhaps she had been tricking us all along.

Still, the little wolf had shown me mercy when she should have ended me.

That was a kindness she would soon regret because I would not repay it. She would already be dead had her packmates not protected her. Dealing with them had been surprisingly difficult. They were too quick and agile to get caught in my ice spray, and the alpha had somehow shielded their minds to block my magic. The canyon terrain was not ideal for my dragon form, but I did not need teeth and claws to defeat them. I had my own gun, loaded with silver bullets, and a sword forged from silver and iron.

Opening my bag, I retrieved the pistol and checked the magazine. It was full.

"What are you doing?" Tyrin asked, his tone alarmed.

"You saw what she did to that Ancient," I replied.

"You don't know that for sure."

"She is the broken beast. I need to destroy her before she fulfills her destiny."

The buzzing started up in the back of my head, indicating the chalice had moved out of range. I headed for the cliff that led to the canyon, but Tyrin leaped into my way.

"You promised Catori you would bring the girl home alive," he said.

I had, and it struck me then what an odd request that was for Catori to make. Not only had she made me promise, she had also informed Tyrin. The dryad had insisted I bring the bastard to protect me, but was it possible she had sent him as a fail-safe for her plan?

"Everyone you care for will betray you," a woman's voice whispered in my mind.

Was Catori finally stabbing me in the back?

I had always known her betrayal would hurt the most, but I had never expected her to side with the beast holding me hostage to my curse. Had she been working against me all along? I did not want to believe it, but I could not deny the possibility. If Catori had turned on me, promise or no, I had to destroy the beast. Now.

"Get the fuck out of my way, Tyrin."

He crossed his arms. "Swear you won't kill her."

I laughed, sounding admittedly unhinged. Did the bastard really believe he had negotiating power?

"I will not hesitate to go through you if I must."

He met my gaze, and I let him see the truth of my words. Although I would never consider us friends, he and I reached an understanding during this trip. He had stopped the car when I was on the verge of hyperventilating. I would never admit it, but I had consciously chosen to save him in that canyon. I was still angry with my húskarl for his betrayal, but I no longer wanted to kill him.

Tyrin swore and stepped aside, shaking his head. "If you kill her, you will regret it."

His words rang true in my spirit, but I ignored them, knocking my shoulder against his as I strode to the cliff's edge. Wrapping magic around me, I stepped off and drifted down to the canyon floor. The chalice was not there, but something magical was at the foot of the dead Ancient, and I needed to find out what it was.

Following the curiosity I could not explain, I found a glowing red orb not much larger than my fist. Someone had pried it open before casting it aside. I pocketed it before following Grace's scent and the call of the chalice through the canyon. When the buzzing in my head vanished, I knew I was getting close.

The canyon narrowed, and a limestone shelf connected the walls, closing in the passageway. I paused at the entrance. The chalice was not far now, and I only had to enter and reclaim it. But as I stepped under the cover of the limestone ceiling, memories of being trapped underground assaulted me.

I bolted back out.

Sunshine beat down on me, and I took a deep breath, considering my options. The wolf could not stay hidden away forever. She would eventually have to leave or starve to death. I could be patient and wait her out. But the dead vegetation of the canyon reminded me what she was capable of.

The beast was dangerous, and I needed to put an end to her before she struck again.

I was a dragon, afraid of nothing, not even tight spaces. It was a lie, but I desperately wanted to believe it. Determined to overcome the fear, I pocketed my gun and drew my sword before easing back into the passageway.

The walls immediately began to close in around me.

No, that was impossible. Walls did not move. Taking deep breaths through my nose, I focused on each one, reassuring myself of their stationary locations. The ceiling was about a foot above my head. I did not have to duck. I had a good five feet on either side of me. Nobody had trapped me. I could escape if I needed to.

I followed the passageway to where it split, scenting the air. Chaz and Rust had gone to the left, which led to the fresh air of an exit, but Grace and Mackiel's scents led to the right, deeper into the darkness. Trying to ignore how the passageway narrowed when I followed their scent trails, I continued on.

Three steps in, panic seized me.

I could not move another step. In fact, it took all my will not to bolt back out the way I had come. Closing my eyes, I envisioned the Ancient, reminding myself of how Grace kneeled, her hand on the trunk, as life drained from the branches.

She was a monster.

I could not allow her to live.

Strengthening my resolve, I filled my lungs and took another step. Then another.

It was my destiny to kill the beast. Nothing else was important. Not even obtaining answers about my father's heritage. I had failed to kill the beast once and had no intention of repeating my blunder.

Another step.

The passageway narrowed to a cave ahead. Smoke thickened the air, but beneath it, I could smell blood. I was close now. Just a little further, and I could end my curse and leave.

Sword drawn, I sprang forward, launching myself through the

narrow cave entrance and scanning the small space. Grace was on her knees, holding the Chalice of Power up toward me in offering. Behind her, Mackiel was asleep in wolf form, his fur matted with blood. Beside the wolf, a being made entirely of fire hovered above the ground.

"Please," Grace said, drawing my attention back to her. Tear tracks streaked her soot-covered cheeks. "I'm begging you not to hurt them. Here's your artifact. I'm sorry I took it. This thing has ripped apart my life. Please take it back."

This was not at all what I had expected. She was kneeling and helpless. All it would take to end her was one slash of my sword.

Yet, something stayed my hand.

"You wish to give the chalice back to me?" I asked.

"Honestly, I wish I could go back in time and not steal it in the first place, but since that's impossible, yes. I want to give it back."

"How do I know this is not some sort of trick?" I sniffed the air, wondering if I was about to be ambushed by Chaz and Rust, but their scents were old, and Grace's smelled of truth.

"I swear on my daggers—the only gift my father has ever given me—that this is no trick. Spare my friends, and I won't fight you. My life is yours to take or spare as you will."

"No, Chip." The fire being drifted forward.

I braced, preparing my attack. I had no idea what my sword could do to the being, but perhaps I could freeze the fire. At least for a minute or two.

Grace held out a hand, stopping the being from coming closer. "You owe me, Ann. In payment for your debt, I ask you to stay out of this and take my friend to our packmates. See him and them safely back to the mainland."

The fire being narrowed her eyes at me. "If you kill her, I will find you."

"No, you won't," Grace said, sounding frustrated. "You will live a long, free life. The life you deserve. The life that was stolen from you by the Sons of Oannes. You will rejoin your people and be happy knowing this was my choice. Please, Ann. Enough people have already gotten hurt because of me."

The fire being looked like she wanted to argue, but resignation filled her eyes, and she drifted back, crossing her tiny arms.

The little wolf was full of surprises. She still held the chalice in one hand, extended toward me. I reached for it, but as my fingertips neared the artifact, I felt a charge of electricity. The hair on my arm stood up, and instincts warned me not to get any closer. Catori had questioned whether I could touch the chalice, and at the time, I had brushed off her concern. Now, I realized the dryad might be correct.

And Catori would be getting what she wanted because I would have to wait until I got home to kill the beast.

I withdrew my hand. "Put the chalice in your bag. You are coming with me."

Thank you so much for reading **Pack of Secrets.** Please take a moment to write a review because I would love to hear what you thought of the first book in the *Celestial Artifacts* series. Grace and Arioch's Journey continues in **Pack of Betrayal,** releasing soon.

Stay up to date on book sales and releases by signing up for my newsletter here at www.amaramae.com

ALSO BY AMARA MAE:

Pack of Betrayal: Celestial Artifacts #2

Pack of Discord: Celestial Artifacts #3

Pack of Change: Celestial Artifacts #4 (releasing 2023)

Pack of Hope: Celestial Artifacts #5 (releasing 2024)

Pack of Vengeance: Celestial Artifacts #6 (releasing 2024)

ACKNOWLEDGMENTS

This book would have never become a reality without the help and support of so many people. Special thanks to my husband, Meltarrus, our boys, and all my friends and family for letting me off the hook when I daydreamed storyline and dialog during our conversations.

Huge thanks to the incredible Gail Goldie, who doesn't mind spoilers and edited this book at least a dozen times, through all the many rewrites. Also, thanks to my fabulous friend Nicole Phoenix for her content edits, suggestions, and ceaseless encouragement. Jood with JS Editorial Service was an incredible editor to work with, asking all the difficult questions and forcing me to nail down character and storyline development. The three of you made this happen!

Thank you, beta and ARC readers for your edits, support, and love.

And, thank you, reader, for embarking on this journey with me!

ABOUT THE AUTHOR

Amara Mae is an urban fantasy and paranormal romance author who has written additional genres under other pen names for more than ten years. Fantasy has always been her first book love, and she's researched and generally geeked out for years to build the Fractured Earth world which will be home to her Celestial Artifacts and several other series. She resides in the rainy Pacific Northwest, where she enjoys real and imagined adventures alongside her husband and their five boys and two dogs.

Printed in Great Britain
by Amazon

22568249R00165